ALASKA
TRANSIT

Michael — Enjoy — Richie

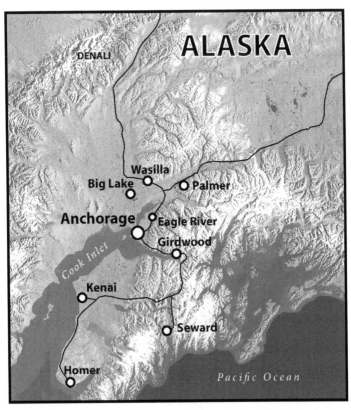

Southcentral Alaska includes the Municipality of Anchorage, the Matanuska-Susitna Valley, the Kenai Peninsula, and Denali National Park.

ALASKA TRANSIT

More crime on the Alaska / Russia border

SEASON 2

by

RICHIE GOLDSTEIN

Contents

ISBN: 978-1-5323-9699-1
Writer's Guild of America West - Registry #2131835
Copyright © 2021 Richie Goldstein
All rights reserved.

Cover design, book layout and maps by Penny Panlener.

Principal Characters

An asterisk (*) is placed after the below-named characters the first time they are mentioned in the text, indicating that there is more information about that person in the Biographical Notes at the end of the novel.

Sgt. Aleksandra (Sasha) Kulaeva — a detective

Lt. Gary Hernandez — her immediate boss

Capt. Stanislav Babiarsz — her principal boss

Sgt. Busby Moranis — her partner

Robin Kulaeva — her daughter

Boris Bunin — a capo

Larissa Bunina — his wife

Leonid Bulgarin — a pilot

Dorotea Bulgarina — his wife

Mehmet Ozil — an expeditor

Artun Ozil — an expeditor

Maj. Tucker Cranston — a US Army officer

Luellen Cranston — his wife

Tamara Stoikova — a nurse

David Osinchuk — a smuggler

Anatoly Suvorov — a commercial airlines pilot

Pyotr Bondarchuk — a border guard

Salar Murad ibn Sayed ibn Habibullah — an Afghani shaikh

Hakeem ibn Salman — an Afghani businessman

Mirza ibn Murad — an Afghani truck driver

Kamal ibn Saifi — an Afghani Army officer

A note on Russian names

Russian men and women have middle names based upon their father's first name.

For women, *ovna* or *yevna* is added to the father's first name to make a woman's middle name. Example: here is Aleksandra whose father is Peter. She would be called Aleksandra Petr*ovna*. If her father were Sergei, she would be Aleksandra Serge*yevna*.

For men, *ovich* or *yevich* are added. Example: here is Boris, whose father is David. Boris would be called Boris David*ovich*. Or if his father is Sergei, he would be called Boris Serge*yevich*.

If I am a friend of Boris, I might drop the *ov* part and call him Boris Davidich. Or if his father is Sergei, I might drop the *yev* and call him Boris Sergeich. This doesn't work for women's middle names.

Almost every Russian first name has a nickname. So Aleksandra is Sasha, Boris is Borya, Valery is Valya, Mikhail is Misha etc.

A note on rendering Russian phonetically into English:

The main problem in rendering Russian into English is with the two (2) Russian letters for the English sound E. One is pronounced, one is not (at least in any way discernable to the English ear). Many Russian words end in both the pronounced E and the so called 'short E.' I have avoided the problem by smushing them together and using an English 'y.' Hence, Yury, Georgy, Veliky. All of which, in Russian, end in *both* the pronounced *and* the 'short E.'

With appreciation

To my corps of volunteer proof readers –
Rick, Michelle, Gerald, Martin, Bobbie, Jeff, Steve,
and especially Linda.

BOOK 1
January 2019

"It's foggier than shit, snowin' like crazy. Witnesses say the guy was goin' way too fast. Musta been travelin' at least forty, forty-five, when he shoulda been goin' no more'n twenty. I mean the road was completely covered with ice. Then this fuckin' moose shows up. Runs between two parked cars onto the road. Guy tries to veer away but hits the moose in the ass. His car spins out, flips a buncha times and slams into a light pole."

It was just past eleven at night. Anchorage Narcotics Sergeant Busby Moranis* sat behind the wheel of his department's unmarked car. The vehicle's headlights illuminated the crash scene: an upside down Ford Taurus, driver's-side door ripped open by a Jaws of Life.

Moranis was talking to Lieutenant Gary Hernandez*, head of the APD's Narcotics Division. They watched through snicking windshield wipers as police and paramedics swarmed around the site. A persistent light snow drifted down upon the first responders. The car's defrost kept the windows from clouding over.

Moranis shifted in his seat, unzipped his wet, yellow slicker, and pulled apart the garment's dripping halves. He dried his hands on his pants and took out a small notebook, being careful not to dampen the pages.

"The witnesses—two old broads drivin' home from a night of bingo—were comin' the other way. They each said about the same thing. The car hit the moose then flipped upside down, and the driver, they said, musta busted through the windshield with his head and had one arm wedged in the driver's-side door, which was part open. They saw him move a little but after a while he stopped movin'. They called it in."

Hernandez shifted in his seat. "OK. But why are *we* here? We're narcotics. Why'd they call *us*?"

"Lemme finish, will ya?"

"Go on." Hernandez smiled, pushed his slicker off his head and leaned against the car door. "I'm listening."

"The trunk sprang open when the car hit the light pole and all the shit *inside* popped *outside*. We've roped off and covered everything. Including—and this is where we come in—a backpack with about twenty kilos of what looks like junk."

"Junk? As in heroin junk?"

"As in heroin junk."

"OK, Busby. Now you got my attention. What about the driver? He the only one in the car, the only fatality?"

"Yeah. Well, no. The only *human* fatality. There was a dead dog, some kinda shepherd. And the moose, o' course." Moranis pointed to a spot on the side of the road, thirty yards away, where several people were salvaging the meat from the moose carcass.

Hernandez stared at the dismemberment. "Cryin' shame the meat has to go to charity. So, what about the guy? Got an ID yet?"

Moranis flipped notebook pages. "Driver's license says he was Houston Dantley Junior. We got him livin' in a condo in back of that Mongolian place on 15th and Ingra. What's it called?"

"Twin Dragon Barbeque. Let's get a patrol car over there, see if anyone's home. No one there, they can secure the location 'til we can get there. Probably tomorrow morning."

"I'm on it," Moranis said. Five minutes later, he was back. "There was an airport staff parking sticker on his windshield. I called over there, tried to reach Personnel but they're closed 'til mornin'."

"Alright. We'll run over there in a little, see if anybody knows him. Let's go check the backpack." Hernandez raised the hood of his slicker.

Moranis did the same. "Where's Sasha tonight? I thought she'd answer the call. That's actually why I phoned in. Hopin' she'd show up."

"She's busy."

"With . . .?"

"Her daughter, Robin. Bad news. Kid's at McLaughlin. Been busted."

"How bad?"

"Very, very bad."

~~~

Anchorage Police Detective Sergeant Sasha Kulaeva* knew both of the cops who had arrested her daughter that afternoon. She found one of them—Patrol Officer Gordy Hoffman—on a smoke break in back of the precinct house on Tudor.

He saw her coming, dropped his cigarette and crushed it out. "Hey, Sash. I'm real sorry about you daughter. It's a shitty deal."

"Yeah, shitty. Thanks so much, Gordy, for the head's-up."

"No prob. So here's the bad news. At about eleven-fifteen this morning, there was a report of someone driving erratically on the Glenn, heading south towards town. Robbie Fishburn and I were on the highway and got the call. We ID'd the car and hit the siren but your daughter sped up and got off at Muldoon.

We followed her into the Bartlett High parking lot. She spun out and hit a parked car. Luckily, there were no other students around, but the young lady in the car with your daughter took a nasty knock on the head and some bruised ribs. An ambulance took her to Alaska Regional. I heard she's okay."

"And Robin?"

"She wasn't hurt but she was belligerent, looked drunk, and refused the breath test. She showed us her learner's permit, but the passenger in the car with her wasn't twenty-one. And the car had been reported stolen from a parking lot in Eagle River."

Sasha shook her head. "What else?"

"Normally, we don't cuff minors in this kinda situation, but she was flailing around, so . . ."

"Sure. I get it. You needed to do that."

"Right. But the worst part, and I'm sorry for you and your kid, Sash, is that when we searched her, we found a vial of white powder. We phoned McLaughlin, per SOP, spoke with the folks over there. They said to bring her to the Youth Center. Which we did. Left her there around one fifteen this afternoon."

"And the white powder?"

"Lab gave a prelim—heroin."

Sasha covered her face with her hands. "Robin, Robin," she whispered. "Jesus Christ."

"It was a righteous bust, all the way, Sash. We're real careful with juvies."

"I'm sure it was, Gordy. Who'd you speak to at McLaughlin?"

"Gracie Vang."

"I know her. I'll go over there right now. Thanks again. I appreciate the call."

~~~

Near midnight. Snow continued to fall on the large green tarp spread over a backpack that held what Busby Moranis had guessed to be upwards of twenty kilos of heroin.

Wrapped in their slickers, hoods raised, the two Narcotics Division cops slushed their way toward the tarp through ankle-deep snow.

Sergeant Jess Stacey greeted them. "I called you soon as I opened the pack and saw what the fuck was in it," Stacey said. "Couple dozen packages. Powder all over. Only me and Billy Rogers—his squad car was first here—have seen the contents."

"That's good, Jess," Hernandez said. "Let's keep a tight lid on it for a while. Tell Billy not a word for now. I'll let Public Affairs know that we'd like the usual—that the vic's identity is being withheld until next of kin . . . and blah blah."

"Got it," Stacey said. "Who's the guy? We know?"

"Airport worker of some kind. We'll drive over there as soon as we're done here. Meantime, can we get a tent over the tarp?"

"It's already happening. Something'll be up soon."

Ten minutes later, an eight-foot high, twelve by twelve open-sided canopy covered the tarp. A quartet of halogen lamps had been jury-rigged to the tent's crosspieces and shone down on the evidence. The snow had turned wet and was now coming down audibly on the tent.

Moranis kneeled and carefully peeled away the tarp, making sure the snow that had collected on top of it didn't spill back onto the partially open backpack beneath. He photographed the bag from half a dozen angles.

"Good, now the contents," Hernandez said.

What the cops found was as advertised by Sergeant Stacy:

twenty-three packages, each measuring eight inches square by three high, and each wrapped in thick red paper and securely taped. One of the packages had split open, its contents powdering the inside of the backpack. Moranis took more photos.

"Grab the NIK kit," Hernandez said. "See if it's the real deal."

"Gotta be careful with those tests. I just read about a bunch of false positives in some police department in Alabama. Or Georgia. Cops there charged some dude with possession. Turns out it was sweetener. Test was wrong and they stopped usin' it."

"I read that," Hernandez said. "So we'll do a prelim, then take the shit to the crime lab for confirmation."

~~~

Detective Sasha Kulaeva kept clenching and unclenching her fists, looking for something to smash. She was trying to control her breathing. She sat across the table from her fifteen-year-old daughter. The fluorescent lighting in the McLaughlin Youth Center's sparsely furnished meeting room sputtered and hummed. The place had an institutional, antiseptic smell. Mother and daughter were alone.

Robin Kulaeva* sat slumped, eyes cast down, her body signaling defeat.

"Look at me!" Sasha said. When Robin didn't acknowledge her mother, Sasha shouted, "Look at me. Now."

Robin raised watery eyes and wiped her nose with her shirtsleeve. She put on an angry scowl. "I'm looking."

"Right this minute, dear girl, I'd love to grab my bitch of a daughter by the collar and smack the shit out of her."

Robin was silent.

"Let me see your forearms," Sasha demanded.

When Robin hesitated, Sasha reached across the table, grabbed her daughter's left arm, turned it over, and checked for track marks. Finding none, she signaled Robin to extend her right arm. She complied.

"I don't shoot up, Mom. I never did."

"Just snort, huh?"

Robin turned away.

"When did you start and how often?"

Still looking away. "A while back. Seven months ago."

"How often?"

Robin sighed heavily. "Maybe three, four times a week."

"And the money for your habit? Where did that come from? You're not working lately, so where?"

Robin remained mute.

Sasha rose from her chair and did a fuming stomp around the room. She returned to the table and hovered. She could almost hear her teeth grinding. She searched for the right words. "The thing with the stolen car . . . joyriding or whatever. And the DUI. And the injury your drunken driving caused your friend. Those are unhappy crimes, stupid crimes, but not fatal. The four grams of heroin you had in your pocket? That, you stupid . . . that's a game changer. At least it is for me."

Robin glared at her mother.

"Yeah. Definitely a game changer. But you won't be tried as an adult. That's not going to happen. You'd have to kill someone or burn down their house to make adult court. But if I had my way . . . . if I had my way, Robin, you'd be slapped with a felony possession charge that would stay on your record forever, could not be expunged. And every time you'd apply for work and they'd ask you if you'd ever been charged with a felony, you'd have to put an X in that box." Sasha tried to tone it down. She took a deep inhalation, held it for three heartbeats, then slowly let it out. "You know you could help yourself by naming your sources for the heroin and the booze."

Robin shook her head. "Unh-uh."

Sasha, surprise in her voice, "You won't name your source?"

"While I'm in *here*, I won't. Help get me out. Just do that for me and I promise I'll give you the name. And I swear I'll never use again."

Sasha's laugh was caustic. "Who do you think you're kidding with that bullshit? You're strung out, Robin. Don't you think I recognize the signs? Trembling, sweaty. Look at you, all pasty and pale. You'd say anything, promise anything to get out so you could score again." Sasha shook her head. "Get you out of here? That's not going to happen. But here's what *is* going to happen if you don't name your source. First off, the judge—and you better pray to God it won't be Bergsen—won't cut you any slack because of your age. That'll probably mean a year and a half here in McLaughlin 'til you're eighteen. Then, who knows? You won't get serious hard time, and, personally, I think that's a shame. Probably probation instead. Maybe you'll even get to wear an ankle monitor, brag to everyone about how you're a con." Sasha hesitated, then gathered herself and leaned closer to her daughter. Robin shrank from her mother.

"And the second thing that's going to happen if you don't name names . . . I will disown you."

Robin raised defiant eyes to her mother. "Disown me? Right. Like you've done since . . . forever?"

Sasha drew back from her daughter's accusation. "That's not fair, that's . . ."

"Not fair?" Robin spat. "Not fair? You want to tell me it was fair leaving me to grow up alone out in Big Lake? Going to school with those know-nothing valley hicks."

"You had your great-grandfather, your family . . ."

"Yeah, mom, but I didn't have *you*, my one living parent. Except for maybe once every couple months you'd fly in to Big Lake, be all affectionate, spend a night, then fly out. And before you'd leave, what did you always promise me, huh, mom?"

When Sasha didn't answer, Robin went on, "'I promise, Robin,' you'd say, 'I promise you'll come live with me in Anchorage as soon as I'm able to work it out.'" Robin, now on a roll. "Tell me, mom, how come you were never able to work it out? How many years does it take? You make enough, and you have a big enough place for me. 'Work it out?' What a fucking liar you are. And a phony parent."

Sasha struggled for a response, then quietly, "You were better off in Big Lake. Your great-grandfather was a better parent to you than I could ever have been."

"You're absolutely right. He was. Ever ask yourself why? No? It's real simple. Viktor loved me. My mom never did. He spent time with me. You? Never. And when he died last year, there was nobody around to love me. And nobody around for me to love back." Robin slumped into her seat. "I have to get out of here. Get me out."

Sasha softened. "You're right, totally, about my parenting. But if I'm a bad mom, then, you girl, are a bad daughter. And a stupid one." Sasha raised a threatening finger. "You're staying inside, you're gonna go cold turkey, *and* you're gonna give up the name of your source. All of that. Got it?"

"Fuck you, mom. None of that's gonna happen. I'll get out of here eventually, and I won't give up the name."

"Your decision, girl. But if you allow your source to skate, you won't see me again. I won't come visit you here at McLaughlin. I won't write. I won't even say your name again."

"Fine with me. We'll end this farce." Robin crossed her

arms and sat back. "I won't give up my source."

Sasha rose and shoved her chair out of the way. "You will! I'm giving you three days to sit here, time to scream and crawl your way through withdrawal. They don't give you Methadone here. You'll eat shitty food, see what it's like being in jail, and get a real taste of what your future will be like in the joint. You'll hate it. You *will* give up the name." Sasha turned and walked out of the room.

"Just get me out of here," Robin yelled after her. "If you do, I promise, I swear I'll give you the name. Promise."

~~~

Artun Ozil's* hands were shaky as he speed-dialed his cousin, Mehmet*. It was close to one in the morning. Wet snow blotted his windshield.

"Yeah? What's up?" Mehmet mumbled, half asleep.

"The guy didn't show."

"Huh? Whattaya mean?"

"The airport guy, he's an hour late. Never been late before. I waited at the drop-off for an hour. Phoned him. Phoned his home. Nothing. Drove to the back-up meeting spot in the Home Depot parking lot. Wasn't there. Right now, I'm outside his place. His windows are all dark. I went up and knocked. No one home."

"Maybe his car broke down," Mehmet suggested. *Please God.*

"Maybe. But he woulda called."

"Right." Mehmet exhaled. "You think . . . maybe the cops got him?"

"Don't go there, cuz. He'll phone. I'll wait here for a little longer, be home in a couple hours."

"OK. Stay in touch. You hear anything, let me know right

away." Mehmet ended the call.

Her husband's anxious tone had jarred Mehmet's wife from her sleep. "Who was that?" she asked.

"Nothing, Nikki," he assured her. "It was just Artun."

Nicole sat up; her long, gray-streaked hair fell over her face. She brushed it away and demanded, "If it was *'just'* Artun at this hour, then something *is* up. Wasn't he supposed to meet the guy?"

Mehmet rolled over to face his wife. "Right. He didn't show."

"Jesus Christ," she whispered, pulling the comforter around her body. "What happened?"

"No idea." Mehmet paused a moment then sat up on the edge of his bed. "Maybe in the morning, Nikki, you could, you know, maybe . . . pack a few things. I'll go to the office, get your passport from the safe. Who knows? Maybe he'll show. Maybe he had a flat tire."

"Passport?" she muttered. "What the hell, Mehmet? I mean, why . . ."

He flapped his hand at her, "Don't start, Nikki. Leave it for now. It'll be OK. Just pack an overnight bag." He fell back onto the bed, drew the comforter over his head and curled up, back to his wife. He stared into the room's darkness for an hour before falling asleep, but an onset of apnea woke him every few minutes. He tried sleeping on his side. No help.

~~~

One-thirty in the morning. The South Terminal at Ted Stevens International Airport teemed with passengers ready to board red-eye flights, all bound for points south.

In quick succession, the two narco cops questioned a trio

of baggage handlers, several counter folks, two TSA agents, and a handful of concessionaires. No one knew Houston Dantley. Then they asked a janitor working the baggage carousels, name-badged 'Diego.'

"Dantley?" Diego asked. "Skeeny dude? Maybe I know 'eem."

"Maybe?" said Moranis. "Think hard. How 'bout a yes or no?'

"Why you thin' he work here?"

"He has a sticker on his windshield says so," Moranis said.

"What color steecker?"

"What color?" Hernandez asked.

Moranis shrugged. "It's red I think."

"Then he don' work in dis buildin'. We got us green parkin' steeckers. Red ones in other terminal."

In contrast to the South Terminal, the North Terminal was almost deserted—no in-coming cargo flights, no international passengers. The cops made their way to the only workers visible—two Icelandic Air ticket agents, closing their counter.

"Ladies. Good evening," Hernandez said, showing them his shield. "We're looking for Houston Dantley. We understand he works in this building."

"He does," one of the women replied. She was young, slender, tan. She wore her long auburn hair in a ponytail. Her almond-shaped green eyes focused on Moranis. Although Hernandez had asked the question, she directed her response to the blond and hunky younger man. "He was here earlier. I think I saw him leave around nine or so. He's not in trouble, I hope." She nibbled at her lower lip and put on a worried look.

"None at all, I promise," Moranis said. He gave the

woman a big smile and leaned on the counter. "We just need to know where he works."

The second woman, older and grayer, with a prominent mole on her upper lip, said, "He works for Customs. He's a K-9 handler. Has the sweetest dog, a police dog. I think they call them Alsatians, or German shepherds. I don't usually like those dogs, so rough looking and snarly, but Brandy—that's her name—Brandy, is so friendly. I mean . . ."

"Dantley's a dog handler?" Hernandez cut her off, then turned to Moranis. "Well that makes sense."

"Lotta sense," his partner agreed.

Both women nodded. "Uh-huh," the older woman said. "He's been working here as long as I've been here. Must be a couple years already. Has he done anything?"

Moranis shook his head. "Not a thing. Just want to talk to him about his work with the dogs."

The blond wiggled her shoulders and smiled at Moranis. "You like dogs, officer?"

"You bet. I've got a mutt. She's a lover." He leaned farther over the counter and winked. "Kinda like me."

Hernandez rolled his eyes. "Detective Moranis, please. Ladies, couple more questions. Who's in charge, who runs the K-9 squad?"

"That'd be Walesa," the older woman said. "She's the Director of Customs at the airport."

"Great. That'd be W A L E S A?" Moranis spelled.

"Perfect," said the blond with a light laugh. "You spell real good."

Moranis leaned even farther over the counter and was about to comment when his boss pulled him by the sleeve and asked the women, "What planes landed tonight? You know?"

"Only one flight comes in on Tuesday nights," the blond

explained. "Troika Aviation."

"Troika Aviation? What's that? Never heard of it," Hernandez said.

The blond nodded her head. "It's a Russian carrier. Comes in every other Tuesday."

"Russian, huh?" Moranis said. "Makin' more sense all the time."

"Oh yeah," Hernandez said.

The cops smiled their thanks at the women, then turned and made their way back toward the doors.

"This could be a big fuckin' deal, Gary," Moranis said. "I mean, this is usually somethin' for the TSA, for Customs, or even the DEA." He smiled at Hernandez. "Or not."

Hernandez grinned back at Moranis. "Not. Definitely not. TSA can't find their asses with two hands and a mirror. Customs is a joke. And the DEA? They're all down on the Mexican border. Unh-uh, we keep this one close. We'll let Stan know. He'll decide if we want to share this with the other agencies."

"You gonna wake him? It's almost three."

"He'd be pissed if we didn't."

~~~

Stanislav Babiarsz,* former Chicago south-side beat cop, former Dutch Harbor Police Chief, and current Chief of Detectives, Anchorage Police Department, couldn't sleep. He missed his wife, Louisa, away visiting family back in Chicago. He'd come to the kitchen in search of good cheer. He found it in a pair of warmed-up cabbage and beef rolls she'd left for him. He sat, wearing only t-shirt and underpants, beer in hand, about to dig in when the call from his lieutenant interrupted his early morning snack. Babiarsz put down the bottle of Tyskie, his favorite lager, turned his cell phone on speaker, and listened while his officer described the discovery of suspected major criminal activity in their fair city.

"Jezus Chrystus." Babiarsz belched. "Let me see if I got all this. A dog handler from Customs, found dead with twenty kilos of heroin. And the smack maybe brought to Alaska on a Russian plane? Oy shit." He took a long swig of beer and poked at his cabbage rolls, getting colder by the minute.

On the other side of the call, Hernandez said, "I hope we're not thinking about reporting this to those fuck-ups at the DEA. I'm hoping we'll handle it ourselves."

"You got that right, Gary. This gonna be our baby. Keep it in-house as long as we can. Sasha know about this yet?"

"She's not answering her phone. She's going through a rough patch."

"What's up?"

"Her daughter's over at McLaughlin. Busted for possession of heroin."

"The hell is that about?"

"Kid got popped this afternoon. Sasha's been trying to get a handle on the situation. She called me a couple hours ago, said she spoke to the arresting officer. Looks like the bust was legit. She said she was going to McLaughlin tonight to talk to her daughter. Haven't heard anything since."

"OK. Give her a little time." Babiarsz checked the wall clock. "It's gone three. Let's meet first thing, say nine. Try and get Sasha there, too. If not, we'll manage."

"Got it. See you in a few."

After Hernandez hung up, Babiarsz returned to his food, now considerably cooler. He stuck the plate in the microwave for half a minute then popped a second bottle of beer. Back at the table with the reheated treat, the detective considered the stories he'd just heard: two tales of heroin, both involving Sasha Kulaeva, one as a cop, one as a mother. He got up from the kitchen table and took a short walk to his den. He fished around until he found a scrapbook of newspaper articles that chronicled the events, three years earlier, when he was Chief of Police in Dutch Harbor, in the Aleutian Islands. He took the album back to the kitchen, sat and ate while re-reading how Sasha and an FBI agent named Charlie Dana had gone to Dutch to find out what happened to a high seas fisheries observer missing off his boat—a Russian boat that was allowed to fish in American waters. Completely by chance, Sasha and Dana had uncovered a cache of heroin and had taken it to their bed and breakfast. Three Russian goons showed up, intent on retrieving the drugs. In the ensuing gun battle, the Russians were killed, mostly by Sasha[1]. Babiarsz scanned a dozen articles in which the Anchorage press had frothed about her heroism, dubbing her, *'The Shootout Queen.'* But as Dutch Harbor's Chief of Police, he'd soon discovered a pile of evidence that pointed to Detective Kulaeva having executed one of the men.

He'd phoned Anchorage to share his findings with his counterpart, Captain of Detectives Jack Raymond, Sasha's former boss. The two men pretty much agreed that Sasha had shot and killed a wounded and unarmed man[2]. They also agreed that since the dead Russian was a scum-sucking Mafioso, they'd sweep this unpleasantness under the rug. *Where it has remained to this day,* Babiarsz thought. *But Sasha knows what she did. I know what she did. And she knows that I know. Makes for an interesting working relationship, knowing that my most able narcotics investigator is a vigilante.* Babiarsz finished his beer and bussed his dishes to the sink.

~~~

After her bout with Robin, Sasha returned to her double-wide trailer home in Bay View Estates.

Although many of the Estates' residences were vintage Minnie Winnies—pre-1980 corroded and wheel-less hulks sitting on timber or cement foundations—Sasha had somehow lucked out nine years earlier. Right after moving to Anchorage from Big Lake, she found and rented the double-wide, a nineteen-year-old two bedroom, one bath whose wall insulation kept out the Alaska winter, mostly.

The day she moved in, she discovered the place was already semi-occupied. A large streaked tomcat lived under her rickety front porch. She learned from a neighbor that his name was Mortimer. New tenant and feline bonded and soon established a routine that defined the limits of their relationship: Sasha provided a once-a-day can of tuna, served outside, near a hay-strewn kennel she kept for the tom below the trailer. And Mortimer, in his way, returned the favor. Every few weeks, he brought her the half-eaten bodies of his prey: voles mostly, with the occasional small bird. He would lay them in front of the entrance so that Sasha had to watch where she stepped. Their *modus vivendi* established, they lived together peacefully.

Returning home tonight, Sasha was greeted by the tabby. Mortimer rubbed against her legs then sat and looked up.

"Dinner's on the way," she told him.

At the beginning of their relationship, she thought to vary his food. She offered him sardines and chum salmon. Mortimer was disdainful of these other fishy offerings. He insisted on tuna, had to be albacore, had to be solid pack.

After tonight's feeding, Sasha got comfortable, sat on her couch, and without thinking, turned on the TV. A remote crew was at the scene of a car wreck out by the airport. She switched to Colbert. His guest was a young congresswoman from California. Sasha turned them off in favor of Jimmy Kimmel, where she found only a commercial for a local mattress store. She switched off the set.

Although she made a good living and could have afforded a much better place in a much nicer neighborhood, she stayed. She hadn't bothered to move because for years she saw no reason to. With few friends and fewer lovers there was rarely a need to entertain, no need to dust or vacuum. But her conversation tonight with her daughter had thrown her for a loop, had revealed the ugly side of her parenting. She'd dwelled on it driving home. She had to admit that the picture her daughter had painted of her was all too true. *I've been a reluctant mother. Reluctant? How 'bout missing?*

She wasn't hungry but went searching anyway, first in the fridge, then in her cupboard. She settled on a bowl of Cheerios, honey-flavored. She added milk, took a single mouthful, then gave up. She poured the food into the sink and ground it up in the disposal. She stood over the basin, head drooped onto her chest. Sniffling, she held back the tears. *Robin. Robin. Robin. I'm so fucking sorry.*

~~~

Mehmet Ozil tossed from side to side for the next few hours. The Turk rose at six and went into his kitchen where his cousin, Artun, was smoking, brewing coffee, and toasting bagels. The TV was on, tuned to *AM Anchorage*.

On the screen, a tripled-chinned young man was reporting. He had curly red hair and fat lips. Mehmet put on his glasses and watched.

". . . . died last night when his car ran into a moose near the intersection of International Airport Road and Jewel Lake. Anchorage AM's Mindy Malone is at the scene. Mindy?"

The camera cut to a long shot of Mindy with a police officer, both bundled in parkas. They were huddled under a large umbrella. Snow was falling.

Malone: "Thanks Phil. I'm here with Anchorage Police Department Public Affairs Officer Gerald D'Arcy. What happened here, Officer D'Arcy?"

D'Arcy: "Single car crash. Single victim. *(Camera pans to wreck of a 1994 dark blue Ford Taurus, upright now but with its hood accordioned and driver's side door missing.)* Witnesses say the driver hit a moose that was crossing the frontage road in front of ABC Motorhomes. The driver apparently skidded, flipped a couple times and hit a light pole, the car landing upside down. The impact with the pole apparently sent the driver halfway through his door. By the time firefighters got there, the man had died from head injuries.

Malone: And do we know the name of the driver?

D'Arcy: "We do but we're holding on to that until next of kin can be notified. That's it."

Malone: "Sergeant D'Arcy, thank you, *(looking into the camera)*. That's all from here. Mindy Malone reporting. Back to you, Phil.

Mehmet stomped around the kitchen, ripping open and slamming shut cabinet doors.

"Piece of shit," he bellowed. He came to a stop at the sink and leaned over, cupping his face in his palms. "Are you sure it's our guy?" he asked between his fingers

"It's him," Artun confirmed. "I heard an earlier report on the radio and went out there just before dawn, checked the license plate. It's him. And the goods were nowhere in sight."

"God Almighty!" Mehmet raised his hands skyward, as if seeking divine intervention. He began circling the kitchen's island, snatching up utensils, then hurling them into the sink, some ricocheting and clattering to the floor. "That means the cops have probably collected the shit? Right?"

Artun nodded. "That's what we gotta assume. But the good news, he's dead and can't talk."

"Small comfort." Ozil smacked his forehead with a palm. "I need to call Brooklyn. See what they want us to do." He reached into a drawer for a burner phone. He had dozens.

~~~

Larissa Bunina* was still breathing hard, sweat dripping down her cheeks. She and her two bodyguards had just returned from jogging their daily twenty-block circuit of a frosty and frigid Brooklyn Heights. It was ten-fifteen in the morning. She removed her hoodie, took a towel and began mopping off her face and neck.

Her husband, Boris*, out cold, slouched in a wheelchair, snoring in an oxy-induced deep sleep. Boris had broken his right ankle a week earlier during a soccer game with their two sons, home briefly from their University of Hawaii studies. His injured leg extended out from the chair, propped up on a footrest.

His head lolled to the side, a bare hint of spittle glistening at the corner of his partially open mouth. His wire frame glasses rested askew on his nose. When the burner in his lap chimed, his wife picked up.

"Yes?"

"Lara, is that you?"

She laughed. "Who the hell else would it be, Mehmet? Boris is napping. What's up in Alaska? How's the weather? And what the hell time is it up there?"

"Weather stinks. Snowy and cold. Just past six here. And I got nothing but bad news. Airport guy is dead. His car hit a moose. Goods are gone."

Larissa's body went rigid. She focused on her breath, determined not to start hyperventilating. "And we're sure it's him? Dead, I mean?"

"Certain. Artun knows the car and double-checked the license plates. It's him."

She squeezed the phone with both hands. *My plan. My beautiful plan.* "Are there more details?"

"None yet."

"Alright. Boris'll wake up soon. We'll talk and get back to you."

"I'll wait for your call. Soon, huh?"

"Within an hour."

"One more thing, Lara. A favor please. I'm nervous. You can understand. I want to arrange for Nikki to fly outta here late tonight. Just in case. She'll fly to JFK."

"Email me the flight number. I'll send someone to pick her up, bring her here. She can stay with us as long as this takes."

"Thanks Lara. Talk to you soon."

When she closed the call, Larissa began a tense pacing of the Bunin living room, banging her sides with her fists. She stopped at the wheelchair and began nudging her husband's shoulder, calling softly to him, trying to bring him back from oxy-land. He roused, still dopey.

"What's up?" he slurred. He looked at his watch. "Thought I'd be out longer."

"Shit news, Borya," she said.

"Like what?"

She needed a moment to gather herself. She sat down on the couch across from him, unlaced and flipped off her Nikes, then peeled off her socks. "Like our fucking dog sniffer guy at the Anchorage airport died last night in a fucking car crash when he hit a moose in the middle of the FUCKING ROAD!" Larissa paused, took a breath "He'd just picked up a load. Shipment's disappeared." She stood, ripped off her t-shirt and slammed it to the floor. "Son of a bitch!"

Boris shook his head and tried to sit up straight. "What the hell's a moose doing in the middle of the goddamn city?"

She rose and walked to the floor-to-ceiling living room windows that gave out onto the East River, twelve floors down. She stared at the Manhattan skyline. "OK. Let's think. When the police discover—and I'm certain they will—that the shipment arrived by plane, they'll figure out it had to come in on Troika." She turned to face her husband.

Boris rolled his wheelchair toward her. "Of course they will. They'll figure it out. And sooner or later, they'll discover that Troika has partnered with Grizzly Air. Leo will be questioned."

"That's exactly what'll happen."

"And if I know my chicken-shit cousin, he'll fling himself on the floor and confess. Or better yet, maybe he'll kill himself."

Lara was able to chuckle. "He won't kill himself before he kills Dorotea."

Now it was Boris's turn to laugh. "He should have shot his wife years ago."

"Seriously, though," Lara said. "Leo *will* be questioned and . . . ." She moved back to the couch, sat, and took off her sweat pants.

"And?" he said. "Say what you're thinking, Lara."

Larissa Bunina stood to her full five-foot, two-inch height, dressed now only in sports bra and panties. Her long, dark hair, released from its ponytail, now flowed onto her shoulders. She put her hands on her hips. "And we have to decide whether . . . whether that happens or not. I know he's family, but . . . ."

When she realized she was being ogled, she stomped her foot. "Dammit, Borya, stop staring at me and pay attention! This is serious! I mean, if Leo meets with the police, he *will* shoot his mouth off. And then the whole damn show, including us, is *kaput,* as the krauts like to say."

"You're right. Hand me the burner. What time is it in Alaska?"

~~~

Six-forty in the morning, Anchorage time. Leo Bulgarin*, a late riser, was deep in REM sleep. He was dreaming of his first solo flight thirty-three years earlier during his student days at the Higher Civil Aviation Academy, in Ulyanovsk, seven hundred kilometers east of Moscow. He'd taken the Yak-18—a military trainer—for a ten-minute flight. In his dream, he remembered the feeling of exaltation when he'd landed and had been embraced by his flight instructor.

The buzzing of his burner phone brought him to a fuzzy wakefulness, but the memory of his dream remained and he smiled as he answered the call.

A short minute later, the smile and the exaltation had evaporated, replaced by a shuddering recognition that within the next few days, everything he'd worked for—and possibly his very life—might come to a screeching end.

Leo listened as his cousin in New York described in hideous detail the far-reaching implications of the death of a dog handler at the Anchorage airport.

"We're not sure what's going to happen," his cousin Boris said. "You'll almost certainly be visited by the police. They'll want to know about your company's connection to Troika Aviation. You need to be ready to answer them. And you'll need to prep Dorotea."

Leo listened, too stunned to respond. The onset of a sudden pulsating migraine made him feel as if his head was being used like a battering ram. Tears formed in the corners of his eyes. He could smell the sweat dripping down his chest. His cousin wanted to know if he understood all that he'd been told.

"Yes, Borya. I got it all."

"And Dorotea? Will she be a problem?"

"No, Borya, no problem." He was surprised by the lack of emotion in his own voice. "No problem."

"Good. We'll stay in close touch. We've already heard from Mehmet. He told me to tell you that if you need anything, you can ask him to stop by."

Within a few seconds of ending the call, Leo was sobbing so piteously that his wife, in the adjoining bedroom, rushed into his room and came to his side. When he told her the news, Dorotea's* head snapped back and she shrieked, "That's it, Leo. Your wonderful cousin has fucked us good and proper. Just like I warned you."

~~~

The morning after the death of Houston Dantley Jr., Sasha Kulaeva stormed into the precinct's detective division, not at all happy to be back at work. She saw her partner, Busby Moranis, intent over his computer's keyboard. She knew that the sight of her would normally make him stop everything and give her his total—and from her point of view, unwanted—attention. She was surprised when he turned to look at her, showing a face full of concern. She dropped her carryall next to her desk and sat.

He swiveled toward her. "Yo, Sash. I hear your daughter's at McLaughlin. I'm real sorry to hear that. What's up?"

She was soothed by her partner's concerned tone. She opened her computer and logged on. Without looking at him, she said, "What's up is that they got her for heroin possession, sixteen grams. That's what's up."

"Uh-oh. Righteous bust? Get off on a technicality, maybe?"

"By the book." Sasha pursed her lips, shook her head. "I saw her last night. She pleaded with me to get her out. Said she'd be good. As if."

Moranis nodded. "Heard that from every junkie I ever busted."

"That's what I told her. She looked to me like she was good and strung out. I told her she'd stay put and could do her withdrawal in the can."

"They don't use Methadone over there. Give the junkies Aleve, or whatever, for pain."

"Right. It's pretty raw. I'm going again in a few days. Give her time to learn to hate jail. She has 'til then to cough up the seller. I told her she has to name her source if she wants any slack from the court."

"She's holdin' out the name? DA'll hate it."

"That's what I told her." Sasha sat and stewed some more, then finally blinked her way back to the moment. "Anyhow, bring me up to date. What'd I miss?"

Moranis filled her in on the recovery the previous night of a large score of heroin. "We did a NIK test at the site. Showed positive. Lupe over at the lab'll let us know later today, then send it down south for further confirmation."

"That's a load of dope. More than we grabbed a few years back in Dutch³. What do we know about the dead guy?"

"Lots." Moranis looked past Sasha. "Here's Gary now. Let him tell you himself. It's juicy."

Lieutenant Gary Hernandez hung up his coat and scarf and walked over to Sasha. She rose and gave her boss a bear hug of a greeting. He returned the squeeze, then held her at arm's length. "How's Robin?"

Sasha shook her head. "Little bitch is strung out. Won't name her source. I threatened her. I'm not sure she got the message."

"You need time off?"

"Thanks. No. I'd just obsess. Go nuts. Meanwhile, tell me about the guy from last night, the crash? Busby says it's juicy."

Hernandez settled his large bulk into a swivel chair and rubbed his hand back and forth over his short-cropped graying hair. "Juicy? No shit. Guy was a US Customs agent. A dog handler of all things. Just come from work at the North Terminal."

"Wow. Customs. Busby's right, it is 'juicy.'"

"Tol' ya," Moranis said.

Hernandez took out a yellow pad of paper, labeled 'Dantley,' and put on reading glasses. "So here's what little we know so far. Houston Dantley Jr. Thirty-four. Loner. No wife, no kids, no family that we could find here in Alaska. Guy and his dog worked last night at the airport. North Terminal. His shift ended at nine. Half hour later, give or take, he crashes and dies. A backpack of heroin is found next to his car. 'Til there's evidence to the contrary, I think we can assume that the stash he was carrying—just under twenty kilos—arrived by plane. I think it's a fair assumption for a starting theory." He looked at the other two members of the APD's Narcotics Division.

"If the stuff got flown in," Moranis said.

Hernandez looked at Moranis. "What are you thinking, Busby?"

"Well, what if he had the dope in his car's trunk for days? Somethin' he picked up a while ago? Or maybe picked up before work somewhere else in town. Or even picked up after work."

"Worth thinking about," said Hernandez, "though you wouldn't imagine someone would be running around with a load of smack in their trunk. So, for now, it got flown in. Okay?"

"For now," Sasha said. "We can go with that as a starting place. I think we can semi confirm if we make a timeline and nail down when he left work. Make sure he didn't stop somewhere to pick the shit up."

Moranis said, "Maybe he had to punch out. Or sign out. Or let someone know he was leaving."

"Exactly," Sasha said, nodding at Moranis. "When we know that, we can find out where his car was parked . . . ."

"He used staff parking," Hernandez said, "according to a sticker on his busted windshield."

"Alright," Sasha said. "We'll be able to learn the time he left work, estimate how long it took to walk to his car, then drive to the crash site. If that works out to be a pretty tight timeline then we can assume he didn't stop somewhere to pick up the heroin before he crashed."

"Sounds a little thin to me," Moranis said. "Still coulda

been keepin' it in his trunk for delivery later."

Sasha raised open palms. "It's a working theory, Busby. So far, at least."

"I guess," he said.

"Maybe we can also assume that he took receipt of the drugs from someone who had just landed," Sasha said.

"That might be kind of a stretch," Moranis said. "I mean, like I said, Dantley could have kept it stored at the terminal."

"Again a possibility," Hernandez said. "On the other hand, keeping that amount of heroin in your locker out at the airport until he's ready to take it to wherever . . . seems to me, at least, a bit far-fetched. The danger of the stuff being discovered, I mean. He might not have wanted to give his own dog a chance to sniff it out."

"I agree with Gary," Sasha said. "If we go on the premise that the dope came in last night, we need to know what planes arrived while he was on duty, and we need to have a passenger list."

"Troika Aviation was the only flight last night," Moranis said. "It's a Russian outfit. I had the passenger list emailed to Gary."

"On top of things, aren't you?" she grinned, and realized it was the first time she'd smiled since she'd heard about her daughter.

"Not on top of everything I'd like to be on top of," he leered at her wolfishly.

Sasha looked at Gary, indicating her co-worker with a thumb over her shoulder. "Busby never stops, does he? Keeps angling for a harassment suit. Lucky for him I like him just enough not to file."

Hernandez gave Moranis a reproachful look. "Grow the fuck up, Busby. You need to stop the kind of bullshit you pulled last night with the blond."

"What blond?" Sasha asked.

Moranis smiled. "Counter attendant. She thought I spelled good."

"I had to drag him away before he took his pecker out," Hernandez said. "He's our cross to bear, Sasha. If he wasn't so goddamn competent, I'd recommend Stan kick his ass down to traffic."

"Do it anyhow," Sasha suggested, then turned to Moranis. "So tell me, mister 'competent', how many passengers arrived? Figure that one out?"

"Two hundred and thirty-two," Moranis said. "Troika Aviation flew in from Vladi . . . something."

"Vladivostok," Sasha said. "Big crime town. I was there three years ago. Escaped, just."

Hernandez tapped his pen on the tablet. "And it's going to be nearly impossible to tell which passenger brought it in since there was no ID attached to the backpack."

"Prints?" she asked.

"Lab is checking," Hernandez answered.

Moranis said, "Maybe *that* bag didn't go through Customs, wasn't brought in by anyone. Maybe it was Dantley's bag. Maybe there was a switch at the airport."

Hernandez looked at Moranis. "Good thinking, Busby. And maybe we'll keep you here and not send you down to traffic."

"Appreciate it," said Moranis, smiling at Sasha. "I'm still here, partner."

She couldn't help but laugh. "So I see. But we still got a serious problem. How do we tie a load of heroin to one of the two hundred and thirty-two air travelers—dispersed over all hell and gone?"

"Hard for me to think it might be a passenger," Hernandez said. "I checked this morning on Google Earth. Vladivostok is over three thousand miles from here. Troika flies every two weeks. A passenger who flew in regularly would stick out, draw attention to himself. Or herself."

"Yeah, hard to imagine it being a passenger," Sasha said. "But it could be if we think this was a one-off shipment. If that's the case, then we'll need to run checks on all of 'em. But if we think this was one of a *series* of drug shipments, like the ones with the fisheries guy three years ago in Dutch Harbor, then a crew member would be a more likely candidate."

Hernandez referred to the manifest he had printed out. "Besides the passengers, there were three in the flight crew—pilot, first officer, and navigator. And eleven in the . . . what's it called . . .?"

"The cabin crew," said Sasha.

"Right," Hernandez said. "I think we start with trying to figure out Dantley's work schedule, fix a timeline, then check out the crew. Hopefully, we can get this done today."

"Agreed," said Moranis. "And we can *also* find out if it was a regular thing or a one-off by checking the dead guy's bank records. See if there's been regular deposits. He was a mule, we think. Most likely paid per shipment."

"Yeah," Sasha said. "But he'd have to be some kind of jerk to be putting a bunch of money into his bank account. More likely he's stuck it away somewhere, or maybe invested it."

Hernandez held up his hands. "OK. Let's divvy up the work. Busby, go get a warrant to search the vic's home and his bank account, if any. Take someone with you. We'll see if you're right."

"Will do."

"Meanwhile, Sasha and I'll go to the airport, to Customs— learn about the vic, try to figure out a timeline. Let's all keep in touch. Meet back here in the afternoon."

"I got a meeting at three," Sasha said. "How about we meet after six?"

"Lucky Wishbone. At six." Hernandez said.

~~~

In Brooklyn, Boris and Larissa Bunin, nominal president and vice-president of their family's worldwide crime syndicate, were worrying about their disintegrating drug importing prospects in Alaska. They sat on opposite sides of their large, oval dining room table.

Larissa bent forward, rigid fingers spread out on the tablecloth. "Things could go to shit, Boris. Real quick," she said. "Yeah, Alaska is the boonies, but the cops up there are top notch."

For his part, Boris dunked his kaiser roll into a large mug of coffee. He kept it in too long and a portion broke off and briefly floated on the surface before sinking. "Shit," he swore, using a teaspoon to fish out the sodden mass and wolfing it down.

His wife couldn't help smiling. "You eat like a *muzhik,* Boris. Finish your breakfast and think about what the hell we're going to do."

He gulped down the rest of his coffee, wiped his mouth with a napkin, and turned to his wife.

"The dog handler is dead and no one around to replace him. For the moment, at least. My cousin Leo's scared shitless and can't in any way be depended upon not to totally freak out. His wife is equally unreliable. What else do we need to think about?"

"The pilot. What's his name?"

"Suvorov," Boris answered.

"Right." Larissa rose and began gathering the breakfast dishes. "He's probably still in Anchorage. The crew always stays over a couple days before flying back to Russia. What do we know about him?"

"He lives in Vlad. Married with a kid. Been doing these runs from the very start, probably year and a half by now."

"Should we have Mehmet contact him while he's still in Anchorage? Tell him what's happened? Let him know that for the time being—until we can replace the dog handler or find someone new in customs—he won't be bringing product into Alaska?"

Boris sat back and crossed his arms. "Sounds right. Let's call Mehmet, see what he thinks."

In Anchorage, Mehmet Ozil and his cousin Artun were watching and listening carefully to TV, radio, and internet news, looking for further information about the untimely death of Houston Dantley Jr. The Turks had heard nothing new beyond what they had learned from the early morning news.

Mehmet's burner rang. Brooklyn again. He opened the call. "Nothing new, Boris. Cops are keeping a lid on any additional information." He listened as his boss spoke about the pilot.

"I agree," Mehmet said. "Problem is, he's disappeared. He's not at the hotel, wasn't there last night, hasn't been there all morning. I keep calling, left messages on his phone to get in touch as soon as he's back in his room. Nothing yet."

In Brooklyn, Boris shook his head at his wife and said, "Gets worse and worse." Back on the phone, "Alright, Mehmet. Keep trying. Lara wants to talk to you." He passed the phone to his wife.

"Hello Mehmet. Listen. Try like hell to get to the pilot,

bring him up to date. And another thing. The cops there are no dummies. They'll certainly connect the dots and figure out cousin Leo's involvement with Troika. Right?"

"Absolutely, Lara. No question about it. The Grizzly Air connection is gonna come up for sure."

"And that means Leo and Dorotea will be questioned." Larissa paused and looked at her husband, then spoke again into the cell phone. "That means Boris's cousin could very well be a liability."

Boris's expression clouded. "Lara . . . wait a second."

She held up a hand to her husband and spoke again to Mehmet. "Keep close contact with Leo and Dorotea. We'll want to know the slightest weakening of their position. Got it, Mehmet?"

In his Anchorage kitchen, Mehmet was on speakerphone. He looked at Artun. They shrugged at each other and nodded. "I got it, Lara, Mehmet said. "We'll keep a close watch on Leo, let you know right away if anything weird happens."

"Great," she said and ended the call.

Boris stared at his wife. "Leo's family, Lara. I know he's a flake, but he's still family."

Larissa didn't answer. She began clearing the table.

In Anchorage, the Turks sat silently for a moment, until Artun spoke. "Might have to," he said.

"Might have to," his cousin answered.

~~~

Detectives Hernandez and Kulaeva took the stairs to the second floor of the airport's North Terminal. They immediately ran into a crowd lined up in front of the U.S. Customs office, everyone holding paperwork and passports.

"Global Entry," said Sasha.

Hernandez scoffed. "All of them anxious to get out of the country."

"Problem, Gary? You got something against traveling abroad?"

"Love traveling." He hesitated. "Can't any more. All my cash goes to Inez and the kids down in L.A."

Sasha held her tongue. She knew Gary's ex, knew her to be a shallow woman without interests, without brains. *But Gary'd loved her just the same. Probably still did. Go figure.*

The detectives went to the head of the line. They ignored the resentful scowls from those waiting. They showed their badges and were allowed into the agency's inner sanctum.

Annalise Walesa took the news stoically, her face impassive. The fifty-ish Director of US Customs in Alaska wore dark framed glasses that she now took off and placed—just so—on her spacious and uncluttered desk. One hand went automatically to a small hank of gray hair that had fallen onto her forehead. She tried to push it back but it wouldn't obey. Her lips grew thin with her muffed and public attempt at styling.

Sitting opposite her, Sasha felt sorry for the woman. *She seems unhappy and desperate. Join the crowd, lady. I've got a daughter facing drug charges and a boyfriend who lives eight thousand miles away. Saw him last year for ten days. See him again maybe next year. Need to decide on the most apt expression. 'Absence makes the heart grow fonder,' or 'outta sight, outta mind.* She came out of her reverie and regarded the customs director.

Hair still rebellious, Walesa straightened the collar of her rose-colored blouse and passed a hand over the small gold cross hanging from her neck.

"Such a shame, really," she said. "Houston was . . . "

Walesa hesitated, " . . . an experienced employee. But if it were only a traffic accident, I'm not sure why you two are here. *Two* detectives?"

Gary took the lead. "You're right, ma'am. Normally a simple one-car fatality wouldn't warrant an interview with the victim's employer. But there are special circumstances in play."

Earlier, on the drive to the airport, he and Sasha had agreed that they needed to keep the heroin angle buried for now. Sasha chimed in with the story they'd concocted.

"You see, Miz Walesa, we found a weapon, an unregistered pistol in Mr. Dantley's car."

The customs director shrugged. "And? Why is that unusual? This is America, after all. He could have purchased it on-line or at a gun show. Simply owning an unregistered gun isn't that unusual."

"You're right ma'am," Sasha said, "but this weapon was identified by the FBI as the same one used in a liquor store robbery last year in Bellingham, in Washington state. Three people were made to kneel down, then shot to death. The perpetrator was never caught."

Walesa's eyes rounded. "Good God! That little twerp . . ." She caught herself. "I mean . . . it's hard to believe. Houston a murderer? My God!"

Gary said, "Yes, well. We'll want to examine his personnel file, his work schedule to see if, in fact, he could have been in Washington when those murders took place. We'll also want to talk to Mr. Dantley's co-workers." Gary waved his hand in the air to show the all-encompassing search the Anchorage Police Department had in mind.

Walesa considered a moment. "Normally, personnel files of federal employees are not made available. But in this case, a murder investigation, a *triple* murder investigation." She smiled. "We'll do anything we can to help."

Sasha thought the woman was a little too thrilled by the whole scenario. *'A triple murder,'* Walesa had said with apparent glee.

"I'll help you access the paperwork you've asked to see," Walesa said. "But I'm not sure how much you'll learn from the rest of the staff."

"Why's that, ma'am?" Gary asked.

"Houston was a very private person, and not . . . how shall I say . . . a particularly likable one. I know it's unseemly to speak ill of the dead, but there it is. He wasn't very well liked. And since the airport has only two K-9 handlers, he really had only a single co-worker." Walesa seemed to realize something, frowned and sat back in her chair, shaking her head.

"Something you remembered, ma'am?" Sasha asked.

"Yes. Well, not really." She paused. "We . . . I lobbied for years before the airport finally got a K-9 unit. Years. And now half the unit is gone." She shut her eyes and breathed out. "We'll never get a replacement."

Both cops showed sympathetic faces.

Gary asked, "Miz Walesa, one more thing. When Detective Kulaeva and I came into the terminal just now we noticed several video cameras on the ceiling and along the walls. I'm wondering if we might review the tapes from the time passengers on last night's Troika Aviation flight began disembarking?"

"I can arrange those for you."

"That'd be great. Thanks."

While Sasha and the customs director went through the deceased's work schedule, Gary sought out Stacy Kimura, the airport's other K-9 handler.

The cop found him in the lunchroom and took him to an

empty baggage storage area for questioning.

Kimura was a stocky man with a small voice and rat-beady eyes over pockmarked cheeks. He had lank brown hair, parted in the middle. He took out a pack of Juicy Fruit and put two sticks of gum in his mouth. He glared at the cop and chewed with a vengeance.

When the policeman told him about his colleague's death, Kimura blew out a breath. "Too bad, but ya know."

"No. I don't know. Tell me."

Kimura looked around the room and sniffed. "I never much liked the guy."

"What was the problem?"

The dog handler let out a loud sigh. "Houston was a dickwad. Pure and simple. We worked together but hardly ever exchanged words. If we did, it was strictly dog talk. And . . ." Kimura hesitated.

"And?"

"And Brandy, his dog. He never treated her properly. Girl was so smart. So sweet. Deserved better than that moron."

"Brandy also died in the crash. Did you know that?"

"That's a goddamn shame."

"Seems you're more sorry about the dog's death than about Dantley's."

"You got that right. I love my dog. Dantley didn't love his."

"Alright, I get it. He worked the Troika Aviation flight last night. Right?"

"Right."

"Did you guys ever trade off? I mean, you ever work that flight?"

"We never traded. Houston and I had fixed schedules. We're the only two K-9 handlers here at the airport, so we never really got to move around, change up the work."

"So who worked where?"

"Me, at South Terminal, domestic flights. Houston, mostly in North, only rarely in South."

"And last night?"

Kimura rolled his eyes. "I thought I just told ya. Houston worked in North. So he caught Troika Aviation, did it every other Tuesday night."

"So you never worked Troika Aviation."

"Like I said, Houston worked all of 'em, for a couple years prob'ly."

"You ever think that was a little strange?"

"How'd you mean?"

"Well, he worked the same schedule, never deviated."

"His choice. He had seniority and was in charge of making out the schedule. Not my place to question it."

"Anything unusual happen last night during his watch?"

"How the hell am I s'posed to know? I was in the other building, half-mile away. Me and Rowdy caught in-comin' flights from Seattle and Phoenix. Worked all night."

"How did you two manage with only a pair of sniffer dogs?"

Kimura turned to the room's near wall and spat out the gum. It rolled under a pallet. He swiveled back to the detective. "Could be hard, for sure. I mean, in the summer, with tons of air traffic into Alaska, it gets tricky. But right now, mid-winter, it's a lot easier. Just cargo and international passengers. And way fewer of them now it's off-season."

Hernandez thought a moment. "Explain something to me. When a plane comes in and baggage is unloaded, how would Houston and his dog start searching?"

Kimura raised his eyebrows. "Is this gonna end any time

soon? I got work."

Hernandez stared at the man. "It'll end when I tell you it ends. Not before. Now answer the fucking question."

Kimura gritted his teeth. "Christ. OK. Baggage is unloaded off the plane, gets put onto carts and brought into the terminal building. Houston and Brandy would do a quick search while the bags were still on the carts. After that, the luggage'd be put on the belt that takes it inside where the passengers collect their bags."

"That's it? That's the inspection?"

"No. Once all the bags are collected, international passengers still have to go through passport control, then baggage inspection. Which is where Dantley would show up again and do a bag by bag S and S."

"S and S?"

"Seek and Sniff."

"Did you see Dantley at all yesterday?"

"Once, for a few minutes, late afternoon in South Terminal where our kennels are."

"How did he seem?"

"Usual."

"What's that supposed to mean?"

Kimura laughed. "This is getting boring. Like I told 'ya, Houston was an asshole. Got it?" Kimura took out another two sticks of gum, peeled, and stuck them, one after the other, in his mouth. He chewed and stared at the detective. "We done?"

"One more question. Dantley ever flash more money than he should have? Buy something that made you wonder how he could have afforded it?"

"No. Guy drove a crummy old car, had a cheap watch, wore cheap clothes."

"OK. Now we're done."

The two cops met up again in an empty office, loaned to them by Walesa. Since there wasn't a single piece of furniture in the small room, they both stood.

Hernandez began. "The other dog handler, Kimura's his name, had no use for his partner. Resented how Dantley treated his dog. Called him a 'dickwad.'"

Sasha laughed. "I get the feeling that's what Walesa felt about him, too. What else?"

"We got Dantley working in the North Terminal every other Tuesday, all the Troika Aviation flights. Whatta you got?"

Before Sasha could reply, a deep rumbling shook the walls. She turned to the room's large window that looked out onto the airport's north-south runway. A giant FedEx transport—a Boeing 777—was just taking off. The roar of the jet's engines made the window glass rattle. When the aircraft was finally aloft and away, she turned back to her partner.

"Dantley's work records support what Kimura said: he worked Troika every other Tuesday night for the past eighteen months."

"Good. You do a time-line?"

"Yeah. I did a walk-through of how Dantley might have left the building last night. He punched out at eleven minutes past nine. Crash happened right around nine-thirty, according to the witnesses. Leaves twenty or so minutes to get to his car and drive to the crash site. I walked from the time clock he used to employee parking. It's far and real icy and I had to walk carefully. Took about ten minutes. Cold last night, and he didn't have an auto-starter. He might have had to let the car warm up. That makes it, I'm thinking, around nine-twenty-two, twenty-three. He died less than ten minutes later. About how long it'd take him to leave the airport, get onto the frontage road, and drive to the crash site. Which doesn't seem to leave him any time to go somewhere else to collect the drugs."

"So we can pretty safely conclude the dope was here, in the building," Gary said, "and that it probably came in last night on the Troika flight. Passengers or crew."

"Unless Busby is right and Dantley maybe stored it here. And only last night got around to delivering it."

"Maybe. That's still a possibility. Though not a strong one. Seems too weird storing twenty kilo of H at the airport. You think?"

"Probably. And if we don't believe it's passengers who are bringing the drugs in, we'll need to get with the FAA, check their lists of crew flying in and out of town. But right now, let's go review the surveillance tapes Walesa's prepared for us."

The customs director cued the video player. The tape showed a set of glass doors at the end of a corridor about thirty feet long. Half way down, there was a pair of doors on the right hand wall.

"Those are men's and women's bathrooms," Walesa said.

The video showed passengers with their luggage coming through the glass doors and walking toward the overhead camera, then passing out of view.

Walesa said, "They've all cleared passport control and customs."

Sasha asked, "Remind me, Gary, how many passengers did Busby say?"

"Couple hundred, maybe more."

"Actually," Walesa said, checking her notes, "there were two hundred and thirty-two."

"Right," Sasha said. "I've been keeping a rough count of how many we've already seen on the tape. So far, just under two hundred have passed through. But no crew yet."

They watched as another bunch of twenty passengers came down the corridor. They were soon followed by several members of the crew.

Gary asked Walesa, "And how many in the crew? We've just seen eight."

"Nine total, three in the flight crew and six in the cabin crew. So there should be one more."

They watched and waited as another dozen passengers filtered down the long hall.

"That should be most of the rest of the passengers," Sasha said.

They waited a few more minutes. Two more passengers appeared, then another three minutes until the last member of the crew came into the hall, wheeling a bag with black straps. He came halfway down the hall, looked back, and went into the men's rest room.

Gary and Sasha looked at each other and grinned. "Just a wee bit furtive, don't you think?" Sasha whispered to Gary.

"Just a wee bit." He turned to the customs director. "Miz Walesa, can you tell what crew member that man might be?"

"Well, he's got chevrons on his sleeve, so he's probably a pilot."

Five minutes later, the man exited the rest room, still wheeling the black bag. He passed out of the camera's view.

A minute after that, a uniformed man with a dog came through the glass doors and into the hall. He was carrying a large backpack that seemed to be full.

"That's Houston," said Walesa.

Dantley came part way down the hall and went into the bathroom with his dog. After four minutes, the two exited. The backpack was slung over Dantley's shoulder.

"The pack is hanging lower," Gary said. "Looks heavier

than when he entered."

The cops exchanged glances again. "Is this too easy, Gary?" Sasha asked.

"We can only hope."

~~~

Detective Busby Moranis found Patrolman Oscar Wasillie standing before the door of Houston Dantley's third story condo in back of Twin Dragon Mongolian Barbeque.

"Yo, Oscar. What gives here?"

"A big fat zero, Moranis. I got here a little after two this morning. No one home. Door locked. Freezin' my ass off."

"OK. Let's go on in. Get warm."

From the building's broad outside landing, they could look down and see across the highway to the Ben Boeke Ice Rink and the Sullivan Arena, the city's largest venue for indoor sports. And if they leaned over the wrought iron railing, not too far, *Crazy Horse,* home of Anchorage adult entertainment at its most legally explicit, came into view.

Moranis took out a key ring—part of the effects of the lately departed U.S. Customs worker. The detective hadn't examined the set of keys closely when he'd collected them from the precinct's evidence lock-up. But now he noted a type that he clearly recognized—a bank deposit box key stamped 'Do Not Duplicate.' He flipped past that one and opened the condo's entrance with the door key. Moranis called out from the threshold. Hearing no response, the two cops entered warily, sight-cleared the small living space, and did the same with the one bedroom and bathroom. They came into the apartment's kitchenette.

"You hungry, Oscar?" Moranis asked.

"Nah, I'm good," Wasillie said.

"Think the guy'll mind if I graze?"

"Too late for him to mind. Knock yourself out."

"Right." Moranis checked the fridge. He took out an orange, peeled the fruit and ate it, section by section. He washed his hands, dried them with a dishtowel, and turned to the living space. "OK. Let's see what we can see."

"What we lookin' for?" Wasillie asked.

"Guy was a mule. So any drugs, paraphernalia, wads of cash, lists of names, diaries, notebooks. Stuff like that."

"Got it."

An hour later, the only things of interest they'd discovered were the dead man's monthly bank statements and a bill from Mutual of Alaska for the yearly rental of a deposit box.

After Moranis locked the apartment and sealed the door, Wasillie stretched orange crime scene tape across the entry. Moranis sent the patrolman back to the precinct house and drove to the dead man's bank.

~~~

Luisa Cortez was a petite and gently rounded Latina. The bank manager was late-thirties, early forties with short-cropped coal black hair. She had smooth, mocha skin, large gray eyes, and not a single ring on the fingers of her left hand.

On the wall in back of her desk, Moranis saw several photographs of the woman with a pair of girls. There was no man in any of the photos. The detective regarded the woman across the desk. He felt drawn to her and imagined his hands in her hair, looking deeply into those pools of gray. He gave her a long smile, then showed her the warrant and passed her the deposit box key.

Cortez gave the warrant a cursory look then declared in lilting English, "It's a Mutual key, and definitely from this branch." She flashed Moranis a perfect set of brilliant white teeth and a smile that made his pelvis tingle. "Can you tell me, please, why you're investigating Mr. Dantley?" Another devastating smile. "I probably shouldn't have asked," she said. "Police work and all."

The pair of smiles had captivated Moranis. And when he leaned in her direction, he caught the barest hint of her scent and felt further bewitched. Moranis had inhaled a myriad of perfumes in his time. But this woman gave off a singular musky fragrance that made his heart skip. He sensed his body lifting unbidden out of his seat, as if by some unseen force of enchantment. He found his voice. "Sorry, Miz Cortez. Perhaps I'll be able to talk about it with you later on. But for now, is it possible to know when Mr. Dantley used his box?"

"That's easy. He'd have to sign in whenever he wanted to access it. We can check." She rose and came out from behind her desk. The woman was no more than five feet tall.

"Right this way," she said. She'd beckoned so sweetly and accommodatingly, Moranis wanted to swoop her up in his arms right then and there and carry her off. Since he wasn't certain where he'd carry her to, he held himself in check.

With the help of a customer service employee, Cortez produced a list of all of Houston Dantley's visits to his deposit box. Moranis was gratified to learn that his hunch was right: like clockwork, the dead man had visited the box every other Wednesday, Thursday, or Friday for the past sixteen months.

Cortez reached out and touched Moranis' sleeve. "Will you want to see what's in his box?" she asked. "I mean, does your warrant give you permission to inspect it?"

Her hand on his arm had an electric effect. He didn't quite

jump with the voltage, but it made his eyes go wide. He struggled for a breath. "It does ma'am. Here's the warrant again. Have a look." He spread the document on the counter and pointed out the relevant part. Cortez, too short to easily see, stood on tiptoes and leaned over the counter.

Moranis watched, spellbound by the diminutive bank executive. "Look," he said, pointing. "You can see for yourself."

She read for a moment, then seemed to lose her balance and tottered briefly. She grabbed his arm to right herself.

"Sorry, Detective Moranis. I'm a little clumsy." There was that smile again and another Taser jolt tingled through his nervous system. At that moment, Moranis had a thought that caught him off-guard: a role reversal had just taken place. This sensational woman had become the hunter, and he the prey. His lothario's confidence had been replaced by a desire to submit to this woman, wherever, whenever, and in whatever fashion she might see fit. He was surprised how thrilled he was by the notion. He gathered himself.

"Not to worry ma'am. Actually, it was . . . it was a total pleasure." He returned her touch with one of his own—the lightest stroke of her elbow. Her reaction included a saucy tilt of her head and another incandescent smile.

"Miz . . . Miz Cortez. Forgive me for being forward, I . . . I don't normally do this." Moranis put his hands in his pockets, took them out. "I mean. . . hardly at all. I'm here on business and I've come to the bank . . . and you're the manager and I'm really not supposed to . . . but . . . maybe you're free some evening. Can I buy you dinner?" He felt like a kid, a high school sophomore seeking a date to his first prom. *Christ. What a doofus.*

She stared up at the tall, blond policeman, the tip of her tongue showing between her lips. "That would be lovely. This

Friday night? Seven o'clock too early?" She once again placed her elegant fingers on his sleeve.

Busby Moranis couldn't remember the last time he'd felt this way, if ever. All the other women he'd chased—missed or captured—faded from his memory. He gazed goofily down at her. "Works for me," he managed to get out.

Cortez raised her eyebrows and smiled sweetly at his apparent discomfort. "But for now, you'd probably like to examine the contents of Mr. Dantley's deposit box."

"Super," the besotted detective said.

~~~

Nelson Alexie was sorting through papers in his office in the Eagle River Tribal Health Center. He looked up when he heard a light knock. He came out from behind his desk and went to give his unexpected guest a hug.

"Sasha. It's been too long."

"Nelson. It's great to see you, too." She held him tightly then stepped back and looked him up and down. "You haven't changed a bit. You look fit. Still trapping? Running dogs?"

"Trapping's not so good lately. These longer summers, shorter winters are changing everything. But the dogs? Little slower but still reliable. They get me back and forth along the trail. And you, you look healthy." He took a quick glance at his wristwatch. "And you've come at exactly the right time. We're going to start the meeting in a minute."

There were a dozen people sitting in a circle of chairs—women, men, young, old. Alexie spoke first and when he finished his few words, he turned and looked to his guest. "Sasha?" He motioned her to stand.

"If you insist," she smiled and rose. "Hello everyone. My name is Sasha. I'm an alcoholic."

The audience responded with a variety of welcoming greetings.

"I've been sober for five hundred and ninety-two days. Six hundred next week."

More supportive comments from the audience.

"I don't have to tell anyone here just how hard it is to stay dry." She shook her head slowly back and forth. "I mean, I'm thirsty *all* the time. But happily for me, and for all of you, we have Nelson here. He's got your back. I know he's got mine." She grinned at the host. "The first time we met was three years ago, not far from here. I was working, had come to work hung over. Nelson took one look at me and knew instantly that I'd been severely shit-faced the night before. But rather than accuse me of being a drunk on the job, he got down on his knees, scooped up a handful of snow and insisted I wash my face and neck with it. 'This'll sober you up,' he said. Or words to that effect." Sasha laughed. "I see a lot of you smiling and nodding. Seems you've all experienced Nelson's hands-on healing. Well, I didn't completely stop drinking that day, but meeting Nelson was the start of my going dry. And I thank him now from the bottom of my heart. And always will."

After the meeting, over coffee and cookies, Alexie and Sasha found a corner and sat.

"Thanks for the kind words," he said.

"You deserve them. These folks here don't know how lucky they are to have fallen into your clutches."

He scanned the small crowd. "Some do. Some haven't realized it yet. We're working on it. But tell me, how you doin'?"

"Generally OK. Sober, like I said. Couple meeting places

I go to in town, two, three times a week."

"So why come all the way out to Eagle River?"

"Some stuff I needed to think about. The drive gives me time alone, time to mull things over. And the chance to see you again. We haven't touched base in a long while."

"Thanks for the visit. You're still a cop?"

"I am. After we cleaned up that mess—the body that you showed us that morning—the Department gave me a six-month leave of absence. I got serious counseling and dried out. I'm OK now." She took a bite of cookie, shrugged her shoulders. "I guess."

He regarded her in silence for a few moments. "You guess?"

Sasha drained her coffee and put down her foam cup. "I got kid problems."

"You have a daughter if I recall. Should be close to seventeen? Remind me of her name."

"Robin. Closer to sixteen."

He waited.

"Well . . . she got busted. Holding. Heroin."

Alexie shook his head. "Oh Lord, Lord." He took both her hands in his own. "Tell me what I can do to help."

"If there was anything, you'd be the very first person I'd call. But no, it's her problem to solve. She has to figure it out."

"No one can do it alone, Sasha. You know that. She'll need you."

Sasha pressed her lips together. "I'm still trying to figure out my role in her rehab. Trying to understand the why and the what for."

"You believe you have some responsibility?"

She nodded her agreement. "As usual, you've gone to the heart of the matter. I ask myself the part I played. Am still playing. Will play."

"You're a smart lady. You'll figure it out."

She blew out a long breath. "We'll see, won't we?"

"We will. Anyhow, can you stay for dinner? Celia's slow-cooking her famous moose stroganoff."

"Oh my God, nothing I'd like better. But I'm meeting my partners for burgers at The Lucky Wishbone."

"Not quite stroganoff," Alexie laughed.

~~~

Early evening. The three cops who make up the Anchorage Police Department's Narcotics Division were in The Lucky Wishbone, the city's most venerable eatery. They had a window booth and were enjoying hamburgers, fries, and Butterfinger malts.

Outside, it was dark, overcast, cold, and windy. Wet snowflakes were being blown onto the diner's windows. A stand of bare birch trees across the diner's parking lot creaked in the wind.

Lieutenant Gary Hernandez wiped ketchup from his lips. "Looks like we got us a pretty clear pattern here. Busby finds out the dead guy's been visiting his deposit box every other week for well over a year."

"Didn't miss a single bi-monthly visit," Busby added.

Sasha asked, "How much cash the guy sock away?"

Busby checked his notebook. "A ton. There were twenty-eight bundles. Total was eighty thousand, one hundred dollars, all in fifties. In twenty-one of the bundles, I counted three grand in each. In another four, there was twenty-five hundred. And in the rest of 'em, there were amounts between two grand and twenty-four-fifty. So my thinking is the guy got paid three Gs each time. And once in a while, he'd take some. Make sense?"

"It does," Gary said.

"Me and the bank manager counted the bundles. We double checked."

"How come you and the bank manager?" Gary asked. "Wasn't Oscar with you?"

"He was there when I got to the guy's apartment. He'd spent the whole night, froze to death, so I sent him back to the station when we finished. I asked the manager to witness the search and I wanted her to check my numbers. I know it ain't proper procedure but I remember what happened a couple years back when Carella was alone and went into the perp's deposit box and came out with the Ruger. All kinds of shit at the trial from the perp's lawyer, claiming Carella planted the weapon. Just enough doubt so the jury couldn't deliver."

"And you got a photo log I'm hoping," Gary said.

"Absolutely. Prob'ly took thirty photos. When we finished, I left the money in the deposit box, but kept the key. I can go back any time and collect all of it. I can go back tomorrow if we need to."

Gary finished off his malt. "Good. We match your info with what Sasha and I learned today at customs." He took a sheaf of pages from his jacket pocket, moved his plate, and spread the pages out. "We were able to track the dead guy's work schedule. It perfectly dovetails with what you found at the bank. Seems Dantley worked every other Tuesday night, on duty in the North Terminal when the Troika planes come in."

"Gee, what a coincidence," said Busby. "Only tell me, please. Who gives it to him at the airport?"

Sasha dipped a French fry into ketchup. "Well, we're pretty much convinced it's the crew. We went to the FAA after we finished at the airport. They keep a list of the names of the pilots and crew of every commercial or passenger flight that comes into Anchorage. We spent a couple hours checking flight and cabin crews." She ate a pair of small fries. "The cabin crews change all the time. Almost every flight. Yeah, there were a few attendants who flew here occasionally, but not in any significant pattern. So we eliminated them and focused on the flight crew." She smiled at Gary.

"And struck gold," he said. "There's one guy, name's Suvorov, who's flown *every* flight as first officer, co-pilot. And it just so happens, the dude is still in town."

"Really?" Busby asked. "Do we know where?"

"We think so," Gary said. "All the Troika crews—pilots and attendants—stay at the Sheraton. They all fly back tomorrow afternoon. We need to visit him tonight. Sasha and I'll go pay him a call."

"Yeah, but he's a Russian," Moranis said. "Can we arrest him? Or even question him? We got no real proof. We prob'ly don't even have jurisdiction."

"You're right," Hernandez said. "I called over to the FBI, spoke to Bob Glazer, their in-house counsel. He said pretty much what you said. Jurisdiction in a drug smuggling case that involves a foreign national can get real complicated. And the pilot's leaving tomorrow. Besides which, we have no hard evidence that he's connected."

"Other than the fact that the customs guy was working every time the pilot showed up in Anchorage," Busby said.

Gary drank down the last of his malt. "Can hardly go to a judge with 'coincidence' as probable cause."

"So our hands are pretty much tied," Busby said.

"Not quite," Sasha said. "We can scare the shit out of him. Let him know he's unwelcome here. And maybe we can even scare him into helping us out."

"Wear your body cams," Busby suggested. "I wanna see this tomorrow mornin'. And what about a visit to the Troika offices. See what they know?"

"We checked on that already," Gary said. "According to the FAA, they don't have their own office in Anchorage. Everything is run out of Vladivostok. We'll have to contact them somehow."

Busby finished the remaining three fries. "Is that something we—Anchorage police—can do or do we have to go through a federal agency? Like the FBI or DEA?"

"I don't wanna do that," Gary said. "Means we lose control of the case. Let's see if Stan knows someone in Russia."

~~~

First Officer Anatoly Suvorov*, co-pilot of Troika Aviation's Airbus 330 long-range passenger aircraft, returned to his hotel room in the late afternoon. Since his arrival in Anchorage the evening before, Anatoly had whiled away the hours with Olga, a thirty-year-old hooker of Russian extraction he had met at Chilkoot Charlie's months before and with whom he coupled whenever he was in town.

They'd gone for dinner the night before at the Seven Glaciers Restaurant, up the mountain from the Alyeska Prince Hotel. She ordered the crab, he, the petite filet.

Not for the first time had Anatoly suggested a more lasting relationship. And not for the first time had Olga been unenthusiastic about the idea. "Be nice to get the hell outta Anchorage. But, I don't know," she said, "where would I go and why?" She snapped a crab leg in half.

After dinner, the fair-skinned Olga took the pilot back to

her apartment in Girdwood and treated him to her six hundred dollar all-night special. Anatoly used the in-between times to press his case. She remained noncommittal.

Now, around ten o'clock on the eve of his departure back to Vladivostok, feeling exhausted and a tad disappointed that his Olga-suit had, once again, been rebuffed, he lay sprawled on his hotel bed. He was caught up watching an episode from the sixth season of Homeland. Claire Danes was off her meds again and having another meltdown. The pilot was working on a quarter pounder and was sipping from a can of Heineken, his second and last. He admired his own forbearance: after all, he was co-piloting the next day.

There was a knock at the door. He ignored it. But when the banging became insistent, he muted the TV, cursed, and shouted from his bed, "Who is?"

A man's voice announced, "Anatoly Suvorov. Police. Open the door."

The first officer's guts turned instantly to water. "W . . . what you w . . . want?" *Is this it? I should never have listened to Sophia.*

The man's voice came again, more determined, "We want to talk to you. Open the door."

The scene at the end of *Fargo*—his favorite American movie—now flashed before the pilot's eyes: William Macy in his underpants tries to escape the police who have rushed into his motel room. Macy attempts to jump through a window but is dragged back in, screaming. Suvorov looked fleetingly at his room's lone window and thought momentarily about jumping. But since it was a top-of-the window, narrow slat-opener, and since he was on the fourth floor, and since he probably wouldn't survive the fall, and since, if he did survive, he had absolutely no idea where he'd go, he dismissed the idea. Now, louder banging.

"Just a minute," he said. He stood, straightened his back as best he could, called up some saliva into his suddenly parched mouth, and cracked open the door. A large man and a woman. But not in uniform. *Secret Police. I'm fucked.*

"Anatoly Suvorov?" the man asked, shoving open the door and stepping into the room. He was huge. A hundred and twenty kilos, at least. The policeman moved toward the pilot, making the smaller man back up. The cop's fists were balled and he glowered. "Are you Anatoly Suvorov?"

The pilot stumbled backwards into the room. The woman shut the door behind her and turned toward him.

"Y . . . yes. I Anatoly Suvorov. But I small English. I no understand too m . . . many," he stammered.

The woman came up to him, a cheerful smile on her face, and in perfectly accented, perfectly idiomatic Russian said, "Not to worry, pal. You and I can speak Russian. I'll handle the translation without a problem."

Suvorov gawked at her. *She must be the one Mehmet told me about. The one who shot Bunin's men three years ago in the Aleutian Islands. Jesus, save my ass.* The pilot focused on trying to keep his knees from buckling. "Y . . . yes," was all he could muster. His bowels gurgled.

"Let's sit, shall we," she suggested in Russian, guiding the man by the arm into the space between the two beds.

He entered the narrow aisle. *They've penned me in. I'm trapped.* He pushed away the pillows and leaned against the headboard, feet on the bed. The woman took the remote and shut off the TV, then sat at the foot of the same bed. Her partner parked himself opposite her on the other bed.

The woman pointed to the man, "This is Lieutenant Hernandez of the Anchorage Police Department, and I'm Sergeant Kulaeva. We'd like to ask you a few questions."

Kulaeva. She's the one. Oh God.

"You fly for Troika Aviation, correct?"

"Yes."

"First officer?"

He nodded.

"You flew in last night?"

He nodded again.

"And came to this hotel directly?"

"Yes."

"You fly to Alaska often?"

He twitched. "Sometime."

"Sometime?" she asked.

He watched as she withdrew several pages of folded paper from inside her jacket. She took her time. When she spoke, her voice had lost its earlier familiarity. It now sounded more accusatory.

"Mr. Suvorov. This is a complete list of your flights into Alaska. My colleague and I got these documents this afternoon from the American Federal Aviation Administration. That organization records the name and flight schedule of every pilot who flies passenger and cargo planes into our country and lands at an American airport."

His mind was swimming. *I'll never see my son again. Won't see Olga. And Sophia? Never should have listened to her.*

The woman cop held the pages up to him. "Have a look," she said. "Says here you've flown to Alaska every other Tuesday for the past thirteen months. Twenty-eight times, to be exact."

The large policeman frowned and spoke slowly in English, enunciating each word. "Every. Other. Tuesday. Twenty. Eight. Times."

Suvorov could only stare at the cop. *They have an immense*

prison system in this country. Bigger even than ours. Or China's. They must have a gulag. And a Lubianka. God help me.

"Have a look," she said, holding the pages up for him to read.

He stared. Although he could hardly read the English, the twice-monthly dates jumped out at him. "Yes . . ." he said.

"Yes?"

"Well . . . I think . . . " *You're enjoying this, aren't you? You whore.* He shifted his weight from one buttock to the other. He was doing his best not to soil himself.

The male policeman took a small envelope from his pocket and removed a photo. He held it up to the pilot. "Do you know this person?"

It's the guy from customs. He looks like he's gotten the shit kicked out of him. Suvorov saw a man with eyes half-closed, lying on a sheet. His head was mangled. A jagged gash ran from his right-side hairline down to the bridge of his crushed nose. His mouth was open and there was a gap in his lower teeth where cuspids should have been.

"Maybe you know him?" the woman asked.

The pilot kept his hands securely under his thighs. He didn't dare remove them to take the picture. He feared he'd quiver himself right into prison.

"No. No. I don't know this person."

"Sure?" she asked.

"Yes. Sure."

"Interesting," she said. "Because he was the U.S. Customs agent who checked your bags at the airport. And actually . . ." here she searched through the pages and selected one, which she flapped in front of the pilot, "This is a schedule of all of the dead man's work for customs. Seems he's been on duty *every time* you fly in. Some kind of coincidence, Mr. Suvorov?"

When he didn't reply, she continued, "Sure you don't recognize him?"

The pilot felt a stricture in his throat, a tightening that grasped his windpipe. His armpits were dripping. His breathing came shallow and rapid. He knew for a certainty that his physical stresses were being communicated—shouted—to the two cops. *I'm cornered. Sophia got me into this mess. Why did I marry her in the first place?* He raised his head and, with effort, focused his eyes on the photo. He looked at the woman. "It's possible. Maybe I do recognize him. But . . . Why is this so important?"

"He was killed in a car crash last night. Ran into a moose, not long after he checked your bags."

He really is dead. My transfer-contact is dead. Hit a moose? What was he doing driving in the goddamn forest? And the goods? Where are they? But wait a minute. If he's dead, then maybe a chance. Any evidence the man could have given the cops died with him in the crash. Suvorov revived a bit, brushed the air in front of him. "Well. I'm not sure how I'm connected to this. A man who works at the airport dies in a car accident. What has that got to do with me?"

The woman scooted closer on the bed. She leaned toward him and hissed, "Listen very carefully. We don't want to see your ugly face again in Alaska. Ever. In fact . . ." She took hold of his shirt lapels and yanked him closer. "In fact, if I ever learn that you're in our country, I'll find you. I'll smash your face to a pulp. I'll break every bone in your motherfucking body. Then I'll take a blowtorch to your nuts. And that'll only be the beginning. Understand me?"

When he couldn't answer, the woman shouted at him, her spittle spattering his face. "I asked you, Mister Suvorov, if you understood what I just said to you."

"Y . . . yes. I understand."

She shoved him back so roughly that his head thunked against the wall.

The two officers rose and stood over him. The male cop opened his jacket and let Suvorov see the pistol holstered on his hip. The cop raised his arm and made a gun out of his fingers. He pointed directly at the pilot's head and mimed squeezing off two shots. Then he and the woman left the room.

As soon as they were gone, Suvorov rushed to the bathroom where he spent a good five minutes giving back the beer and burger.

Outside, Sasha and Gary sat in his pickup. They were smiling.

"Think we'll ever see him again?" Gary asked.

"I'd love to see him again."

"You might have to go to Russia to do that. That in your plans?"

"Not in this present incarnation. Plus I got shit here at home to tend to."

Gary started up the pickup. "How's Robin doing?"

"I'm seeing Jepson tomorrow morning."

"Why a public defender?"

"I'm gonna ask him to talk to her, try and scare her into naming the guy."

"Think it'll work?"

"I'm not sure. Robin's being a hard ass."

"Apple doesn't fall far from the tree."

"That's little consolation, Gary."

After throwing up his guts and washing his face, Anatoly Suvorov phoned Mehmet Ozil. He began screaming as soon as the Turk answered.

"Secret police come my room. They now go. They say kill

me I come America again. What I do?"

Mehmet was in the bedroom, watching his wife pack. He took a deep breath, rose and as casually as he could manage, sidled out of the room. *First the customs guy dead in a car crash. Now the cops have found their way to the pilot. How did they do it so goddamn fast?* He gathered himself and tried to keep the panic out of his voice.

"OK, Toly. Tell me exactly what happened. What cops? Were they wearing uniforms? Yes or no?"

"No. No. Secret police no wear uniform. Wear normal clothings. One man, big, scary. One woman, more scary."

At once, Mehmet realized the bitch was back. *Kulaeva. Shit!* "OK. Tell me what they asked. Tell me the questions."

"They ask I know customs man, Dantley. I say no. They show photo where he dead. They have papers say I fly Alaska Tuesday. And another one paper say Dantley work when I come Anchorage."

"Did they tell you that you broke a law?"

"No. But say I not come Alaska. Woman cop say kill me if see me."

"When do you fly back to Vladivostok?"

"Tomorrow. In afternoon. I can no come back to America, Mehmet. She kill me."

"Yes, I understand."

"So what I do?"

"Don't come back. Good bye, Toly." Mehmet closed the call and returned to the bedroom. His wife was still packing and unpacking.

"Thank God I'll be out of here in a couple hours," Nikki said, folding a pair of sweaters and placing them with shaking hands in an open suitcase. She stopped long enough to tap out a Gauloises from a pack, lit up, and inhaled deeply. She didn't bother trying to blow the smoke away from her non-smoking husband. It encircled his head. "I mean, it's dangerous here, right?"

"A little, maybe," he hacked. "On a scale of one to ten, ten being extremely dangerous, I'd say the situation was around . . ." he shrugged, "five, maybe."

"Five! Five is not the number I was hoping to hear." She crushed out her barely smoked cigarette in an ashtray on the night table. "Five is . . . a little too dangerous. So who was it on the phone this time? Artun again?" She took out the two sweaters she'd just packed and tossed them on the bed.

"No. Suvorov."

"The pilot?" she croaked. "The Troika pilot? He was just here for dinner last month for Christ's sake. What was that about?"

"It's about the two narco cops who visited him tonight, showed him a photo of the dead dog handler, then threatened to kill him if he ever came back to America again."

Nikki dropped onto the bed, hands clasped between her knees. "Narcotics cops? She gasped. "That means that Russian witch, what's her name . . . ?"

"Kulaeva. Aleksandra Kulaeva."

"Right. If she's involved . . . Jesus." Nikki shook another Gauloises out of the pack and lit it with shaky fingers. She picked up the two discarded sweaters and threw them back into her open piece of luggage. "Why hasn't somebody gotten rid of her by now? I'd do it myself if I had the chance."

Mehmet stared at his wife. In all the years of their marriage and through all of his numerous criminal activities, he'd never heard her make such a declaration. "Really, Nikki? You'd do it yourself? You sound like Artun. He's wanted to kill her for the last three years. Since that clusterfuck out in the Aleutians."

"And why hasn't he?" she demanded.

"Bunin has ordered her off-limits. She has dirt on him."

"What kind of dirt?"

"Something to do with Zhuganov, Bunin's strong-arm guy. Remember him? The one Bunin sent to Vladivostok three years ago for some bullshit reason. Zhuganov kills the Americans, gets caught and is tossed into prison. Gets offed the first night. So for some reason I don't understand Bunin says, 'Hands off Kulaeva.'"

"But she's dangerous, Mehmet."

"Don't I know it. I have to let Brooklyn know about the pilot. They won't be pleased, especially Lara. This Troika thing was all her idea in the first place."

~~~

Public Defender Bobby Carl Jepson, a tall, ex-Alabaman with a paunch, leaned back in his office recliner and sucked on a toothpick. A worried mother sat across from him in his small office.

Sasha regarded the PD, wondering—as she did every time the two had business together—why a man in his forties looked like he was seventy. *Maybe because he doesn't have any eyebrows,* she thought. *Strange looking dude, but a capable PD.*

Jepson was good at expressing much-practiced sympathy, especially to a mother whose daughter was in extremely deep shit. He did so now.

"It's plum awful what's happened to that girl of yours, Sasha. What can I do to help?"

"Thanks, Bobby Carl. You can help me make her see the light. I talked to her JPO, Gracie Vang. Gracie says she can't even begin to consider dismissal, informal probation, or an informal adjustment if Robin doesn't help the court with some kind of plea deal. If she doesn't name her source, she'll be at McLaughlin 'til she's eighteen. And after that, who knows?"

Jepson craned forward in his seat. "Unfortunately for Robin, Gracie's right. Ya'll know Sasha, we got real crime here."

"I know we do. I heard most of it from the arresting officer, but let me have it again, all the details."

Jepson sat upright and opened the file in front of him, *Robin Kulaeva. Juvenile.* He ran a finger down the list of alleged offences.

"It ain't purty but here it is, from the top." Jepson tossed the toothpick onto his desk. "She steals a car in Eagle River, drives drunk to Bartlett High where she's arrested in the school's parkin' lot after hittin' a car. The passenger in the car with Robin, name of Marci Sunderland, takes a knock on the head and some bruised ribs. Not serious for Marci, but complicates things for your daughter."

"Was Marci drunk, too?" Sasha asked.

"One point five on the PBT. Which *she* agreed to take. Unlike Robin, who refused. Not smart."

"No. Not smart."

"Now, 'bout the vehicle. If it hadda been a relative's car, that's one thing. Coulda passed it off as joyridin'. But she stole a stranger's ride and that makes it a whole different shootin' match. Plus, she dint have the sense to shut her trap and told the arrestin' officer that she *'wanted to keep the car.'* Those were her exact words I'm readin' from the arrest report. So now we got us a case of grand theft auto."

"Ah, Jesus."

"Well, GTA is one thing. But the dicey part is the sixteen

grams in a plastic vial in your daughter's back pocket."

Sasha held her head in her hands, the full realization of her daughter's criminal behavior bearing down on her.

Jepson said, "No previous trouble, no record of any kinda trouble. But Gracie's right. What I just read is enough to get your daughter good and fucked."

"Tell me what you can do. Robin refuses to name anyone. She told me she wants to take her medicine."

"Tough kid, Sasha. But that dog won' hunt. Fact, judge won' cut her any slack iff'n she don' help the court." Jepson tipped back in his chair. "This whole thing reminds me of that Rudy Castro bozo. The guy you and Gary caught up with in that heroin bust, three years ago. He dint cooperate either, and there was no way I coulda convince him otherwise. Told him he was lookin' at a serious mandatory iff'n he dint come clean."

"Rudy was a jerk. And it was a different story, Bobby Carl. Mob threatened to kill him if he copped a plea."

"And they did, too, dint they? Caught up with the sucker at that hotel in Palmer. Three in the head, I heard." Jepson retrieved the toothpick and stuck it back in his mouth. "Well, that was then and I'm sorry to say, Sasha, that your Robin's headin' for a heap of trouble 'less she helps the court."

"Bottom line?"

"McLaughlin 'til she's eighteen. After that, up to the judge. Might be probation. Might be released into your custody. Or, she could get lucky. Hard to say."

"Who'll be the judge?"

"Again, she could get lucky and come before Sanzoni. He likes kids. Got half dozen hisself. Catholic dude. Or she gets unlucky and gets stuck with Angela Bergsen, the spinster. She *don'* like kids. Mean lady. Tell me 'bout your daughter's home life. Maybe we can plead emotional problems."

"Well, she misses her great-grandfather. A lot. They were super close. He really was the one who raised her. Raised me, too. They had a wonderful relationship. And when he died she began to lose focus."

"I heard 'bout your granddaddy. I'm sorry for your loss. He was a kinda famous guy, wasn't he? Great pilot, I heard."

"Yeah, Viktor was one of a kind[4]. He was ninety-three when he laid himself down last year and went to sleep. God, I miss him."

"What about Robin's school? Good grades?"

"Used to make pretty fair grades. But they dropped when she fell into a bad crowd of kids at Eagle River High after Viktor died. I was here in Anchorage." Sasha paused, Robin's scathing comment about her mother's absentee parenting echoing. "She was pretty much on her own, and couldn't manage."

"Well, lemme go on over to McLaughlin tomorrow, talk to her, let her know just how seriously deep in shit she is. The prospect of jail time often works wonders to change people's ideas about plea bargainin'. She hears how long she might get, the conditions inside, she might cooperate."

~~~

Leo Bulgarin didn't know what was worse: that his participation in drug smuggling was about to be the main order of business for the Anchorage Police Department, or having to absorb the constant bombardment from his wife about how stupid he was to have agreed to get involved in Boris's plans in Alaska.

He remembers the afternoon, years earlier, when he went to meet Boris for lunch in Manhattan. His wife had pleaded, begged, threatened him not to go. He'd sloughed off her warnings and now was paying the price for the trust he had placed in his cousin.

Seated now in the den of their small south Anchorage home, Leo and Dorotea were silent, Leo fearful of saying something that would re-ignite his wife's fury. And Dorotea, seething, knowing she had been right all along but realizing that no amount of browbeating her husband could alter this situation, so fraught with obvious danger. She opted to focus on the immediate present.

"Have you spoken again with the Turk?"

"Mehmet called earlier. Said to sit tight until Boris and Lara figure out what to do."

"What can *they* do from three thousand miles away?" Dorotea rose and began pacing, circling the table where her husband sat, his head bowed, hands in his lap.

Look at him, she thought. *He's got 'loser' written all over him.* She stopped her table circling. "There might come a time, Leo, when we'll have to fend for ourselves, not wait for those two in Brooklyn to tell us what to do. Like they've been doing since you agreed to drag us to Alaska."

Leo, seeking to maintain the temporary peace, readily agreed. "You may be right. Time may come."

"When are you supposed to fly out to St. Lawrence Island again?"

"In two days."

"No way. It's clear you can't go. You'll have to let the Eskimo guy know to sit on the stuff 'til he hears from you."

Leo felt numb but knew his wife was right. And if he continued to agree with her, she might ease off on her personal onslaughts. "Good thinking." He reached for his cell. "I'll call the guy. Tell him to cool it for a while."

Six hundred and sixty miles due west from Anchorage, Buster Kopanuk ended his cell phone call.

Buster's wife, Lorena, looked up from her sewing.

"That was Anchorage," Buster said. "The pilot. Said he's not coming out any time soon. Said for me to store the stuff until he tells me he's on his way."

"That's a first," Lorena said. "He's never done that before. Did he say why?"

"Engine trouble. But I'm not sure that's the reason. He sounded really nervous, stuttering. Seemed to be making up stuff as he was talking."

"Maybe we should move those bundles out of the shed. Maybe over to my brother's place?"

Buster collapsed into a stuffed easy chair. "Not there. Not yet, at least. I wouldn't want to involve Jessie in our business."

"Not as though he doesn't know what's going on, Buster. I mean, everyone on the island probably knows by now. You regularly travel—several times a year—over to Chukotka. Always bringing back cartons that we store in our shed, then taking them to the Grizzly Air guy. People here aren't dumb, Buster. They know what's going on. Even the Village Safety Officer knows."

"Yeah, but he's getting his cut, too. I wouldn't worry about him."

Lorena Kopanuk shook her head. "I'm worried. This is not good. How many cartons in the shed?"

"Two."

"Two too many," she said.

~~~

They were back in McLaughlin's meeting room. Breakfast was over, but the smell of hash browns and oatmeal lingered.

"How are you?" Sasha asked, but didn't need her daughter's

answer. Two days into withdrawal, Robin looked wrung out, a wreck. Her face was pale and beaded with sweat, eyes rheumy, her body shaking spasmodically. She was hunched over, both arms wrapped around her stomach. Her long hair hung in knots. She sniffled. "I'm a royal screw-up, mom," she mumbled.

Sasha nodded, pleased that her daughter had taken the first step: admitting her mistake. "Good that you know it. And what do you plan to do about it?"

Robin raised her eyes, and in a small voice, "Do? Do the time, I guess. Hope to survive. Turn over a better leaf when I get out."

"Really? I don't think you fully understand what being locked up means. It's rough."

"That's *my* problem, mom. I'll survive."

Sasha hesitated, knew the topic she was going to raise was a sensitive and hurtful one, but pushed it.

"Your father was killed by a couple assholes strung out on crack. You know the story well enough. You heard it from me, from Viktor, and from the rest of our family out at Big Lake."

Robin's face contorted. "Why are you telling me this?"

Sasha leaned toward her daughter. "It's real simple. I'm telling you so you'll know the kind of people you've done business with are the same kind who shot and killed your father. My husband."

Her daughter's eyes teared up and Sasha continued. "You're protecting a drug dealer. Every damn day me and Gary and Busby, the three of us, try to find these bastards and get them off the street. Because you insist on sitting on a name, you hinder our work and allow all these drugs—H, and crack, and meth, and fentanyl, and the opioids to circulate. When you don't cooperate, you make it easier for the dealers to kill kids.

You made a bad choice, girl, getting involved with heroin. But you're making an even worse one protecting the son of a bitch who sold it to you."

Robin's shoulders shook. Snot dribbled out of her nose.

Sasha handed her a handkerchief. "And I told you the other night where I stand. Just so you know. You don't help out here, then you're gonna have to do this on your own, without me. And that, my daughter, is something you will not enjoy."

"Mom, I can't. I can't. The guy said . . . he said he'd kill me if I ratted on him. Said he'd rip my eyes out."

Sasha's body began to shake. She had to take several deep breaths to control her growing rage. She put her forearms under the table, balled her fists and tried to relax her face. "I can protect you. We can protect you. Tell me the name, we grab him, throw him in the can, keep him there for years."

Robin looked wonderingly at her mother. "Whattaya mean, mom? He's got friends. I'll never be safe."

"Trust me, Robin. I'll fix it. And then you can work with Jepson, the PD, work with the DA, and try to avoid serious punishment."

"I don't . . . I can't . . . listen mom . . . please." Robin fell silent, collapsed back into her chair. Her body gave up. Through sobs, she whispered, "B.J. B.J. Lewis."

Sasha breathed out. "Who is he and where do I find him?"

"Eagle River High. He's a senior."

"Description?"

"Tall. Skinny. Glasses."

"White guy? Black guy? Native?"

"White guy. Good looking."

Sasha paused, didn't want to ask the next question but couldn't help herself. "Good looking, huh? You have sex with him? Trade sex for H?"

Robin didn't answer, averted her mother's eyes.

"Were you *fucking* him, Robin?"

Her daughter recoiled at the direct question. "No Mom. I wasn't *fucking* him," she spat out. "And if I did, it's my fucking business, isn't it?"

Sasha wanted to end the discussion of her daughter's sex life but the words spilled out. "So only hand jobs and blow jobs, huh?"

Robin didn't answer, looked away.

"Right." Sasha counted to ten. "This B.J. He sells to other kids?"

"I think he's the school's main source."

"How many score from him?"

"I don't know. Maybe a half a dozen."

"I want their names."

~~~

A.W. Heating and Plumbing in Eagle River was owned by Antoine Washington. His highly-regarded and fair-priced work was well known not only in his hometown, but in other communities north of Anchorage. His business was located on a two-acre parcel of woodland off of a sparsely populated Pole Line Road.

In his thirty-year career, he'd nursed back into operation every kind of faulty Alaskan heating system: forced air, baseboard, wood stove. He'd plumbed the depths of professionally installed or DIY drainage systems, toilets, septic tanks, and leach fields. And with longer and hotter Alaskan summers brought on by climate change, Washington now included 'air conditioning installation and repair' on his web page's menu.

He was busy throughout the year. But never too busy to

visit his other two homes, both paid for in hard cash: the condo in Cozumel, in Mexico, on Calle 17 Sur; and the bungalow on Mint Meadow Lane, on Orcas Island in the San Juans. The repairman vacationed in each at least once a year, enjoying the life of a well-to-do single man on the make.

Some of his neighbors speculated that the plumber must have an additional source of income. Those were the clever ones. But if they suspected anything, they never broached the topic with the mean-looking, six-foot, four-inch former Colony High tight end, All-State three years running, 1985-1987.

His suspicious neighbors never imagined the full extent of Washington's misdeeds: for the last twenty-some years he was the Mat-Su Valley's pre-eminent heroin dealer whose product was distributed throughout the fastest growing and most addicted population center in the state.

Washington had no illusions about the devastating effects of the product he was pushing. "Theirs not to reason why," he said of his customers. "Theirs but to shoot and die." While plumbing afforded him a decent living, selling heroin made him rich.

All of his sub-contracting distributors, including one B.J. Lewis, understood the horrific nature of the drug. None, however, really gave a shit. The money was just too good.

~~~

As soon as Sasha walked out of McLaughlin, she phoned her boss and gave him the name of the heroin dealer.

"I'll send Busby to get a warrant," Gary said. "Then he and I'll go and collect him."

"I want to go," she said.

"Don't be crazy, Sash. Against the rules. You, working on

a case involving a relative? Unh-uh. We were even stretching it some allowing you to interview Robin. Me and Busby'll go. We'll be in touch later."

She found a bench outside the Youth Center, used her scarf to slap away the snow, then flopped down. She drew her watch cap over her ears and buried her hands deep into her parka pockets. The high pressure zone that had settled over the city covered the Anchorage bowl with very clear and very cold air.

Sasha's mouth was dry. *What I wouldn't give for a beer. Or two. Or three.* Next week is the anniversary of my sobriety—six hundred days clean.

She thought about Robin and how their lives would be changed by her daughter's arrest. She regretted the ferocity with which she'd come at Robin just now. But she didn't regret the results: the identity of her daughter's source. What Sasha hadn't told Robin, had never told anyone, not even her shrink, was that when the two men who killed Robin's father were set to be released, she planned on being there to meet them and mete out to them the punishment she believed they deserved. *But didn't get from our overly lenient legal system. I'll make sure that justice will be done.*

She tried to move her thoughts to another time and a happier place: the past summer when Tomás, her Chilean cop, had come to visit.

She'd met him in 2016 at a conference in Anchorage when they'd talked for a total of four minutes. The next time she saw him was a week later, in Vladivostok, where he saved her from being murdered by the Russian mob. And then here in Alaska last year, ten amazing days together, never out of sight of each other for more than a few minutes, devouring each other like starving beasts. And the promises. To meet again, soon. To figure out a way to be together.

~~~

School was over, kids pouring out the doors, getting on their bikes, climbing onto buses, heading for their cars. Gary leaned against the student parking lot fence while Moranis stood near B.J. Lewis's green Subaru Outback. They were alerted when the car came to life by auto starter. A moment later, Lewis walked into view. He stopped short when he saw a man standing next to his car.

"Brian John Lewis?" Moranis challenged the tall young man, holding out his badge.

Lewis stared at the cop, blinking rapidly.

"You're Brian Lewis, aren't you?" asked Gary, his voice coming from behind the suspect.

Lewis whirled and saw an unsmiling and very large man walking quickly toward him.

"Don't stand there like an idiot. Answer the goddamn question," Gary snapped, stopping an arm's length from the boy. He saw the young man's body tense, as if preparing to run.

"Go ahead, moron. Make a dash. Give me a chance to beat the shit out of you. Or better yet, you're a dope dealer trying to escape. I could put three rounds in your butt before you got twenty feet. Go on. Make a run for it."

"Gary. Cool it," Moranis laughed.

Lewis was trembling. "W . . . what? Dope dealer?"

Moranis showed the suspected heroin dealer an arrest warrant. He shoved him against the Outback, searched him, then secured his hands behind his back with a plastic cable tie.

Several students had gathered and aimed their smart phones at the excitement.

Gary noted their presence. He read the suspect his Miranda rights.

Moranis got into Lewis's car. He didn't have far or long to search: a baggie of white powder showed up in the glove compartment. "Look at this, Gary. Wanna guess the weight?"

Gary took the bag on his nitrile-gloved palm, assessing it. "If it's what I think it is, then I'd guess it weighs about eight to ten years, 'specially since he's been selling to minors." He put the powder into an evidence bag.

The preliminary search of the suspect's vehicle soon completed, Moranis locked the car, phoned back to the station to arrange for a tow to the precinct garage for a more thorough search.

Gary yanked Lewis toward the police cruiser. "No tellin' what else we might find," he whispered, shoving the young man into the car's back seat.

The detectives took their time driving back to Anchorage. A heavy wire mesh separated Lewis from the pair of cops.

As Moranis drove, he spoke into the rear-view mirror. "You're over eighteen, buddy. An adult. Gonna go down for 'possession for sale of a Schedule I controlled substance, to wit: heroin in powdered form.'" He winked at Gary in the passenger seat. "Not bad, huh?" Then to Lewis again, "It woulda been McLaughlin just a couple months ago, when you were still seventeen and a minor. But you've had a birthday, so it's jail. Hard time, kiddo." Moranis watched the suspect squirm in the back seat before continuing. "Good looking kid like you? Well, I don't have to spell it out for you, do I?" Moranis glanced briefly at his partner. "Whattaya think Gary? B.J. here's a pretty good lookin' young white boy. Think he'll last a day with the grown-ups before he becomes someone's bitch?"

"Might last a night. Maybe."

"Nah, not that long," Moranis said. "But listen up B.J. You gotta understand somethin'. You're not only on the hook for the smack, but you also threatened to kill some people if they named you. We know about the six kids you sold to. They're all gonna give you up. Count on it. So, besides however many years you're lookin' at for the dope, they'll be a bunch more added for each kid you threatened. Max in this state for threatening to kill someone is five years. Six kids times five is thirty. Plus the heroin. Jesus, you'll be an old fart by the time you see the outside. That's if you don't die of AIDS first. Yeah, and since it'll be such a long-term confinement, you can forget Goose Creek, up on the highway, close to your home. Nah. You'll get shipped down to the lower forty-eight. Colorado or Arizona prob'ly. That's where we usually send our serious bad guys. That'd be you, knuckle head. But maybe you know some stuff we'd like to hear."

B.J. Lewis, hands laced tightly behind his back and body tilted uncomfortably in his seat, would have loved to play the tough guy, loved to tell these two dumbass cops to suck off, loved to tell them that, because his father was a hot-shot lawyer, there was no way he was going to do any time. But the attitude was missing and the words wouldn't come. He was royally screwed and he knew it. He swallowed. "I know a lot."

~~~

Artun Ozil was by nature a supremely cautious master criminal. His caution had been learned—often the hard way—growing up in Istanbul's slums. There, a false step, an unintended slight, or a lack of paid respect might result in serious physical pain. Or worse.

Artun's close attention to detail had not always been appreciated by his partner in crime, his older cousin, Mehmet. And because of Mehmet's looser way of operating, Artun judged himself to be the more adept of the two, the more clever, the more capable. In proof thereof, he often reviewed the times that his cousin had not shown the proper amount of caution and had seriously screwed up.

Artun remembered in vivid detail his cousin's first misstep. In 1986, against all advice, Mehmet chose an outsider to help with a project. Up until then, they'd relied strictly upon their own cohort—family members—to abet their crimes.

But a large consignment of high-end furs on their way to the Avanti store in Corfu had tempted Mehmet into allowing an outlander into the Ozil inner circle. The man was a former Avanti employee and a Lebanese Christian. He'd come highly recommended by someone with whom the Ozils had worked successfully on several occasions.

What the recommender did not know—and what Mehmet discovered only too late—was that the Lebanese was a wanted man. He had been one of the Christian Phalangists who helped massacre several hundred Palestinians in 1982 in Beirut's Shatila refugee camp. A price had been placed on his head by the PLO. Unfortunately for the Ozils, but more unfortunately for the man, Yasser Arafat's minions caught up with the Phalangist in Athens. They spirited him to their headquarters in Tunisia where they exacted their revenge. The man reportedly took days to die.

Mehmet's planned fur heist had to be aborted at the last minute, leaving the Turk to pick up the not inconsequential tab for promised, but unfinished, work.

Artun had berated his cousin. "Stick to our own family, depend only upon our own kin."

Mehmet reluctantly agreed. For a few years, at least.

But in 2004, he again broke the rules and dealt with unknown actors. Mehmet agreed to broker an arms sale between ETA Basques, the unknown buyers, and a French group of mercenaries in Marseilles, the unknown sellers.

"We don't know a single person from either of these groups," Artun argued. "This is bad business. Remember the Phalangist."

"I know, Artun, I know," his cousin had argued. "But Nikki wants to take the girls to Bermuda and we're a little short," Mehmet explained.

"So we once again break Rule Number One so you and your wife and kids can go on vacation?"

Mehmet was abashed but remained adamant. Artun finally relented, against his better judgment.

That the shipment of French-supplied arms wound up at the bottom of the Bay of Biscay was no one's fault really except the incompetent captain of the boat who had put to sea in the face of a very threatening Atlantic Ocean.

When the irate Iberians demanded their money back from the Marseilles gang, the Frenchies told them to go suck on a rock and get the money from the broker.

Mehmet claimed the fault was in the stars—an act of God—and refused payment. The Basques wouldn't take no for an answer and forced Ozil and his family to flee Europe for the colder climes of Alaska. There, thanks to his old friends, the Bunins of Brooklyn, he found work expediting smuggled heroin.

And then three years ago, in 2016, Mehmet suggested that he and Artun join the ranks of heroin salesmen.

"Are you out of your mind?" Artun roared. "We are *not* sellers. We're middlemen. Expeditors, for Christ's sake. We handle the stuff only long enough to move it along. We're not in the growing business like those zombies in Afghanistan, the Murads, or whatever the hell their name is. Nor are we buyers, like our bosses, the Bunins. No, cousin. This is folly."

Mehmet tried to explain. "The Bunins have excess product coming into Alaska. Boris offered us a kilo a month. I figured we could both use the extra money."

"Speak for yourself, Mehmet. I don't need more," Artun answered. "If you do, say so, but don't tell me that 'we could both use' to justify your greed." Artun regretted the harsh words the minute they were out of his mouth. "I apologize, cuz," he said. "Didn't mean it."

Mehmet seemed mollified. "I know this guy in the Mat-Su. Antoine Washington's his name. Black guy. Deals all around the Valley. Very low-key. Works as a plumber. I've been in touch. He's open to talking. So let's talk."

They talked, agreed to work together, and for the next three years, things went smoothly: Mehmet sold the kilo of very good Afghani product to Antoine Washington, who stepped on it before moving it to his lower-level buyers, who themselves stepped on it and then resold the compromised drug to the Valley's end-purchasers.

Because Artun's innate caution had screamed at him at the outset, he'd insisted that Washington provide the particulars of all of his sub-contractors: names, addresses, phone numbers, car makes, and license plate numbers.

"So we can keep track of who's moving the shit, and if anything happens, we'll know quick. Be safer that way," he told Mehmet.

Because of this precaution, Artun was able to see the tsunami before it swept them away. He was watching the evening news. The reporter, a pumpkin-faced young woman with spikey brown hair, told of a drug arrest at Eagle River High School. She took special pride in announcing that her TV station had acquired smart phone video taken by an anonymous student. The video showed a young male—his face pixelated—being spread-eagled over a car. Artun noted the license plate, went to his computer file and rushed to tell his cousin the horrifying news.

"One of Washington's sellers has been grabbed. He'll talk, name his source, who'll name *his* source, which, my foolish cousin, is you and me."

Which is why Artun Ozil was on his way to Eagle River, to find Antoine Washington. The Turk's favorite Walther pistol was neatly stowed under his seat.

~~~

Quentin Lewis was a junior partner in the Anchorage offices of Sooby Whattem Gluck—eight hundred lawyers in sixteen cities all across the United States and Canada.

Lewis had received a call about three that afternoon, telling him that his only child, Brian, had been arrested, booked, and charged with possession for sale of just over one hundred and eighty-four grams of heroin. The attorney went to Google, found a conversion table, and learned that his good-for-nothing progeny had been caught red-handed with six and one-half ounces of a Schedule I drug.

Since he was in corporate law and not criminal, Lewis made a few phone calls to colleagues and further learned that his eighteen-year-old Brian would probably be spending a good deal of time in the slammer. At the same time, his own hopes of someday running Sooby's Anchorage office seemed dashed. The lawyer was tempted to call his ex—Brian's mother, Marci, now residing in Palm Desert, California—to let her know just what her coddling, enabling, and smothering parenting had led to. *Goddamn Marci. Never let me have a go at the boy, never let me show him that his lying, cheating, and arrogance would have consequences.*

B.J. Lewis was sitting, sandwiched between his father, a corporate lawyer, and Harvey Zipser, a criminal lawyer.

On the other side of the table were Assistant District Attorney Janice Fitzhugh and the APD's Chief of Detectives, Stan Babiarsz. The five were in a small conference room at the Tudor Road police station.

Fitzhugh began. "Your client, Mr. Zipser, has already orally waived his Miranda right to keep silent, and has made it clear that he wants to deal."

Lewis looked at son. "Is that so, Brian?"

When B. J. Lewis nodded, his father threw up his hands in disgust. "I wish you'd have kept your mouth shut. But you never could do that, could you?" He turned to the DA and sighed, "What do you want from him?"

"Simple," Fitzhugh said. "The names of the people he gets the heroin from."

Harvey Zipser spoke, "And for that information, what does Brian get?"

The Assistant DA sat back in her chair. "He gets not to go to trial. See, with no deal, Brian is looking at six to ten for the heroin, and three to five for each charge of threatening to kill his sales people if they turned him in. Who are all minors, by the way. So bottom line, when we convict him, he'll be looking at twenty-four years, at least."

Zipser blew out a 'phhh.' "Who are you kidding, Jan? Twenty-four years? You'd never get anywhere near that if we go to trial, even if you *did* convict him. And we all know just how capricious juries can be."

Fitzhugh shrugged. "Not buying it, huh? Selling heroin to six juveniles. All willing to testify. All good, white, Valley families. Brian here getting those kids hooked on smack. Jury would love nothing more than to nail him to the wall. And remember," Fitzhugh looked at the suspect's father, "he's the son of a prominent attorney. One who's angling to take over Sooby's local office. You want to go to court, Mr. Lewis? Let's go."

The elder Lewis leaned in back of his son and motioned for Zipser to meet him. They whispered for a moment, then Zipser said to the Assistant DA, "And if Brian gives up the name of his source?"

Now it was Fitzhugh and Babiarsz who whispered for half a minute. When they finished, she turned back to the Lewises, "Seven years in jail. Five for the heroin, two for a single count of threatening. With good time, he's out in just under five. Three years probation."

"Let's go for six years to serve, two years probation." Zipser countered.

Fitzhugh shook her head. "Seven and three."

"Seven and one," said Zipser.

Fitzhugh pushed back in her chair and made to rise. "Seven and three. Take it our leave it."

"I'll take it," said the suspect.

The suspect's father sank into his seat.

Babiarsz looked at B. J. Lewis. "The name."

The now confessed heroin dealer closed his eyes and spoke the name.

~~~

Steering his white Toyota Tundra towards Eagle River, Artun passed the time by reviewing the twenty-two people he'd killed during his life in crime. In the same way that many folks keep lists of their sex partners, the killer kept a mental list of his victims in alphabetic order[5].

He hadn't murdered them. Artun had killed them. In point of fact, he refused ever to use the word murder, claiming that murder often involved emotion and passion. He insisted that it was never, ever personal, always and only business. People who interfered with his and Mehmet's illegal affairs needed to go away. Those who cheated, stole, encroached on the cousins' turf could not be allowed to live. Just that simple.

He'd dispatched most of his victims with his trusty Walther. But some—his very first and a few others—he'd eliminated using a variety of other weapons, some improvised.

He always went about his work with great care and precision. And so, after parking his pickup well away from Washington's home, he walked the snowy mile to his target. A half moon darting in and out of the clouds lit up the road, allowing him to avoid slipping. He purposely walked on the roadside or on the ice so as not to leave fresh footprints in the snow. Coming in sight of Washington's cabin, Artun found a copse of willows in which to hide and observe the compound of the soon-to-be doomed drug dealer. He heard occasional barking echoing through the still night air.

He waited, checked the Walther, threaded on the suppressor, took the pistol off of safety, and went to pay Antoine Washington a final visit.

~~~

Sasha rushed home after learning the name of the man who had supplied B.J. Lewis with the heroin he had supplied to her daughter.

She gathered the same kind of gear she had used once before, in 2013: a six-foot by nine-foot rug, bailing wire, and a Taser.

Her plan was essentially the same as when she caused to disappear a sex offending and murdering local evangelical pastor who had raped and then drowned his two nine-year-old stepdaughters. The man had been out on bail when Sasha abducted him, wrapped him in a rug, and took him flying in her floatplane. They'd landed on a small lake north of Anchorage into which she had deposited the be-rugged holy man. It was her first venture into vigilante-ism and she had zero regrets.

Driving now to the home of Antoine Washington, she puzzled over how to dispose of the body. She knew him to be very large, someone clearly too big for her to heft into her Cessna. Even lifting him into her pickup would probably prove impossible. *Might just have to Tase the SOB to death. Or burn down his house with him in it. Or shoot him with Old Faithful, my unregistered and very cold, never-been-used, thirty-eight-caliber revolver.*

It was past two in the morning when she slowed to a stop a quarter of a mile from the Pole Line Road cutoff that led to Washington's compound.

She took her TaserX2, set it for max—50,000 volts—pulled up the hood on her parka, and made her way to the heroin seller's home. The night was cold and intensely silent. Not a sound. When she peered through the shrubbery that fronted Washington's log cabin, she understood at once why it was so quiet: the moon's light illuminated two Rottweilers, still tethered to long chains, lying next to each other, unmoving. She tossed a snowball at one of the dogs. No reaction. She emerged from her vantage and slid quietly into the yard. Both dogs were awash in their own blood and the smell of their feces was strong. One hand on her Taser, the other gripping her pistol, she walked, hunched over, toward the cabin. The front door was ajar, a low light coming from within. Sasha climbed onto the porch and gently eased the door fully open.

Antoine Washington lay on his back in the middle of the small room.

She cleared the cabin, then returned to the body and knelt down beside it. She knew there was nothing to be gained by assessing the man's pulse, yet force of habit took over and she put two fingers on his carotid artery. Nothing. She guessed a medium caliber weapon judging from the size of the three neatly spaced entry holes—one over each of the dead man's eyes, and the third just above the bridge of his nose. *Good shooting! Guy who did it obviously knew what he was doing.*

The deceased's blood was drip-dripping into the very large pool that had collected under his head. The victim's eyes were open, an expression of surprise still registering on his face. *Someone you know, guy? Or knew, actually. Past tense required here. You went to answer the door, and kablooie. Lights out.*

Sasha felt mixed emotions: pleased that a bad man had received a bad fate. But unhappy about the means of his demise. She felt disappointment and even a little cheated that it had not been she who had done the deed. She left the scene.

~~~

Mid-morning. Detective Gary Hernandez paced back and forth in front of the log home of the late Antoine Washington. Sasha and Busby leaned on the hood of their car. All three were dressed in heavy parkas and wool caps. All wore gloves. A police forensic team was scouring the area. The sky had clouded up, threatening snow.

"What are we to understand from this unfortunate event?" Gary asked. His breath hung in the air. He pulled his collar up around his neck.

"Pretty simple, I think," Moranis said. "Looks like he was

offed before we could get to him and have a talk."

"I agree with Busby," Sasha said. "This isn't a random killing or robbery. Nothing appears to have been stolen and the bullet holes in the dude's head were perfectly spaced. Guy who shot him was a pro, knew what he was doing." Her previous night's assessment made her smile internally.

Hernandez nodded. "Yeah, that seems to be it. Meaning the guy was probably killed by whoever he was getting the drugs from. And where does that leave us?"

"Shit outta luck," Moranis said. "Unless the forensic team comes up with something." He looked around. "And out here on this road to nowhere, with no neighbors nearby . . . No one really to question . . ."

One of the forensic techs approached. "Morning all," she said.

"Morning, Lizzie," Gary said. "Got anything?"

"Not a whole hell of a lot. A buncha sets of boot prints. Too many to probably be determinative. We're taking impressions but I don't hold out much hope."

"Fingerprints inside?" Sasha asked.

"Too soon to tell. We still have all these sheds and outbuildings to go through. We'll let you know."

"Keep an eye out for drugs," Gary said. "Guy was apparently a dealer."

"Will do." She turned and went back to the cabin.

Gary stretched. "Nothing else to do here. Meanwhile, I got a call from Stan last night. He said he heard from Vladivostok police. Investigator over there says Troika Aviation has a partner here in Anchorage, out at Merrill Field."

"Who'd that be?" Moranis asked.

"Outfit called Grizzly Air," Gary said. "Someone called Bulgarin, the owner. You two go on over, ask some questions."

~~~

Her nameplate said 'Dorotea Bulgarin,* Assistant Manager. Grizzly Air.' Her pallid complexion matched her dyed blond hair that she wore in a bun. Wire-rim glasses were perched on her nose. A long-sleeved purple blouse, open to the sternum, revealed much of the woman's substantial bosom. She had scarlet-painted fingernails and was entering numbers into an adding machine. When a man and a woman entered the office, she looked up. The man spoke first.

"Good morning, ma'am. I'm Sergeant Moranis, Anchorage Police. This is Sergeant Kulaeva." The two cops showed their badges. "Is Mister Bulgarin in? We'd like to talk to him."

This is it, Dorotea thought. *They're here sooner than I expected. And now the Kulaeva slut shows up. I told my moron of a husband years ago, I told him this project wasn't going to work. I warned him about that goddamn Boris. Shit!*

"Talk to him? About what?" Dorotea squeaked through a crooked smile. She hoped the abject terror in her quaking voice wasn't apparent to the cops.

"Just some questions, ma'am," Sasha said. "Routine stuff. Is your husband . . . I presume he's your husband . . . is he available?"

"Yes, he's my husband. Of course he's my husband! But I'm not sure he's here." Her eyes darted, flickety-flit.

Moranis glared at the woman. "He's your husband and you're not sure he's here?" Now to Sasha, "She's not sure, Detective Kulaeva."

Sasha stifled a yawn. "Well, I wouldn't worry. We can wait."

The two cops looked around, saw seats by a large window, walked over and perched themselves. They picked up copies of

Aviation Week and settled in.

Dorotea couldn't take her eyes off the policemen. She tried to resume her calculator work but her fingers had lost motor control. They jerked and jumped wherever she put them—in her lap, on her desk, hanging by the side of her chair. She gave up after a few moments, stood, and walked to a door in the rear of the office. She glanced quickly at the cops. The man waved sweetly. Dorotea shuddered and went through the door into a large storeroom. She grabbed a jacket, then darted out the building's rear exit. She scurried to the Grizzly Air hangar as fast as her two-inch heels would allow, fresh snow collecting on her shoes. She found her husband inside the building, talking to their mechanic.

Leo saw his wife rushing toward him. Her frantic expression made his innards rumble.

"Police. In the office," she sputtered. "That Kulaeva woman." With both hands, she grabbed hold of her husband's bare right forearm, her fingernails sinking into his flesh. Leo tried to shake off her grip. He winced, but she held tight.

"Leo . . ." Dorotea wheezed, hardly able to get the words out. "Leo, you gotta go talk to them. They know you're here." She noticed the mechanic watching them closely and switched from English to Russian. "They're waiting in the office. You need to get it together." She increased the pressure on his arm.

The mechanic, an older man with a full white beard, dressed in oil-stained dungarees and a watch cap, stared at his suddenly crazed bosses.

Leo was able to shake off Dorotea's death-grip. His forearm was deeply indented, but no blood. "What the hell am I supposed to say?"

"Just answer their goddamn questions," she shouted. "It's probably about the car crash." She searched the hangar, wild-eyed. "They've connected it somehow to Troika. They want to talk to you." She cast a quick glance at the mechanic, and in English, "Take a hike, Billy. Go get yourself some coffee."

Billy scratched his whiskers and walked off.

Leo couldn't catch his breath. "I don't know *anything* about the crash."

"Right. That's *exactly* what you tell them. You don't know anything. About the crash or about the dead driver."

"Jesus," he said rubbing his palms into his eyes and shuffling out of the hangar. "Jesus. Jesus."

A long two minutes later, Leo swallowed hard and entered the Grizzly Air office. "Good morning, officers. You wanted to talk to me." He was astounded at how cool and collected his voice had come out.

"Don't I know you, Mr. Bulgarin?" Sasha asked, rising from her chair. "Three years ago, didn't you fly me from St. Lawrence Island to Anchorage? Remember?"

Leo assumed a questioning expression. *How could I forget? You're the Anchorage cop who created such a shit storm in Russia. Catching Taras Zhuganov. Shooting those drunken Kerensky brothers[6]. Then you show up on St. Lawrence Island. Want to catch a ride home with me. Wind up sitting on forty kilos of our heroin all the way to Anchorage. And me piloting the plane. Almost had a stroke. Do I remember you, you bitch? Go fuck yourself. I remember you.* "What was your name again?" he asked.

"Kulaeva. *Detective* Kulaeva." Sasha stressed her title and watched as Leo Bulgarin licked his lips and sat down in his wife's vacated chair. "Right. I recall now. Well, what can I do for you two?"

The male cop leaned on the counter. "Mr. Bulgarin.

We're investigating the death of a United States Customs agent. Houston Dantley's his name. He died in a car crash couple nights ago. Did you know him?"

Of course I knew him, you moron. He was our man at the terminal. Helped us bring hundreds of kilos of pure heroin into America. "No, Officer . . . what did you say your name was?"

"Moranis, sir. Did you know the gentleman?"

"Who? The man in the car crash?" Leo shook his head. "Unh-uh. No. No. I didn't know him. How would I know him?"

"Just wonderin'." Moranis took out the post mortem photo of Houston Dantley. "Maybe this'll jog your memory. It was taken yesterday mornin' at the morgue."

Leo didn't want to look but couldn't help himself. He darted a glance at the photo, at once recognizing the man who had visited them right here in the office, more than once. "Don't recognize him. Sorry."

Moranis gave Leo another few moments to look at the customs agent before returning the photo to his jacket pocket. "Actually, there's also the pilot, or rather the *co-pilot* from the Troika Aviation flight that landed a couple nights ago. Name is Suvorov. Anatoly Suvorov. Since your company here, Grizzly Air, is partners of a sort with Troika Aviation, perhaps you know *him?*"

Yeah, asshole. I know him, too. He was over at our place a month ago. Brought us a bottle of Stoli Blueberi.

Leo sat back in the chair and looked up to the ceiling, as if searching for the pilot's identity. He scratched his chin in contemplation. Finally, "Nooooo. Unh-uh. Can't say I know him either. Sakuroff you said his name was?"

"Close. Suvorov. It's spelled S U V O R O V. Don't know him either?" Moranis asked.

"Definitely not. I'm sure." Leo was now gnawing at his lower lip. He licked it and tasted blood. Licked again and sighed. *Why don't I just confess? Maybe they'll only deport me back to Russia. Maybe Dorotea will leave me. Please.*

Moranis looked at Sasha. "Anything else right now for Mr. Bulgarin, Detective Kulaeva?"

"Yes, one more thing, Mr. Bulgarin. We're conducting a wide-ranging investigation into the death of the customs agent. There's a chance your partner, Troika Aviation, might be somehow involved. So, we ask you to please *not* alert them to our being here today. Best if they don't know about our chat. OK?" Sasha gave Leo a conspiratorial wink. "OK, Mr. Bulgarin?" She zipped her lips with her thumb and forefinger, smiling at the man.

Leo nodded once, then nodded some more. "Certainly. I'll keep it to myself."

"Atta boy," said Moranis.

After the police left, Leo searched for his wife. He found her prostrate on a couch in the back room, sobbing into a balled up handkerchief. She stopped long enough to look up at him through tear-filled eyes. "I told you, Leo. Didn't I tell you? Your fucking cousin is gonna be the death of us."

Leo clenched and unclenched his hands. "I gotta call Brooklyn."

~~~

Boris listened to his cousin's frenzied recounting of the visit by the police and recognized at once who the woman cop was—Kulaeva. His entire heroin trafficking enterprise, from Vladivostok to Brooklyn, had been seriously and adversely affected by her for the past three years. If the woman didn't possess a set of photographs that incriminated him and Vladivostok's mayor, she'd be long dead[7].

"Did they ask about Troika?" Boris asked.

"Yes. And about Suvorov, too. The Pilot. Jesus, Borya. I'm shitting in my pants. If they know about him and if they collected the stuff from the custom guy's wreck, then they'll put it all together. They're close."

"Wait a moment Leo. I want to put you on speaker. Lara wants to talk to you."

Leo Bulgarin waited, knowing the tougher of the two was now engaged.

"Hello Leo," Lara said. "Did they demand to see any documents? Did they have a warrant of any kind?"

"No, Larissa. No warrant. They said they might be back later. And they didn't ask to see any documents."

"OK," she said. "What about Dorotea. Did they talk to her?"

"Yeah, they did. But just long enough to tell her to come and find me." Leo's voice began to crack.

Boris came back on the line. He spoke soothingly. "OK, Leo. Let's not panic quite yet. We have a little time. Sit tight for now. I want to talk to Mehmet. I'll get back to you in a couple hours. OK?"

Leo Bulgarin knew better than to argue with his cousin. "Yes, Borya. I'll wait for your call."

Boris hurled his smart phone onto the couch. It bounced onto the floor. His wife came around to the back of his wheelchair and began massaging his shoulders.

"It's not working, Borya," she said calmly. "The whole thing is collapsing. At least the Troika part. What are you thinking?"

He exhaled loudly. "I'm thinking, Lara, that you are a wonderful masseuse. Work my neck, please, dearest."

She walked her fingers onto his upper nape.

He moved his shoulders in sync with her touch. "It's unfortunate, but it seems that all good things, at some point, must come to an end."

"*'At some point?'*" She squeezed his neck.

He squirmed under the pressure. "I guess I'm not yet totally convinced we've reached that point." He craned around so he could see her. His beautiful wife wore an ugly sneer. "Such a face, my dear."

"It's not the time for smiling, Borya."

As Larissa worked on her husband's neck, Boris closed his eyes and recalled the events that had led them to this point. It began as a lunch date in 2004, at Lanza's, one of Manhattan's premier Italian kitchens. Over the calamari, he'd proposed to set his cousin up in an air-taxi service in Alaska. At first, Leo had balked, but by the cannoli, he'd been persuaded.

Grizzly Air began operating the next year with a handful of four- and six-seat planes. Boris arranged for the business to expand, and by the end of their fifth year of operation, the air taxi service was flying all over the state in a fleet of a dozen various sized aircraft.

Soon after, came the flights out to St. Lawrence Island to collect product smuggled to the American island from Chukotka.

And finally, the operation's crowning achievement—a partnership with Troika Aviation, the Russian carrier, and those carefully orchestrated twice-monthly shipments.

Boris reached up and gently took his wife's left hand, moving it high on the back of his neck. "Right there, please, Lara. Go deep for a little. And when you're done, we'll spend some time considering our options."

Larissa dug into her husband's neck. "We don't have a lot of time, Borya. Nor a lot of options. Leo sounded like he's ready to break." She kneaded his flesh even harder. "You're tense, dearest. We have to get rid of this trouble spot. Perhaps a call to the Turks."

Boris breathed out and let his head bend forward. After a minute, he pointed to the floor, where his smartphone was lying. Larissa picked it up and gave it to her husband. He let it rest in the palm of his hand.

"Make the call, Borya," she commanded.

Boris dialed, and in a minute, "Mehmet. I'm worried."

"Join the crowd."

"Leo is vulnerable."

"No shit! He's more than vulnerable, Boris. He's toxic. He probably already phoned you."

"Right. He did. He said the police visited him an hour ago. That Kulaeva woman. Showed him a picture of the dead customs agent. Talked to him about the pilot. Police're putting the whole thing together. Leo's freaking out."

"Absolutely freaking."

"What about Suvorov, the pilot?

"He finally showed up. The cops visited him last night, warned him not to come back to Alaska. And they were at the custom guy's condo. Artun was gonna clean up the place. But when he gets there, he sees two policemen go in, spend an hour. When they leave, they cover the door with that orange crime tape. One of the cops is carrying a bunch of envelopes. Artun followed him. They wind up at the dead guy's bank. Christ, Boris. It's unraveling."

"I can see that."

"We may need to take . . . eh . . . drastic steps. If we want to continue, I mean."

"Drastic? Wait a second, Mehmet. Larissa wants to talk to me. Hold on." In Russian, Boris began talking with his wife.

In Anchorage, Ozil waited. He could hear his boss and his boss's wife talking. Larissa was speaking forcefully. Though Ozil didn't understand, he had a notion what the topic was—who was arguing 'for' and who 'against.'

In Brooklyn, Boris Bunin was fighting to save his cousin's life.

"He's family, Lara. Leo's my first cousin. My uncle Misha's son. I can't let Artun have him. Let's pull him and Dorotea out of Alaska as soon as possible. We'll do something with them."

"Really? We'll do something with them? Is that what you said? What will we do with them, Borya? They'll be wanted, on FBI posters. International drug traffickers. Do we bring them to Brooklyn to live with us? Or maybe we send them back to Russia? Or here's an idea: we put them in the Bunin's witness protection program, give them phony IDs, hide them on some farm in North Dakota."

When he didn't respond, Larissa ramped it up, "Oh, wait a second. I forgot. We, in the serious crime business, we don't have a witness protection program. Ours is a little different from the feds. We hide our problems in the BOTTOM OF THE FUCKING HUDSON RIVER," she screamed.

Boris leaned over his knees with his forearms on his thighs. He shook his head back and forth. He whispered, "He's family, Lara."

She took a deep breath and pushed a chair next to her husband's wheelchair. She sat and with both arms hugged him to her. Quietly, she said, "Leo is weak, Borya. As much as he loves you, as soon as the cops apply the thumbscrews, he'll give you up. He'll give us up. He'll hate himself for doing it, but it won't matter. Leo gets arrested, Borya, we're sunk. And you know it, don't you, dearest?"

He nodded, fumbled for his smartphone and re-connected with Alaska.

"Mehmet. Listen . . . I . . . I mean . . . Larissa and I think . . . We, ah . . ."

Larissa gently took the cell phone from her husband's hand. "Mehmet. Take them both out. Immediately."

"Yes, Lara. Right away."

The capo's wife ended the call and walked around in back of her husband. "Let me finish the massage, Borya. I'll work out that kink in your neck."

Three thousand miles away, in Anchorage, Mehmet Ozil broke his burner phone in two and tossed the parts into the trash compactor. He turned to his cousin. "You were listening. Go do it."

"Good as done," Artun said.

~~~

The Bulgarins were frantic in their dining room after racing home from Merrill Field. Leo sagged in his chair. He alternated biting his lower lip and biting his cuticles.

Dorotea was hyperventilating, holding both hands over her chest, trying to catch her breath.

"Didn't I tell you not to have anything to do with your cousin?" she panted.

Her husband cowered, not daring to meet his wife's eyes.

"Don't look away, Leo, goddamn it. Look at me. Didn't I tell you? For years I've been telling you." She paced in and out of the dining room, swaying. "When you told me he'd invited you for lunch that day in Manhattan, I told you *not* to go." Now, stopping next to his chair, leaning over him, "Didn't I Leo?"

"Yes, dear. You told me," he muttered, sinking lower into his seat.

"But you went anyway," she smirked, curling her lip. 'He's my dear cousin,' you told me. 'I owe his family,' you told me. 'Don't worry,' you told me." Dorotea hovered over him, wanting to wring his neck. "And look where the hell we are now," she bawled. "Cops this morning, sniffing around. They know most of it, Leo. Probably'll know everything soon. We're in serious trouble." She took a deep breath, walked to an antique hutch and pulled out a bottle of peppermint schnapps. She took two long swallows from the bottle, then wiped her mouth with the back of her hand, all the time glaring at her husband. "And when you came back from that lunch and told me Boris's great idea—that he wanted to set you up in an air taxi business here in Alaska. What did I tell you about this icebox of a shithole? About this place where I can't even get a decent fucking perm? Remember, Leo, what I told you then? I told you that if you took his offer, that he'd be the *death* of both of us. And god damn it to hell if that isn't happening."

Leo's heart felt ready to burst through his chest. He stared down at his hands, lying inert in his lap.

His wife drank again from the bottle. "And *he's* always been the one in charge of what goes on at Grizzly. Not you. Not me. Him. He tells you to fly out to St. Lawrence Island, pick up some packages. What'd you think was in them? Huh, Leo? My idiot of a husband. As if you didn't know." Dorotea guzzled another two swallows of schnapps.

Leo rubbed his fingernail-bruised forearm. The indentations were still plainly visible. He was on the verge of tears, understanding that his screaming know-it-all wife was one hundred percent correct: his cousin Boris was going to be the death of them.

Dorotea put the bottle down. "We gotta get the hell outta here, Leo. I mean, right now! You know that Mehmet spoke to Boris. And what's worse, he probably spoke to Lara, too, that little shit-hook. Always pretending she's so goddamn educated. Mentioning her degree from university every goddamn chance she gets." Dorotea picked up the bottle, considered another drink. "She's never liked me, Leo. Never liked you. I'll bet she's put a bug in her husband's ear: 'Leo and his wife are loose cannons.' 'Tell Mehmet to do what he needs to do.'" She put the bottle on the table.

"It's possible," Leo whispered. He reached for the schnapps, took a long slug. "It's possible."

"Possible? Shit, Leo. We're toast. What are we waiting for? The Second Coming? We gotta do something. You gotta protect us from Mehmet and from his cousin, Artun. That piece of shit'd kill us just for kicks."

Leo took another gulp of the schnapps, looked wildly around his dining room, and stood. "You're right. You're right. We gotta go. Now. Right now. Get your passport, cash, jewels. Pack whatever'll fit into a single bag. Make it fast."

"Where to?"

"We'll leave from Merrill Field. The Citation's gassed and ready to fly. We can get to Canada, Seattle. Doesn't matter. We'll figure it out."

They rushed to pack.

~~~

Artun opened his safe, pulled out a shelf and examined his armory. Although he had a dozen handguns, he opted, as usual, for the Walther. It was a favorite of his since he saw

Sean Connery use one in *From Russia With Love*. That would have been 1969. He and Mehmet had snuck into the Emek Sinemasi in downtown Istanbul. He was eight-years-old.

Artun took three magazines, put two in his pocket and pushed the third into the butt of the pistol. He made sure the weapon was on safety, jacked a round into the firing chamber, and put the Walther in the pocket of his windbreaker.

Just to be on the safe side, he grabbed a second handgun, a Springfield 9 mm and pushed a full magazine of sixteen rounds into the pistol's grip. He chambered a round then slipped the heavy weapon into a holster and attached it to his belt. He used the windbreaker to hide the pistol.

He checked himself in his den's mirror, smoothed down his sparse hair, and put on a baseball cap. He was now ready to go kill Leonid and Dorotea Bulgarin, folks he'd known for years. *Nothing personal*, he told himself. *Just business.*

~~~

Sasha and Busby returned to Merrill Field to find an empty Grizzly Air office. They walked over to the taxi service's hangar. They found a mechanic.

"I don't know where they're at," Billy said. He rubbed oily hands up and down the sides of his overalls, then scratched his beard. "Haven't seen 'em in a couple hours."

"No idea, huh?" Moranis stepped close to the man. "Maybe gone home? Where do they live?"

"Not sure," Billy said. "South Anchorage somewhere. Maybe. I dunno."

Moranis laid a palm gently on Billy's shoulder, pulled him closer. "Listen to me, Santa Claus. We're looking for your bosses. Police business. Important stuff. You hold out any info, you could become an accessory. Not only that, but if you don't tell me where they live, I slap the shit outta ya. Right here. Right now."

~~~

It took Artun fifteen minutes to drive to Leo's Sand Lake neighborhood in south Anchorage. When he turned onto Caravelle, he saw Leo's blue Audi a block in front of him, turning north on Terry. Artun followed him at a safe distance and watched as the Audi swung onto the Hickel Parkway. He phoned Mehmet. "Missed 'em at home but I caught up with 'em. We're on the parkway, goin' fast. I'm thinkin' they're headin' back to Merrill Field. Maybe plannin' to skip on outta here."

"OK. Want some help?"

"Nah. I got it. I'll call when it's done. I'll bring some baklava home from Turkish Delight."

"Yum. Be in touch."

"Will do."

~~~

"The garage is empty, door's wide open," Moranis said.

"The front door's ajar."

The two cops quickly exited their police car, drew their weapons and advanced toward the home of Leo and Dorotea Bulgarin.

While Sasha poked her head around the side of the single-car garage, Moranis stepped quietly onto the porch, sidled up to the front door, and called in, "Police. Anybody home?"

No reply. They entered the home, calling out and identifying themselves. When they had cleared all the rooms in the small home, they went back to the owners' bedroom. They found small piles of clothes spread over the bed.

"Somebody packed in a hurry," Busby said.

"Right. These guys beat it."

"Let's get back to Merrill Field."

They ran to the door.

~~~

Leo and his wife roared into Merrill Field and rushed into their Grizzly Air office. Billy was at the Mr. Coffee, helping himself. He was taken aback by the panicked vibes his bosses were giving off. "What's goin' on?"

Leo ignored him, went to the till, took out all the paper cash he found, stuffed it into his pants pocket, and yelled to his wife who'd gone into the back room, "Get a move on."

Billy asked again, "What's happenin' boss? Need some help?"

Leo became aware of the mechanic. "Citation ready to fly?"

"Yeah. Fully gassed it yesterday. Why?"

Dorotea came out of the back room holding a heavy fur-lined jacket and a small valise. "I'm ready."

Leo turned to Billy, "We're gone. Anyone . . . I mean *anyone*, cops included, asks where we are, don't tell 'em anything. Me and Dorotea gotta leave. Right now."

Billy, coffee in his hand, stared and nodded an OK.

The Bulgarins ran from the office and hurried to the Cessna Citation, parked close to the airport's taxi-runway.

~~~

When Sasha and Busby careened into Merrill Field, they saw a blue Audi parked in front of the Grizzly Air office. And nearby, a white Toyota Tundra with the driver's door wide open. Moranis braked the cruiser hard. Almost at once, the cops heard shots. They spilled out, ducked behind their police cruiser, and pulled their pistols. They scooted to opposite ends of the car and peered out. Sasha saw the plane first. It stood near the Grizzly Air hangar, forty yards away. "Busby," she pointed. "Look at the stairs."

"Jesus. Looks like a body. She's half way into the plane. I think it's Bulgarin's wife."

The hangar door crashed open and a man dashed out and ran toward the plane. More shots. The man half-stumbled and kept running toward the aircraft. A second man had emerged from the hangar and sprinted after the first man, firing as he ran. Sasha and Moranis rose up and shouted, "Police. Drop your weapon."

Artun Ozil, slowed down, astounded! He'd never, ever been accosted by the police. A lifetime of high crimes and here was an unprecedented and wholly unexpected first. But there they were, shouting at him to drop his weapon. *My beautiful Walther? Drop it? I don't think so, motherfuckers.* Artun fired off a volley at the policemen. *Let's see who's a better shot.*
The cops opened up on the shooter. From her hunkered-down position behind the cruiser, Sasha fired off a three-shot volley and watched the dirt in front of the man kick up. *Low.* The man turned and began running back to the hangar. She raised her Glock and fired again.

Artun felt bits of gravel pelt his legs. *They're shooting low.* Christ. Twenty yards from the hangar, a bullet caught him in the foot. *Shot! I'm fucking shot!* He continued to run, hobbled now, looked down and saw a bullet-gash across the top of his shoe, blood slowly darkening the leather. *A scratch.* He returned fire at the cop car, saw and heard the 'ping' as his bullets ripped into the police car. Two more shots and his clip was empty. He thought to change magazines on the fly, but opted for the heavier weapon. In mid-hobble, Artun stuck the Walther into the pocket of his windbreaker, then reached in and yanked the Springfield from its holster. He fired wildly, hoping desperately to reach the hangar.

Moranis had come out from behind the cruiser and was making a long circle toward the man, firing as he went. "Drop your weapon," he screamed, weaving toward the shooter. "Now. I mean now! We'll kill your ass if you don't drop your weapon." When the shooter aimed at Moranis, the cop fired twice and caught the man again. The shooter fell, but kept firing.

Artun felt the immense impact as another slug tore into his right calf, above his already bloody foot. *The pricks shot me in the leg. I'm not gonna make it.*

Sasha ran forward and knelt down in back of a baggage cart. She'd halved the distance between her and the shooter. She steadied her pistol on one of the cart's wheels and methodically fired at the crawling man, now just twenty-five yards away. The first shots missed. She adjusted her aim slightly and fired again. The 9 mm round caught the man in his right shoulder.

Jesus Christ, I'm hit again. I'm on the ground. God, it hurts. I have to keep crawling. Mehmet. Help. Here's the hangar door.

Just let me get inside. Mehmet! There, I'm in.
Sasha watched the man crawl into the building. She rose up and ran toward the hangar, paused briefly, then swung into the room.

Three quick shots rang out. Moranis rushed up to the door as Sasha exited the building. He was stunned to see that his partner was smiling and calm. "He's done for," she said. "Call it in. Get an ambulance. Let's see if anyone's still alive."

~~~

Despite his cousin's assurances that he could handle the execution of Leo and Dorotea, Mehmet decided to lend a hand. He was on 15th Avenue, still half a mile from the main entrance to Merrill Field when he heard sirens wailing behind him. *A bad omen.* He phoned Artun. No answer.

His disquiet ramped up when he had to pull over to allow an ambulance, a fire truck, and three police cars to roar by. He phoned his cousin again. The same empty result.

Mehmet followed the wailing vehicles, hoping against hope they wouldn't turn left into the airfield. When they did, he stopped, phoned again. "Come on, Artun. Answer the goddamn phone. Please, cuz." When his plea went unanswered, Mehmet Ozil, heroin expeditor extraordinaire, phoned Brooklyn. Boris Bunin liked to get bad news right away.

~~~

Mindy Malone, *AM Anchorage's* on-air talent, read the early morning news with excitement, her hands giving emphasis to her words.

"A shooting yesterday afternoon at Merrill Field has left four people dead, three employees of Grizzly Air, and the suspected shooter. The three victims are Leo Bulgarin, owner of the air taxi service; his wife, Dorotea Bulgarin, who was Grizzly Air's assistant manager; and William Frady, the company's chief mechanic. The alleged shooter, whose identity is still unknown, was himself shot dead by two Anchorage Police Department Narcotics Division officers. A police spokesman said that no motive for the crime has been determined . . ."

Back in his kitchen, Mehmet Ozil used the TV remote to shut out the awful news. He and Artun had been more than just cousins. They'd been partners for over forty years; partners when they'd been kids and had lifted cartons of Marlboros off of a US Army truck headed for Incirlik Air Force Base; partners in their first big-time arms smuggling, stealing all those weapons from the Bulgarian armory in Sofia; partners when they borrowed those 4th Century Greek amphorae from the home in Ephesus and sold them to the museum near Santa Monica; and partners for almost fifteen years here in Alaska, moving hundreds of kilos of Afghani heroin into America. Mehmet sobbed.

~~~

Boris Bunin hobbled around his large living room, trying to rehabilitate his ankle.

Larissa sat on a sofa, head back and eyes closed. "It's a debacle, Borya. The dog handler is dead. The pilot, according to Mehmet, was told never to return to America. Artun was shot and killed at the airport."

Boris grunted his way through the third lap around the room.

"But not before he killed Leo and his wife," Larissa added. "It seems almost everyone who can connect us is dead. Except Mehmet." She lifted her head and looked at her husband.

Boris returned a long stare. "Don't even go there, Lara. Remember, no Mehmet, no heroin. And all your wonderful plans . . . up in smoke."

"You're right, of course. We need him." Larissa rose, went to her husband, took him by the arm. "Enough exercise for now. Come and sit. Let's think more about this train wreck."

With his wife's assistance, Boris eased into his wheelchair. Larissa knelt and propped his injured ankle back onto the leg extension then rose and handed him a tall glass of lemonade.

"What did Mehmet say about the shipments coming into St. Lawrence Island from Chukotka?" she asked.

Boris drank half the lemonade. "He said there were at least two parcels waiting on the island. Ready to be picked up. Normally, Leo would have collected them by now. Since that didn't happen, we can assume the Eskimo still has the stuff, stuck away God knows where. And it'll probably stay there until we can figure a way to get it to Anchorage."

She laced and unlaced her fingers. "OK. Phone Mehmet. Have him call the guy on the island, tell him to sit on whatever he has until further notice. Assure the Eskimo that we'll figure out some kind of alternative and re-start as soon as we can." She looked at her husband. "Best we can do, Borya."

"You're right. Can't do much else for now except hunker down. I'll call Mehmet. Let me have an oxy, please, Lara. My ankle is killing me."

~~~

Buster Kopanuk had a splitting headache. The pilot he was expecting still had not shown up in Gambell, his St. Lawrence Island home. The pilot—Leo he called himself—should have collected the parcels Buster had brought from Chukotka in his welded aluminum skiff. In payment for which, Leo would have passed him an envelope containing two thousand dollars.

Instead of the pilot showing up, Buster had gotten a call from someone he didn't know, telling him that Leo would not be coming any time soon. The man told him to store the goods until further notice. Although he'd never asked Leo what was in the packages, he had a clear notion. As did his family. Especially his daughters and grandchildren, all of whom he had helped put through the University of Alaska using the money Leo paid him. They'd always suspected, though never fully acknowledged Buster's criminality.

Feeling anxious, but not wanting to engage with his wife, Buster sought out his granddaughter, Julia, the last of the Kopanuks who was benefitting from Leo's payoffs. He found her in Gambell's health clinic where she worked as a medical assistant. She was alone, riffling through a filing cabinet.

Buster got straight to the point. "The pilot should have been here by now. I just got a call telling me he wouldn't be coming for a while."

Julia continued to thumb through files. "Maybe, Grandpa, he has engine problems. What's the name of his company?"

"Grizzly Air."

Julia looked startled and quickly closed the file cabinet. "We need to go online. I saw something the other night on state news."

They went to a computer where Julia searched the Alaska

Daily News website. Buster watched as his granddaughter typed in *Merrill Field. Shooting. Anchorage.* The Kopanuks read.

Buster grabbed his head and began circling the small room. "My God. He's dead. The stuff in my shed. What the hell am I supposed to do with it?"

Julia bit her lip. "Is there anyone at Grizzly you can contact?" she asked.

"No. The only contact I've had in all these years has been Leo, the pilot. He's dead. My God."

— **Two Weeks Later** —

Special Agent in Charge Emmitt Esterhazy ran the Anchorage field office for the FBI. He was a short man, dapper, modestly efficient, usually jolly but with sporadic bursts of temper. He had a special dislike for the Drug Enforcement Agency, which he regarded as an archrival.

Esterhazy generally played by the rules, but was not above a once-in-a-while deviation from policy.

Before he came to Alaska, he'd been the SAC in the Bureau's Albuquerque field office. He fell afoul of Quantico when he purposely gave the FISA court bad intel in order to gain a warrant to investigate a techie from Santa Fe. When no incriminating evidence against the man was found, Esterhazy's warrant application was reviewed and found wanting. Because he was usually an able officer of the law, he wasn't booted from the Bureau. Instead, he was simply shipped north in the hope that the cold winds blowing off the Bering Sea would convince the man to retire. He did not. Rather, he found Alaska to his liking and remained on the job.

Esterhazy was working on his fifth divorce and was deeply

enamored of Detective Sasha Kulaeva, nearly thirty years his junior. She met his advances with a smile, a sweet "no thanks," and her usual genial put-down, "You're too short for me, Emmitt." Undeterred, Esterhazy carried on with his unrequited quest.

Sasha entered the SAC's private office wondering what he wanted and who the other man was, the one in the beautifully tailored suit.

"You're looking lovely, as usual, Sasha," the SAC began, even before she'd shucked her parka.

She gave him a set of rolled eyeballs. "Leave it, Emmitt, and introduce me to this gentleman."

Before Esterhazy could manage, the second man rose to his well-over-six-foot height and bent at his narrow waist. "Igor Semyonovich Konovalov," he said in perfectly inflected English. "I am very pleased to meet you, Detective Kulaeva. Your reputation precedes you."

Sasha considered a downcast head, a toe swish, and an 'aw shucks' but resisted. She looked long at the Russian and scoured her memory banks. She recognized the name, but couldn't place the gaunt, ruddy-complected face.

"Thank you, Mr. Konovalov." Sasha shook his outstretched hand. "I've heard your name, sir, but . . ."

"I am a Deputy Minister in the Russian Ministry of Justice." When he smiled, he showed a gap between his tobacco-stained yellow front teeth. "I've come here with the express purpose of meeting you."

Sasha raised her eyebrows. "I'm frankly puzzled why a Russian deputy minister would travel to Alaska 'with the express purpose' of meeting me." She sat. The two men followed suit.

Esterhazy jumped in. "I got an email from Minister Konovalov last week. He's here because both of our countries share a similar and very serious problem."

"Heroin," said Konovalov. "Thousands of Russians and thousands of Americans are suffering from heroin addiction. In Russia, it's one of our fastest growing medical health issues, next to alcoholism and TB."

Sasha nodded. "I fully appreciate your concern, sir. We work on it here in the United States every day. To fight the problem, my police department created a special task force last year. But help me out. Where do I fit into your problems?"

The minister interlaced his long fingers. "Two weeks ago, you and your colleagues broke up a very sophisticated smuggling operation. Heroin was being brought in by air from Vladivostok on a Russian airline. We're watching the pilot, Suvorov, though, so far there is no hard evidence against him. We're still unsure how our end of this trafficking operation works." The Minister sat back in his seat and dropped his hands into his lap. "I am deeply embarrassed by my country's law enforcement shortcomings. And by our criminality. We are trying to determine how this could have gone on for so long." He inclined his head toward Sasha. "But, because of your excellent work, Detective Kulaeva, you were able to close down this particular illegal enterprise. My congratulations. This was your second successful effort."

Sasha smiled. "If a moose hadn't crossed the road, and if the customs agent hadn't hit him, and if the heroin he was carrying didn't fall into our hands, no telling how long that 'enterprise' would have continued. We had good fortune."

"And very good police work," Esterhazy added.

"Indeed. Excellent police work," Konovalov agreed. "Similarly, three years ago, you and FBI agent Dana were instrumental in shutting down another heroin operation here in Alaska. Again, one that originated in Russia." Konovalov turned to Esterhazy. "It is with deep regret that your agent, Mr. Dana, died while in my country."

"Murdered, you mean," Esterhazy said, a testy note coloring his voice. "By orders of Roman Kollantai, the mayor of Vladivostok. I'm frankly surprised, Mr. Konovalov, that your ministry allows someone as corrupt as that piece of shit mobster to remain free."

Konovalov laughed lightly and raised his palms and shoulders. "May I speak now off the record, Mr. Director? Yes?"

When Esterhazy nodded, the Russian went on. "That 'piece of shit mobster,' as you have very correctly labeled him, and our president, Mr. Putin, are, shall we say . . . close. Similar perhaps to your president and any number of people, indicted recently and in jail."

Esterhazy chuckled. "Forgive my rash assessment, Mr. Minister. I'll be less accusatory next time."

"Nothing at all, Mr. Director. We all have our private burdens. But let me please explain to Detective Kulaeva my reason for coming here." He bent toward Sasha and cleared his throat. "We would like you to come to Russia for a short, working visit. It would be strictly unofficial."

Sasha recoiled slightly but remained silent, waiting for further explanation.

"We understand your situation with Vladivostok's mayor," Konovalov said. "He doesn't like you. Not at all. In fact, if he had his way . . . But that's not at issue here. The work we have in mind for you would not require you to go to Vladivostok."

"Where then? And why? And what kind of work?" Sasha asked.

"The exact same kind of work you've done here in Alaska so effectively—interdiction and disruption of heroin trafficking."

"We got lucky this last time, Minister Konovalov. While I appreciate your kind words, it was luck, nothing more."

"That's a lotta bullshit, Sasha," Esterhazy interjected. "You got a nose for this kinda work. You're the reason the APD created a Narcotics Division in the first place. Gary might be running the show but you're the division's heart and soul."

Sasha blew the SAC an air kiss. He didn't quite swoon.

Konovalov said, "Ninety-five percent of the heroin in Russia comes from Afghanistan and enters my country through our border with Kazakhstan. Once in Russia, most of it is funneled through Chelyabinsk. You are familiar with our geography?"

"Certainly. It's a good-sized city not far from the Kazakh border. It's also on the TransSiberian rail line, and because of that, it's the perfect place to receive and then distribute Afghani heroin to the rest of your country."

"Precisely," said Konovalov. "Because you are unknown in that city, we would like you to come and investigate exactly how the drug is received and moved."

Sasha fidgeted in her seat, looking back and forth between the two men. "You want me? Why don't the local police or the militia handle that job?"

"They are totally corrupt. The cartels own them. In the same way that the Sinaloa cartel owns many officers in Mexican law agencies."

"Sounds to me, Minister Konovalov, that you're reaching, desperately reaching. I mean, bringing an *American* police officer to one of Russia's drug centers sounds like a crazy idea."

"I realize it's crazy, Detective Kulaeva. Totally crazy. Still, you have shown yourself to be resilient, clever, resourceful, and dedicated."

"Thanks. I'm some of those things. Some of the time. But on my own turf, here in Alaska, where I know my way around.

I've never lived in Russia, visited only a couple times, don't really know how things work there. I'm not at all sure that what you've said about me would count for a whole hell of a lot in Chelyabinsk."

"In my ministry, we think differently. Your Russian is native and your expertise and success in this field absolutely qualifies you. We would provide virtually unlimited assistance: a team of my ministry's top agents, ready to assist you in any way." He paused and sat back. "Would you please consider coming?"

"I have to tell you, Mr. Minister, that I'm not in love with the idea. Besides which, I'd have to clear it with my bosses."

Konovalov nodded in Esterhazy's direction. "We—the Director and I—have already spoken to your superiors. Like you, they are not *crazy* about the idea, but they have generously left it up to you to decide. And if you agree, there will be a cash payment to you, personally, of fifty thousand dollars, whether or not you succeed in helping us."

"Fifty grand, Sash," Esterhazy said. "That ain't chump change."

Sasha blew out a breath, then looked at Esterhazy. "No it ain't, Emmitt." She paused and pointed a finger at the SAC. "This is your doing, isn't it? Throw a little cash her way and watch her jump."

Esterhazy smiled. "Well . . . ."

"If the bucks weren't there, I could refuse with a clear conscience. But now . . . Jesus." *Money enough for a down payment on a place. Get me out of the trailer park. No more double-wide living. Get Robin to come live with me.*

Esterhazy moved his chair closer to Sasha's. "You won't be there alone. Minister Konovalov is offering several of his Ministry's staff to help you out. They'd be in close touch with us at all times. We'd be able to keep tabs on you."

"Thanks a lot, Emmitt. You can be at the station to wave goodbye when I'm shipped off to the gulag, or dumped into the Volga with cement boots." She looked at the minister. "Fifty grand, huh? When and for how long, Mr. Konovalov?"

"You would leave in a week and you'd be there for at least two months."

"Fifty thousand's your best offer?"

"Don't be greedy, Sash," Esterhazy warned.

"Mind your business, Emmitt. It's not gonna be your ass on the line in Russia."

Konovalov said, "I can try and squeeze some more out of our budget, but for now, that seems to be it. If I could promise more I would."

Sasha sat back and stretched her legs in front of her. "Where are you staying in Anchorage?"

"At the Captain Cook."

"I'll let you know by tomorrow. Will that be OK?"

"Excellent, Detective Kulaeva." Konovalov rose, shook hands with the two Americans and left Esterhazy's office.

With the Russian gone, Sasha turned to the FBI Director. "So tell me, Mister smart-ass SAC, what do you know about this 'virtually unlimited assistance' Konovalov said I'm supposed to get from the guy's ministry? From what we know about the Russians and their promises, they could leave me high and dry."

"Three or four agents, all English speakers. A couple technical geeks. You'll have access to some of the best Russian spyware. A muscle guy will physically follow you, always within hailing distance. And another Russian will be your gofer. But let me ask you something. Off the subject."

"No, I won't have dinner with you, Emmitt."

"I didn't think you would. It's not that. Tell me why you didn't let us know about the dope the minute you found it?

Why'd you hog the investigation?"

"Talk to Stan. His call. And as far as I can tell, the right one. We did good, didn't we?"

Esterhazy gave her a concessionary nod. "You did. What else you want to know about Russia?"

"A lot. Since Konovalov said the local gendarmes are all corrupt, I suppose I can't expect any help from them."

"Right. As a matter of fact, they won't be told about you at all. You're to remain out of sight, totally undercover."

"And I'm supposed to track shipments of heroin into and out of a city I've never been to? Piece of cake."

"You're good at it Sash. You found that huge stash in the restaurant in Dutch Harbor three years ago."

"Me and Dana. I already told you it was pure luck. *And* it almost got us both killed."

"But you were quicker on the draw, Sash."

"Lucky again."

"Don't downplay your talents. You can do this. You'll get there, figure something out. Maybe even shut down the flow."

"Get real, Emmitt. You think anything I do over there is gonna seriously stop the flow of heroin into Russia? Forget it. Afghanistan is just one enormous poppy farm with a bumper crop this year, I hear. The Russkies love their smack and they got a border with Kazakhstan that goes on forever. Best I'll be able to do, if anything, is to put a momentary stopper in the bottle."

"True, Sash. But you'll be fifty-thou richer."

"I should live so long."

~~~

Detective Captain Stanislav Babiarsz stared at the policewoman sitting across from him. "I've wanted to talk to you for a good long while now, but I never found the right time. Been hedging."

"About the Officer Involved Shooting report?" Sasha asked.

"Yeah. But not about the OIS connected with the guy you shot at Merrill Field."

"No? What then?"

"About the Russians you shot three years ago in Dutch Harbor."

Her stomach suddenly knotted. *Christ.* "That's old business, Stan," she said. "The OIS in Dutch cleared me."

"Bullshit. You were cleared, Sasha, only because Jack and I agreed to clear you. No other reason."

When she didn't respond, he went on.

"The two guys from my squad in Dutch who I assigned to the OIS? I let them know what's what before they even started. They soft-pedaled the investigation. Pretty much at my direction."

"Yeah, but . . ."

"Yeah but nothing, Sasha." He straightened in his chair. "There were witnesses who contradicted your account of the shooting of the Russian guy in the parking lot. Did you know that?"

She shook her head.

"No? I didn't think you did. The couple who lived next door—a doctor and a nurse—they reported they heard shots coming from the B and B. But in a different sequence from what you reported. A difference that cast serious doubts on what you told me immediately after."

She was silent, her stomach churning. *Where is this going?*

"And I bet you also don't know that I spoke to your boss

the next day, told Jack how iffy your account of the shooting was. Did you know that?"

Another shake of her head. *Jack knew. And never said word one to me.*

"I laid it out for him, what you'd done in the B and B and out in the parking lot." Babiarsz fixed his eyes on his detective. "Upstairs, Sasha, where you finished off the Russian with one in the heart? It was a through and through from close range. Actually, you were standing directly over him. We know this because we dug your bullet out of the floor below him. Do I have that right?"

When she didn't answer, he went on. "But that's a minor problem. Guy was probably dying anyway. The real heavy shit took place in the parking lot, when you went after the third Russian."

"He fired at me, Stan."

"Is that right, Sasha? Really? Jack and I don't think so. Our thinking is that you fired off a round from his pistol after you'd shot him."

She tried to relax her facial muscles, but she couldn't unclench her jaw and couldn't stop her teeth from grinding. Her boss was glaring at her.

"If you could see yourself in a mirror right now, Sasha, you'd see that I've nailed it." Babiarsz relaxed back into his chair. "But not to worry. This conversation won't be repeated or reported. Nor will anyone other than you, me, and Jack ever know the details of what you did out in Dutch. I just wanted you to know that *I* know. And as your boss, a warning, Sasha. Keep your nose clean. I don't mind a heavy hand from my detectives once in a while. But yours is way too heavy. You're a great cop but you gotta calm the fuck down if you want to keep your badge. Understood?"

Sasha nodded.

"Say it, detective. Say you understand. I want to hear it."

"I understand."

"You can go."

She stood and left.

~~~

Mother and daughter were back in the Youth Center's meeting room.

"I like your new do," Sasha said.

Robin ran a hand over her inch-long hair. "Yeah, I figure no sense trying to do anything with it while I'm in here. I'll keep it short like this. Manageable."

"I have very good news. I spoke to the assistant DA. She's pleased you gave up Lewis. She says he's looking at some serious jail time. I don't think you know it, but *his* source was killed a while ago. We kind of know who did it but it's complicated. Bottom line, none of those people can bother you."

Robin took a deep inhalation. "So all I have to worry about now is how I'm going to survive here 'til I'm eighteen. And after that . . .?"

"You may get lucky. Judge Sanzoni's gotten your case. According to Jepson, Sanzoni likes kids, has a soft heart. The PD says when you go before him, be as contrite as you possibly can be, acknowledge your mistakes. Jepson thinks you might be able to get away with less than a year here at McLaughlin."

"And after that?"

"Hopefully you'll be released into my custody."

Robin sat back, crossed her arms. "And what's that supposed to mean?"

"It means you'll come live with me."

Robin laughed. "In the double wide? You've got to be kidding."

"No. I'm not. You want to come live with me, the door's open. And I'm moving. Gonna look for a house."

Robin let her arms unwind, stared hard at her mother. "A house, huh? Lemme think about it."

Sasha gave her daughter a half-smile. "OK. Think about it."

"And? What else?" Robin asked. "You look like something else is on your mind."

"You don't miss a trick, do you? Actually, there is something. A big something. I need to go abroad. Work related."

Robin frowned. "Abroad? Abroad for you is probably Russia. That it?"

Sasha shook her head. "Can't say. I might be leaving as soon as next week. I'll be out of touch for a while."

"It *is* Russia, isn't it? What's going on?"

Sasha rose and drew her daughter up from the sofa. She took Robin's hands. "I really can't say. But it's definitely *not* dangerous work. And it pays huge bucks, so when I'm back and you're out of here, if you like, maybe we can go somewhere."

"I'm game. How 'bout Chile? Know anyone there?"

Sasha laughed. "Chile sounds great. You'll love it."

"You might, too, Mom."

~~~

Two Anchorage Police Department lieutenants sat opposite Sergeant Busby Moranis. A small office in the Tudor Road precinct house was the site of the meeting.

Lt. Noreen Polito had a folder open in front of her. "A

busy time for you, Detective Moranis, what with everything that happened over at Merrill Field."

Moranis was silent. He knew Polito, at one time considered asking her out. But her higher rank had always made him leery. And right now he was dating someone. *Too late, Noreen.*

"You're handy with your weapon, detective." said Lt. Vince Robinette.

Moranis stared at him. "I didn't hear a question mark at the end of that sentence, lieutenant. When you got a question, I'll be glad to answer."

"Don't wise-ass me, Moranis. This is your third OIS. We know all about you."

Moranis sat back, waiting for the man to reveal what everyone knew. He looked at Polito, who was the senior officer in the room. That was confirmed when she turned to Robinette. "Let's stay on track, Vince." Then to Moranis, "Why were you at Merrill Field, Detective?"

Moranis smiled at Polito. "Finally, a question." He blew out a deep breath. "Sergeant Kulaeva and I went to Merrill Field to interview Leo and Dorotea Bulgarin, the owners of Grizzly Air."

"Why did you want to talk to them?" Polito asked.

"We wanted to know whether either of them knew the US Customs worker who died several nights before."

"The one in the car accident?" asked Robinette.

"Yeah."

"The one who was found in possession of about forty pounds of heroin?"

"Yeah, that one. Oh, by the way, Lieutenant Robinette. In our police department, we measure heroin in kilos not in pounds. Just so you know." Moranis smirked.

"Fuck you, Moranis. That was the same heroin that you

and your boss never reported to the FBI, the DEA, Customs, the TSA, Homeland Security. That heroin?"

"Yes."

Polito again, exerting her senior status. "Vince, we're not here to talk about jurisdiction. We're here to establish this officer's role in the death of the unidentified man at Merrill Field." She turned to Moranis again. "Have you figured out the guy's identity yet?"

"Still workin' on it."

"Okay. So, you and Sergeant Kulaeva arrived at the airfield. What happened?"

"As soon as we arrived in front of the Grizzly Air offices, we heard shots. We exited our vehicle, drew our weapons, took cover, and tried to see what was going on."

"What'd you see?"

"Well, the first thing we saw was the body of a woman sprawled half-in the door of a nearby plane. She wasn't moving. We later identified her as Dorotea Bulgarin, the wife of Grizzly's owner. Then we saw a man running from a hangar and a second man chasing him, firing a pistol at him. The guy running away was hit and fell. Sergeant Kulaeva and I rose up and shouted at the gunman to drop his weapon. He shot at us and began running back to the hangar. We returned fire and apparently struck the gunman three times before he entered the hangar."

"And after that?" asked Robinette.

"After that, Sergeant Kulaeva pursued the shooter into the hangar."

"Where were you?"

"I was running toward the hangar and heard three shots from inside the building. I arrived at the hangar just as Sergeant Kulaeva exited."

"Did she say anything to you?" asked Polito.

"She said, 'He's dead. Let's take care of the wounded.'"

"How did Sergeant Kulaeva appear?"

"She looked like she'd just been in a deadly fire-fight and had been shot at repeatedly."

"Can you describe her more accurately?" Robinette demanded.

"Her face, her body, you mean? She was shaky, pale, kinda wild-eyed. You ever been in a shooting Lieutenant Robinette? Lieutenant Polito? It's no fun. You're crappin' your shorts the whole time. That's what Sergeant Kulaeva looked like. And if you'd ask her, she'd probably say the same about me."

"Did the shooter fire at you, Detective?" Robinette asked.

"Several times. From his Walther, and then again after he went to the Springfield. Several shots."

"Did you fear for your life?" asked Polito, writing on the report in front of her.

"Yes, I absolutely did."

Polito looked at her partner. "Vince?"

Robinette glared at Moranis. "You look OK for this one, Moranis. Your partner also. But like I told you. This was number three. You should try to avoid a fourth OIS."

Moranis rose up from the table. "That's my hope and my prayer, Lieutenant Robinette. Just tell the bad guys to stop shooting at me."

~~~

For their second meeting, Konovalov was dressed more casually: slacks, a pullover, and slippers.

"Thank you for coming, Detective Kulaeva. Please," he

said, waving her in.

Sasha entered the Captain Cook's premier penthouse suite. She dropped her parka, watch cap, and scarf on a chair in the entryway. She walked across the spacious living room to the floor-to-ceiling windows. The city below was white and relatively still, the past evening's heavy snowfall slowing the sparse downtown traffic. Five miles to the east, the Chugach Range was totally blanketed.

"Can I offer you something to drink or something perhaps to eat?" the Russian asked.

"Coffee'd work. And maybe a sweet roll?"

Russia's Deputy Minister of Justice was already on the house phone. "Done," he said in a moment.

"Great." She did a quick stroll around the airy, well-appointed room and found a deep armchair into which she settled with a contented sigh. "Fifty thousand, you said, Mr. Minister?"

Konovalov smiled. "That's what I said."

"Well, I guess you can sign me up. Although it's absolutely against my better judgment. Between you and me, I didn't much enjoy myself the last time I was in your country. And I made a vow after I'd escaped—I had to escape Russia, for crying out loud—that I'd never go back. But here I am, a slave to cash." She grinned.

"I can appreciate your hesitation about returning. I know mostly everything about your last visit. Perhaps too much excitement in Vladivostok?"

"You know about my time in Vlad? Were you there?"

"Not quite. When you and the other man—the detective from Chile, I believe—captured Zhuganov in the hotel, I was in Moscow. The authorities in Vlad contacted me. I was ordered to go and collect him, bring him back to Moscow. But somehow, between the time I boarded the flight and nine hours later when I landed, Zhuganov had been stabbed to death in the Partizanskaya, one of our infamous prisons. So I never got to meet the gentleman. I had a few questions I wanted to ask him."

"Questions that certainly would have compromised the mayor out there, Kollantai," Sasha said.

The door chimed. Konovalov went to open it. A young Latino rolled in a tray with coffee and assorted pastry. The Russian tipped him a five. When the waiter left, the minister served. Sasha was charmed by the man's good manners.

"Thanks so much, Igor Semyonich."

"A pleasure, Detective," he said, putting coffee and cake on a table next to her armchair. The minister retired to his own chair, sitting opposite her. "I regret to say that your Mr. Esterhazy was correct yesterday when he described Kollantai."

"Kollantai is bad news. The mayor's just a goon in an expensive suit. And, in fact, he *does* get away with murder." Sasha sipped her coffee. "Zhuganov strangled the director of our local Drug Enforcement Agency and shot two friends of mine in the hotel room at the Hyundai. But he couldn't have done it without the direct knowledge and the stamp of approval from Kollantai. Am I right?"

"Absolutely right. You know, whatever success you might have in Chelyabinsk will affect Kollantai. He's the last link in the heroin trail before it starts its journey across the Bering Sea."

She paused in mid-sip. "I hadn't really seen it that way, but . . . you're right. Added incentive for me. Beyond the cash, of course." She smiled and took a bite out of a chocolate croissant. Crumbs spilled onto her blouse. She looked down and brushed them off. Konovalov watched her with deep pleasure.

"Your border with Kazakhstan?" she asked. "What can you tell me?"

The Russian breathed out, shaking his head. "It's porous.

Always has been. There are literally thousands of places you can walk across, out of sight of any kind of frontier security."

"But we're talking major loads of heroin, aren't we? I mean, shouldn't we focus on the main highway into Chelyabinsk?"

"That's what I would suggest," Konovalov said. "As a starting point, perhaps focus on the FSS frontier guards. Many are corrupt."

"Sounds a likely starting place." Sasha rose, brushed cake crumbs from her lap, and walked to the window. "What do you know about the origins of the heroin? I mean, it's from Afghanistan for sure, but more than that, how does it get into Russia?"

"We know that our frontiers are not safe. There have been numerous instances, throughout our history, of all kinds of contraband smuggled into Russia—into Imperial Russia, into communist Russia, and into today's Russia. All from the south. When the Soviet Union broke up, Kazakhstan, Uzbekistan, and Turkmenistan—former Soviet republics—all achieved a great deal more independence. And with independence, Russian influence in those three countries was severely diminished."

"Allowing all kinds of hanky-panky on those borders," Sasha said.

"Hanky panky?"

"Illegal activities."

"True. The traffic on the highways connecting those countries is heavy. Lorries by the thousands."

She wagged her head. "Sounds like I'm undertaking a mission impossible."

"We have hope. We trust that you'll succeed."

"Perhaps."

"Yes, perhaps. And perhaps someday we'll even be able to go farther south, and cut off the production and processing of the product at the source, in Afghanistan."

"I'm not so sure. Heroin is what Afghanistan is all about." She gave him a sly grin. "How did your last venture into Afghanistan go? Not too well, if I read my history properly."

Konovalov returned her smile. "Our own Vietnam. But happily for us, not as long nor as costly as yours."

~~~

Busby Moranis and Luisa Cortez were enjoying another meal together, their fourth, this time at Simon and Seafort's. All the window booths were full, so they decided to eat at the bar. The bank manager ordered crab-stuffed halibut, the cop, BBQ baby-back ribs.

"Why did they interview you again, Busby? Didn't you have to make out a report and tell what's his name, your boss, what happened?"

Moranis was pleased by Luisa's genuine interest in his well being. *First time any woman has ever given a real hoot about me.* "It's standard practice, Luisa. Whenever a police officer fires his weapon, there's an investigation. Nothin' to worry about. I was cleared. So was Sasha." He glanced down at his plate. He loved ribs, ordered them often. But now, recognizing what a mess they were making of his hands and face, he regretted his food choice. *Shoulda ordered the chicken. Coulda knife and forked it. Hard to look cool with bar-b-que sauce all over my face.*

His dining partner wasn't calmed by his explanation. "You must be a wreck, Busby. All that shooting. So scary." She reached across the table, covered one of his hands, gave it a squeeze, and favored him with one of her radiant smiles. The sixteenth since they met in the bank. He'd counted.

Luisa tilted her head. "Maybe, Busby, if you'd like, we

can have coffee and dessert at my place. I made flan."

"Sweet of you to offer, but I wouldn't want to intrude, Luisa. I mean, your kids . . ."

"It's Friday. Both the girls are at their friend's home. A slumber party."

"Well, if it's not too much trouble," Moranis said.

"No trouble at all," she assured him.

~~~

"Place hasn't changed much," Sasha said.

Katherine Manfredi chuckled. "I try to keep it *un*-changed. I believe the folks who come to see me need an environment they can count on, comfortably the same."

"Makes sense," Sasha said. She walked over to the long bay window that gave out onto an icy Cook Inlet. She scanned the several dozen succulents and cacti that spread along the window's inner sill. She smiled. "Is there still a place for me on the sill?"

The psychologist nodded. "You did some great work sitting there at our very first meeting, three years ago. Remember?"

"Like it was yesterday. I told you about my husband's death. Up until then, I hadn't really shared that story with anyone not in the family." Sasha passed her hand over a Christmas cactus beginning to show a few blooms. "It's been sixteen years since he died . . . was killed." She looked out the window. The outside drizzle became more insistent. "I think I told you, last time I was here, about the cop I met at that crime conference. Tomás. He's from Chile. Santiago. It's a long story but . . . we're . . . an item, I guess. I'd like to think so. He came up here for ten days last summer. It was great. More than great. Fabulous. Been a long time for me between lovers, Katherine. Long time." Sasha smiled at the memory. "He told me he loved me. And I believe him. I told him I loved him, and I believe I do. But . . ." She shivered. The room had gotten chilly. "But. Must there always be a 'but'? I mean, can't we talk about relationships without using that word?"

"'But' is what creates the drama, Sasha. If there were no buts, everything would go smoothly and neither of us would have a job."

Sasha grinned and straightened in her sill-seat. "Right. *But* he lives and works in Santiago, almost eight thousand miles from here. He loves his work, loves his city, and has a large and wonderful family there. And me? Same thing. Love Alaska, love my work, have my family here. So neither of us is gonna pick up and join the other. Truthfully, I wouldn't feel right about asking him to give up his life there to come here. And I know he feels the same reluctance about asking me to move south. Neither of those things is likely to happen."

"So?"

"So. We're stuck. Although it's not totally unrequited love, it's not very rewarding. Kinda sucks, actually. See, love by email doesn't work. Skype-love stinks. Sexting stinks. All I want to do is to be able to touch him. To lay my fingers on his neck. To lean against his shoulder." She laughed. "To sit on his lap."

"Do you have plans to see him again? A trip south, perhaps?"

"Nothing firm. We talk or text two, three times a week. It's later there, by five hours, so it's hard sometimes to connect."

"I wish I had an Ann Landers solution for you, Sasha. Sorry, but I don't."

"No, I know you don't. Nobody has one. But it's been good to air it out. I've told you before, Katherine, you're a good listener, a good shrink." Sasha rose from her seat and stretched her arms to the ceiling.

Manfredi said, "You also once showed me a photo of your daughter. How's she doing?"

Sasha's dropped her arms and let her shoulders sag. "How's she doing? Not so hot. She was busted last week for possession of heroin."

Manfredi collapsed back into her chair, shaking her head. "Oh no. I don't know what to say, Sasha, other than I'm sorry. Very sorry."

"Me, too. Came out of the blue. Total surprise. She's at McLaughlin. I was crazy angry at first. Couldn't believe that a kid of mine . . . But I saw her again yesterday. She's OK and so am I. At least, I can live with it. She'll spend the next year and half, 'til she's eighteen, in the Youth Center."

"And after that?"

"I want her to come and live with me. She's thinking about it. I'm still in the double wide, in Bay View Estates. No bay. No view. Not exactly your up-town residence. But I'm looking for a house where the two of us can share space. I just took on extra work, something with a big pay-off. Could make the down payment for me."

"Extra work?"

"Yeah. Still police work, but I can't say what." Sasha did a short tour of the psychologist's office then sat again on the windowsill. "This seems the best place for me to lay something else on you, something I avoided talking about three years ago. You remember, after the shooting in Dutch Harbor, I asked you about the crimes some of your patients had committed?"

"I remember it distinctly, Sasha." Manfredi pointed with a pen. "You were right over there, leaning on the kitchen doorjamb. You had a cup of coffee in your hand. We were talking about the shooting, but you veered off-topic and began asking about my other patients."

"Right. I was debating with myself how much I should tell you about what really happened in Dutch. I was worried about patient-client privilege."

"So you wound up *not* sharing what was on your mind. Okay, I get it. That was then. And here you are again. Similar sequence of events."

"Meaning?"

"Meaning, three years ago, you were in a shooting in Dutch Harbor, then you came to see me, almost ready to talk about something. Then, a couple weeks ago you're in another shooting. This time here in town, at Merrill Field. In the aftermath of each of those horrific events, you call up and make an appointment to see me. Actually, when I read the news about what happened at Merrill Field, I half-expected to hear from you."

"You thought I'd show up?"

"I did. The session after Dutch Harbor, you left a lot unresolved. I imagine that these similar circumstances—another shooting—would again raise those same unresolved issues. Am I right?"

Sasha bowed an acknowledgement toward the other woman. "I'm wondering if I should go lean on the door jamb. The 'jamb of denial.' But you probably won't let me," she laughed.

Manfredi joined her laughing. "I can't stop you, of course. But I don't recommend it. Not unless you're interested in avoiding once more the reason you've come here."

The detective smiled. "So you'd like me to stay here, sitting on the window sill?"

"That's my recommendation. I think it's the appropriate spot for whatever it is you want to share today. Move the aloe vera a little and get comfortable."

Sasha rose, repositioned the plant, then sat again, taking care not to get impaled by a large and spikey crown-of-thorns. She took a deep breath and blew it out. "I got a big surprise yesterday. My boss, the Chief of Detectives, told me stuff about the Dutch Harbor shooting that I didn't think anyone else knew. Well, besides Charlie Dana, the FBI agent who saw the whole thing. And he was killed the next week in Vladivostok."

Manfredi leaned forward, elbows on her desk, head cupped in her palms. "What did the chief of detectives tell you?"

Sasha hugged herself with both arms. "He told me that he knew . . . well, suspected, though he was pretty right on . . . he knew that my account of the shooting was . . . was not truthful."

"Not truthful?"

"Yeah. A lie." Sasha turned her body to look out the window. She whispered, "It was a lie, Katherine. My account was a lie. And Stan, my boss, knows it."

"What was the lie?"

Sasha turned back to the room, looked at the psychologist. "The man I killed, the one in the parking lot? I testified to the cops who ran the Officer Involved Shooting investigation that he shot at me first and I killed him in self-defense." She shook her head. "I lied. He never shot at me. My boss guessed what happened. He said that I fired the weapon *after* I shot the man. After I killed him."

"And is your boss right?"

Sasha nodded. "Yeah, he's right. He was the Chief of Police in Dutch at the time. Now he's my boss here in Anchorage. And he knows all about me and all about what I did out there. Interesting working for someone who knows I'm a liar. And a killer."

Psychologist and patient maintained a long silence.

Finally, Katherine asked, "What'll he do with the information?"

"He promised he wouldn't do anything. Just warned me to watch my step. Take the foot off the pedal a little."

"What else?"

"He said he's known about it from the very beginning. Said he talked to my former boss, Jack Raymond. Jack's retired now, in Arizona. Said he and Jack doped out what they thought really happened in Dutch. Smart cops, those two. Not much gets by 'em."

Manfredi waited for Sasha to continue. When she did not, the psychologist asked, "And the shooting at Merrill Field? A couple weeks ago?"

Sasha shook her head and stood. "I think I'm gonna go lean on the doorjamb, Katherine. If it's all the same to you."

Manfredi smiled at her patient. "Really? The windowsill is still available. No other patients scheduled today."

Sasha stood. "I think we're done for now."

"So be it. I have only one more question."

"Shoot."

"Why have you told me this? Your new boss knows. Your old boss knows. You said it's just the three of you. And your new boss assured you that neither he nor your old boss would ever breathe a word. So why tell me?"

"A great question, Katherine. I hadn't thought about it before, on the way here. Didn't ask myself 'why?' Wasn't even sure what we were going to talk about today. Everything just seemed to bubble up. Let me think on it and we can maybe talk about it next time."

"Do I have to wait for another shooting to see you again?"

Sasha went to the coat rack and donned her parka and wool cap. "Hopefully not. Thanks for your time, Katherine."

Sasha glanced toward the bay window. "Your plants have grown. They're thriving. And you've added some new ones."

"There's always room on the sill, Sasha."

~~~

Breakfast downtown at Snow City Cafe. Chief of Detectives Stan Babiarsz was treating his three Narcotics Division staff. Between bites of his spinach omelet, he looked at Sasha. "When are you gonna tell these guys?"

Hernandez was in the middle of a mouthful of Tundra Scramble. "Tell us? Tell us what?"

Sasha put down her fork, let her eggs Benedict sit. "I guess sneaking off isn't going to work."

"Where you sneaking to?" Moranis asked.

When she hesitated too long, Babiarsz announced, "Our Sasha here is on her way to Russia. Special assignment."

Hernandez dropped his fork onto the table. "You're going to Russia? I mean, two weeks ago you told me not in your present incarnation. What the hell's changed?"

Sasha played with the hash browns on her plate. "What's changed is that a guy from the Russian Ministry of Justice made me an offer."

"One you gobbled up, obviously," Moranis said. "Kind of an offer?"

"A shit load of rubles to go and help them figure out how so much heroin is being smuggled into their country."

"They can't do it themselves?" Moranis asked.

"Apparently not. Seems the place I'm going, the crime fighters are all on the take. So, I'm elected. I'm leaving in a couple days. Be gone for . . ." she looked at Babiarsz, "maybe three months."

"And what are we s'posed to do in the meantime?" asked Moranis.

Babiarsz said, "I'll see about getting you guys a fill-in for the duration."

"Not the same thing, boss," Hernandez said.

"We all know that," Babiarsz agreed. "But she's made a commitment. That's it."

"Let's have the details, Sash," Hernandez demanded. "You going alone? I mean, how are you gonna do what they're paying you to do?"

Sasha put up her palms. "Sorry, Gary. Not only can I not give you the specifics, I really shouldn't even have given you this much. It's kind of hush-hush."

"Right," Babiarsz said. "What little you two just learned stays here at the table. Anyone asks, Sasha's on extended leave. We don't know where or why."

"Not crazy about the idea," Hernandez said. "Sounds way too risky. I mean, last time you went, you got your ass in a sling and barely escaped." He looked at his boss.

Babiarsz said, "It's her decision."

Sasha nodded. "Yep. My decision. How 'bout we change the subject? The shooter at Merrill Field? Still no word on who the hell he was?"

"No word," Hernandez said. "Forensics said his clothes were European, and the ID in his wallet—his driver's license, social security—were phony. Same with his car registration. All made out to someone named Armand Osorio. And both weapons—the Walther and the Springfield—were unregistered. But here's the really interesting thing. The ballistics on the Walther showed it was a weapon with a long history. It killed the three people at Merrill Field, right? It also killed Antoine Washington out in Eagle River. And . . . this here's the fun part .

. . it's the same weapon used to kill Rudy Castro in that Palmer motel, three years ago."

"Same gun, same guy," said Moranis.

"But I'm not through," Hernandez said. "I got a call this morning from Lupe, over at the crime lab. She says the heroin that was found in B.J. Lewis' car, and the heroin your daughter was holding match the smack you and Dana found three years ago in Dutch."

"Jeezo," Sasha said. "Is she sure?"

"Absolutely. She says the FBI's analysis of all three samples shows the identical chemicals used in the processing. The feds have determined that all three batches most likely came from the same processing plant in Afghanistan. They think in Jalalabad, east of Kabul."

"Afghanistan," Sasha said. "Poppy heaven."

~~~

BOOK 2
Earlier, 2017-2018

They drove the pitted, one-lane dirt road in an open Jeep, dust billowing in their wake. The two blade-thin men sitting in the back were bearded, turbaned, and dressed in simple white shirts, baggy pants, and sandals. Their AK 47s were propped in front of them, muzzles skyward. A heavy wooden box rested on the floor between them.

The driver, Farouz, a man in his early fifties with a deeply lined face of burnished copper and eyes of the richest blue, was also turbaned. But unlike his two cousins sitting behind him, he was clean-shaven and armed only with a Russian Tokarev pistol, in a holster, draped across his chest.

The fourth man, in the passenger seat, was Kamal Saifi ibn Murad*, a robustly stout major in the Afghan Army, dressed today in a light green turtleneck sweater and beige Dockers. On his feet, his favorite Birkenstock sandals. Kamal's Afghan Army fatigues were stuffed into a burlap bag under his seat. Because this trip today with his clansmen was off the books, and since wearing his army uniform would only draw suspicious looks from the farmers—and perhaps even draw fire from any of the Taliban in the area—Kamal chose mufti. When they'd return to Jalalabad this afternoon, he'd change back into his fatigues.

The major's head was uncovered. He loved the country breeze in what remained of his thinning hair. Driving along this rough and hilly, stream-side road, he got caught up in the memory of the times he and his cousin, Samir, used to swim here in waters that were bone chillingly cold even in mid-summer. He sat back in his seat and regarded the meandering stream and the tall, red flowers that grew in profusion, extending up from the water's edge. Over the past several years, he'd come to love the color red.

Samir Mahmoodi, hoe in hand, heard the Jeep before he could distinguish it from the cloud of dust it created as it navigated the rocky road up to his hilltop farm.

"Reina," he yelled back to the house. "Guests."

Samir's wife stood in front of her stone home, her bare arms dusted white to the elbows with flour. She was kneading dough on a rude, wooden board. She wiped her hands and arms on her apron and shouted to her son, "Malek, quickly. Get the sheep off the road, then clear the table in the backyard. Your uncle is coming."

The seventeen-year-old hobbled barefoot toward the flock of eighty fat sheep that had parked themselves in front of the entrance to the farm.

Reina hurried into the house and went to an ancient chest of drawers. She took out a simple, dark blue *hijab* and stood in front of a mirror. She wrapped her head in the scarf, hiding her long, gray hair.

The Jeep from one side, and Malek from the other reached the sheep at the same time. Farouz slowed the vehicle to a stop and leaned on the steering wheel.

"Good looking flock," he called out to Malek. The boy smiled and expertly herded the sheep off the road.

"Thank you, my prince. Very well done!" Kamal called to him.

"You are welcome, uncle," Malek said, standing as proudly

straight as his twisted leg would allow. "Father and mother are waiting by the house."

Kamal winked at his driver. "With any luck, Farouz, mutton for lunch."

In the shade of a large walnut tree in back of the farmhouse, the men sat at a plank table, sipping hot tea, smoking, and enjoying the honey and pistachio cakes that Kamal had brought from Jalalabad. The dishes from their lamb stew were cleared by Reina, who now retired.

Kamal let his gaze wander. In the distance, on the slope of a sparsely wooded hill, a simple piece of white stone marked a grave. "What a boy. I miss our Bashir."

"As do I," Samir answered slowly, remembering every second of the day years earlier when his clansmen brought back the body of his thirteen-year-old son, shot dead by a Russian helicopter gunship.

By way of easing his cousin's grief, Kamal began recounting a story all of them had heard often, and from which he knew Samir would take comfort.

"So there we were," Kamal began, "just outside of Herat, pinned down by automatic weapons fire from that Soviet half-track. We're taking a hell of a beating. Your Bashir . . . he's what? Barely twelve? He jumps out from behind the rubble, runs across that melon patch, grabs the RPG from the dead Russian. It's as big as he is. Stands up, brazen as a mukhtar, aims and fires. KA-BLAM! You could hear the explosion in Kabul. The half-track's all in flames. I'm watching the whole thing half a kilometer away, on the side of a hill. The captain's standing next to me. Hamid Ali . . . you remember him, don't you? That old piss-pot with a tic in his left eye. He yells out, 'Who the hell is that kid?' I say, 'That's Bashir, my cousin's oldest.' The captain says to me, 'Now there's a warrior to make a father proud.'"

"Truly," said Farouz, giving Samir's arm an affectionate squeeze. The two bodyguards nodded to Samir, their hands over their hearts.

Overhead, the walnut boughs rattled in the breeze.

"Thank you, all," Samir said quietly, stepping out from the table. "Let me get you something."

Kamal looked to his two bodyguards. "Fetch the box, set it up here on the table."

Kamal helped to spread a clean tarp across the length of the table, then carefully withdrew a set of Bausch and Lomb digital scales from its protective padding in the wooden box. He placed the scales in the center of the tarp, then put a heavy plastic container, capable of holding up to ten kilograms, on the scales. He zeroed out the dials.

Samir returned with a large cardboard carton containing nineteen clear, gallon-sized Ziploc bags, each holding a dark brown, resinous, and lumpy ball. He passed the balls, one at a time to Kamal for weighing. For the next twenty minutes, armed with identical TI 363 calculators, each man kept a tally. When the last of the balls was weighed, Kamal stepped back and showed the results of his calculations to his cousin: "Sixteen kilo, one hundred twenty-one grams."

Samir consulted his calculator. "Exactly," he said.

"Times today's current rate," Kamal said, entering some figures.

"Less of course," Samir added, smiling from ear to ear, "eight percent for uncle."

They both chuckled at the thought of their eighty-four-year-old Shaikh, Salar Murad ibn Sayed, their tribal patriarch, counting his eight percent from each of the more than fifteen hundred clansmen/farmers who swore fealty to him.

"Inshallah," Kamal said. "May he live and profit until one hundred and twenty years." He finished his calculations and turned to Samir.

"So cousin, it seems you are due one thousand, nine hundred and eighty-nine American dollars and thirty-six American cents." He showed his calculator to Samir. "Let's call it an even two thousand and let me get going. My escort back to Jalalabad is waiting down by the highway. He looked to his driver, "Ya, Farouz. Count out two thousand American for our cousin and his lovely family."

The scales back in their box, Kamal took Samir aside. "How's Malek doing?"

"They've scheduled the operation for the end of next month. That's when a team of doctors from the European Red Crescent will be visiting. From the x-rays they took at the clinic in Charikar, the doctors are optimistic."

"How much?"

"Three thousand American."

"Manageable. If you come up short, let me know. The Shaikh also asked about Malek. He said to keep him up to date. And of course, he would pay any price for the health of your son."

"Thanks to you, cousin, and when you see him, thank our uncle. Tell him I'm grateful. Now then, you have a long trip back to Jalalabad. So, on your way."

Samir embraced each of his four clansmen and bade them safe journey. They drove slowly out of the farm and low-geared themselves cautiously down the rocky mountain road.

~~~

Tucker Cranston* leaned over the pommel of his saddle and stroked the smooth neck of his horse. It was getting towards three and he would have to start back soon. There was family waiting and a meal to be shared.

He had ridden out from his home at noon, making for the Susitna River. The rough trail was bordered on each side by low-hanging willows and stunted alder. The weather matched his depressed mood: dark skies, weeping clouds, a chilling breeze sweeping up from Cook Inlet.

Tucker usually didn't hold with finding omens in the weather. Still . . . he felt something was speaking to him on the eve of his departure for his third battlefield tour. His stomach was knotted. Wind-whipped tears shone in Major Tucker Cranston's eyes.

Years earlier, he'd done service in Iraq. In 2003 and 2007. He'd hated going, believed the whole undertaking was a criminal waste cooked up and sold to a gullible president. And now, in 2017, he was getting shipped to Afghanistan. *Another totally idiotic mission*, he thought. But he would obey orders. No choice. He would go. Tomorrow.

They'd rise at daybreak, he and Luellen. He'd say goodbye to his five children and leave his home in Palmer, Alaska. He and his wife would head east into the late spring sunrise, past Eagle River, over the bridge spanning Knik River and then on to JBER, Joint Base Elmendorf Richardson. There, Tucker would join two hundred other unfortunates, all back in uniform after the six days allotted to them for leave-taking. They would wrestle their gear into duffle bags, board a trio of C-130 Hercules aircraft and continue east. Twenty-six hours later they'd land at Bagram Air Base, Parwan Province, Afghanistan. Major Tucker

Cranston would spend the next twelve months commanding the 2nd Battalion of the 142nd Infantry Regiment.

Without his five children.

Without Luellen.

A distant bolt of spring lightning followed by a clap of thunder made his horse jitter. He turned his mount homeward and thought about the void the army was creating in his life. He'd miss the graduation from Colony High School of his twin daughters, Raylette and Tessa. He wouldn't be there to help his daughter, Elizabeth, in math. He'd be gone when his young sons, Rory and Trent, prepared for the Alaska State Fair. He'd not be there for his wife.

Luellen Cranston* spoke quietly, almost whispering.

"Dear Lord. We are gathered before you tonight, seven of your children. Lord, please cast your loving gaze upon us as we send our husband and father into a dangerous and uncertain future. We place his life into your keeping and ask that you give us the strength and guidance to continue to do your good works."

"Amen," said Tucker and his five children. Luellen raised her head, keeping tight grips on the hands of her husband and her youngest son. "Amen," she murmured.

Late afternoon, 20,000 feet, the coastline bordering Virginia and the Barrier Islands was a thin white line where it met the blue of Chesapeake Bay.

Ten hours into the flight, Tucker Cranston looked out a portside window of the aircraft that was carrying him and seventy-two other members of his battalion's airborne infantry to Afghanistan. He was trying to work out—for the umpteenth time—how his life had taken this wholly unwanted turn.

Twenty-five years earlier, while a senior at Colony High,

he was turned down by the Air Force Academy, the place his family of pilots hoped he'd attend. Plan B was the University of Washington for a degree in history and a teaching credential. Plan C was Texas A & M, a degree in history, and a four-year stint in their Corps of Cadets.

Tucker's father had attended A & M and upon graduation, had gone to Vietnam. Two tours there earned him a Silver Star, three purple hearts, and left the little finger of his right hand paralyzed. He lived through Tet in 1968 and returned home relieved to have survived, yet half-crazed by a war he admitted could not be won. Despite his open disillusionment with the conflict in Asia, he urged his son toward a career in the military. Tucker grudgingly honored his father's wish and allowed himself to be sold the dream the old man was selling.

Although he enjoyed his first semester at A & M., his interest ebbed with each year. The regimented life of a soldier chafed. Having to salute and pretend to respect people he knew were self-serving bootlicks chafed. Having to render blind devotion to American foreign policy, a policy he knew was deeply flawed, chafed.

During his studies at A & M, he'd found time to read the *People's History of the United States* by Howard Zinn. Although he found some of Zinn's assertions about American policy weakly argued, in the main, he agreed with the author: Americans, Tucker felt, had a lot to answer for.

In his junior year, he declared his major in Middle Eastern History and learned of his country's participation in Operation Ajax, the 1953 CIA/MI6 coordinated overthrow of Iran's popularly elected prime minister and the installation of the hated Shah. *Yeah, we're no angels.*

As an academic, Tucker excelled. His senior thesis was a sharply focused analysis of Bismarck's strategic policies, which

Tucker believed were a direct cause of the First World War. The fifty-page document was widely admired in his department and beyond.

As a soldier, however, Tucker was less than brilliant, never really buying into the *esprit de corps* A & M attempted to instill. He followed orders, fulfilled his duties, and learned what he needed to become an able, if undistinguished, commander of men. He graduated in the second quarter of his class, but the doubts about his future in uniform lingered and gnawed at him. He also came away less healthy than when he entered A & M: he learned to smoke and his serious study habits left him needing reading glasses.

In 2003, during Desert Storm, Lieutenant Cranston gained his captaincy due to an unanticipated and unearned battlefield promotion: his company commander was relieved of duty for insubordination.

Tucker's running his mouth at the wrong time and openly criticizing President George Bush kept him a captain. His repeated questioning of the President's dubious service with the Texas Air National Guard could not fail but come to the attention of his superiors. Doubting the Commander in Chief's valor and judgment proved a distinct obstacle to advancement.

And when Bush landed on the aircraft carrier Abraham Lincoln and declared 'Mission Accomplished,' Tucker was openly derisive. "Dummy hasn't got a fucking clue," he opined way too loudly in the officers' mess. "Jackass paints the situation in blacks and whites, instead of the gray tones that've colored the Middle East forever."

Circumspection had never been Tucker's long suit, and when Bush challenged the world with his ultimatum, "You are either with us or against us," Tucker seriously considered leaving the army.

As much as he doubted the utility of his service, the ever-present bottom line loomed: he had eighteen years in, two to go before he could retire. And when he broached the topic at home, his wife helped him crunch the numbers. The verdict was determinative: the amount of money they'd lose if he decided to cash in early would hardly begin to cover the growing needs of his young family. No choice but to soldier on. And since promotion in the military is made up of equal parts *gung ho* and ass-kissing, and since he scored low in both, Tucker stagnated at his captaincy rating for years. It was only in 2017, with his combat deployment to Afghanistan, that he received his major's gold oak leaf.

~~~

After graduating from the Kirov Military Medical Academy in St. Petersburg in 1987, Tamara Ivanovna Stoikova* was sent directly to the front—to a makeshift, blood-soaked, and limb-strewn tent, near Khost, Afghanistan. The brutal war the Russians were making on the Afghanis was in its eighth year.

She arrived at her duty station just after one o'clock in the afternoon. By four-thirty, she had helped restrain an eighteen-year-old from Tula as his left leg, above the knee, was removed; she had handed the attending physician the instruments he needed to extract cluster bomb shards from the back of an hysterical twenty-two-year-old corporal from Omsk; and she had embraced a veteran Russian infantry sergeant from Volgograd as he slipped from life, begging for his mother.

Over the next two years, Tamara had to deal with all manner of physical and mental trauma. She treated gunshot, mine, and IED wounds. She worked in the improvised burn ward where screaming soldiers had to endure skin sloughing from their charred bodies. She regularly assisted in the removal of limbs and became expert at fashioning *ad hoc* prosthetics. She ministered to victims of psychological trauma—soldiers who had become incoherent and even incontinent because of lives lived in constant fear. And on an almost daily basis, Tamara was called upon to comfort dying young men, men who hadn't the faintest idea why this battle zone and this time had been selected for them as the place to breathe their last.

The experience was unforgettably harsh, but for purposes of furthering her nursing career, it could not have served her better. Because after being demobilized in 1989, and with two years of combat zone duty on her resume, she was hired by the first hospital to which she applied—Municipal Polyclinic #2 in Chelyabinsk, in southern Russia, not far from the border with Kazakhstan. She was assigned to the ER, appointed over the heads of many nurses with more seniority but with not nearly her hands-on experience in trauma care.

In 1996, Tamara married Artur Vinogradov, the volleyball coach at the city's Locomotiv Youth Sports Club. Their son, Marco, was born a year later.

But when it was discovered that the coach had been diddling the long-limbed and very blond spiker for the women's under-21 team, Tamara's marriage headed south. And when both coach and blond went missing on the same day, everyone put two and two together. Rumor had the runaways holed up in Smolensk.

The leggy spiker returned home after only a few weeks. No one was surprised that she had quickly tired of the older and going-to-paunch coach.

Artur returned to Chelyabinsk the next month, tail between his legs. He first asked, then begged Tamara for forgiveness. His soon-to-be ex-wife showed him the gate.

Left on her own, Tamara and Marco had to move into a one bedroom *Khruschoby*—the tiny cracker box apartments named for Nikita Khrushchev by an outraged and sardine-packed population.

The single, working mom found that her nursing salary barely managed to get by in Vladimir Putin's post-communist regime. She needed a lucky break.

Through the '90s and into the new century, Tamara continued as an emergency room nurse—just a lumpen Russian citizen/ worker who, since her divorce, had a hell of time making ends meet.

Despite her steady work at the hospital, her inadequate nurse's salary needed constant supplementing. So, like all enterprising Russians, she found a few extra rubles a month *'na levo,'* on the left, that extra-legal place where nearly every former Soviet and current Russian citizen has had to make do— tiptoeing between legal and illegal.

Years earlier, while still in high school, Tamara's facility with languages allowed her to pretend to be a foreigner, a European, in order to gain admittance to the state-run Intourist foreign goods stores, off-limits to run-of-the-mill Soviets. She'd dress up in western clothes in order to gain entry. Once in, she'd buy European and American products and later sell them at a profit to Russians hungry for a Swiss bar of chocolate or an American bar of soap.

And in the summers, she and her friends would cruise the Moskovsky Vokzal train station, waiting for a careless tourist to leave unattended—even for a few seconds—a piece of baggage.

Later, while a nursing student at the Medical Academy, she drove a 'gypsy cab,' a beat-up Gazelle van owned by her uncle. In his off hours, he let his niece use the meter-less taxi to earn money for her tuition.

Even now, well into her nursing career, her fortunes needed to be augmented. A slight uptick occurred in 2010, when she was promoted to Dispensary Charge Nurse and became responsible for all medication in her eighty-bed facility. It was a job she had angled for, because she was now able—every so often—to raid her pharmacy for painkillers and other prescription drugs. Her son, Marco, had no trouble selling the stolen pharmaceuticals to friends. Not a huge step up, but enough to allow mother and son to treat themselves to a restaurant meal once a month.

Tamara continued to search *na levo* for other opportunities.

~~~

Boris Bunin had been in an on-and-off funk for months—the death of his brother-in-law, Taras, the year before, the reason. A funk that was impossible to shake since Boris had been the instrument of the man's death.

His preferred place to brood was his Brooklyn Heights west-facing balcony, twelve floors above the East River—which is where his wife, Larissa, found him this morning. He was standing, turned toward the Manhattan skyline, half-leaning on the railing. He was swaddled deep in his robe.

Larissa came onto the balcony, closed the French doors behind her, and gently called to him, "Borya, dearest." He didn't react. She came to the railing and leaned into him. "I know you miss Taras. So do I. Terribly."

He kept turned away from her and shook his head. "I never should have sent him to Vlad. He was determined to go. All he could think of was those two Alaskan cops—Kulaeva and that FBI agent—who had killed his brother. When I told Taras they'd be attending the crime conference in Vlad, he felt he had to go. I could have stopped him. I didn't."

"You gave him a choice. You didn't *order* him to go. He could have refused."

Still unable to face his wife, "No, Lara. Taras needed revenge. And I was stupid enough to let him try and take it."

Larissa fell silent, unable to assuage her husband's anguish over the death of his most trusted lieutenant.

She knew all of the awful details. After Taras arrived in Vladivostok, things quickly fell apart. The Bunins learned that he had murdered three people in the Hyundai Hotel: the FBI agent he was targeting, the Drug Enforcement Agency's director in Alaska, and an American translator. Those last two were innocent bystanders—wrong place, wrong time. Larissa remembered Vladivostok's crime boss, Roman Kollantai, screaming over the phone, "Boris, I let your guy come over and he's produced a clusterfuck of epic proportions. What have you done to us?"

And when Kollantai later reported that Taras had been captured by the Anchorage policewoman and tossed in jail, Larissa understood that her husband had no choice: he had to have his friend silenced before the Russian authorities could question him. With Boris's acquiescence, Kollantai arranged to have Taras killed in prison.

Larissa said, "You did the right thing, Borya. At the end, I mean. I know how painful it was. But you had to protect us." She reached out her hand to him. "Come inside. I'll make us something."

Two cups of coffee and a heavily buttered Kaiser roll later, Boris was in a slightly better mood. "Last year, Lara, when Alaska was giving us problems, we discussed alternate routes. I've made an appointment with the congresswoman for next week. Thoughts?"

"The Russians are still fully on board with the idea?"

"Totally. I've already received assurance from their version of the FAA. They're ready whenever the government here gives a green light."

"And Leo must be thrilled."

"Ecstatic. He says even Dorotea likes the prospect of flights to Vladivostok."

"That'll be a first. She hasn't liked much of anything since they moved up there." Larissa stood and gathered up the dishes. "Perhaps I should go with you to D.C.," she suggested. "Stars of the Bolshoi are at the Kennedy Center."

"Actually, I've already ordered tickets."

~~~

Night over the Atlantic. The aircraft's interior lights were out, stars clearly visible over the wings.

During his first combat tour in Iraq, in the autumn of 2003, the questionable decisions by J. Paul Bremer, America's pro-consul, intensified Tucker's skepticism about 'Operation Iraqi Freedom.'

His second tour, in 2007, only served to deepen and solidify his doubts. He took part in two combat operations—Dixon and Commando Dive—in which General David Petraeus's new tactics in counter insurgency were put to the test. Although the press made much of the new commander, to Tucker, not a whole hell of a lot changed on the ground.

Now he was on his way to Afghanistan, thirteen years after the US first intervened in an attempt—so far futile—to oust the Taliban. *Same old shit.* Tucker looked down at the gray, early morning coast of Ireland. *Folks just waking down there. Going about their lives. No IED worries. No year-long tour in Afghanistan awaiting them.*

They landed and refueled at Lakenheath Air Base in England. The men poured out of the aircraft and made straight for the mess hall, the phones, and the computer banks.

Tucker called home and spoke to his daughter, Tessa.

"No one else is here," she said. "Mom took everyone to the movies." The line went silent for a moment, and in a breaking voice, "We miss you so much, daddy."

Tucker heard his daughter fighting to hold back her tears. His own were flowing freely down his cheeks. He tried to comfort her, to assure her that all would end well. He promised to call again when he was at Bagram. He hung up, cursing his fate and unable to imagine a life without his darling Tessa.

On the glide pattern into Bagram, the C-130 broke through the clouds at 8,000 feet. Afghanistan's terrain came into brilliant focus: craggy mountains framing exquisite green valleys; rivers swollen by spring runoff that cascaded through steep canyons. Tucker was stunned by the beauty of the Afghan landscape and recalled his father describing just how lushly verdant Vietnam was. The old man often questioned how such violence and such beauty could coexist. Tucker heard the wheels lock into place. His heart constricted.

They landed at Bagram just after four on an overcast afternoon. Besides a sea of U.S. Air Force personnel, the immense, mile-high facility was teeming with American Army, Navy, Marine, and Coast Guardsmen, as well as foreign military from half a dozen countries. And civilians—spooks, black-ops mercenaries, and contractors making ungodly salaries for doing the dirty work the U.S. and other western governments out-sourced to them.

Three hours after landing, and after seeing to his men, Tucker sat in his new digs—a one-room, sparsely furnished pre-fab bungalow containing a pair of beds, a single chest of drawers, a small refrigerator, a hot plate, a standing closet, and a card table with two folding chairs. A trio of bare overhanging bulbs illuminated the room. The place stank of lived-in-too-much: sweat, dirty laundry, beer, and gun oil. Tucker leaned back in one of the chairs and sipped from a frost-beaded can of Pepsi. He regarded the man sitting opposite. "What's with the poppies, Major McHenry? The ones I see in the lapels of some of the men here on base? I'd have thought that would've been bad form."

The other man allowed himself a wry smile. "Call me Jed, please. We're only gonna know each other for a day or two. Soon as you officially replace us, me and my 10th Mountain guys are outta here. But in the meantime, it's Jed."

"I'm Tucker. Happy to know you. I'm hoping you'll help me learn some of what I'll need to know. Still, I'm wondering about the poppies. Thought we're here to eradicate those flowers." He'd tried to keep his tone light, but it came out more officious than he'd wanted.

McHenry shrugged his broad shoulders and scoffed. "Poppies, huh? We kinda think of it as the wearin' of the red. Kinda like the Irish and their green. Men here are ordered to do somethin'—eradicatin'—that most of 'em don't give a shit about. It's not that many of them are big fans of opium. Some are, for sure. A couple even may be strung out. But the majority couldn't care less, and wearin' a poppy in their lapel is them sayin' so." McHenry took up a Styrofoam cup, spat a stream of black tobacco juice into it, then took a tin of Skoal from his shirt pocket and offered it to Tucker. "It's Long Cut Straight. Care to try?"

"Smoked a lot in the past, but never dipped. Been off tobacco for twelve years now. But thanks. And the officers? They feel the same about the wearin' of the red?"

"Goes right up through the ranks. Not quite to CentCom, but pretty near." McHenry tipped back in his chair. "But, first things first. You wanna know what gives here and I'm more'n happy to help. So here's lesson number one. You don't wanna be *too* gung-ho." McHenry paused and looked steadily at his replacement. "You gotta trust me on that one."

Tucker returned McHenry's gaze and added a set of raised eyebrows. "I'm not sure what I'm supposed to understand from that."

McHenry went to the fridge and came back with a Dr. Pepper. Tucker took a moment to assess the officer: a large man, well over six feet, with mottled, pink skin and a mop of unruly fair hair. He had light, hazel eyes, and a boxer's busted nose. He was jowly and had immense hands. Tucker noticed them when they met and shook. He'd also noted that McHenry's fingernails were fastidiously clean and buffed though his fatigues were crumpled and dirty. The out-going commanding officer wore a side arm, a Smith and Wesson 9 mm.

McHenry noticed Tucker glancing at the weapon. He patted his sidearm. "This pistol here's lesson two. Don't you dare go *anywhere* without one of these guys. Might even come a time when you'll hafta use it right here on base."

"Green-on-blue?"

"Exactly. Some Afghani soldier shouts 'Allahu Akbar' and draws down on ya. Happened in 2015, just outside the base. Guy in uniform on a scooter killed six US troops. Could happen any time again."

"So how do you tell who's on our side?"

"Can't. And that's a real problem. Has been since day one.

Hard to keep track of who puts on Afghani Army fatigues and for what reason. And besides their army, there are several hundred locals, civilians, who work here on base. We vet 'em before allowin' 'em in. But you never know. So, third lesson. Keep your eyes open all the time." McHenry paused, leaned forward. "But there *is* one local in particular, someone who you'll *really* want to meet."

"Who's that?"

"A good guy. Name's Jabari Hajji Murad. Assistant cook in the Officer's Mess. He's not on duty now, and not a great cook, either. But someone important for you."

"Important? How?"

"Guy'll set you straight. He'll get in touch. Prob'ly t'morrow. Listen to what he says, then *do* what he says to do."

Tucker played along, suppressing a chuckle. "And what'll he tell me to do?"

"I'm serious, Tucker. He'll tell you that his uncle, Shaikh Murad, the local warlord, will want to meet with you *right away.*"

"OK. I've read up. I know those kinds of links are important. But 'right away?' What's the rush?"

McHenry took his time responding. He worked on his soft drink. "You got my letter, I hope."

"Couple weeks ago. But why a letter? Why didn't you just email me?"

McHenry narrowed his eyes. "Too easy to snoop," he said.

"Got it. You told me to buy an expensive gift for Murad."

"Right. I hope you did."

"I did."

"Great. When Jabari offers to drive you to meet the man, take your gift and make a big deal about it. You'll score points.

You'll learn that's the way it works out here." McHenry rose, stretched. "You'll be in-country for a year. That right?"

Tucker frowned. "So it seems."

"Meet Murad, talk to him, *learn* from him, and your time here'll be a whole helluva lot easier. I guarantee. And that's all I'm gonna say about it." McHenry made to leave. "Gotta get my men ready for t'morrow's passin' the baton ceremony. Such bullshit. But if we're not too busy, we can talk again before we fly outta this shit hole."

"Absolutely. I got a lot more questions. And maybe you can introduce me to the general, if he gets back to base in time."

"I can do that. Though between you and me and any of the spooks who're listenin' in on us, the man is a grade-A fuck-up. And chicken shit, to boot."

"I've heard that. How much longer is he here?"

"Rumor has 'im bein' bumped up to CentCom. Can't happen too soon." McHenry pointed to the beds. "Take whichever bunk you like. I had the sheets changed on each this mornin'. See ya later."

~~~

Congresswoman Rachel Feinbaum came out from in back of her cluttered desk and walked, right hand outstretched, toward the man—the generous campaign contributing man—who had just been shown into her office.

"Mr. Bunin. How nice of you to stop by, sir. It's always a pleasure to meet with my constituents, and I understand you've been a consistent supporter of mine. My chief of staff tells me you helped raise more than fifteen thousand dollars for my last election, bundled with the help of your colleagues. I'm frankly surprised we haven't met before. *Just another mob gumba. Only a Russian gumba.* My apologies for this very tardy meeting and a belated thank you." Rachel Feinbaum gestured to a deep leather chair. "Please. "

Boris Bunin nodded, took the offered seat and gave the woman a long smile. "Thank you so much Representative Feinbaum for taking the time. You are very kind."

"Can I offer you something to drink? Coffee, tea, bottled water?" she asked, settling into her chair. "I've a bottle of Stoli, Blue Label," she winked. "Perhaps a small glass?"

Boris Bunin raised a hand. "Thank you so much, but, no. I'm meeting my wife soon. I wouldn't want her to discover I'd been having too good a time."

Feinbaum dutifully chuckled. "Well then, Mr. Bunin, what brings you to my office this morning? How can I help you?"

Boris Bunin adjusted his glasses and cleared his throat. "Representative Feinbaum. I have a good friend in Alaska, in Anchorage. He's been in the aviation business for years. Currently he operates an extensive air taxi service all across Alaska. Back and forth from Anchorage to Fairbanks and villages all over the state. Regular flights to the oil fields on the North Slope. Even out to St. Lawrence Island, close to Russia. My friend would like to expand his business. He would like to be able to fly directly from Alaska to the Russian Far East."

Boris noted that Feinbaum's smiling lips turned downward and her body seemed to cave into itself, a "no" seemingly in the offing.

No matter, the Russian man thought. His own smile widened and he continued, "As you know, anyone who wants to fly these days from Alaska to Russia across the Bering Sea must pay several thousand dollars for a charter. The alternative route is a tedious one, the very long way around, through Seattle or Minneapolis, and then over the Pole. It's so silly, really, since

Russia is just a few hours flying time from Anchorage. I was hoping you might use your influence on your committee to help my friend."

Representative Rachel Feinbaum, hands resting gently on her desk, fingers laced loosely in front of her, raised then lowered a set of disappointed shoulders.

"It's a great idea, Mr. Bunin, and one that I've supported in the past. You know that in the 1990s Alaska Airlines flew to Vladivostok and Irkutsk. But, unfortunately, politics and Russia's economic problems got in the way." Feinbaum picked up a pen and began fiddling with it. "So, at this time, there is no Russian airline willing to take the risk. Nor are the members of the committee which I chair currently disposed to recommend to the FAA that they open up those routes. It's simply not a viable plan at this time. I'm truly sorry."

Boris nodded. "I'm fully aware of the history of those flights from Alaska to Russia. But there are now two companies that have partnered—my friend's company, Grizzly Air in Anchorage, and Troika Aviation, out of Vladivostok. They can be ready to fly in a matter of months. Troika has begun the process of leasing a pair of Airbus 330 aircraft. They can easily fly the three thousand miles from Anchorage to Vladivostok. All that my friend in Alaska needs is for your committee to make a positive recommendation to the FAA. I would hope you might change *your* mind and convince your friends on the committee to change *theirs*."

Rachel Feinbaum had long ago mastered the politician's talent of simultaneously saying "no" while leaving hope that a "yes" might materialize at some undesignated future date. She was also adept at deflection, assigning the "no" to another authority.

"Having the FAA approve my committee's recom- mendations, Mr. Bunin, is one thing. Having the Russian government agree is quite another."

"That will not be a problem. I've already received assurances from the Russian State Aviation Authority that they are agreeable to these routes being reopened. I can provide you and your committee members with translated documentation to that effect."

Feinbaum gave out a sigh of resignation. "If it were up to me, Mr. Bunin, I'd sign off on this idea right here and now. But the solution to your problem is not to be found in this office. The Federal Aviation Administration has carefully assessed the situation and feels that it's simply not feasible at this time for flights back and forth from Alaska to Russia. I'm sorry."

The congresswoman sat back, signaling an end to the conversation. She was surprised when her visitor didn't begin to pack up and leave. Instead, the man reached into the inner pocket of his sports coat and withdrew an envelope.

"Representative Feinbaum. Here is a check for ten thousand dollars. I have left blank the place where I'm supposed to write in the name of the recipient. If you would be interested," he trailed off, laying the envelope on her desk, and gently pushing it toward her.

United States Representative Rachel Feinbaum licked her lips. For her, ten grand was good money. Not great money, just good money. Great money was what she'd made six months earlier when she'd arranged for her brother-in-law to win a no-bid paving contract for twenty-two miles of highway near Saranac Lake. That was great money. This offer of ten thousand—not quite.

"Mr. Bunin, while I appreciate very much your exceedingly generous offer, I'm afraid that my committee is simply not ready to entertain the opening of such a route. As I said, sir, I am *very* sorry."

Boris Bunin didn't appear to be discouraged. He left the envelope on the desk, the check half visible.

"Representative Feinbaum. Your work occasionally takes you far from Washington, does it not?"

The woman squirmed restlessly in her chair. She brushed some unseen lint off of her sleeve. She wanted the meeting to be over. She had a racket ball game scheduled in thirty minutes, downstairs in the basement of the Rayburn House Office Building. Her playing partner was Jennifer McClarnon, one of the NRA's more persuasive favor seekers and money donors. With the slightest bit of impatience creeping into her voice, the representative answered, "Yes, Mr. Bunin, I often travel. On behalf of my constituents, you understand."

Boris Bunin let several seconds go by. "And two years ago, in December, you traveled to St. Petersburg, if I'm not mistaken."

Feinbaum hesitated, her past flooding across her memory banks. "Yes. A beautiful city. The Hermitage rivals our own Met." The faintest bit of hesitancy crept into her voice.

"You stayed at the Hotel Astoria for three nights. The first night after your arrival, you retired early. The second night, however, you spent time in the hotel's wonderful bar. A special place, wouldn't you agree?"

Feinbaum's face took on the appearance of a Renaissance death mask—ashen and rigid. She gave the man a single, wooden nod. "Yes. Special," she managed.

"Quite," said Boris Bunin. "You sat at the bar, alone that night. The weather outside was dreary. Typical St. Petersburg December. You drank two vodka gimlets. Not my favorite mixture. Down the bar from you, there was a man, a good-looking man. Sergei, he called himself. You surely recall him?"

Representative Rachel Feinbaum could not reply, her teeth

clenched, the fingers on her desk now clasped tightly together.

Boris Bunin reached into his jacket once more, this time producing two letters, hand-written. "I believe I've told you enough, Representative Feinbaum, but in the interests of full disclosure, let's finish the story, shall we?"

When she didn't reply, he went on. "You struck up a conversation. He was a good listener, charming and witty. He told you he was an airline pilot. Naturally, he lied. In fact, he's a chauffeur for close friends of mine in Moscow. On special assignment, you might say."

Rachel Feinbaum remained mute, unmoving.

"You invited him to your room. He agreed but asked you to wait. A friend of his was meeting him in the bar. Soon, the friend arrived. Another good-looking man. Asian. Sergei told his friend—Benny, he called himself—that you had invited him to your room. The friend said it sounded like a party. The three of you went up to your room and spent the next four hours apparently having that party. At least that's what these letters seem to indicate."

Boris Bunin placed the letters gently on the desk in front of the representative. "Here are two of the seven rather graphic letters you wrote to Sergei in the months following your evening together. I completely appreciate your preferred use of snail mail. Anyone, these days, can hack into email. The Russians seem quite adept at it." Boris paused. "You may keep these two."

Rachel Feinbaum stared at the evidence of her debauchery.

Boris Bunin's voice, up until then warm and cordial, now turned as hard and cold as a gun barrel. "If you cannot arrange what I have asked, Representative Feinbaum, then copies of the remaining five will go to your husband, Morris, to your three children, to the National Enquirer, to the Speaker of the House, and to the Washington Post."

"This is blackmail," sputtered the congresswoman.

"Of course it is," said Boris Bunin, looking around the room. "Correct me if I am wrong but this *is* Washington D.C., is it not?"

Representative Rachel Feinbaum picked up the damning evidence and quickly scanned the two letters. Then she smiled. A sad smile. A smile of abject defeat. She exhaled. "A new air route from Alaska to Russia? A great idea, Mr. Bunin. And about time, too. I'll do everything in my power to make it happen."

"I am certain of it, ma'am. I have every confidence in you. I'll let my friend in Anchorage know that he can plan for direct flights to begin in—shall we say—six months?"

"Six months should be ample time, Mr. Bunin. I'll be in touch. Good luck to you and your colleagues."

Boris Bunin rose and bowed graciously to the congresswoman. Before turning to leave, he took up the envelope with the check and put it back in his coat pocket. He gave the woman a final smile and left her office.

Rachel Feinbaum sat stony-faced for two full minutes, then buzzed her intercom. "Call the bitch from the NRA and cancel," she ordered. Then she swiveled in her seat, reached into her cabinet and came out with the bottle of Stoli. She filled a shot glass to the rim and tossed off the clear liquid. Then she poured herself another.

~~~

Houston Dantley Jr. came into the world by C-Section five and half weeks early. He weighed in at three pounds, fifteen ounces. His parents, Houston Sr. and Monica, were naturally worried by the early birth. But because of the care the infant received—spending a month in the hospital's neonatal ward—Houston survived his first months. But not without a problem that continued and worsened throughout his early years: melanocytic nevus. And although these unattractive spots usually appear on the limbs, in Houston's case, he had the misfortune to have three very visible discolorations take root on his right cheek, jaw, and neck.

By the age of twenty, the young man's self-worth had vanished under a lifetime barrage of being called 'mole-man,' or 'cheeky' or 'dirt-face.'

He never dated, had never even been kissed. He found a bare semblance of sexual gratification in pornography and the occasional visit to The Hung Pony. There, runaway nymphets, with obviously feigned enthusiasm, lap danced on Houston's thighs, trying their best to avoid eye contact.

Things changed on September 11, 2001. On his way to work as a stocker at the Quik Korner Market, he listened on his car radio to a vivid description of an attack on the American homeland. Although never much of a patriot, Houston somehow intuited that this national catastrophe would somehow, in some way he couldn't begin to imagine, change his life for the better.

When the PATRIOT ACT was passed a few months later, the Department of Homeland Security was created, and the Transportation Security Administration began hiring, Houston grabbed his chance. After a surprisingly minimal amount of training, he became a TSA agent, one of the crew at Ted Stevens International Airport in his hometown of Anchorage, Alaska.

After a lifetime of shame and indignity, Houston joined a mostly under-educated group of louts who were legally allowed to make life a living hell for air travelers. And of all the insensitive yahoos on that Anchorage airport crew, Houston

Dantley Jr. was the most purposefully insensitive, the rudest, and the most profane. He could now happily wreak his revenge upon a society that had denigrated him his entire life. 'Mole-man' was replaced with, "Yes sir, Agent Dantley." The ugly boy's horrid younger life became the ugly man's revenge. Houston was earning a kind of respect, one born of fear and loathing.

In 2013, he was able to move laterally, to U.S. Customs. A better job. More pay. More credibility. And more opportunity to humiliate the flying public.

Then, in 2014, another advancement. Despite never having owned a dog and not being particularly fond of them, Houston applied for and was accepted into the K-9 training program in Virginia, at the Canine Center Front Royal. At the end of the nine-week course, he was matched with Brandy, a three-year-old German shepherd. His starting salary was $55,000 a year. He returned to Anchorage and began his new career.

Late one night while working the red-eye shift in the airport's North Terminal, he spent several minutes over-aggressively sorting through the luggage of a just-arrived traveler from London. The man had attempted to bring five Swiss-made Toblerone Fruit and Nut bars into the United States. The passenger, foreign looking by his clothes, was Armand Osorio, according to the name on his passport.

"Osorio?" Houston demanded, snarkily. "Kinda name is that?"

The passenger calmly replied, "I was born in Istanbul, in Turkey, but I am now an American citizen."

Houston turned up his nose. He had never met a Turk and eyed the man with deep suspicion.

Osorio was, in fact, the alias of Artun Ozil, a life-long

criminal with international creds who also happened to be a superb reader of men. He now found the words that surprised the dog handler, words Houston had never heard.

"Good job, Agent Dantley. Very professional search. I commend you on your thoroughness. It was my mistake to try and bring chocolate back home. I apologize."

Never having received anything but dirty looks and muttered-under-the-breath curses, Houston was stunned, but was able to respond, "Just trying to do my job, sir." The agent actually shyly smiled at the passenger.

Ozil returned the agent's smile and reached into his coat pocket. He pulled out a business card with his name and phone number. He offered it to the dog handler.

Houston stared at the card. "What's your business, Mr. Osorio?"

Artun Ozil let a moment lapse before answering. "I'm a recruiter. Perhaps you'll give me a call."

Agent Dantley was dumbfounded. The last time he had been recruited for anything was in 1993, for the Fourth of July Pie Eating Contest. He came in last, of course. He read the card again and tucked it into his pocket.

"Call me, please," Ozil said, then collected his baggage and walked away.

Houston Dantley Jr., starry-eyed, watched the Turk depart.

~~~

The evening after the capo and the legislator met, Boris Bunin phoned his cousin Leo, owner of Grizzly Air.

"Great news," Boris began. "The FAA's going to give you and Troika the go-ahead. Flights should be happening, hopefully, within six, eight months."

On his end, Leo Bulgarin began jumping up and down. "Oh my God, Borya. This is incredible. How did it happen?"

"I pulled in an IOU, long overdue," Boris said. "You ready to start flying to Russia?"

"Borya, I've been ready to fly to Russia since we started this business. It's a dream."

"I'm glad you're happy. Dorotea should be, too."

"She's going to love the idea. Can't wait to tell her."

"Great. I'll be in touch with the details. Meanwhile, when are you scheduled to fly again out to the island?"

Leo slumped. A topic and a job he wanted to avoid, but could not.

"In a few days, Borya." He hesitated. "Not my favorite part of the program. Dorotea and I both think it's still too hot. All that shit out in Dutch Harbor last year. And Taras getting killed in Vlad." Leo knew he was treading on thin ice, venting to his cousin, but it came spewing out. "I tell you, Borya. I'm freaked."

Boris listened patiently. He'd heard his cousin whine before, and often. He debated the glove or the fist. He chose the glove.

"I know how difficult that job is for you, Leo. But it's important to the operation. And it's not as though you and Dorotea aren't getting well paid." He left it there, wondering if he'd have to be rough with his relative. "We're working on other ideas, Leo. Stick with it while we figure out different routes. OK?"

Leo understood there was no 'give' with Boris. Never had been. "OK. We'll . . . we'll carry on. Bye, Borya."

"Bye for now, cousin."

Leo found Dorotea outside their office, smoking. She

screamed on hearing the Troika news, embraced her husband, then asked, "Does this mean we can move back to Russia, to Vlad, and leave this shit-hole? Tell me, Leo. Please. I'm so sick of Alaska."

After explaining to her, once again, how their economic future was tied to Alaska, she dropped her cigarette, stamped it out, and began to pout. The sun dipping behind the clouds and a sudden gusty breeze made her hug her shoulders.

He sought to change the subject, allay some lingering doubts about their future. "Mehmet assured me there wouldn't be any blowback from Dutch Harbor or Vlad."

"No blowback? Really? Who the fuck is he kidding? Three of Bunin's men killed in Dutch Harbor. And those three Alaskans murdered in the hotel in Vladivostok. Then Bunin's brother-in-law shanked in the Partizanskaya. No blowback? Christ, Leo, I'm still shaking in my fucking boots every time I see a cop car."

"Boris says it's cool. And . . . he says I have to keep flying to St. Lawrence Island."

She looked at him in horror. "You're gonna keep flying with a plane full of heroin? Are you nuts? And the local cops here in Anchorage with their new narcotics division, starring guess who? What's her name? The one that knows you? You met her, right?"

He shuddered. "Kulaeva. Yeah, she knows me. She shows up on St. Lawrence Island last year, wants to fly back here to Anchorage. Plane is full so she winds up sitting on fifty kilos of heroin. I almost crapped my pants."

Dorotea patted her pockets, not finding what she was looking for. Leo pulled a pack of Kools out of his pocket, tapped one out for her. She lit up and took a deep drag, then made a face. "I hate Kools." She blew smoke into the air and gestured broadly with her cigarette-holding hand, "And I hate this place, this freezer." She looked him straight in the eye, sneering, "And I really hate that you let yourself be snookered by your lying, mother-fucking cousin and his cunty wife."

He'd heard it before and knew he'd hear it again. "Nothing to do about it now." He turned from her. "I need to check the landing gear on the Citation."

~~~

Where Samir Mahmoodi's rutted dirt road descended to join a two-lane blacktop leading back to Jalalabad, a pair of army transports and ten heavily armed men awaited the return of their four clansmen. The men, all in Afghan Army uniforms and all Ghilzai kinsmen of Shaikh Murad, were there to escort Kamal and almost four million dollars worth of raw opium to a factory in Jalalabad. There it will be processed into ninety-five-percent pure heroin. The world's favorite drug will then be packaged and driven north through Turkmenistan, Uzbekistan, Kazakhstan, and finally across the Russian border, to the TransSiberian rail station in Chelyabinsk.

What happened to the heroin after that, the men guarding it could only guess. They were not told. They did not ask. It was none of their business. Their only job was to protect the treasure in Kamal's Jeep. And for that they will each be given an American fifty-dollar bill.

Several of the more curious were intrigued by the face on the bank note. A few argued that this Grant person reminded them somewhat of their own Shaikh (sanctified be his name!).

The skeptics conceded that the beard *did* bear a faint resemblance to that of their sainted patriarch, especially in his youth. But the detractors pointed to Grant's nose. Possibly

Semitic, but nothing at all Afghani!

And a small handful, somewhat better versed in American history, compared General Grant's ruthless war-making to their own struggles in the 1980s against the invading Soviets (may they be forever damned to eternal hell!).

All, however, were in agreement: the twice and sometimes three times weekly excursions into the countryside earned them an immense supplement to the exceedingly meager salaries provided by the Afghan Army.

Certainly, there was danger—this *was* Afghanistan, after all.

Fresh in each man's memory were the horrific details of an incident that occurred a year earlier when rogue elements of Shah Ahmed Khan's breakaway clan ambushed a drug convoy near Panjwai, on the outskirts of Kabul. The attackers slaughtered all ten of the Baluchi men protecting the drug and made off with more than twelve kilos of unprocessed opium.

The Baluchis—noted for their centuries-long vendettas— were quick to react. The war they made on Shah Ahmed Khan's family was vicious, even by Afghani standards. In the end, a deal was brokered. The opium was returned and all of the still-living attackers, including two of Ahmed Khan's young nephews, were turned over to the Baluchis.

After that brief, but bloody clan war, Kamal had insisted on greater armed protection before entering the dangerous warrens of Jalalabad.

That extra protection—an armored personnel carrier with a dozen men and three Jeeps with mounted 50 calibers— made rendezvous with Kamal at the village of Kalakan, twenty kilometers from Jalalabad.

The newly enhanced caravan proceeded cautiously, snaking through rolling valley farmland that slowly gave way to the shanty houses on the city's outskirts. With every passing kilometer, the detritus of war—left over from both the Soviet and American conflicts—grew into larger and larger heaps that littered the landscape in all directions: burned-out tanks and armored personnel carriers; destroyed artillery pieces of all caliber and vintage; blown-up trucks stripped of wheels, axles, tail gates, and doors; overturned Jeeps, their chassis torn and twisted; and even the charred carcass of a Soviet Mi-10 heavy transport helicopter, its rotor-remnant sticking straight out of the ground.

Entering the city proper, the men were now on full alert, their weapons bristling. The soldiers warily eyed the impoverished, noisy, and noisome neighborhoods of Jalalabad. Masses of people overflowed streets crowded with corrugated tin and cardboard homes, crammed against each another. Hawkers shoved and dragged pushcarts, all the while dodging vehicles dating from every decade since the advent of internal combustion, each honking and belching choking exhaust fumes. Added to this was the full menagerie of animals: donkeys, horses, sheep, goats, chickens, the occasional camel, and packs of dogs of every stripe and shape.

And, of course, the competing smells: the sweet, oily odor of diesel mixing with the savory aroma of lamb kabobs being prepared by street vendors squatting by their braziers; the stench of untreated human sewage mingling with the scent and feel of cement dust and a myriad of other gritty industrial particulates that floated around construction sites, giving the air a bitter, acrid, and centuries-old taste.

Noise, dirt, shit. Jalalabad.

After a ten-kilometer creep through the city, the armed procession carrying Samir Mahmoodi's harvest arrived at the far end of town. In clear view was the Abdullah Bin Masood Mosque, crowded at this hour with the devout, coming for *Asr*, the afternoon Muslim prayer.

Farouz looked questioningly at Kamal who quickly replied, "Can't stop now. Keep driving."

Farouz grumbled.

Kamal recognized his cousin's unhappiness. "You can catch up after sunset, at *Maghrib*."

"There's no catching up, cousin. One either obeys the commandments or does not."

Kamal pronounced a testy, "Tsk – tsk. That's all well and good, cousin, for those of us who are *not* involved in the business we make our money from. The two of us are unworthy. After all, we traffic in an illegal, addictive, and deadly drug. What did the prophet say about *that*?"

The corners of Farouz's mouth turned upward slightly. "You are too clever for me, cousin. As usual. You are right, of course. We *are* criminals. I admit it. I have killed. I have broken the sacraments. I have done all manner of evil. But our god is a compassionate one. He will forgive even *my* transgressions."

"Don't hold your breath, cousin," Kamal said, poking Farouz in the ribs until the driver squirmed away, laughing.

The convoy slowed to let a crowd of chattering uniformed schoolgirls pass in front of them. Farouz turned to his cousin, his employer, his life-long friend, and his co-religionist. "But prayer, Kamal. Prayer allows me to feel like a good man, despite my sins."

"Dear Farouz, listen to me. *I* say you are a good man. Your loyalty to me as a cousin and friend, and your devotion to our Shaikh are things of rare wonder."

Farouz sighed and smiled, just as the last of the girls crossed the street in front of them.

Kamal pointed to the road. "It's clear ahead, cousin. Drive, please."

Twenty minutes later, Kamal's convoy turned into a cul-de-sac, a tree-lined and much quieter residential section of Jalalabad. At the street's entrance, several Afghani Army soldiers leaned against an American armored personnel carrier and watched the convoy approach. They hardly reacted as Kamal rolled by.

The street continued another hundred meters and ended at a high brick wall capped with mounds of broken glass shards glistening through swirls of concertina wire. Motion sensors and floodlights were embedded in the walls.

The convoy passed through a pair of heavy steel doors and entered a dusty yard dominated by a three-story brick building, all of whose windows were boarded up.

Men in army fatigues were scattered about the yard, some playing an enthusiastic game of soccer, some squatting and sipping cups of tea, a few playing shesh besh.

Kamal's escort vehicles parked just inside the compound's gates, while Farouz nosed the Jeep around the side of the building. He pulled to a stop next to a brightly colored lorry with a large golden eagle painted on the side.

~~~

David Osinchuk* had nose problems. He'd broken it or had it broken for him on four occasions.

The first occurred in 1980 when he was a seven-year-old at Gymnasia #4 in Odessa, on the Black Sea. He got smacked around for trying to defend his older sister, Devorah, from being pawed by a twelve-year-old. David's chivalrous defense was successful but his previously straight and unblemished nose now assumed a more corrugated appearance.

The second time was during a soccer match when he was thirteen. He jumped for a header and collided with an opponent's elbow. His coach provided an on-the-field straightening. David returned to the game, but by then, his nose had developed a downward hook to go with the crinkles.

The third re-arrangement happened when he was twenty-two and he'd moved to Chelyabinsk to become a go-to guy in the city's underworld. He was driving a refurbished IZH Planeta sports bike. The usually reliable Soviet-era motorcycle blew a front tire, sending its driver over the handlebars and skidding across the pavement. David hoped he'd avoided major damage, but the motorcycle had gone airborne, and the rear tire crashed onto his face. His nose was splattered and required plastic surgery. The operation wasn't even moderately successful, leaving David resembling some kind of fairytale grotesquery.

The fourth and final time his nose came into damaging play was when it was stepped on by a three hundred pound Kazakh goon. He and David had argued about the ownership of a large amount of uncut heroin. David was in his garage-headquarters when the man burst in. The gorilla threw David to the ground, kicked him in the ribs a few times, then stood on his face, the brute's clodhoppers squishing the fallen man's nose. Although David's head was pinned to the ground, his hands were free. He pulled his switchblade from his dungarees, flicked open the razor-sharp knife, grabbed the man's offending foot by the ankle, and neatly sliced the assailant's Achilles tendon. The man crashed to the ground, screaming. His yelling lasted only a few seconds, however, as David buried his knife's entire four-inch blade in the attacker's eye. The Kazakh died instantly. David examined his nose and realized it was forever de-constructed. He refused further surgery and lived with it.

Despite his all too obvious disfigurement, women never stopped flocking to his side. There was something attracting (if not necessarily attractive) about the man: maybe it was his large and deep-set gray eyes; perhaps his freckled-specked skin and his mop of red hair; it could just as well have been his soft-spoken baritone. His nose never got in the way.

~~~

Anatoly Suvorov and Sophia Kress were married on a bright spring morning in front of the Monument to Solzhenitsyn, next to the harbor in Vladivostok. It was a compromise location.

The bride had objected to the place, suggesting that she wasn't a big fan of the dissident Nobel laureate. "He wrote all this depressing, commie-hating shit that I never liked reading. Booooring! And besides which, Toly, the Most Holy Mother of God Church in Pokrovsky Park would be a much better place for us to get married."

The groom fumed. "You want to drag *my* family into a *Catholic* church. Christ, Soph. Are you kidding? They'd never come to the wedding. Unh-uh. If we're gonna be on good terms with my folks, we need to be married by a Russian Orthodox priest."

"Forget it, Toly. That is *not* going to happen. *My* family would boycott the ceremonies and hate you in the bargain."

After weeks of back and forth they came to an agreement: they'd have a civil ceremony to be performed by Dmitri Nikolayevich, the senior flight commander at Troika Aviation, the groom's employer.

"My mother's going to have kittens when she hears," moaned Sophia.

"As will mine. But Dima's done it before. Couple times,

actually. It'll be fine."

And it was.

The big day dawned bright and sunny. The breeze skimming off the harbor's waters was refreshing. And the families seemed mollified by the comforting words delivered by the groom's boss who spoke of harmony and friendship between the families of the betrothed. At the end of the ceremony, it was all smiles and good wishes.

After a hurried honeymoon at a private lodge on Lake Baikal in central Siberia, the couple returned to Vladivostok and to their work: Sophia as a beautician, and Anatoly as a pilot for Troika Aviation.

Prior to his marriage, Anatoly believed his betrothed to be sensitive, accommodating, pliable. But almost immediately upon returning from their honeymoon, the groom began to have serious doubts about his previous assessment. Sophia seemed a changed woman: hard-edged, rough talking, and insistent. She began demanding things that threw the pilot for a loop. Like extra money. A lot of extra money. *Where the fuck is that supposed to come from?* he thought.

The new groom went drinking one night with Dmitri Nikolayevich. Anatoly explained to the senior pilot the problems at home. "New shit keeps showing up in the apartment. Useless crap. We got no room to put it. She's essentially *ordering* me to make more money so we can get a bigger place. What the hell am I supposed to do, Dima? Start printing rubles?"

Dmitri sipped his rum drink. "Money? I know it can be hard with women, giving them what they want. Hard to figure sometime. But listen, there's a guy I know. Maybe he can help you out. No promises, mind you. But . . . . you should go see him."

Toly perked up. "Guy? What guy? What'll he have for

me? Can't be a second job, Dima. I mean, I'm maxed out right now flying for the company."

"I get that. No, no other job. Just . . . . go see him. You know the Slavianski Bazaar. That flea-trap on the dock?"

"Sure. When I was a teenager, we'd go there to get laid. Why? What's there for me?"

"Talk to the desk clerk. Guy at the front, behind the mesh. Tell him I sent you. Tell him you fly. He'll put you in touch with some folks."

Anatoly finished off his gin and tonic, signaled to the bartender for another. He felt a little better.

~~~

On a balmy, early April morning, Tamara Stoikova's need to be ever-scheming, her need to scrimp her way through life, evaporated.

She'd taken a smoke break to enjoy one of the two cigarettes a day she allotted herself. She sat outside the hospital's ER, enjoying the dawn breeze.

The sound of squealing tires split the air. A dark red van swept into the hospital's driveway. Barely coming to a stop, the rear doors were flung open and a body dumped onto the pavement in front of her. It bounced and audibly thudded before rolling to a stop.

Tamara yelled through the doors of the ER for help then rushed to the crumpled body—a man of about fifty, still alive, but just. His shirt was drenched in blood. She ripped it off and exposed his wounds: two serious punctures, one in the right upper chest, and one in his left lower abdomen. From that upper wound, Tamara heard a sucking sound. She diagnosed a tension pneumothorax, a puncture to the lung that was allowing outside air to enter the chest cavity. She put her right hand onto the bloody wound and felt the jagged end of a shattered rib poking through. She shoved it back inside, then pressed her hand down over the hole, sealing it. Something she had done on a dozen previous, wartime occasions.

She knew he was close to terminal shock. With the fingertips of her other hand, she felt his carotid: tachycardia off the charts as his heart, sensing diminishing blood volume, attempted to compensate by pumping even harder.

The man was only minutes from death when the ER team came running: doctor, two nurses, and three orderlies pushing a gurney with an oxygen canister and a rolling IV set-up. They scissored off the rest of his clothes, used wide dressings and put direct pressure on his wounds, began a double IV drip of normal saline, shot him full of morphine, raised his legs, gave him oxygen, and swaddled him in a warm blanket. *Exactly how we tried to do in Khost. We even succeeded. Sometimes.*

The orderlies moved him expertly onto the gurney, then rushed him into the ER, where the man, later identified as David Iaklovich Osinchuk, forty-nine-years-old, clung to life through the night, was semi-lucid the next day, and soon made the woman who saved him an offer that would change her life.

"What's in the packages, David?" Tamara asked. "Just curious."

David Osinchuk, ten days removed from intensive care and recovering nicely from a pair of knife wounds, sat in a wheel chair, being pushed through the hospital's extensive gardens by his favorite nurse. It was early afternoon. The sun shone through a layer of gauzy clouds.

"What difference does it make?" he answered lightly. "Listen, Tama. We've talked the past week about ourselves.

You've allowed me to know you. You told me you need extra money. I can help."

A light breeze sprang up. She leaned over and wound his woolen scarf more tightly around his neck.

"I'd just like to know, David, if I get caught, into what kind of gulag I might be thrown. If it's only American toothpaste I'll be carrying, that's one thing. If it's gold bullion, well, that's something else, isn't it?"

She stopped the wheeling in front of a pond around which tall cattails swayed. She sat on a bench and leaned back. The sun passed out from behind a bank of clouds and shone down on them. She closed her eyes and turned her face skyward.

David regarded closely the woman he had come to seriously admire. Tamara was tall and wiry, but surprisingly strong. Straight brown hair, cut short. Big, honest black eyes over raised cheekbones. Full lips under a Roman nose. Smart as a whip and with a brilliant sense of humor. He thought she was close to his age—late forties—but knew better than to ask. He considered her question.

"I promise you, Tama, it's neither the one nor the other. And if it'll make you feel any more inclined to agree, I can tell you that there are many people who work for me, doing the exact same thing. All without incident. All safely."

"Why do I not feel reassured?" she asked, still leaning back onto the bench, eyes closed, face upturned. A moment passed, then, "So, something between toothpaste and bullion, is that it? Or something infinitely more illegal?" She opened her eyes and turned to him, searching his face. "Remind me again of the money."

"A thousand American dollars per trip. Every other month. Plus expenses—train fare there, all your food, an overnight in Vladivostok, and air fare back."

She cocked her head to one side, thought a moment. *I really could use the extra money. I'll probably regret it, but what the hell.* "Let's go fifteen hundred and expenses for one more, my son, Marco."

David didn't need long to consider. "Done," he said. And then, not quite as an after-thought, he added, "Oh, one more thing . . ." He wagged his head and shrugged a 'no big deal.'

"Do I really want to hear this? All right, tell me. That 'one more thing' would be . . .?"

David, almost apologetically, "I have a pistol for you."

"What the hell!" she said loudly enough to attract the attention of two hospital orderlies walking nearby. They glanced her way, saw who it was, grinned, and went about their business.

"Am I carrying state secrets? Will I have to shoot someone?"

"Hopefully not. But . . ." he left it suspended. Then he asked, more as a tension breaker than a real question, "Ever shoot anyone, Tama?"

She frowned at the memory, then looked him straight in the eyes. "No David. I came close once. But passed on the pleasure. You?"

"I shot *at* someone. But I don't know if I hit him. Or them."

"Where was that?"

"In Chechnya, Christmas time, 1999. We were in Grozny. My squad was in ambush at the edge of the city. We were supposed to shoot anyone who came through our zone of fire. There was no moon, totally overcast. All the electricity in the city was out, so it was pitch black. I put my hand right in front of my face—a few centimeters away—couldn't see my fingers." He rolled his eyes at the memory. "There were five of us. We could hear cannon fire thirty kilometers north of us. But around our area it was dead quiet. I was half asleep. Then the guy next to me, Antonov, jabs me in the ribs, whispers to me he hears something. I nudge the legs of the other guys. They come awake and thankfully don't make a sound. Then from off to our left we hear a bit of talk, then footsteps. Someone's coming our way. When they're fifteen, twenty meters in front of us, we open up, spraying the entire area. After a good half minute, I call a cease fire." He paused.

"And . . .?"

"And? Nothing. No one wanted to leave our safe position to go investigate in the dark. We couldn't shine a flashlight to see if we hit anything. So we waited."

"For how long?"

"'Til first light. At dawn we were able to see the entire area. Nothing. No one. I don't know what we were shooting at. But to this day, I'm thankful that there were no bodies to see. I didn't shoot anyone, and I'm grateful."

"I envy you your clean conscience."

"Now your turn."

She sat up straight, closed her eyes, and began. "In 1988, I was working in a field hospital near Khost. An Afghani soldier was brought in to be treated." Tamara laughed ruefully at the memory. "That, in itself, was unusual. The enemy's wounded hardly ever made it that far. Our soldiers never had much use for the Geneva Conventions." She paused, wondering how much to share with David.

"Go on," he encouraged.

"The wounded man, an officer I think, was placed on the operating table. Table? It was a door someone had taken off a nearby shack. He'd been shot in the thigh, bleeding right through a makeshift dressing. Apparently no one had bothered to search him because he pulled a pistol. We wrestled for it." Tamara paused. "I've never told this story to anyone, David. Not even Marco has heard it," she said.

"It'll be just you and I who will know, Tama."

After a few moments, she took a deep breath. "I won the wrestling match, grabbed the gun and pointed it at him to keep him quiet. I called out for help. A sergeant rushed in, saw what was going on, took the pistol out of my hand and shot the man in the head." She paused, the memory vivid. "The thing is, David, he didn't need to die. I had the gun trained on him. He was helpless, wounded. He wasn't going anywhere. I called for help, help arrived, and the man got shot. Some nurse I am, huh? So much for the healing arts."

"It wasn't your fault. Could you have stopped the soldier from shooting the man? Are you sorry? Do you regret it? Do you lose sleep over it?"

"Sorry? Certainly. Regretful? Yes, absolutely. Do I lose sleep? I did for a while. Then I was too busy to remember. This is really the first time in years I've bothered calling up the memory."

"How does it feel?"

"I'm still regretful. But I've put it behind me. You're right, of course. Nothing I could have done. War stinks. People die for all kinds of stupid reasons." She fell silent for a moment. "And you want me to carry a pistol to protect whatever the hell it is I'm carrying to Vladivostok. Is that it?"

He didn't answer.

"Well, as I've already told you, I'm strapped for cash. Marco wants to study. So I'll be your mule, David. But the pistol? I won't carry it. I'll do without."

"So be it," he said. "I can live with that." He looked long at her. "You're something else, Tama. You know that?"

She leaned over, picked up his wrist and lifted his left hand gently in her two. She began taking his pulse, looking into his eyes the whole time. She answered in a quiet voice, "Yes, David. I know. Thank you for noticing." After thirty seconds, "Oh, one more thing," she wagged her head and shrugged, mimicking him.

"What's that?"

"Strong pulse," she said.

~~~

Jabari Hajji Murad was a toothpick of a sixty-year-old man, skin and bones hanging off a leathery, stooped frame. He had a stubble beard and close-cropped graying hair. His coal-black, piercing eyes, set deep under bushy brows, glowed warily. He approached a breakfasting Tucker Cranston with a deferential step, pausing several feet away. "Major Cranston, sir?"

Tucker looked up from his eggs and bacon, smiled at the man and beckoned him to come nearer.

The cook took a few tentative paces closer. He stood stiffly. "I Jabari Hajji Murad. I please to meet with you."

"And I am pleased to meet you." Tucker offered the man a seat, but Murad declined.

"Not permitted," the Afghani said.

Tucker nodded his understanding. "You are a hajji," he said. "When did you go to Mecca?"

Murad's eyebrows shot up in surprise. "You know what hajji mean? I glad. I and my old brother make Hajj in 1979. I was young man. I was bless to go."

"Seventy-nine? Wasn't that the year insurgents attacked? Hundreds died, I think I read."

Murad leaned closer to Tucker, a warm smile on his face.

"Not many except in *Ummah* know this. How *you* know, Major Cranston?"

"I study history. Especially history of the Middle East."

Jabari nodded. "Many died. It was long time to stop bad *mahdi*. But I and brother far from shooting. My brother sick and we live in hotel. We lucky." Jabari placed a hand over his heart. "Major Cranston, sir. I own deep impression by your knowing of our history. And my uncle, Shaikh Murad, will also have impression. He like meet with you."

"Thank you, Jabari. And when might I be so lucky as to meet with your uncle?"

"If in two days, Thursday, is proper for you . . ."

"I'll make sure I'm free. Thursday will be fine."

"Good. South Gate nine in morning? Is suitable?"

"I'll arrange for an armored escort."

Jabari grinned. "Not needed, Major. All in Parwan and Nangarhar know Jeep I run. No one shoot. Trust me."

"Major McHenry told me to trust you."

"Major McHenry wise man. He learn much here. We miss him in Parwan."

"I hope to learn as much as he did."

"I sure by it, Major Cranston, sir."

"Jabari found me at breakfast," Tucker told the man he was replacing. "We're set to visit the Shaikh on Thursday."

"That's a good thing," McHenry said, popping open a bottle of Heineken and tossing the cap on the ground.

They were walking the inside perimeter of their fenced-in compound at Bagram. Eight-foot high Hesco wire barriers, stuffed with straw and sand, kept them hidden from the Taliban, and allowed them to stroll in relative safety. Near at hand, several empty Hescos were piled one atop the other, ready to be opened and filled.

"Like I told ya, Tucker. Listen to the old man, butter him up, and you'll leave your meetin' feelin' just fine."

"You know that for a fact, do you, Jed?"

"Absolutely. It's a question of trust. Trust Jabari to get you there in one piece, and trust the old man's judgment."

"It's the 'one piece' part that scares the shit out of me. I mean, here I am, alone with a cook—assistant cook, whatever the fuck he is—driving through the Afghan countryside as if I belonged here, as if I know what the hell I'm doing."

McHenry smiled and shook his head. "Sometimes you gotta just take shit on faith. This is one of those times."

They'd reached a corner of the company's compound and took a turn, now heading south. A vast plume of gray and black-streaked smoke billowed up from the far side of the base, staining the bright blue sky.

"What's going on? I didn't hear any in-coming," Tucker asked.

"Burn pit."

"What's getting burned?"

"Anythin' and everythin'. There's at least three of 'em here on base. God only knows what gets tossed in. Always smolderin.' And when a *simoom* blows in from Arabia, or wherever the fuck those dry winds come from, the whole base gets covered with smoke. You'll be breathin' that shit and spittin' and gaggin' 'til the air clears. I hear some vets are tryin' to sue the army."

"Good luck with that," Tucker scoffed.

A K-9 handler with his sniffer best friend approached. The dog trotted along the Hesco fence, muzzle down, searching.

"Sirs," the non-com said as he got closer. He stopped and saluted.

McHenry threw a finger toward his forehead. "Whatcha

got here, sergeant?" he asked, nodding toward the dog.

"This is Gypsy, sir. Malinois. Belgian," the burly non-com answered. "Got her trained to sniff and seek just about any kind of explosives these camel-jockey motherfuckers might be thinkin' of usin'."

Tucker cringed internally at the man's language. *This mission is so fucked.* He bent over and extended his fist toward the dog. After checking with his trainer, the Malinois took a step forward and allowed herself to be petted.

Small pleasures, Tucker thought, *for both me and you, girl.*

"Carry on, soldier," McHenry told the man.

Tucker rose and the K-9 handler returned to his work. The two majors continued strolling.

"What am I supposed to wear when I visit Murad?" Tucker asked. "I mean, I don't want to stand out while we're driving. But, at the same time, I want to appear at least somewhat official when I meet the guy."

"Keep it informal. Don't let your fatigues give you away. Murad understands that. You can show up at his place in civvies, as far as he's concerned. Believe me when I tell you that he already knows more 'bout you than you can imagine. He won't give a shit what you'll be wearin'. And don't forget your gift."

"I won't."

They turned and looked up as a Learjet cruised high over the base.

"That could be the general," McHenry said. "We should get over there so's you can meet him straight away."

"He's been at CentCom? That what you said?"

"Right. Been at Al Udeid for a week. Your fingers ought to be crossed. Maybe the asshole's been bumped up."

"Let's hope," Tucker said.

The Learjet had to mark time in line behind a pair of circling Galaxies before being allowed to land and deliver Major General T.R. Cunningham, commander of all U.S. Army forces at Bagram.

Tucker and McHenry waited on the tarmac with several of Cunningham's staff officers.

"Tell me about his nickname. How'd he get it?" Tucker asked.

McHenry smiled. "Now there's a story. And a good one, too."

The first Galaxy landed, sending great puffs of dust and gravel in its wake.

"Three years ago, Cunningham is at FOB Buckeroo. Place used to be way up north, hard by the border with Pakistan 'til they shut the firebase down last year. Anyhow, he's there with three U.S. senators, in-country to see what the fuck. They come by chopper in the afternoon and get weathered in. So they gotta overnight and start drinkin' right away. One of the senators is a recovering alky and doesn't join in. But Cunningham and the other two hit it hard and pretty much collapse. 'Bout midnight, the Taliban start throwin' flares over the place. Followed by mortar rounds. The FOB lieutenant, guy called Reynolds, goes to wake the general, let him know. Accordin' to the sober senator, Cunningham screams at Reynolds, 'I'm trying to sleep here,' then turns over and snores through the attack, which fizzles after a couple hours. Needless to say, word spreads and our commandin' officer is now known to one and all as General *'I'm tryin' to sleep here'* Cunningham."

They watched the second Galaxy land.

"And he lives up to it, huh?" Tucker asked.

"Oh yeah, does he ever. You'll find out."

The Learjet landed a minute later and taxied toward them. When the cabin door opened and the stairs dropped, a squat man wearing a red beret and brown paratrooper boots appeared. Thick glasses clung to a bulbous nose.

"That's our guy," McHenry said, straightening up.

Cunningham stood unsteadily in the door, made a sun-screening visor of his hand, then carefully managed the three steps to the tarmac. His staff officers all snapped to attention, saluted, and formally shook hands with their commander.

"I'm not sensing a lot of love between him and his staff," Tucker whispered to McHenry. "Everyone looks pretty grim."

"You got that right," McHenry said, nudging Tucker toward the general. "It's our turn."

"General Cunningham, sir," McHenry said, saluting. "Welcome back, sir. I'd like to present Major Tucker Cranston, 142nd Infantry. He'll be replacing me and the 10th Mountain."

Cunningham seemed to have trouble focusing. He looked first at McHenry, then at Tucker.

"Cranston?" the general asked.

"Sir," Tucker answered, coming smartly to attention, and executing a crisp, textbook salute.

The general eyed him through his bottle-bottom thick glasses that made his watery blue eyes bulge. A close up of his thread-veined and rosy nose showed him to be a heavy drinker. A blast of booze-breath confirmed Tucker's suspicions.

Cunningham extended his hand.

Tucker reached out and shook, being careful to gauge the general's squeeze and respond in kind, neither too strong nor too weak.

"Come on," Cunningham ordered.

When McHenry also fell into step behind the general,

Cunningham said, without turning, "McHenry. Not you. Go tend to your men."

"Yes sir," McHenry said, exchanging questioning eyebrows with his replacement before peeling off.

Tucker, trailing his commanding officer, now had time to observe the man. Cunningham was short, maybe five-foot six. His appearance, however, was distorted by a body that was all torso built upon very stubby legs. The combination made his arms seem longer than they were, especially since he hunched forward when he walked. Tucker wondered if the general ever dragged his knuckles.

They entered the commanding officer's bungalow. Cunningham went straight to his desk, opened his brief case, took out his computer, and spent the next five minutes staring into the screen. Tucker stood at attention.

Finally, "Be at ease, Major," the general said.

Tucker noted three padded chairs in the room. He was not asked to sit.

Cunningham turned from his computer and looked up. "You here for twelve months. Right, Cranston?"

"Yes sir."

The general sighed heavily, picked at a zit on his chin, and returned to his computer screen. "Try not to fuck up too badly. That's all."

"Sir," Tucker said, coming to attention, saluting, about-facing, and quick-stepping to the door. Once outside, he wanted to take a deep, cleansing breath, but a sudden hot wind surrounded him with a cloud of burn pit smoke that made him gag. He pulled out a handkerchief, tied it around his nose, and returned to his new quarters.

~~~

During czarist times, those who guarded Russia's borders were among the country's most feared men—Don River Cossacks, famous for their unfailing allegiance to the crown.

When the czar was replaced by the Bolsheviks, oversight of the frontiers shifted. Under Lenin, the notorious NKVD, the People's Commissariat for Internal Affairs (read: secret police) protected Soviet borders. Later, its successor, the KGB, the People's Committee for State Security (read: secret police) took over the job.

Today, in post-Soviet times, the FSS, the Russian Federal Security Service, (read: secret police) with its 170,000 men and women, is tasked with protecting the homeland's frontiers.

But since the salary paid to these folks is so paltry, FSS members are often tempted to look elsewhere, *na levo,* in order to make ends meet. Which is the reason that ninety-five percent of the heroin enjoyed by Russians arrives in the country through its porous southern border with Kazakhstan.

Oftentimes, when a car or lorry or van carrying goods of dubious legality arrives at that long frontier, FSS border guards are not above taking a gratuity, an occasional *'mordida,'* as they call it in Tia Juana, a *'lagniappe,'* if you come from New Orleans, or where the Russian border with Kazakhstan meets, a *'baksheesh'.*

The penalty, if caught, will be severe: internment in a Russian prison, possibly in Lefortovo or Vladimir Central, or in one of the penal colonies in Mordovia—all with well-deserved reputations as places to be avoided at any cost. On the other hand, the *'baksheesh'* . . . .

Pyotr Alexandrovich Bondarchuk*—Petya to his friends—

was a thirty-three-year-old FSS sergeant whose job entailed the examination of the papers and baggage of those travelers wishing to enter Russia from Kazakhstan through the Bugristoye border crossing. Bondarchuk had been stationed there for more than six years. He enjoyed his job, depended on it, and lobbied hard to retain it.

At the beginning of his posting, when he was a lowly corporal, Bondarchuk took his work seriously: he matched photo ID with the traveler's face, asked leading questions about where, why, for how long. He even went so far as to check on the contents of the entering vehicles, searching the cars' trunks, glove compartments, and under the seats. He assiduously read the vehicle's manifest, often climbed into the backs of semis, opened the odd carton, and at times, even checked through bins of produce in refrigerated vehicles.

That devotion to duty ended in March, 2015, when an Afghani lorry driver, one Mirza ibn Murad, offered him a *'baksheesh'* no honest Russian could turn down: ten American fifty-dollar bills. Five hundred American dollars, for God's sake! Bondarchuk's eyes blurred at the sight of the greenbacks. He'd never seen that much money, never dreamed he'd be offered such a sum. *And for what?* he asked himself. What could this man, this poor Afghani driver possibly be secreting in his lorry that might be harmful to Bondarchuk's fellow Russians? He could guess, but did he really care? In a word: no. He pocketed the money, allowed the driver to enter Russia, and went home. The next day, he bought himself a used, but still serviceable Vespa motor scooter from friends who ran a chop shop.

The Afghani driver showed up a few days later as he exited Russia. He made Bondarchuk an offer that caused the Russian to gasp.

"I'll be coming back and forth several times a year. I can't promise the same amount, but . . ."

Petya Bondarchuk readily agreed.

That was two years ago. The Afghani had passed through a dozen times since, pressing three or four fifty dollar bills into the guard's palm each time.

After some early profligacy (the Vespa, an HD TV), the border guard began saving, stuffing the fifties into the hollowed-out middle of a book—*Crime and Punishment*—that he had fashioned into his private mini-vault. He had always meant to read Dostoevski's classic, but since the frontier guard felt zero guilt about his *own* crimes, he didn't see the point of empathizing with someone—this Roskolnikov jerk—about *his* sense of guilt.

Bondarchuk was saving for the marriage dowry he'd have to pay to the grasping and greedy parents of Svetlana, his high school sweetheart. She'd kept him waiting for years.

Just a few more times, a few more *'baksheesh'* from the Afghani lorry driver and he'd be ready to propose!

~~~

With Kamal leading the way and Farouz carrying the box of unprocessed opium gum, they entered the factory through another heavy metal door. They passed into a huge open room where teams of men and women were transforming raw opium gum first into morphine, then into heroin. The workers were dressed similarly, in very clean, very white garments, their hair in nets and their hands in nitrile gloves. Many wore respirators.

The place was all noise, mostly from a powerful ventilation system that exchanged fresh outside air with the noxious fumes of ammonium chloride and hydrochloric acid used in the processing.

Farouz delivered the wooden box with its precious contents to a young woman standing in front of large digital scales. She weighed the bundles, made a notation in a ledger, had him sign it, then gave him a receipt.

Kamal nodded toward the far end of the factory floor, forty meters away. A wall was blackened, windows were blown out, and shredded plywood casings hung in tatters. Sunbeams streamed through a hole in the ceiling.

"What's with the destruction?" he asked the woman.

"Someone got sloppy. An unhappy reaction. We're still finding her body parts."

Hafez Ghafoor, the seventy-year-old manager of the largest heroin processing plant in Jalalabad, lowered his ample rear end between the arms of his desk chair and smiled up at his guest. "You've come just in time for coffee."

Kamal sat opposite and brushed dust off of his pants. "What's that contraption?" he asked, pointing. "That's *not* your Mr. Coffee."

"It's new. It's called Nespresso. Taste this and you'll never go back to Mr. Coffee. It's my latest western indulgence."

They both laughed.

Ghafoor poured his guest a steaming, dark cup of coffee made in his Western indulgence.

Kamal sipped. "Wonderful."

"I knew you'd like it. Try the baklava, it's still warm."

Kamal reached for the pastry. "I stopped by Samir's. Collected over sixteen kilo."

"A hard worker, that one. How's his son?"

"They're saving for an operation next month. I told him not to worry about the cost. Three thousand American. He says he'll have it.'

"Let me know if he's short," said the head of heroin processing in Jalalabad.

"Thank you," Kamal said, at the same time gazing out the window where the lorry was still being loaded. "Where's it going?"

"Mirza's taking a load of rugs north tomorrow. Through the 'stans' and that leaky Russian frontier just south of Chelyabinsk. Most of the goods'll go to St. Petersburg and Moscow. A small shipment'll go east, on the TransSiberian. Then across the ocean to Alaska."

"They're developing quite a business over there, aren't they?"

"What do you mean 'developing?' They've always loved heroin in America." Hafez sat back and sighed. "But we have a small problem. This may be the last shipment north for a while."

"The last? Why? What's happened?"

"What's happened is the fucking US Army is changing personnel at Bagram. The major in charge is going home. Someone new is replacing him."

"Much of a problem?"

"Maybe, maybe not. Depends on the soldier."

~~~

Seeing Tucker Cranston's mystified expression as he entered his new quarters, McHenry was seized with the chuckles.

"Guess it didn't go so well with 'I'm tryin' to sleep here.' He get to ya?"

Tucker dropped into a chair. McHenry's amusement was infectious—Tucker joined him, laughing quietly, shaking his head back and forth, and blowing out a breath.

"Like my granny used to say, 'What can't be cured, must be endured.' I'll have to put up with the dumb shit."

"Just make yourself scarce and do your job. You'll be tempted to yell at him, tell him what a total cock-up he is, but hold your tongue. Meantime, grab yourself a beer."

"That's exactly what I'm needing," Tucker said, going to the fridge. "When are you and your men leaving?"

"Maybe tonight, or so I've been told. We'll collect our duffels, mount up, and get the fuck outta Dodge."

Tucker popped the cap on his bottle and tipped it toward McHenry. "Safe flight home, Major."

McHenry returned the toast. "Safe tour, Major."

They drank.

"So far, Jed, you've given me a lot of advice, most of it, I think, pretty fair. I'm supposed to wear my sidearm at all times, watch out for green-on-blue attacks, trust Jabari, and do what Murad tells me. Anything else you'd like to share before you leave?"

McHenry leaned forward, hands around his beer bottle. "Yes, there is. I was saving it. It's kinda in line with what I told you about not being too gung-ho."

"Go on."

"Well, here's how you and your men, at least most of you, will survive this place." McHenry took a long swallow of beer, then set the bottle back down on the table. "A couple years ago, stateside, I met three old-timers, jar-heads who'd served in 'Nam. They figured out a way to survive a situation that was as fucked up *then* as this one is *now*."

"What'd they tell you?"

"They told me they changed the mission in Vietnam."

"From what to what?"

"From 'Search and Destroy' to 'Search and Avoid.'

They'd leave base with a mission to hunt up VC and engage them. Instead, they left base, walked a couple clicks, found a safe haven, and hunkered down. When they returned to base, they reported, 'No contact.'"

"I've heard that story. And that's what you're suggesting we do?"

McHenry locked eyes with his replacement. "It's what *we* did, Tucker. And it's what *you* should do." McHenry finished his beer, rose and retrieved a second bottle from the fridge.

When Tucker made no response, McHenry continued. "Now, I'm not particularly proud of the fact that we didn't follow orders, didn't work to advance Washington's political agenda. A deeply flawed agenda, by the way, us trying to impose democracy on a people that don't get the concept, have no interest in the concept. But I *am* extremely proud of the fact that durin' my time here, the 10th Mountain didn't suffer a *single* KIA. Not one. And only four of my guys were injured badly enough to earn a trip to Ramstein. I may not be able to look the President in the eye—fuck that moron anyway and the horse he rode in on. But, tomorrow, or the day after, we'll get home to New York, to Fort Drum. And with a great deal of comfort and pride, I'll stand in front of the hundreds of family members of my men and be able to tell them, mission accomplished. See, my mission, as I saw it, was to bring their family members—sons and husbands, daughters and sisters—back alive. And, except for those four wounded men—all still back in the states, and mostly rehabilitatin'— we were successful beyond my wildest dreams. I leave this place a happy man."

"I envy you, Jed. But I'm not totally convinced you did the right thing. I'll need to think about it."

"You'll do fine, Tucker. You're nobody's fool. If you think

more about the safety of your men and less about the mission, you'll be OK."

Tucker smiled "But whichever way I decide, Cunningham's sure to be a pain in the ass."

"Oh, yeah. You can take that one to the bank."

~~~

"I got Danish from the Almondine," Larissa announced at the doorway. She brought the bag of pastry into the kitchen. Her husband was on his cell phone, listening and smiling.

"Thank you again, Congresswoman Feinbaum," Boris said. "I applaud your diligent and highly successful work. Congratulations. And the FAA?"

He listened. "Excellent. Yes, thank you again. I'm obliged to you. Please expect a FedEx with the other five letters." He closed the phone and turned to his wife. "That was our favorite congresswoman. She said her committee voted today to approve the Troika flights."

Larissa shook her head in disbelief. "It took her only three months. You must have really scared the shit out of her." She put the Danish on a plate, plate into the microwave.

"Nothing more than full exposure of her fucking around to every newspaper in DC, her husband, kids, Nancy Pelosi."

Larissa laughed. "You kept copies of her letters, I hope. I want to read them again. Sizzle."

"My lustful wife. Of course I made copies. We may need her again."

"What did she say about how soon flights can begin?"

"Feinbaum said she's strong-arming the FAA, so shouldn't take more than a couple weeks."

"And then?"

"Troika has already leased the planes. The two aircraft are in Vlad right now. And with the Russian side already signed off, it's just a matter of a few weeks, maybe a month before the first flight."

"Who's the delivery boy over there?"

"Kollantai said they're working on a pilot."

"Terrific. And on this side, up in Alaska?"

"Thanks to Artun, we have a K-9 handler at the airport ready to take possession and be our courier."

"How did Artun find him?"

"Mehmet said he fell into their lap. Artun was coming through customs and spoke to the dog handler, complimented him on his work ethic. The guy apparently fell right in line."

"I can't believe it's gone this smoothly and so quickly," Larissa said. "Amazing."

The microwave dinged. "I'll butter the Danish, Boris said. "Wanna make a fresh pot of coffee?"

"I will if you go get Feinbaum's letters. I'd rather read them this morning's Times."

"Agreed."

~~~

If **Mirza ibn Murad*** had been an Italian-American Mafioso, he'd be a 'made guy,' untouchable, his safety from rival gangs guaranteed. Being the oldest nephew of his Shaikh, Mirza enjoyed the status his family name brought him, although he was probably ignorant of the 'made guy' designation enjoyed by his American colleagues-in-crime.

If not a 'made guy,' Mirza was recognized as a 'good guy,' possessed of a generous nature and a happy-go-lucky disposition. In recognition of his winning ways, the Shaikh had placed his nephew in work that allowed him to succeed marvelously—as a long-haul truck driver.

Mirza's only job, undertaken every other month, was to head north in his 1995 Mercedes Benz Atego. He'd drive his eagle-decorated lorry through Turkmenistan, Uzbekistan, Kazakhstan, and finally across the Russian border to Chelyabinsk. There he'd deliver a large pile of rugs to a Russian, someone the Afghani suspected of being a Jew. Despite that obvious-to-Mirza birth defect, the driver knew the Russian to be a reliable businessman.

The drive from Jalalabad to Chelyabinsk covered thirty-two hundred kilometers and took six or seven days, depending. On the way, Mirza would befriend, joke with, share coffee with, and most importantly, suborn the frontier guards and customs officials who attempt—without much success—to secure the four international border crossings between Afghanistan and Russia. It was the kind of work perfectly suited to the jolly Mirza ibn Murad.

The early evening sky was a fiery red-orange. A sudden swirling dust devil in the factory courtyard made several of the armed guards bend away, covering their eyes. Above them, a trio of mallards squawked their way west, toward the Shina River.

Inside the factory, on the ground floor, the evening shift had just arrived, continuing the work of processing raw opium gum into pure heroin.

In Hafez Ghafoor's office, he and Mirza were finishing off a light dinner of hummus and pita, eggplant salad, honeyed apples, and tea.

"You're all loaded and ready to go." Ghafoor said. "You should be in Chelyabinsk in a week."

Mirza scooped up some hummus with a wedge of pita and

swallowed the piece.

"Tomorrow's a long day," the driver said. "Eight hundred kilometers to Herat, but after that I can manage six hundred a day. Not a problem. Never has been. I'll start tomorrow before first light, be on the road by four." Mirza wiped the last of the hummus off the plate with a crust of pita.

"And the gifts you've arranged for your friends at the border? Anything special?" Hafez asked.

Mirza sat back, licked his fingers, then wiped them on his dungarees. He stroked his scruffy beard with one hand and rubbed his large and rounded stomach with the other. "Mostly the usual stuff. Always works."

"Great. Have a safe journey. Best to Medina and the girls."

By four the next morning, Mirza was ready to roll. On the passenger side of his truck's cab were his usual two companions during these long drives: a huge wicker hamper and an ice chest.

The first brimmed with bags of nuts, dried and fresh fruits, a whole roasted chicken, a bag of grape leaves stuffed with lamb, an assortment of cookies and cakes, and two Thermoses of sweetened coffee.

The ice chest was stocked with yoghurt, kefir, rice pudding, baklava, skewered kebabs, meatballs, a carton of hard-boiled eggs, another two roasted chickens, and bottles of juice and soda.

His wife, Medina, had prepared the food with the help of Yasmin, at sixteen, the youngest of their five daughters.

Before climbing the steel steps into the Atego's cab, he briefly embraced his wife and blessed his daughter. "See you in two weeks," he told them.

"Drive carefully. Call every day. And for my sake, please

don't forget to pray," Medina said.

"I'll drive carefully. I'll call. I'll pray," he promised. *At least the first two,* he thought.

"Bring me something from Russia?" his daughter asked.

"Have I ever forgotten?"

Ten minutes later, working the shift stick and the vehicle's horn with equal vigor, he slowly honked his way out of his home town, driving through streets that even at this early hour were already clogged with hundreds of lorries, all belching diesel fumes into Jalalabad's stinking air.

~~~

Following the advice of his boss, Anatoly Suvorov went to the Slavianski Bazaar and spoke to the desk clerk behind the meshed wire cage. The man was expecting him and wrote down a place—the Café Pyatnitsa; a time—3 pm; and a day—next Tuesday when he'd meet with someone who might ease the pilot's financial burdens.

A driving rain was sweeping across the city when Anatoly got off the autobus that delivered him to the Café Pyatnitsa. The place was in a section of Vladivostok he'd never visited before—the far eastern edge of the city, close to Ussuri Bay. He entered the café soaked to the skin.

The only person in the eatery at this mid-afternoon hour was round, hairless, and drinking a large beer.

Anatoly hung up his dripping coat and cap, pushed his hands through his hair, and approached the man.

"I'm Suvorov. The desk clerk at the Slavianski Bazaar said you might have extra work for me. Who are you?"

The man gestured for Anatoly to slide into the booth and

sit opposite.

"Who am I? Not important. Something to drink?"

"Thanks, no. I'm good. I'm just curious . . . about . . . ."

"About how you might earn enough to keep your life from going into the toilet. That it?"

Anatoly gave the man a sad smile. "That's it."

"So. Anatoly Maximovich Suvorov. You're a pilot, fly for Troika, getting ready to be first officer on your company's new route to Alaska. Have I got it?"

"What are you talking about? Alaska?"

The man seemed surprised. "You don't know yet? Your airline's going to begin flying regularly to Alaska, to the big city over there, Anchor . . . something. You apparently haven't heard."

Anatoly shook his head. "No. How do you know this?"

The man chugged the rest of his beer, wiped his lips and smiled. "Not important how I know. What I *do* know is that you've been penciled in to be first officer on those flights."

Anatoly couldn't shake the puzzled expression off his face. Finally, "OK. So I'll be first officer. When do these flights begin?"

"Within a few weeks, I hear."

Anatoly now realized what he'd be called on to do to earn the extra money. "So, I'm to be a smuggler."

The man chuckled. "You've guessed it. And you'll be paid three thousand dollars every time you fly to Alaska. And since you'll be heading there every other week, that's six thousand a month. Guaranteed. Interested?"

Anatoly suddenly couldn't breathe. He felt as if a great vacuum cleaner had sucked all the oxygen out of his lungs. His eyes bugged. He fell back in his seat, unable to respond.

The man signaled to the waiter. "Bring my friend here

something to drink. Got Coke?"

"Unh-uh," the waiter called back. "Only Pepsi."

"Bring one."

Anatoly and the man sat silently facing each other, the one smiling, the other too dumbfounded to be able to talk. The waiter placed a bottle of Pepsi and a glass in the center of the table, then left. The man poured the soda and pushed it toward Anatoly. "Go on, Toly. Drink some. It'll loosen you up."

Anatoly downed half the glass and sputtered, coughed. "Three thousand dollars? Every two weeks?"

The man winked. "That should keep Sophia happy."

Startled, Anatoly asked, "How did you know my wife's name?"

"Again, not important. More important is if you are interested."

"Of course I'm interested."

"Of course you are." The man studied the pilot's face. "You're a bright guy, Toly. You've already guessed that for the amount of money I'm offering, I'll almost certainly ask you to do something illegal and dangerous. You understand that, don't you?"

Anatoly breathed out. "I guess. I mean . . . right. What . . . what do you want me to do? I mean, what do I have to carry into America?" A question to which he already knew the answer—something illegal and dangerous.

The man gently raised his palms. "You can guess, but best if you don't know precisely. Here's how it'll work. The night before you fly, you'll pick up a piece of luggage—probably weigh no more than thirty kilos. You'll take it on board with you and fly to America. You'll hand it to someone in US Customs. That's all of it. When you return home, you'll go back to the Slavianski Bazaar for the payoff. Three grand. Simple."

Anatoly's brain was swimming. He managed to finish the rest of his Pepsi.

~~~

Tucker and his driver left Bagram just after nine Thursday morning and headed southeast, driving on a winding and deeply pot-holed blacktop. They were riding in Jabari Hajji Murad's distinctive green and white striped closed Jeep. A green triangular banner, attached to a tall antenna, fluttered above them.

Tucker had taken McHenry's advice and exchanged his army fatigues for Levis, a sweater, a Red Sox baseball cap, and a light windbreaker. He felt for his Colt 1911 9 mm pistol, holstered on his belt.

"My uncle is practical man, peaceful man," Jabari explained. "He understand why Americans being in Afghanistan. He hate Taliban."

His passenger, in-country barely three days, hardly acknowledged the driver's declaration. Tucker was too busy searching the passing countryside, looking for—but hoping *not* to see—anyone with an automatic weapon pointed his way. *I must be out of my mind. Driving through Taliban country with an Afghani cook. This is the craziest fucking mission I've ever been on.*

Jabari glanced over at Tucker, noted his nervousness. "We safe, major. I promise. We come soon to home of uncle. I speak to uncle last night. I tell about our meeting. He very wanting to meet you."

"And I would like to meet him," Tucker replied. *But why now? Why so soon after I've gotten here?*

Despite Jabari's insisting that they would be safe, that the Taliban wouldn't dare attack this vehicle, Tucker's knee jittered up and down while his sweaty right palm never left the butt of the Colt. With his left hand, he felt for and found a lump in his jacket's large pocket—his gift for the warlord.

A quarter of an hour later, the Jeep still intact, they turned off the pavement onto a dirt road and drove into a valley, barely two hundred meters across. Stunted pine trees grew on both steeply pitched hillsides. Partially hidden within the scant forest, Tucker noted a variety of concrete pillboxes. They'd been sited at varying elevations, in places where each had a wide range of fire. *They're watching us. Count on it.*

Higher up, on the crests of both hillsides, Tucker saw complex arrays of antennas and satellite dishes. *Looks like NSA headquarters.*

The deeper into the valley they drove, the more serious the protective measures became. Swinging around a blind curve, they came upon a high metal gate, fortified on either side with thick sandbagged walls. And behind the walls, a squad of armed men. Tucker thought the Jeep would be stopped and inspected, but the gate swung open and they were waved through without a word. Tucker looked at his driver and finally let himself relax.

"I guess we're expected."

"I drive to here each week. They know me," Jabari said. "The home of uncle is most safest home in Nangarhar."

Immediately after Jabari's Jeep cleared the security gate, the road became a smoothly paved two-lane. After a kilometer, they entered a wooded pasture of ponds crowded with ducks and swans. A stand of mature date palms shaded grassy lawns. And beyond the palms, on a small hill, Tucker saw a large, artfully crafted stone building, a terrace sweeping around the structure's perimeter. Dozens of men roamed about, AK 47s slung casually over their shoulders.

Jabari pulled to a stop in front of a flight of stairs that

led up to the building's entrance. A tall man in dark pants and a white shirt, open at the neck and with sleeves rolled up, stood halfway down the stairs watching them.

Jabari jumped out of the Jeep and waved to the man. "This my nephew, Hakeem ibn Salman*."

Tucker saw a good-looking man of some forty years, clean-shaven, hawk-nosed, with bronzed skin, short-cropped black hair, and dark eyes. He arrived at the bottom of the stairs in time to take the hand that Tucker extended out to him.

"A pleasure to meet you, sir," Tucker said.

"And mine equally, Major Cranston," the man answered in perfectly accented British English. "I hope you had a pleasant drive here from Bagram."

Tucker smiled. "I confess, I was nervous at first, but your uncle insisted I was safe."

Now it was Hakeem's turn to smile. "And did you believe him?"

"Not entirely. But when we entered your lovely valley, I began to relax."

"And that is what you must continue to do while you are here, as a guest of my grandfather, Shaikh Murad." Hakeem turned to Jabari and spoke to him in Pashto. The driver nodded, returned to the Jeep, drove to a shaded copse and parked.

"My uncle will wait right there, Major, until you are ready to depart." Hakeem indicated with his hand the broad set of marble stairs that led up to the home of Shaikh Murad. They took their time ascending.

Tucker said, "By your accent, I'm guessing you've spent serious time abroad, in England, I'm thinking."

"Indeed. When I was eleven, my grandfather felt it necessary—for the good of the family, of course—to send me there. My objections did me little good. Disagreeing with grandfather is a losing proposition. So, I went and suffered through ten years at public school—Harrow, of all places—and then university, Cambridge."

"What did you study?"

"The same as you, Major Cranston. Middle-Eastern history. And English. And Russian." Hakeem frowned. "Russian. Brrr. A horrible language spoken by equally horrible people. We had our fill of them in the eighties."

Tucker smiled. "A difficult language, that's for certain. People? I've actually met some decent Russians. Not many. Some."

"To tell the truth, so have I."

Tucker paused near the top of the stairs and turned back toward the well-tended grounds. "It's a small paradise here, Mr. Salman."

"We think so, and we work hard to maintain it. But please, Major, call me Hakeem."

"Certainly. I'm Tucker."

"Thank you, but calling you by your given name is an informality that I cannot assume. In England, of course. But here, no. You are our honored visitor, a person of rank and reputation, Major Cranston. It would be presumptuous and ill-mannered of me to address you as an equal."

"Rank and reputation? OK, I guess I have rank. But reputation? You flatter me."

"Not at all. Both grandfather and I have read your paper on Bismarck, done while you were at university in Texas. We found it well-argued and instructive."

Tucker stopped, his eyebrows arching in surprise, and when he seemed to be having trouble replying, Hakeem continued. "Truly, Major. A clever re-thinking of history."

"I appreciate the kind words, Hakeem. I hadn't thought

about my thesis for a good long while. I appreciate you having read it." *McHenry said they'd know more about me than I could imagine. How the hell could they have found it to read? And what else do they know?*

At the top of the staircase, the two men walked slowly onto a broad, covered terrace that stretched off in either direction. Thick marble columns extended the length of the porch and supported overhanging eaves. Floral mosaics decorated the flagstone floor.

"The building has been our family's home for more than one hundred and fifty years," Hakeem said.

"Built around the time of the Second Anglo-Afghan War, perhaps?" Tucker suggested.

Hakeem stopped short and regarded his guest. "My uncle said your knowledge of our history was extensive. I commend you, Major Cranston."

"Nothing any student of this region wouldn't know," Tucker said. "This part of the planet has always had a particular fascination for me."

Hakeem pointed to a long marble bench, covered with a thick, upholstered mat. "Let's sit for a moment, shall we, Major? And tell me the root of this 'fascination' of yours."

They sat and faced out, leaning on the balcony's balustrade. A light breeze ruffled the palm fronds below. From somewhere hidden in the trees, a muster of peacocks squawked at each other.

"I'll try and think of a way to explain without offending," Tucker said.

Hakeem brushed the air in front of him, as if to dispel his guest's reservations. "No offense will be taken, Major Cranston, I assure you. I lived in England, home to perhaps the most caste-conscious, racist, and bigoted people I've ever met. I learned to let each slight, each subtly pointed barb—and the British are past masters at such innuendo—float away. So, please, you may speak bluntly."

Tucker removed his baseball cap and massaged his scalp. "Well, my fascination is rooted partly in just how thorny—I think that's the appropriate word—your countrymen are." He looked over at his host. "And I use the word 'thorny' with precision *and* with appreciation."

Hakeem considered, then grinned. "Go on, Major. Explain our thorniness."

"Well, I believe it's an apt metaphor for the way you treat any and all of the invaders who've attempted . . . and still attempt . . . to come into your country and tell you what to do, tell you how to live. The Persians tried it around five hundred BC. The Greeks under Alexander after them. The Arabs, Romans, Mughals. Then the English. Russians not so long ago. And now we Americans have come into Afghanistan with the intention of bending you to our ways. A few of the invaders had some success, others not so much. We Americans? The jury is still out, and will probably remain that way. You've treated all of them—all of *us*—with an extensive and painful diet of thorns."

Hakeem threw his head back and laughed for a full minute. When he had caught his breath, "It's true. We deeply resent intruders. I think your metaphor is apt, Major. And I believe my grandfather, whom you will meet shortly, will be pleased and amused."

"I'm ready to meet your kinsman, Hakeem."

~~~

The lorry driver took Highway NH01, the ancient 'ring road' whose origins are lost in pre-history. After a long day behind the wheel, Mirza arrived in Herat. He needed to gas up, make serious use of the toilet at the service station, and stretch his legs in the park across the highway.

Half an hour later, chores done, he returned to his truck. The Atego was parked in a shaded grove of trees. Directly across the road was the Herat-Afghan Girls High School. He took his Nikon binoculars out of their case, adjusted them slightly, and was ready to ogle to his heart's content.

A few minutes past two o'clock, the school's wide doors flew open, young girls flooding out. Most used *burqas* to cover their faces. But there were a few—the select few whom he had come to recognize and appreciate—who allowed their *hijabs* to fall free and drape their shoulders. It was those daring young ladies who drew Mirza's attention and longing stares.

The driver maintained his self-imposed discipline, never leaving his vehicle nor allowing his voyeurism to extend beyond his self-imposed time limit—fifteen minutes.

Not that the fifty-two-year-old was the sort who might take advantage of the girls. After all, hadn't he helped his wife raise their five daughters? *Five daughters,* he thought. *I'm cursed, son-less.*

At these moments, he kept in mind the most serious disincentive to any kind of silliness he might consider—a warning from on-high, from the Shaikh, himself. The patriarch absolutely forbade any deviation from *Naamus*, the part of their Pashtun code that commanded the protection of women from sexual harm. And in this regard, Murad's notorious ruthlessness had been brought to bear on his own family.

Mirza recalled with shivering clarity the incident three years earlier when one of the Shaikh's great-grandsons, fifteen-year-old Farjaad, was caught with his pecker out, abusing Dara, his ten-year-old cousin. By order of his great-grandfather, the boy was tied hand and foot to a fence, suffered fifty lashes with a knotted, leather thong, then had his private member unceremoniously removed. He was left tied up and ultimately bled to death. Shaikh Murad had insisted that the ordeal be witnessed by the boy's family. News of Farjaad's ritual execution spread through Nangarhar like wildfire, and not a single violation of *Naamus* had occurred among the Shaikh's kinsmen since.

So Mirza simply watched. And waited. And licked his lips. Ten minutes into his allotted quarter hour, *She* came out. *Her. The One.* The driver had first spotted her two years earlier and had been immediately struck by the girl's wild beauty. She wore a *hijab,* very loosely draped around her head, allowing her curly, raven-black hair to spill tantalizingly across her face.

She was tall, with cream-colored skin, pitch-black eyes, high cheeks, and a mouth that he dreamed about, longed for. A mouth that knew how to smile, how to laugh, how to taunt. He'd seen her ten, twelve times, and by now, knew her moods, how she walked, how she ran, how she pouted. Last year, he'd seen her play soccer on the school's front lawn with several of her girlfriends. She had worn shorts that day and the sight of her bare and shapely legs was unbelievably delicious. He couldn't deny his lust for her, made obvious by the bulge in his pants. Nor, being the father of five girls, could he deny his shame. In the throes of his unrequited ardor, he'd repeat to himself a quip he'd read somewhere, *'Just because I'm on a diet doesn't mean I can't look at the menu.'*

Mirza watched as the nameless teenager skipped down the school steps, arm in arm with a girlfriend. She whispered something into the friend's ear. Mirza imagined, hoped, it was something sexual. The friend seemed to blush, but his favorite smiled knowingly in a manner, a very mature and totally feminine manner that made the voyeur gulp. *'Look at her. My God. What I wouldn't give to see her strip. Simply take her clothes off. I swear I'd never touch her. I swear. Just let me watch.*

The buzzer on his smart phone's timer rang the fifteen-minute mark. He took a last look at her, let out a small groan, then put down his binoculars, started up the Atego and, reluctantly, very reluctantly, resumed the drive north, to Towrgondi and the border with Turkmenistan.

~~~

After his meeting with the unknown, unnamed man at the Pyatnitsa Café, Anatoly Suvorov was deeply torn between the money—which was spectacular, and the risk—which was more than hideous. And right now, the risk seemed to dominate his thinking. He'd tell his wife only part of the story. They were in their bedroom, late at night.

"Met some guy couple days ago," the pilot began.

Sophia was sitting in front of her dressing table mirror, brushing her hair. She was naked under a partially open bathrobe. She looked at her husband's reflection. He was sitting on their bed, bent over, his elbows on his knees. "A guy? What guy?"

He took a long breath. "Someone who has a gig for me." Then in a whisper, "Could be a lot of money."

"Really? What's the gig?" She began searching her hair for split ends.

"He wants me to smuggle some stuff into Alaska."

She paused in her split ends search, made mirrored eye contact. "Smuggle?" she questioned. "What the hell are you talking about? Smuggle what?"

He took a deep breath. "Smuggle . . . drugs . . . into America."

Sophia swiveled around. "Drugs? Smuggle drugs into America? He must be out of his mind. Why would he think you'd do that?"

Toly wanted to clam up right now, change the subject. Sorry he'd even brought it up. He knew if he mentioned the amount of money being offered, Sophia would flip. He remained quiet.

"Toly, I'm asking you, why would someone who you hardly know think you'd be up for something so dangerous?"

He straightened, exhaled, then flopped back on the bed, the back of one hand covering his face.

She rose, hairbrush in hand. "Toly. Answer me."

"Because, Soph . . . because he knows we need the money."

"Sure we do. But so what? I mean . . . how much is he offering?"

"A lot."

She came to stand over him next to the bed. "A lot? A lot doesn't tell me anything. Exactly how much is this guy suggesting?"

Anatoly, by now well versed in his wife's profligacy, low-balled the amount. He whispered, "Two thousand."

"Two thousand rubles? He must be nuts. Who would do something like that for two thousand shitty rubles."

He knew he should stop talking, let her believe what she wanted to believe. But he thought of the one thousand dollars per voyage he'd be skimming for himself. He couldn't hold back. "Two thousand *dollars*. Every other week." There. He said it. It could not be retracted.

Sophia went wild-eyed, fell back two steps as if shoved, found her balance, and began laughing ecstatically. She went close to the bed, let her bathrobe fall to the floor, went on to her knees, and began unzipping her husband's fly.

He lay there, supine, flaccid. *What have I done?*

~~~

They followed the porch around the building to a pair of swinging doors that opened into a vast, glass-roofed greenhouse, twenty meters wide and fifty long. Halfway down the center aisle, an old man, dressed in work clothes and a gardener's apron was reaching into a pomegranate tree with a pair of pruning shears.

"Grandfather is an avid gardener," Hakeem explained.

Tucker appraised the Shaikh. For an eighty-four-year-old man, one who reportedly had survived numerous life and death struggles, Shaikh Murad* seemed to Tucker surprisingly youthful, anything but the vicious war-lord he'd studied in the CIA's on-line archives during the weeks before his departure for Afghanistan. *More St. Francis in his garden, tending his lilies of the valley, than Ghengis Khan leading his Mongol armies.*

The expression on the old man's face—tongue tip between his lips, right hand lovingly caressing the pomegranate branch he intended to clip—was all concentration, all intention, all gardener. The totally peaceful view of the small, stooped man, certainly no taller than five-foot, four, set Tucker's mind at ease.

"Grandfather," Hakeem called.

Murad didn't react at once. Instead, he used his shears to clip off two ruby-ripe pomegranates. He laid the fruit and the clippers on a small cart, then turned and advanced quickly to his guest. He took Tucker's hand in his scarred and gnarled ones, and pressed.

"Major Cranston," he said in English. "You are welcome to my home."

Without thinking, Tucker placed his other hand on top of the old man's two. He felt an immediate bond with Murad, so different from what he'd been expecting. *On the other hand, the guy's reputed to have killed, slaughtered, and annihilated hundreds. That's why he rules in Nangarhar Province. Not because he's a sweet old man and a gracious host. But because he kills better.*

Murad led his guest to three deeply cushioned wicker chairs, set around a wooden table. The Shaikh took a moment to settle, affording Tucker a moment to breathe in the heady aromas of the garden—oranges, jasmine, and gardenia.

When Murad spoke to his grandson, Tucker noted the high register of the Shaikh's voice, at odds with his dominant reputation. At the same time, however, the man's demeanor was one of commanding authority. He spoke a few words to Hakeem, who gestured to an unseen, off-stage, someone. Within a few seconds, a teenage boy carried in a tray laden with an assortment of dried and fresh fruits, breads and jams. Amid the food stood a dusty green bottle, uncorked, with a set of crystal glasses. He placed the tray on a nearby bench, then cast a quick glance at Hakeem, who nodded at the youth. The boy smiled shyly before departing.

"My son, Akbar," Hakeem said to Tucker. "He is my grandfather's favorite great-grandson."

The old man must have understood, because he smiled and nodded.

"Will he also be sent to England to study?" Tucker asked with a grin.

Hakeem translated. Murad laughed and shook his head, then spoke a few sentences to Hakeem in Pashto.

"Grandfather says that that punishment was reserved specifically for me. To correct my wayward behavior."

Hakeem and Murad conversed again, both laughing. Tucker caught the word 'Cambridge.'

The Shaikh directed his grandson to the tray of food.

"Grandfather wants you to know that all this fruit was grown here, in Murad orchards. And the wine, also, in our vineyards." Hakeem took one of the glasses, poured it half-full of the amber liquid, and passed it to Tucker. "Grandfather is deeply proud of this wine, more than sixty years old." Hakeem filled the second glass and handed it to the old man.

Tucker wondered why despite Islam's prohibition on alcohol, they were about to imbibe. *So be it. There's bound to be a Pashto or Arabic adage about forgiveness for sinning, the usual accommodations where real life meets religious dogma.*

Tucker lifted the glass to his nose. The smell of the sixty-year-old vintage made his breath catch and his eyebrows rise. *Heaven must smell like this.*

Murad raised his glass toward his guest, and in English, "To friends, Major Cranston."

Tucker nodded. "To friends, Shaikh Murad. And to family."

"Family all," said Murad.

"I agree, sir. Being away from my own is painful." Tucker stared off into space. *How soon will I see mine again? If at all.* When he came back to the present, he sipped the wine, then hugged himself with satisfaction.

"Ummm. Like nothing I've ever drunk. I could give up beer for this."

Murad beamed, spoke to Hakeem, who translated, answering Tucker's unspoken question.

"We are instructed to avoid alcohol, as you know. But in certain circumstances, we feel obliged to deviate from custom. Your presence in our home is one of those circumstances. Please don't think ill of us, Major."

"On the contrary, Hakeem. I appreciate your family's ability to adapt, to be flexible. And, of course, it is *I* who feels honored to be in *your* company."

Hakeem translated back and forth, then spoke again. "Grandfather feels you are more eastern than western, Major. And he means that as a supreme compliment."

As Tucker was about to respond, Murad rose, nodded to his guest, and took his leave.

Hakeem explained. "After working in his garden, grandfather always takes a short rest. He'll rejoin us in an hour. Will you excuse him?"

Not much choice for Tucker, since his host, with surprising agility, was already disappearing behind a banana tree.

~~~

Leo Bulgarin hated flying out to St. Lawrence Island. Today would be the twelfth time he'd make the trip. Throughout the six-hour flight in his Beechcraft Bonanza he'd fret, bite his lip, try to keep the contents of his stomach from welling up into his throat. He knew what he had to do, what his cousin Boris insisted he do, and what his wife, Dorotea, hated him doing. And the knowledge made him feel bitterly used. Since last year's problems in Anchorage and in Vladivostok, he'd seriously considered getting out. Leaving Alaska. Leaving Grizzly Air. Going back to Russia. Only his fear of his cousin restrained him.

He'd taken off from Merrill Field early this morning carrying five passengers. He set course for Gambell, one of St. Lawrence Island's two villages. As far as he was concerned, the place was the end of the world—within sight of the frozen and desolate mountains of Russia's Chukotka Peninsula.

After takeoff, the weather was tolerable. He flew west under Visual Flying Rules up to and over the Alaska Range. But once on the other side of the mountains, it was Instrument Flying Rules pretty much all the way. Not quite a white out, but close to it. His five passengers laughed nervously, especially when Leo took his hands off the yoke and sat back, allowing the autopilot to do its thing. He knew there was little danger since there were few mountains from the west side of the Alaska Range out to the coast. Rolling tundra pretty much all the way.

When he hit the Bering Sea, the weather cleared slightly. From there, it was a fairly simple task navigating over the water.

Nearing the far northwestern tip of the island, the village of Gambell came into view. From his current altitude, two thousand feet, Chukotka's mountains across the sea stood out bleak and foreboding.

An overnight storm had dropped four inches of snow onto Gambell's narrow, waterside landing strip. The airport's ground crew had not yet fired up the snowplow. Leo handled the plane on the slushy surface without incident and taxied to the end of the runway. He got out of the Beechcraft, stretched, and helped his passengers deplane. He opened the baggage door, unstrapped the bags, and pulled them out. The passengers took their gear, thanked the pilot, and went to the snow machines and ATVs awaiting them.

Leo walked around the aircraft, going through his post-flight checklist. A minute later, one of the airport workers showed up to refuel the plane. It took ten minutes.

When the refueling was completed, an ATV, towing a sled, brought four outbound passengers to the plane. Leo helped them off the sled, then picked up their luggage one piece at a time, estimating the weight and how he would stow the baggage so the aircraft would be balanced.

Two of the four passengers were men from the Alaska Department of Transportation, come to St. Lawrence Island to see about the feasibility of building a deep-water port. Climate change was thinning out Arctic ice and the Northwest Passage above Canada was now a traversable reality. A new St. Lawrence Island port would serve the large volume of expected shipping.

The other passengers were two young Eskimo women: one pregnant and on her way to the Alaska Native Hospital in Anchorage; the other, someone he knew—a nursing student at the University of Alaska Anchorage. Leo helped them onto the aircraft then went to see about their baggage.

The two DOT staffers each had a daypack and a small suitcase. The pregnant woman had a small duffel. Only the student had serious luggage: a carryall, a suitcase, and two oilskin-wrapped parcels, each weighing about fifty pounds.

Leo carefully loaded the luggage and strapped it down. When he finished and climbed back into the cockpit, he verified that everyone was properly belted in. He warmed up for a brief minute then taxied to the end of the runway. Keeping the breaks on, he slowly gunned the engine. He watched the controls and at the precise right moment released the breaks. The Bonanza lurched forward and slowly gained speed. Well before the end of the runway, it lifted into the air.

Leo Bulgarin, four passengers, their personal baggage, including eighty-six pounds of Afghani heroin, were on their way to Anchorage.

Buster Kopanuk was a contented man. He'd just watched his granddaughter, Julia, deliver to the Grizzly Air pilot the two parcels he'd brought the week before from Chukotka.

Within the next few days, he'd receive a small package—two thousand dollars in fifty-dollar bills. His granddaughter would use the cash to make a payment on her student loan.

Buster's wife, Lorena, had prepared lunch for her husband. She studied his face when he walked in. She was relieved to hear him whistling.

"Good meeting?" she asked.

"No problem," he answered. "Julia got right on." He appraised the steaming, fishy broth his wife had set before him. "Smells great." He looked up at Lorena. Her compressed lips had fused, an expression he knew well.

"You need to stop," she said. "It's too dangerous."

He took a spoonful of soup. "Soon as Julia finishes nursing school, I'll stop. I promise."

"We both know what's in those bundles."

He put his spoon down and sat back, crossing his arms over his chest. "I've never looked. Never asked."

She chuckled. "You think that'll convince a jury? You're gonna testify that you didn't know what you were bringing from Russia? 'Yes, Your Honor, I got two thousand dollars for every shipment I brought in, but it never occurred to me to ask what was in those packages.' That's your defense?" She snorted another laugh.

Buster Kopanuk, smuggler of unknown goods, couldn't resist his wife's humor. He broke out laughing and uncrossed his arms.

She reached across the table and took his hand. "When Julia's school is paid off, you're gonna stop."

He didn't respond.

"Buster. Listen to what I just said. I'm not joking. When we finish paying for her nursing studies, you're done."

"Two more years," he said.

~~~

While Shaikh Murad rested, Tucker got the grand tour of the grounds. He and Hakeem strolled across expansive lawns and through thick groves.

Throughout Hakeem's descriptions of the out-buildings, stables and orchards, Tucker thought about the royal treatment he was receiving and why he needed to meet the Shaikh so quickly. Though Murad seemed genuinely glad to meet him, Tucker sensed a darker purpose behind the man's apparent benevolent nature. *The warlord has more on his mind than he was letting on.* Tucker suspected he'd been invited here to accept an offer. But what kind of offer? Of cooperation? To help fight the Taliban? And most importantly, at what cost to him?

With it all, however, he couldn't help feeling a connection to Murad and to the travails—historic and present-day—this country was forced to endure. Before coming to Afghanistan, he'd reviewed the CIA archives chronicling the ten-year war with the Russians, from 1979 to 1989. Brezhnev was the first of four Russian leaders who had misread history, thinking the Soviets might subdue the Afghani mujahedeen and install a communizing government. *Clearly, the invaders had not read about the previous attempts to conquer this mountainous region. What made them believe they could do what others had failed to do?* Tucker spat out a bitter laugh. *It's the same hubris that since 2001 has infected my own, supposed freedom-loving country. It's exactly as Murad has so far indicated. Only family, bloodline, and clan count for anything in this country. Democracy in Afghanistan? Who's kidding who?*

"Try one of these apples, Major Cranston," Hakeem offered.

They were in the middle of an orchard. Rows of apple trees reached out in every direction.

"Did you know that the apple began here in Afghanistan? There are literally hundreds of wild varieties. But this, our own, we have cultivated for over a century."

Tucker took it and shined the fruit on his sleeve, drawing an appraising look from the other man.

Hakeem imitated his guest. "A good idea, Major. We can learn every day, if we are only open."

The apple now shined, Tucker took a bite. It was as if someone had injected honey into the crisp fruit. "Unbelievable," he said, juice dribbling down his chin.

"In twelve months, when you are ready to leave our country, you'll take some of these back with you to Alaska, to Willow, for your wife Luellen, and your five children. And perhaps you will even share some with your brothers, the pilots."

Tucker kept his face impassive, didn't react to the fact that they'd investigated him, knew about his personal life. He took another bite out of the fruit.

They walked out of the orchard, back toward the house. Hakeem was watching him closely.

"Major McHenry visited us here often. We enjoyed his company. He was a wonderful storyteller. One time he told us how he used to play poker with other officers when they were in Iraq. He said he won hundreds of dollars because of his 'poker face.' You know the expression, Major Cranston?"

"I do," Tucker answered. "I played a lot when I was in high school and at university."

"And did you succeed?"

"You mean, did I win? Yes, I won most of the time."

"And what is the key to winning?"

Tucker thought about it through several paces and another bite of apple. He stopped and said, "Knowing your opponents. Being able to assess them correctly. Knowing when they are telling the truth and when they are not."

"A valuable talent, wouldn't you say?"

"Maybe one of the *most* valuable, Hakeem."

"When I shared with you, just now, information about your family, you didn't even blink. Showed no surprise. Congratulations. I believe that your poker face is even better than Major McHenry's."

When Tucker kept mum, Hakeem laughed lightly, then continued. "I'm wondering how you might react if I told you that your two daughters, Tessa and Raylette—both of whom have applied to Columbia University in New York City— received letters of acceptance earlier this morning. I suspect you have not heard yet from your family."

This time, Tucker blinked and couldn't help but smile. "There goes my poker face, Hakeem. I don't know how the hell you found that out, but I thank you for that wonderful news. I'm thrilled to hear it."

"I'm glad you are pleased, Major."

They arrived at the broad stairway and paused a moment.

"The news, however, is not all positive," Hakeem said. "We also learned that your family's air service has *not* been awarded the three-year By-Pass Mail contract they have been seeking. Something, I believe, your family was counting on." Hakeem let this last statement hang for half a minute, then, "And with the loans you have outstanding for the two Cessna aircraft you purchased earlier this year, your family's business might be in jeopardy."

In a flash, Tucker now saw the handwriting on the wall. It could not have been clearer. It screamed out at him. The only question now was what he would have to agree to in order to earn the bribe-money to pay for his daughters' tuition and to keep his brothers' flight service from going bankrupt. He re-assumed his poker face and didn't reply.

"Come, Major. Grandfather has certainly finished his nap and awaits us for lunch."

~~~

Towrgondi, the customs station on the Afghani border with Turkmenistan, is a surprisingly large town perched in the middle of exactly nowhere. Its only purpose is to control the passage of large caravans of wheeled vehicles that pass between the two countries.

In a part of the planet where smuggling and bribery are the life-blood of the population, the presence of scores of huge lorries, full of desirables, sends the locals into a lather. Chief among the participants in this centuries-old thievery are those who guard the borders. Mirza arrived at the frontier late at night. He'd called ahead and confirmed that the Turkmeni side of the border would be staffed the next morning by two men with whom he'd established a mutually beneficial relationship. He pulled his rig to the side of the road and ate his supper—cold stuffed grape leaves, eggplant salad, kefir, and coffee. He found a secluded ravine where he relieved himself then returned to the Atego and prepared his bed on the truck's long seat. He undressed, took a handful of tissues, and thought about *Her.*

The Turkmeni guards, Rakim and Hanchik, were in an excited state. Waiting for the arrival of their special friend, the two men could hardly contain themselves. They were both young, unmarried, and shared a single, desperate passion: porn. They craved porn. They lived for porn, and if pressed, would probably have died for porn.

The friendly guards joined Mirza as he waited in line around eight in the morning. The three of them climbed into the back of the lorry. The driver handed them a box which they tore open: six DVDs, all American-made, and all featuring huge-busted and huge-butted blond women doing things the two men could hardly think about without spontaneously ejaculating.

"Thank you, Mirza, thank you," Rakim gushed.

"You are the most benevolent of our Afghani friends," Hanchik said. "When will you return? Soon, we hope."

"In a few weeks. I'll see if I can find something to surprise you," he added, winking at the men.

Because of this bountiful largesse, the two frontier guards had not given even a cursory peek at the truck's cargo. A quick scan of the manifest—*Rugs. 46. Afghani. Hand woven, Afghani cotton and wool*—had satisfied them.

Nor had either of the guards dared to joke about what the driver might be secreting in one of the rolled-up carpets. Given the wonderful gifts they regularly received from this very generous gentleman-driver, such a joke would have not only been in bad taste, but would certainly have killed off the fatted calf. They got down off the back of the lorry. Mirza closed the doors, walked toward the lorry's front end and raised himself back into the cab.

"See you next time, my friend," shouted Rakim as he swung open the heavy steel border-blocking barrier. "Drive safely."

"Come back soon," Hanchik said. "Thank you to the heavens, once again."

"You are most welcome, my good friends," the driver replied. He put the lorry in gear and rolled into Turkmenistan. Once there, he immediately called the factory at Jalalabad.

~~~~

Hakeem guided his guest back up onto the building's terrace. They passed through the main set of thick wooden doors, removed their shoes, and entered a room with a twenty-meter long pool in the center. Koi swam amongst water lilies and sedge. At one end of the pool, Murad sat at a round table, chairs placed on either side of him. He beckoned to his guest and indicated the chair to his right.

Tucker was relieved to see that he wouldn't have to eat in the more traditional Afghan style—seated on cushions with his legs somehow bent beneath him. He wasn't sure how long his knees could manage such a pose.

He took his seat and wondered what the next hour might bring. He was a believer in nano moments—those evanescent instances that can turn one's life upside down, give it a whole new direction. He knew, without a doubt, he'd soon be presented with one of those life-altering moments.

He surveyed the table and felt relief once again. His host had seemingly deferred to his Western guest: there was no communal dish out of which he might have to eat with his fingers. Instead, a dozen dishes—open and covered, heated and cold—were spread before him on the table. Meats, fowl, rice, vegetables, bread, a large basket of fruit, and a cut glass pitcher of lemon water.

He wondered if he should serve himself and whether he'd have to eat solely with his right hand. He knew that the left hand in many Middle Eastern cultures was considered unclean. He turned to the Shaikh. "After you, sir."

Following Hakeem's translation, the old man smiled, took with his right hand but once the food was on his plate, he used both hands. Tucker followed suit and dug in.

The guest stayed on his best behavior during the meal, sampling everything, doling out compliments when he found the food delicious, smiling and finishing courses even when he found the food unappetizing. He'd read up on proper dining etiquette and remembered that leaving a bit of food on the plate was considered polite. He left two green beans and a forkful of rice. He sat back and considered waiting for his hosts to clarify why he'd been invited. Hakeem had made an obvious and very correct assessment of his financial situation. *Where's the follow-up? What'll the offer be?*

But then, rather than wait, Tucker decided to take the initiative. He took a cloth bag from his jacket—his gift for the Shaikh. He placed the bag on the table and pushed it toward the old man. "Something for you, Shaikh Murad," he said.

The patriarch initially feigned astonishment—big eyes, huge smile, and a nod of thanks. But when he opened the bag and withdrew its contents, his happiness could not have been more genuine. He glowed as he took up the pair of spurs. He caressed the finely etched metal, and spoke through Hakeem.

"Grandfather is astounded by your gift. He wants to know where they are from, where they were made."

"They're from Mexico. They're hand-forged iron made in Azomoc, south of Mexico City. The rowels are silver, mined in a town called San Luis Potosi."

"And to whom did they belong, do you know?" Hakeem asked.

"There are always stories about ownership. These spurs were supposed to have belonged to Pascual Orozco, a Mexican revolutionary who was captured by Texas Rangers in 1915 and executed."

Hakeem translated for his grandfather. Murad held the spurs as he would a precious jewel. A faraway light shone in his eyes. He spoke at length to Hakeem.

"Grandfather is more than enchanted by your gift, Major. He told me that you have taken him back seventy years, to the first time he ran *buz kashi.* You know the game?"

"I know it's your national sport—groups of riders competing to pick up a goat carcass and carry it off safely. It's a rough game. I made it a point to watch a video on it before I came to Afghanistan. That's where I got the idea for the spurs." Tucker turned to Murad and slowly, in English, "Your first *buz kashi*? How did it go?"

Murad must have understood, because he shrugged, laughed, then spoke to his grandson.

"He fell off his horse," Hakeem said. "And then got paddled by his father."

"I know the feeling," Tucker said, "when I fell off my first mount. Four times."

Murad put the spurs back in the bag and handed it to Hakeem with an explanation.

Tucker thought he heard 'Akbar.'

Hakeem said, "Grandfather says his *buz kashi* days are long behind him, but Akbar, my son, will be forever in your debt. He'll be the envy of every other horseman." Hakeem sat back. "And now it is our turn, Major."

The long, dark wood box was decorated with gilt and inlaid with blue lapis lazuli. Arabic script covered the top. Tucker looked at Hakeem for a translation.

"It's a quote from Muhammad. It says, *'A man is the*

guardian of his family and is responsible for his flock.'

Tucker felt the rope being drawn tight around him. *They're pushing all the buttons.* He opened the box and discovered a beautifully carved scimitar in a tooled leather sheath. A small ruby glistened in the handle. *It's lovely, but it's only a foretaste. What else?*

Hakeem explained, "It belonged to Wazir Akbar Khan, a distant clan member who helped force the British to leave our country in 1842."

"I've read some history, but I'm not familiar with that name. How did he help expel the English?"

"He killed most of them as they attempted to retreat through a very snowy Hindu Kush. There were nearly sixteen thousand British and their allies who were either killed or captured. A very small number succeeded in escaping."

Tucker removed the knife from the box and then took it from its sheath. The blade shone brightly and appeared unused. He looked at the old man.

"I'll treasure this gift, Shaikh Murad. As you passed the spurs to your great grandson, so I hope to pass this on to one of my grandchildren."

When Murad heard the translation, he said in English, "Very good," then he nodded at Hakeem.

"Major Cranston. We would like to provide you with a daily update, delivered by my uncle Jabari, on Taliban movement here in Nangarhar and in the neighboring provinces of Laghman, Konar, and Lowgar. We believe that knowledge would benefit both of us."

Tucker considered a moment. "It would, Hakeem. I'd be grateful for such information." *The kind of intel that could earn me a silver oak leaf. Lieutenant fucking colonel. Now what do I have to do to get it?*

"I'm happy to hear this, Major. And in return we would appreciate your cooperation."

Here it comes. "What would that be, Hakeem?"

"Immunity for our clansman from your poppy eradication program."

Tucker raised his brows. *Christ. What do I do now?* "That might prove difficult for me, Hakeem. I get my orders. I have to obey them. If I'm told to go to a particular place, perhaps the fields of your kinsman, and destroy all the poppy plants, my hands are pretty much tied. *Lame, for sure. But true, nonetheless. My hands really are tied.*

Hakeem didn't seem to be bothered by Tucker's declaration. "Major McHenry taught us another poker phrase," Hakeem said. "The need to occasionally 'sweeten the pot.'"

Tucker felt a pounding begin behind his eyes. He shut them. *If I ask about the 'sweetening' . . . won't that mean I'm available?*

Hakeem and Murad waited patiently, relaxed in their chairs. Tucker sat for a long minute. He crossed and uncrossed his legs. He thought about his girls, off to Columbia, sure in the knowledge that their father had the cost of tuition covered. *Like hell.* He sat up straight and looked at Hakeem. *Fuck it.* "Tell me about the sweetening, please."

Hakeem opened a manila folder and riffed through a few papers.

"This is an application to open an account in a very small, very old and respectable bank in Lausanne, in Switzerland. *DuBois Freres.* Our family has used them for over eighty years. They are more than discreet." Hakeem paused, allowing the information to percolate.

Tucker recognized that this was the nano moment that could turn his life in a wholly new direction. He fought to remain stoic.

Hakeem watched his guest closely and smiled. "You have put on your poker face, Major. Congratulations once again. Your thoughts remain your own. Shall I continue?"

Tucker sat back into his chair and turned inward. He knew—as did Hakeem, as did Murad—that if he agreed to listen, he'd be hooked, good and solid. He gazed at the two men, both watching him and waiting calmly. He closed his eyes. The faces of his wife and children flooded his thoughts. He tried to regulate his breathing, but his heart was thumping. After what seemed to him an eternity, he opened his eyes. "I'll need to think about it."

The expression on Hakeem's face didn't change. He remained smilingly cordial. "Of course, Major."

But Tucker noticed that Murad's face had hardened ever so slightly and his smile didn't appear as welcoming. Tucker shuddered internally and was taken aback when the Shaikh rose, bowed and spoke quickly to Hakeem. Then the old man turned, bowed once again to Tucker, and left his guest.

"Grandfather is tired," Hakeem said. "And a trifle disappointed. But he is a patient man and an understanding one. He will not be offended in the slightest if you refuse his offer. And of course, should you accept, you will find him a generous benefactor. But that is your decision, Major Cranston."

Tucker sensed the meeting was over. He picked up his jacket. "Tell your son that I hope he puts the spurs to good use."

"I will tell him. And I assure you, he will always remember you and your gift."

They walked out onto the broad veranda where Hakeem signaled to Jabari. The cook started up the Jeep and drove it to the foot of the steps.

"And now, Major Cranston. Farewell. We look forward to seeing you again. Soon, I hope."

"Goodbye Hakeem. Please tell the Shaikh how glad I am to have met him. I hope we'll have a successful relationship."

Hakeem smiled. "That is our hope, too, Major Cranston." He accompanied Tucker half way down the steps. "Safe drive back to Bagram."

At the bottom of the stairs, Tucker turned and looked again at his host. *What's he thinking? Have I done the right thing?* When he got in the Jeep, Jabari was frowning and seemed out of sorts. They drove away.

Hakeem watched his guest leave, took out his cell phone and made two calls: one to Jalalabad and one to Brooklyn.

~~~

They were at the dinner table. Boris had made cabbage, beet, and potato soup. "Not quite borscht," he described it.

"Probably because you use za'atar," Larissa suggested. "Not sure about your choice of spices, but excellent, Borya." She finished her soup, cleaning the bowl with a crust of black bread. "A minute ago, I saw you fuming on the phone. What's up?"

He stopped eating and put down his spoon. "The bad news keeps happening."

"Not more problems in Alaska? I thought we'd pretty much got that sorted out."

"Alaska? No. The fisherman and his three friends are all gone."[8]

"And Leo? A problem with St. Lawrence Island?"

"No, that's still happening. He flew out there three days ago, collected over forty kilos."

"Then what?"

"Afghanistan," he said, paused, then added, "A small

- 229 -

problem in Nangarhar." Another pause. "Maybe medium sized."

"Go on."

"Hakeem called. The army's changing commanders. Murad's met the new soldier in charge at Bagram. He's resisting."

"Really? Hard to resist Murad."

"Hard indeed. He can be very persuasive," Boris said, his mood softening. "But on the bright side, the new commander is from Alaska."

"You're kidding?" When she saw he was not, she laughed out loud. "Incredible luck."

"Not only from Alaska. But Hakeem says he's a pilot. His family operates a small air taxi service."

"Amazing," she said. "The possibilities . . ."

~~~

Tucker arrived back at Bagram after dark and found McHenry relaxing in their pre-fab, sipping a beer. "I'm hopin' you had a nice visit with Murad," he said.

Tucker didn't answer, gave the man he was replacing a noncommittal shrug. "I thought you and your guys'd be gone by the time I got back."

"No such luck. We're here couple more days until transport can be rustled up."

Tucker stripped off his civvies and began changing into his army fatigues.

McHenry said, "I notice how you're not answerin' me 'bout how your visit went."

When Tucker didn't reply, the other man shook his head. "Uh-oh. I think, Major Cranston, sir, you might need a story. I considered tellin' it to you before you went to see Murad, then thought better of it. But now seems you need to hear it."

"A story, Jed? Does it have a happy ending? I really need to hear one with a happy ending."

"Happy for one, not so happy for another."

Tucker got himself a couple bottles of beer from the fridge, sat opposite McHenry, and popped open a bottle, draining half. "Lay it on me."

"So. Year ago, I replaced a guy called Stevens. A major and a very good guy. He left Bagram a happy man. You might have an inklin' why, seein' as how you've just had lunch with Murad. But Stevens wasn't *originally* the commandin' officer of the group we were replacin'. That guy was called Contreras. From Reno, I think. Story I heard is that Contreras and his infantrymen were out in the boonies destroyin' poppy fields. Diggin' 'em up and burnin' 'em down. They even were thinkin' about doing an aerial sprayin' but nixed the idea when they caught heat from the locals." McHenry paused, finished his own beer then reached over and took Tucker's untouched second bottle. He paused before opening it. "Anyhow. Choppers take 'em east, close to Tagab, drop 'em off for a few days of eradicatin'. They're clearin' fields all along the highway. Fertile ground. And of course you know whose lands those are?"

"They're Murad lands, I'm thinking."

"All of 'em. Every field that Contreras destroys is on Murad land."

"Oooops," said Tucker. "I got a bad feeling where this story's going."

"No shit. On the third day of this particular operation, 'bout four in the afternoon, there's a single gun shot. Everyone ducks, goes on alert, but no more in-comin'. Just the one shot."

"Contreras?"

"Contreras. Bullet catches him in the Adam's apple, rips out the rest of his throat. He was standing next to a farm door, so they were able to dig out the slug. High velocity fifty BMG, probably fired from a Barrett."

"Jesus. Sniper. Sounds like a message."

"That's what I'm thinkin'. With a weapon like that, a marksman could just as well as hit Contreras in the head. Kill him right off. But it looks like the sniper *chose* to shoot him in the throat, make him last a few seconds. Time enough to contemplate his poor decision makin'."

Tucker took his still frosty bottle and placed it on his forehead, rolling it side to side.

McHenry continued, "When I came on, I asked Jabari about the guys who came before me. He spoke about Contreras. Said the man, and these were his exact words, said the man 'didn't enjoy meetin' the Shaikh.'"

Tucker's shoulders drooped. "Fuck. And looks like he paid for it."

"Oh yeah. Did he ever. So, Tucker, my new friend. I ask you once again, how'd your visit go with Murad? And I hope to hear a satisfactory answer."

"Well, he loved the spurs I brought him."

"Spurs? A great idea. Good goin'. And the rest?"

"The rest?" Tucker sighed. "I told him I had to think about it."

"Jesus H. Christ. I hope he was smilin' when you told him."

"Not really." Tucker rose, walked to the door of the bungalow, and looked out into the night. "I guess I should think about another visit."

"I should hope to God," McHenry said. "And soon."

The next morning, Tucker let Jabari know he'd like to see the patriarch again as soon as possible.

By noon, the two were at Murad's compound. Once again, Hakeem was at the steps, a cautious smile on his lips. "We didn't expect you back so quickly, Major. But we are, nonetheless, very glad to see you."

"I hope I haven't surprised you with such a speedy return."

"Not in the least. Grandfather is waiting. I hope you bring us good news."

"I hope so, too."

Hakeem opened the manila folder, placed it on the table, and swiveled it so his guest could easily see. "When you fill out this application and establish your account—an absolutely and totally private account, I assure you—we will make an initial deposit of thirty thousand dollars. Then, each month, and for the next twelve months of your tour here in Afghanistan, we will deposit ten thousand dollars. The math is simple—one hundred and fifty thousand dollars growing at a handsome five percent a year." Hakeem sat back and regarded the prospective bribee.

Shaikh Murad cleared his throat and smiled sweetly at Tucker, and in English, "Family is all, Major. Yes?"

Tucker had a hard time returning the old man's smile, but answered, "I couldn't agree more strongly, sir. Yours is considerably larger than mine. Still, I treasure mine as I'm sure you do yours. Life is full of surprises, Shaikh Murad."

Hakeem translated for the Shaikh, who leaned back, in no hurry.

After a lengthy silence, Tucker spoke, "You're right, sir. Family *is* all." He took a deep breath. *Here goes.* "But for me to agree to this arrangement," he paused and looked at Hakeem, "the pot needs to be sweetened."

Hakeem smiled, translated for the Shaikh, then turned back to the American, "We are listening, Major."

"I'll need twice as much. The one hundred and fifty thousand will not even cover half of my daughters' university tuition. So, I'll need an initial deposit of sixty thousand dollars and a monthly payment of twenty thousand. If you agree, I'll sign the application right now and open my account."

Hakeem spoke to his grandfather. The old man's face slowly became wreathed in a huge smile. He spoke to his grandson who translated for Tucker.

"My grandfather will agree to *forty* thousand initially and monthly deposits of *twelve* thousand dollars. He hopes you will find that agreeable, Major."

Tucker thought about his wife, his children, and the risk. He considered a counter-offer, but instead reached his hand across the table. The Shaikh leaned over and took it. For an eighty-four-year-old man of such slight stature, Tucker felt his hand in a vise.

After signing the new account application, Hakeem took his guest to the greenhouse. On a large table, a map of Nangarhar Province lay unfurled and weighted down at the corners.

Hakeem nodded and smiled his pleasure. "Thank you again, Major Cranston, for agreeing to work with us. We are deeply appreciative."

Tucker didn't especially enjoy being thanked for becoming a traitor to his country. And since he was unsure how to respond, he kept mum.

"So," Hakeem continued, rising and moving to the map and pointing. "These are the lands on which you and your men will be asked to work your eradication. The ones outlined in red are Murad lands. The blue belong to the Barakzai. The yellow to the Tokhi, and the black to the Hotak."

Tucker leaned over the map and studied it carefully.

"We understand, Major, that it would be impossible for you to completely avoid our kinsmen's property. It would draw suspicion."

"Of course. How do we get around that?" He winced internally at his use of "we." *I'm now a partner. I'm complicit. I've been bribed and I'm a traitor.*

"We don't avoid it. At least not totally. My uncle Jabari will let you know those particular Murad properties on which your men *should* work their eradication. We make arrangements with our kinsmen well in advance, letting them know of your arrival. They understand the problem. We compensate them in full for their lost revenue. Many of them actually enjoy the process, being relieved of the burden of the harvest—a difficult task."

"Just out of curiosity, Hakeem. Over what percentage of Murad lands will I be able to deploy my men?"

"A fair question, Major. There are over one thousand five hundred parcels of land here in Nangarhar worked by my grandfather's kinsmen. Each eradication raid of yours will include no more than two such parcels." When Tucker didn't reply, Hakeem continued, "I've brought these maps out for a second, perhaps equally important reason."

"And that would be?"

Hakeem used a pointer on the large-scale map. "Here are the headwaters of the Kalakan River. You can see there are several rivers that all have their origins in these mountains. For centuries, this has been an often-used gateway into Parwan, and then south to Kabul. During the war with the Soviets, the Russians used this valley in 1984 and again in 1988. But without success."

"Without success? Why?"

"Because the locals know every boulder in those mountain

valleys. And when the Soviet infantry thought to use that passage, we caught them in a crossfire and slaughtered them to a man."

Tucker closely assessed the map and took the pointer from Hakeem. "And I'm guessing you caught them at these points here, Hakeem. And here. Am I right?"

"Exactly there. Foolishly, the Soviets tried to pass through during the day. In plain sight. They didn't have a chance. And you can see the cliffs on both sides of the narrow valley limit the ability of helicopters to maneuver. At least those Soviet helicopters from the '80s. Several tried to support their troops but were either shot down by our RPGs, or gave up trying."

Tucker blew out a breath. "A bitter end for those Russian soldiers. But why the history lesson?"

Hakeem laid the pointer down and waved to a pair of armchairs, inviting his guest to sit. "We have received word that a force of about forty to fifty Taliban will be attempting to infiltrate the area through that valley. Their goal is an attack on Kabul. But, if your forces are arrayed strategically, the Taliban will meet the same fate as the hapless Russians."

"How reliable is this information?" Tucker asked.

"Very reliable. It comes from the highest possible source."

Tucker raised an eyebrow. "OK. Can you be more specific about the day and time?"

"It will happen next week, but I'll know more by tonight. I'll let Jabari know and he'll relay the information. Will that work, Major?"

"It will. And thank you, Hakeem."

"My total pleasure, Major. And good hunting."

His driver was silent, smiling, calm. Tucker sensed that Jabari knew of his having been woven into the Murad web and seemed happy about it.

The word TREASON, in capital letters, kept cycling through Tucker's brain. There was simply no other word for the crime he had just committed: conspiring with the enemy.

Certainly, the money was great. The chance he was taking, however, and the danger to his family was only now sinking in. He remembered shaking Murad's hand. Strong and unforgiving.

His knee once again began jittering—not from fear of a Taliban bullet, but rather from the prospect of an extended stay in the United States Disciplinary Barracks, a military facility located close to the Fort Leavenworth army base in Kansas.

He imagined the ways he might get caught, how his crime might be discovered, who might tumble to his treason. He realized the only way suspicion might arise would be from the IRS. But if he were careful about his new-found wealth, secreted away in a hopefully untraceable Swiss account, then he ought to be safe.

He began to relax. His knee slowed its up and down. The more he thought about it, the more he felt confident that the only way he could screw up was by being too overtly spendy with the money.

He sank into the Jeep's passenger-side seat and recounted the small and medium sized illegalities that had peppered his own and his wife's histories.

When he was sixteen, he was offered a chance to buy a large quantity of Matanuska Thunder Fuck, the particularly potent strain of cannabis that grew in numerous well-tended patches in his Palmer, Alaska neighborhood. He'd jumped at the chance, and in no time he'd made himself a cool several hundred dollars selling to his classmates at Colony High. Criminal money that he successfully hid. *Same as I'll try to do here.*

In his senior year, he became an adept joy rider, borrowing

neighbors' cars, trucks, tractors, even a semi one time, and taking them for a quick spin before leaving them intact and undisturbed. He and his then girlfriend, Joanne McGuinty, grew adept at undressing one another in those vehicles.

After marrying Luellen, she came into a sizeable inheritance: an uncle left her a house on thirty-three acres of productive farmland. She sold the property but overlooked mentioning the capital gains to the IRS.

And at the beginning of his first year-long tour in Iraq, in 2003, the Palmer Chamber of Commerce sent his battalion five hundred cartons of cigarettes. He signed for the shipment and stored the cigarettes in a shed. They remained there for months until he sold them to the Iraqi street vendors who lined the streets of Fallujah.

He'd never been particularly clever with money. He'd always left that to his wife. Luellen graduated from UTEP with a bachelors in business administration, which is how Tucker met her when he was a lieutenant, stationed at Fort Bliss, near El Paso. He'd gone drinking one night and happened to be in a bar whose owner was going over his taxes at one of the tables. The person crunching the numbers was Luellen O'Hara, a senior at UTEP. They dated for a year and when she finished her degree, they married.

Although Luellen had always managed their family's finances, this was a much riskier venture than anything she'd have willingly undertaken. He knew she would react to the sudden and illegal influx of cash in much the same way he had: overjoyed to have it, but fearful of the consequences. He'd have to let her know right away. And it would have to be in person, the usual texting, phone, email or even snail mail too dangerous. As soon as Jabari dropped him off inside Bagram, Tucker texted his wife.

"Need to see u ASAP. Pls PLEASE drop everything and meet me in Delhi, India. I can take 2 days. Dying to see u. Pls come. VERY important. Love U Lulu, always and forever.

Her follow-up happened a minute later.

"WTF Tuck? U want me 2 come 2 Delhi? India? 4 a tryst?"

"Exactly. Can't tell U how IMPORTANT it is for u 2 come, if only for 2 days. Pls. We need to see each other. REALLY important."

"If it's REALLY important, I'll have to break into the piggy bank."

"Do it. It's VITAL we see each other."

~~~

Mother and father were allowed into the hospital's post-operative ward only after eleven that night. They'd been awaiting news of their son's surgery since early afternoon. They entered the room and saw that Malek was still unconscious. A doctor was present and signaled to one of the nurses as the two concerned parents approached.

The doctor spoke to the nurse in French. The woman translated for Reina and Samir.

"Are you the parents?" the nurse asked.

"Yes," Samir said. "Malek is our son."

The nurse confirmed to the doctor. He extended a hand to Samir, then asked the nurse to again translate.

"Tell them that I'm doctor Henri LaBouche, from Doctors Without Borders and that I have good news for them about their son." He looked to the nurse, who translated.

The parents returned the doctor's smile and listened eagerly as he explained that their son's deformed leg would take several months to heal completely, but he should be able to walk properly within a year.

Reina was overcome, leaned into her husband and wept. Samir comforted her and thanked the doctor, vigorously shaking the man's hand.

Once outside, the parents walked toward a waiting Jeep. Kamal and Farouz rushed forward. From the smiles and tears of Malek's parents, they understood the news was good and they rejoiced.

~~~

No sooner had Tucker entered his quarters back at Bagram, when McHenry asked, "And . . .?"

Tucker shrugged. "We shook." Then he slumped into a chair and opened the beer McHenry brought him.

"I am so *very* happy to hear that," McHenry beamed. "Really, I am." He leaned over the table and affectionately grabbed his replacement's arm. "And like I already told you, you can trust Murad. I went on line today, to my bank. You prob'ly know which one. Checked my account. It's all there. Every dime."

Tucker went to the fridge and retrieved a half dozen more beers. He stood them in a row on the table. "Risky business we've undertaken, Jed. I mean, you're done here in-country in a day. What happens after you're back in New York? You think you won't still be on the hook to do the Shaikh's bidding?"

McHenry popped open a bottle of beer. "If I was in for the long run, maybe. If I thought about a new tour here in Afghanistan, then, yeah, prob'ly. But I got a year to go in this man's army before I change back into civvies. I'll do my time at Fort Drum. And after that, there's a houseboat on Lake Powell with my name on it. Middle of Colorado. I'm a single guy, Tucker. I plan to be outta sight and outta touch."

"I envy you your sense of impending freedom. But I'm not so sure, Jed. The two of them, the old man and Hakeem are serious guys. I can't imagine I'll be able to escape quite as easily."

"You're from Alaska, right?"

"Right."

"Seems to me a place that's just about as far away from drug traffickin' as you can get. Don't you think?"

"Yeah. Maybe, you're right. I probably worry too much." Tucker opened a beer and took a long pull. "One more thing, a great thing, actually." He drank again. "Hakeem gave me a piece of serious intel about a bunch of Taliban due in the area. Jabari'll have the details."

"And you're gonna be there to meet 'em?"

"That's the plan."

Four days later, thirty-six Taliban died in a withering and murderous cross fire of automatic weapons delivered by Tucker Cranston's men. The Taliban fighters who survived the initial onslaught were strafed by three Apache helicopters that went up and down the valley, reducing everything to its component molecules. An additional sixteen Taliban, all wounded, were taken prisoner.

When news of the successful mission filtered back to Bagram's HQ, General Cunningham sent a terse note to his junior officer: "Good work Cranston."

~~~

She met him in the arrival lounge at Indira Gandhi International Airport. They fell into a long embrace, kissing, hugging, fondling, and groping each other until Luellen, laughing, pushed her husband away.

"Whoa there, big fella. Save some of that romancin' for tonight."

"Tonight? Not waitin' that long, Lulu. We're heading for the hotel right this minute where I plan to have my way with you."

"Well, if you must," she said, letting the back of her hand brush his crotch.

"Harlot."

"Better believe it, big boy. Grab my bag and let's get goin'.

Later, in their fifth floor suite at the Andaz Hotel Delhi, sweaty and exhausted, Luellen Cranston pronounced the words she'd rehearsed on the Cathay Pacific flight from Hong Kong: "What the hell is so important that I needed to drop everything, fly thousands of miles, and spend almost two grand on a one-way ticket?"

When he hesitated too long, she hastily added, "Don't get me wrong, sweetheart. The sex was sensational, but two grand's worth? I'm not sure."

Tucker rested his head gently in the crook of his wife's elbow. "Do I need to tell you right this minute, Lulu?"

She ran fingers through his thick hair. "I guess not. At least not right this *exact* minute. But I'd dearly love to know the reason sometime before dinner."

He lifted himself up and sat on the edge of the bed. "Tell

you what. Let's get some shorts on, take a walk down by the pool. We'll sit and soak our feet."

The evening was balmy and unusually starry. A strong, warm breeze—a *loo*—blowing off the Thar Desert, had cleared the almost permanent haze out of India's capital, one of the planet's most air-polluted cities.

They sat up to their shins in the hotel pool's deep end. A gaggle of children in the shallow end, forty meters off, splashed and screamed. The smell of jasmine filled the air.

"Awright, I'm listening," she said. "Let's hear it."

He took a deep breath and began telling about his meeting Shaikh Murad. Tucker spoke of the man's family members, drew word pictures of his sumptuous estate, described the exotic lunch in detail, told of the man's influence . . . . then trailed off, leaving his wife with knitted brows.

"OK," she said. "Looks like you've brought me five thousand miles to tell me about a local bandit and what you had for lunch. That it?"

He placed an arm around her shoulder and pulled her toward him. "You hungry yet?"

She pushed away from him. "Hungry? Bullshit, Tuck." She punched him lightly on his upper arm. "Stop fartin' around, Major Cranston. Let's hear it."

He straightened and kicked the water. "Well then . . . here it is." He looked his wife directly in her eyes and took both her hands. "I've been successfully bribed, Lulu. There's a load of money—forty thousand dollars—been deposited in a Swiss bank account in my name. Our name, really, as soon as you go there and co-sign. And more'll be deposited regularly until the end of my tour. Twelve thousand every month."

She fell silent, stayed that way for several minutes, staring into the pool. Finally, "Am I gonna be scared shitless when I hear all the details?"

"Prob'ly."

She leaned back into him. "Fuck. Then I better hear 'em right away."

~~~

Just off the Rue des Tanneurs in downtown Lausanne, a three story, stone building stands back from the narrow, cobbled sidewalk. The building has windows only on the top floor. The single attempt at architectural *haut décor* is a gently fluted cornice whose upper edges seem to flow into the deep blue and cloudless late morning sky.

Back at street level, there is a thick glass door attended by a single good-looking man dressed in an obviously tailored gray suit. He wears dark glasses and stands relaxed, but alert, hands clasped behind him. He wears an unobtrusive ear bud. He nods to the occasional passerby. Above him, cameras are mounted along the walls. There is no indication what goes on in the building other than the burnished copper plate set in the wall to the right of the door: *DuBois Freres – 1804.*

Luellen Cranston approaches the man. He sees her and nods a friendly greeting, as if he has been expecting her. She shows him her passport and a letter. He examines both quickly then escorts her to the door. Luellen is surprised when it swings silently open, seemingly unbidden. She is momentarily taken aback by the portal's automated response, but when a smiling older woman dressed in a dark burgundy pants suit meets her at the threshold, Luellen is set at ease.

"Madame Cranston," the woman says in French-accented English. "How lovely to meet you. I am Giselle Bisset. I will be your private agent. Please." The older woman gestures with her hand and escorts Luellen into the confines of *DuBois Freres*.

They ascend by lift to the third floor and walk across a thick-pile dark blue carpet. They enter Madame Bisset's tastefully furnished office: a mahogany desk, a scattering of three-tier wooden filing cabinets with a vase of fresh flowers on each, walls of compelling modern art, and a pair of cushioned arm chairs set in front of a low table. And on the table, Luellen sees a folder labeled CRANSTON.

Before sitting, the visitor surveys the room. Luellen notes that Madame's lone window is protected by a tracery of thick wire. The view through the window is unimpressive—the four story apartment house across the street. On the wall in back of Madame's desk hangs a small painting. Luellen approaches and admires. "It's lovely."

"Isn't it. It's a signed oil by Giuseppe Salvati. I was in Rome with my husband in 2010. We went to Porta Portesi, their wonderful open-air market. I found it there at the end of the day."

"Looks like it might cost a small fortune."

Madame Bisset laughs. "On sale in an art gallery, it might command a *very* small fortune. At Porta Portesi, only five Euros."

"A bargain. You have a good eye." Luellen sits in one of the armchairs.

Madame Bisset asks if her guest would like coffee? Tea? Luellen has eaten only airline food for the past thirty hours. First, Delhi to Moscow, then to London, then to Basel, followed by a two-hour train ride to Lausanne.

"Coffee would be lovely," she says.

"And perhaps a light breakfast?" Madame suggests.

"If it wouldn't be too much trouble."

"Pas du tout. Not at all," smiles her hostess, who makes no move to place the order. Yet wondrously, within three minutes, a rolling cart is pushed into the room by a thin, older, and wispy-haired man. He wears thick bifocals suspended low on his long nose. He is dressed in starched whites and a black bow tie. He places a tray on the table. On the tray there is a carafe and two ceramic mugs, sugar cubes and a pitcher of cream, a dish of butter, three jars of different jams, a plate with an assortment of cheeses, and a small bowl of red and green grapes. He removes the cloth napkin that covers a large basket, revealing an array of breads, rolls, and scones. The café/bakery smells inundate the room and Luellen begins to salivate in happy anticipation.

The previous night during the Moscow to London leg, she practiced pronouncing the limited number of phrases she has retained from three years of high school French. "Merci beaucoup," she now says to the man. "Je suis tres reconnaisant."

He bows graciously. "De rien, Madame." He inclines his head slightly, turns and wheels the cart away, leaving the tray and the light breakfast on the table.

Madame Bisset joins Luellen in their small repast. They chat. Luellen tells about her children. Madame talks of her own two sons, both studying medicine in the United States.

When their meal is finished, they turn to business. Madame opens the CRANSTON file and over the next hour explains in great detail everything her new client needs to know about her and Tucker's secret Swiss bank account, to which Luellen Cranston is now invited to become an official signatory.

Later that night, from her second floor bedroom at the Hotel de la Paix, Luellen sends her husband a short text: "Signed, sealed, and delivered. Good luck to us! We'll need it!"

~~~

It was the eve of Tamara and Marco's first train ride to Vladivostok. She'd offered her son a vague explanation why they were going.

"We're taking a package to Vlad, to a friend of David's." Although she didn't elaborate further, she was certain that her street-savvy son would connect the dots. He was already a ten-year veteran of hustling prescription meds, meds his mother had liberated from her hospital's dispensary.

"How much is David paying you for this errand?" he asked.

Tamara shrugged. "Enough. A goodly sum."

"A goodly sum, Mom? I think you're reading too much Tolstoy. How much, exactly, is a goodly sum?"

She chuckled, surprised by her son's literary insights. "It so happens that I'm re-reading *Anna Karenina*. I think Stiva uses the phrase. I suppose you should know how much David's paying me—one thousand five hundred dollars."

"Impossible. There's not that much money in all of Chelyabinsk," he laughed.

"There is, in fact. And David's promised it for this favor I'm doing him."

"A favor, huh? I can imagine what kind of favor. Feels like a dangerous and risky one. But, it's a ton of cash. Maybe even enough for a year of carpentry."

"Maybe even three years, the full course."

The next day, Friday, was their traveling day. Tamara didn't go to work. She and Marco spent the morning and afternoon packing, preparing for the five-day trip to Vladivostok. Well before their evening departure, they arrived at the steamy Chelyabinsk

Railroad terminal. An ear-aching din filled the air: chuffing trains, unintelligible loudspeaker squawking, the conversations in a score of languages of hundreds of arriving and departing passengers, and vendors hawking finger foods, cakes and tea, smoked fish and beer.

At half past nine, Tamara and Marco waded into a packed Red Flag Tea Room. Both were wearing heavy fleece coats, wool pants, and high, fur-lined boots. A bright blue scarf was draped around Tamara's neck. They each wheeled a suitcase. A heavy, brown canvas bag with a strong zipper and a set of black straps sat atop Tamara's roller. Marco shouldered a large carryall.

They stopped next to a bubbling samovar, stacks of white saucers and mugs close at hand. They waited for a booth to come free.

Three women—Azeri by their dress—vacated a small table in the room's far corner. Marco raced to it, beating a young Kazakh man by a nose. The loser swore at the winner, but retreated. Tamara came to the table and placed the strapped bag beneath it.

A large wall clock with a sweep-second hand hung over the café's entrance. It now showed a quarter to ten. They had forty-five minutes before their train to Vladivostok.

Marco went to the buffet, grabbed a tray and piled on cups and saucers, cutlery, four small berry tarts, three long rolls, sausages, cheese, butter, two lemon-flavored yoghurts, and a carton of six hard-boiled eggs. They'd have a quick bite now and save the rest for the days ahead. He drew boiling tea from the gurgling samovar and gathered sugar cubes and lemon slices. He paid the cashier, and returned to their booth.

They ate and drank quickly. Every two minutes, Marco

looked at the clock. "Are we going to be late?"

"Calm down," Tamara answered. "He told me ten." Despite her assurances to her son, she was jittery. For weeks, David had tried to convince her that she had nothing to worry about. In spite of his downplaying the risk, she understood that the danger was very real. But then, so too was the money she would earn. Fifteen hundred dollars. Six times a year. A fortune.

The loudspeaker came alive, announcing the first call for the departure of the train to Yekaterinburg, Tyumen, Omsk, Irkutsk, and points east.

Just then, at the entrance to the café, a familiar face, carrying a brown canvas bag of some weight with a heavy zipper and black straps. He paused and surveyed the crowded room, entered, took a mug, paid the cashier, and drew himself a cup of tea from the samovar. He searched casually for a place to sit. He saw a seat next to a woman wearing a bright blue scarf. He made for the table and stopped in front of it.

"May I?" he asked, nodding to the empty seat.

"It's a free country," Tamara answered.

"So they keep telling us," he countered.

They all smiled. He put his mug on the table, placed his bag next to Tamara's, and slid into the booth. They chatted until Marco tapped his wristwatch. "We should go, mom."

Tamara nodded to her son. He stood, took David's bag from under the table and draped it over their roller. She rose and turned to the man.

"Good bye. Nice meeting you. Have a happy journey."

"You, too."

The novice drug mules, luggage in tow, stepped quickly out of the café.

~~~

The two Troika pilots were back in the Knevichi Airport's staff lounge rehashing the same topic: Sophia Suvorova's incredible talent for disposing of her husband's money.

"Nothing's changed, Dima. Soph is still going through everything I earn. And the shit she buys. My God. She's totally filled up the apartment with crap and now says she wants a bigger flat. But that's not the worst of it," Anatoly continued. "There's more."

"What's up?" Dima asked, leaning over the table.

Anatoly dropped his head and mumbled, "I think Soph is . . . she's . . . she's fucking around."

"Sophia? I don't believe it. What makes you think that?" Dima wiped beer foam off his upper lip and put down his bottle.

"Just a feeling. Well, more than a feeling. A suspicion, I'd say."

"What do you suspect? And why? And who with?"

Anatoly finished off his beer and signaled to the waiter for two more bottles. "I don't know who and I don't know why, but for the past several months she's often out when I get home. She leaves our son at the sitter's. When I'm not flying, I get home usually about six. A lot of the time she's not there, and later, when I ask her where she's been, she tells me at a girl friend's. Or getting her hair done. Or having a fucking pedicure."

"OK, those are reasonable answers, aren't they?"

"Of course they are. I ask her how *long* she's been gone, she tells me 'only an hour or two.' But when I ask the sitter the same question, what time Soph dropped off Marat, the sitter tells me about noon. Something's screwy, Dima. It doesn't add up."

The waiter came with their new beers, collected their empties, and left.

"I guess I can see where you might be suspicious. Have you thought of following her? I don't mean *you* personally. But hiring someone to follow her."

"I thought of it, yeah, but haven't done it. If she'd catch wind of it she'd skin me alive. I'm fucked if I follow her and fucked by not knowing." Anatoly took a long slug from his bottle. "Shit."

"You guys'll work it out, I'm sure. But meantime, tell me. What came of my suggestion to see the guy at the hotel? Anything happen?"

Anatoly didn't answer right away. He didn't want to tell Dima it was a successful visit. Certainly didn't want to tell his boss just *how* successful, that he was now smuggling drugs into the United States and raking in six thousand dollars a month doing it. But a part of him, the suspicious part, felt Dima already knew of his involvement and was probably getting some kind of finder's fee for having steered him to the hotel. Anatoly killed time by drinking from his bottle, then lighting a cigarette.

Dima asked again, "Did you go to the hotel? Find out what they needed?"

"Yeah, I went there." Anatoly shrugged his disinterest. "Guy was vague about what he wanted. And the money he offered was lousy. So I turned him down."

Dmitri Nikolaevich knew his employee was lying, knew exactly what Anatoly was making *na levo*. And, through discreet channels, he'd discovered that the husband was short-changing the wife. He knew the whole story because he, himself, had been on the take for years. Because he and Sergo, the man who met Anatoly at the Café Pyatnitsa, attended the same high school, were both on the Admiral Vladivostok Hockey Club's junior team, and been drinking buddies for thirty years. Dima smiled at his employee. *Just keep delivering the shit, Toly. Try not to get caught. And best if you don't pursue your idea of following your wife. You just might discover something unfortunate.*

~~~

In the seventh month of his tour, Tucker met once more with Hakeem for another map-search, followed a week later by another mission against the enemy. The slaughter this time took place about twenty kilometers north of Bagram, above Jabal us Saraj. Hakeem provided Tucker with unerringly accurate intel: date and time. He and his men arrived two days early, dug in on both sides of the shallow valley and waited. The enemy arrived right on schedule. An even two dozen of them died moments later, and twenty-two were taken prisoner.

This time, General Cunningham was somewhat more effusive in his praise: "Very good work, Cranston," he wrote in the short memo to his junior officer.

Tucker was pleased by the 'very' and amused by the follow-up military communiqué about *" . . . the two brilliantly laid ambushes orchestrated by General Cunningham, resulting in the deaths of more than eighty-five Taliban and the capture of over one hundred of the enemy."*

Tucker smiled at the gross exaggeration of the enemy's casualties. *Command has been doing that forever. Inventing unreal body counts just like they did in 'Nam.*

The communiqué further noted that Cunningham was being transferred to CentCom where he would take command of CERP-A, the Commander's Emergency Response Program for Afghanistan.

Tucker knew all about CERP-A's mission: the distribution

of immense amounts of money for Afghani humanitarian aid. Money for the rebuilding and reconstruction of clinics and schools. Money for roads. Money that had to be used for the benefit of the Afghani people.

He also knew about the hundreds of millions of dollars siphoned off by local tribal leaders, anxious to increase their own influence. He was certain that the choice of Cunningham to lead CERP-A ensured half-assed, half-completed projects, snafu-ed timelines, stolen money, and a generally botched job.

Two days before his transfer to Al Udeid, the general summoned Tucker.

Contrary to their first interaction, the general told his junior officer to be at ease.

Tucker stood, hands clasped behind his back, wondering what was on Cunningham's mind.

Eyes glued to his computer, fingers scratching at his unshaven chin, the general spoke. "I'm recommending you for a bump up to colonel."

The best a very surprised Major Cranston could manage was, "Thank you, sir."

Cunningham continued searching his computer, finally looked up. "That's all Cranston."

"Sir," Tucker responded, saluting, executing an about face, and quick-timing it out of the general's office. Once outside, and at a safe distance from Cunningham's office, Tucker let out a single 'whoop,' then texted his wife.

~~~

In 1989, when Tamara began working in her hospital's emergency room, she was counseled by one of the older doctors. "Your trauma care is wonderful and on the battlefield, I'm sure you saved lives. But here, back home in urban Russia, you need more. You need to be able to recognize—by sight, by smell, and even by taste—the drugs your patients will have taken."

Two days later, the doctor showed her what he meant. Early that morning, a teenage girl was admitted to the ER. She was disoriented, flailing wildly, incoherent. Tamara searched through the girl's clothes, found a vial of crystalline white powder, and handed it to the doctor. He poured some onto his palm and licked a few grains. "PCP, angel dust," he said. He ordered the patient restrained, sedated, monitored her airway, ordered a full blood panel, and administered activated charcoal to hinder further absorption of the drug.

After the patient was stabilized, the doctor took Tamara aside.

"Like I was telling you, you have to know what these kids are taking these days. Which means, you, yourself, need to experiment. If we had the time, we could have sent the powder down to the lab and toxicology would have eventually told us what the hell it was. But we didn't have that luxury. She was *in extremis* and we needed to know right away."

"You knew it was phencyclidine?"

The doctor sighed. "My foolish grandson was a PCP user. Up until his father found out and beat the shit out of him. My son confiscated the stuff and gave it to me. I tasted it. Now I know what angel dust tastes like. You need to know, too."

That was in 1989.

Now, on the train, it took Tamara less than five minutes to determine what, exactly, she was carting to Vladivostok. As soon as she and Marco had settled in their compartment, she lugged the strapped bag into the bathroom at the end of the carriage. She locked herself in and opened it up. She counted twenty-two packages, each measuring about thirty centimeters square and eight centimeters high, and each wrapped in heavy red packing paper, taped at the corners.

She took a nail file from her purse and gently poked a thin, almost invisible, hole in one of the packages. When she withdrew the file, it was covered with a dusting of powder. She licked her finger and ran it along the file. Then the taste test and the certainly: heroin. She'd tasted it in the ER at least twenty times.

David had alluded to her cargo, but had never come right out and told her. *He should have,* she thought. *He's put me and Marco in a dangerous situation. But then again. I had a choice, didn't I?*

She closed the bag, and returned to her compartment. Marco looked at her, a question in his eyes.

"You were right," she said, handing him the strapped bag. He stood on the seat and hefted it into the overhead.

"How much did you say we're getting for this grand adventure?" he asked.

Tamara slumped into her seat and stared out the window. "Not nearly enough. Not by half."

As their train pulled away from the platform, Tamara's trepidation had grown into something almost tangible. Although Marco appeared to take the prospect of the upcoming five day, seven thousand kilometer trip to Vladivostok in stride, she wasn't able to tamp down her fear.

Barely seven hours into the trip, and not yet dawn, Tamara asked Marco to fetch them food and beer from the station at Tyumen. While he was gone, and desperate now for a hit of calming nicotine, she lit up, despite knowing that smoking was prohibited on Russian trains and a stiff fine a possibility. She opened the long, lower window and bent over to blow away the evidence of her crime. It was her fourth in the last hour. *There goes my self-imposed limit of two a day.* The cigarette didn't help and neither did the food when Marco returned with kabobs and beer. She couldn't stomach the sight of the over-cooked meat wrapped in greasy paper. And the alcohol had the opposite effect she desired—it only heightened her dread, made her thinking fuzzy, and caused her sweat to stink like the guilty person she knew she was. She left their compartment and struggled down the corridor to the bathroom where she had a half-wash and changed her blouse. *If I survive, I swear I'll never do this again.*

Early that afternoon, at the stop in Omsk, she almost came apart when two militiamen joined her and Marco in their second-class compartment. Her panicked state reached a crescendo when the older soldier sat himself directly beneath the black-strapped bag, stored just above him in the overhead.

At that point, her terror turned to fatalism. *A lurch in the train, a sudden stop, and the bag will come tumbling down. It'll spill open onto his lap and reveal to the world my crime. Fuck it. I deserve it.*

The only thing that kept her sane was her decision *not* to take a pistol. Had she been carrying one, she would have tossed it and the bag of heroin off the moving train.

The soldiers seemed affable and tried to make conversation, but Tamara's monosyllabic responses soon shut down the small talk.

She was desperately tired but couldn't allow her exhausted body to doze while the militiamen shared their compartment. She spent most of the time wondering what could have possessed her to undertake this insanity. She personally knew two men and a woman who'd done time in Russian prisons. Each told her the same story: Vladimir Central and the IK-14 Prison for Women were indescribably horrible, the last places on earth anyone would want to get sent.

When the two soldiers finally disembarked in Novosibirsk, Tamara let out a breath she felt she'd been holding for days. Marco crossed over to her. He took a cushion, laid it on his lap, then took his mother by the shoulders and eased her down. "They're gone, Mom. You can relax."

They remained happily alone for the next two thousand kilometers—more than a day and a half of travel—until Irkutsk and the arrival of more compartment-mates: an elderly woman taking her grandson to Khabarovsk. The crone was a chatterbox who insisted on sharing recipes with Tamara. Marco and the grandson occupied themselves playing video games.

After the woman and her grandson left the train, Vladivostok was just another ten hours away.

"Courage, Mom. We'll make it," Marco said.

Tamara bit her lip and exhaled. "I don't know, son. I don't think I'm cut out for this."

"And if David asks for another 'favor'? What'll you say?"

"I'll thank him. And . . ."

"And?"

"Let me get to Vlad in one piece. I'll let you know then."

Near midnight at the end of their fifth day of travel, they rolled into Vladivostok. Tamara was punchy, sleep-deprived, buoyed only by the knowledge that she'd be able to hand off the bag in just a few minutes.

They made their way to the back of the terminal, to the mosaic of St. George near the building's eastern façade. They found a bench along a lamp-lit and snowy path. After dusting off the bench, they sat. It was now close to one a.m.

At a quarter past the hour, a man showed up. He was blond and good-looking. He wore a uniform of some kind under a full-length wool coat. He carried a brown bag with a heavy zipper and straps. He placed it on the ground, next to hers, then sat and turned to her. "Unusually shitty weather this year," he said.

She breathed a sigh of relief. *Thank god. The correct password.* She joyfully spoke the counter-password, "It's an American plot."

The man gave her a broad smile and a nod. "Good work," he said. He bent down and relieved her of almost twenty kilos of Afghani processed heroin.

Watching him carry away the illegal drug, Tamara relaxed for the first time in five days. The tension gone, her entire body went limp. She collapsed onto her son's shoulder and sobbed, "Never again."

David had arranged for their overnight at the Hyundai Hotel, one of Vladivostok's finest. Mother and son arrived there by gypsy cab just after two a.m. They entered an almost deserted lobby. Marco escorted his mother to the bar to eat whatever leftovers the barman might produce. After a throw-together meal, they took the elevator to their room on the third floor, bathed, and collapsed.

The two heroin mules slept until ten, enjoyed a sumptuous breakfast in the hotel's rooftop restaurant, and cabbed to the airport.

Five hours later, flying home over central Siberia, Tamara was feeling refreshed. The fear that had clutched at her heart during the train trip was gradually melting away, replaced by the knowledge that in a few hours, David would put into her hands one thousand, five hundred American dollars.

Next to her, Marco was absorbed in a video game.

She nudged him with her elbow. "We can afford the voc tech institute. Still interested, I hope."

"Carpentry," he answered, not leaving his game.

"It's a three-year course, you know."

He paused, looked over at her and smiled. "Shouldn't be a problem, should it? I mean, now that we're flush."

~~~

Although Anatoly Suvorov was psyched to co-pilot the maiden flight of Troika Aviation's new route to Alaska, he was totally crazed by what he had agreed to smuggle on board. He found no sympathy at home.

"You'll be fine, Toly," Sophia assured him. "You just hand the stuff to the guy in American customs. I mean, what could go wrong?"

"What could go wrong?" he shouted. "What if the guy's sick and not working that night and someone else has to check my bag? 'Holy shit,' he'd say. 'What do we have here? Looks like this Russian bozo is smuggling drugs.' What could go wrong, Soph? How 'bout everything."

She had stopped listening. She was trying on a new wool pullover she'd ordered from Aran Sweaters. She admired herself in a full-length mirror and spoke to his reflection. "Just do it, Toly. When you get back, we'll celebrate."

In the very early morning hours before that first flight, he made a stop at Vladivostok's central train station. He carried a heavy, brown canvas bag with a strong zipper and a set of black straps. He was crazy nervous, his head twitching back and forth, as if searching for a way out. *What the fuck am I doing? Sophia will spend the money as quickly as she gets her hands on it. And if I get nabbed . . .*

He walked to the back of the station and saw a woman

and a young man sitting on a bench. With relief, he noted that they'd brought with them a piece of luggage exactly matching his own. He walked up to the couple, placing his bag next to hers, and sat.

"Unusually shitty weather this year," he said, the words almost sticking in his parched mouth.

"It's an American plot," the woman answered.

Anatoly breathed a huge sigh. *Thank god. The correct password.* "Good work," he said. He sat for a moment, looked around, saw they were alone, then reached down and took her black-strapped bag. He rose and left quickly. He found a taxi to Knevichi International Airport. He boarded the Troika Aviation Airbus 330 with the rest of the flight crew and stowed his luggage. He then helped fly a planeload of passengers across the Bering Sea, fifty-three hundred kilometers to Alaska. He de-planed at Anchorage's Ted Stevens International and entered the airport's North Terminal. As he pushed a cart with his luggage, his heart was racing, sweat trickled down the nape of his neck. His breathing was labored. *Jail is waiting for me. God help me.*

He and the rest of the crew eased their way through Passport Control and followed the signs to US Customs. There he saw a K-9 handler. The man's dog, a shepherd, was actively sniffing the baggage of the just-arrived passengers. As Anatoly moved up in line, he exchanged a fleeting, if worried, smile with the man. The crewmembers who preceded had no trouble and as Anatoly shuffled toward the head of the line, the K-9 handler nonchalantly walked his dog to a group of three passengers at the other customs inspection area. The pilot's luggage went through without incident. He almost feinted with relief.

Clear of customs, his next planned stop was the first available bathroom. He entered a stall where he found a backpack hanging from the door hook. He spent several minutes repacking his luggage. He left the terminal and traveled by shuttle to the Sheraton Hotel in downtown Anchorage, feeling an intense need to let loose. The bellboy suggested Chilkoot Charlie's, a local watering hole. The pilot showered, popped a five mg Dexedrine tablet, and taxied to the bar. There, he found Olga, a Russian-speaking prostitute. He spent the night in her arms and between her legs.

When Anatoly returned to Vladivostok three days later, he stopped back at the Slavianski Bazaar, entered the dingy lobby and went up to the meshed-in front desk. The hotel clerk was smoking and reading from a worn paperback—poems by Pasternak. He looked up from his reading. "I heard everything went okay."

"Clockwork," Anatoly answered.

The desk clerk handed the pilot a fat envelope.

The smuggler took a cab to the Primorye Bank on Okeanski Street where he placed a thousand dollars in American one hundred dollar bills into a newly rented deposit box. The remaining two thousand dollars he'd take home. *Hopefully, I'll see some benefit before Sophia'll piss it all away.*

~~~

Petya Bondarchuk was living the dream. With the money the FSS border guard had been scamming over the past couple of years, he had been able to enhance not only his own dreary soldier's life, but the lives of his family.

He treated his father to a new stereo system and a high definition television. The old man, a former frontier guard himself, was thrilled at the gifts, despite knowing exactly how his son was finding the extra cash.

"Don't get too greedy, Petrushka," his father cautioned.

"You think you're floating in the clear, not a worry. Then, all of a sudden there's a knock on the door and the roof caves in. It's over. That's what happened to your uncle Nikita. Worked at Barshoo for years, that crossing with Mongolia. Spent money like a drunken Cossack. FSS caught him, sent him to Lefortovo for seven years. Killed him."

"Not to worry dad. I'm careful."

"Careful is good. Your wife, son? Does she know about any of this?"

"Well . . . kinda."

"Not good, Petrushka. Not good. The fewer people, the better. So be *super* careful. By the way, your sister called me, wants to know about Sochi again."

Petya grinned. The year before, he'd paid for his grumpy and overweight sister's vacation to Sochi, on the Black Sea. He'd splurged for an ocean view room at the Hotel Pullman, right on the beach. She came back tan, slightly less grumpy, but still overweight.

"She called me, too," he said. "Asked me if Sochi was going to be a 'regular thing.' I told her not to count on it."

Father and son laughed.

Petya's philanthropy also extended to people outside of his own family. Looking for a way to ingratiate himself with his girlfriend's parents, he presented the potato-farming couple with a workable MTZ-80 tractor. They were delighted, even though he knew they harbored a deep mistrust of him because of his Ukrainian roots.

Nor did he stint on himself. He traded in his Vespa for a 1969 BMW motorcycle with a sidecar. He and Svetlana regularly rode east of Chelyabinsk, cruising the city's 'Lake District.'

And, best of all, when Svetlana accepted his proposal, he moved out of the dismal FSS barracks at the border crossing at

Bugristoye and rented a one-bedroom flat in Troitsk, a city of 90,000, just up the road from the frontier. The flat included a gas stove, refrigerator, carpets, and curtains.

He quickly arranged for a landline phone in their apartment, something he'd always associated with being an adult.

"Let the kids use their smartphones," he told Svetlana. "This is a real phone, just like my folks had."

His fiancé smiled but continued using her Samsung 5.

Svetlana worked as a teller in the Russian Agricultural Bank in Troitsk. When, by chance, she discovered his *Crime and Punishment* cash hideaway, she convinced him to rent one of her bank's deposit boxes. She went with him when he put eight thousand, two hundred and twenty American dollars into their new, jointly held security box.

"So much safer here, Petya," she told him. "No one can steal from us."

They were married in the summer in front of Chelyabinsk's World War II victory memorial, a Soviet-era tank. They honeymooned in Moscow, first time for either of them in the capital city. They ooohed at the Faberge eggs in the Kremlin armory, gawked at St. Basil's onion domes on Red Square, and waited in line for an hour for the obligatory one minute shuffle-through, in and out of Lenin's mausoleum.

"He's so short, Petya. I always thought Lenin would be way taller. And he's yellow. Why is he so yellow?"

"Weird," he said.

~~~

David Osinchuk rushed into Tamara's apartment and greeted her with a ferocious hug.

"You're back. You look great. I heard from Vlad. A smooth

meeting with the pick-up guy. Everything apparently went as planned. Right?"

"Right. Except I was scared to death the entire time. Didn't sleep. Couldn't eat. Then these two militiamen decided to camp in our compartment for over eight hours. I could hardly breathe."

"But here you are. Job well done." He took a fat, rubber-banded wad of bills from his pocket and handed it to her.

Tamara gave him the slightest of smiles, unbanded the bills and proceeded to count out a quantity of American twenties.

"Twenties are easier to deal with," he said as she made the tally.

"It's all here?" she asked.

He retreated a step and looked at her, half-frowning, half-amused. "Did you think I'd cheat you, Tama?"

"No, David. I knew you'd be good for it. I just was never sure *I'd* be here to collect. It seemed to me much more likely that I'd be arrested, that I'd be spending the next twenty years in some forced labor camp in Siberia, working next to Navalny."

He laughed and embraced her again, nuzzling into her hair. "I'd come visit you every week. Promise," he whispered. "They allow conjugal visits now."

She shoved him away. "You beast. I'm in the slammer and you'd be free? Don't make me laugh. I'd give you up in a heartbeat if it meant a lighter sentence." She couldn't help grinning. "And I would, too."

"I absolutely believe you." He took her hands, raised them to his lips, and kissed her fingers. "So. Will you be ready to do it again in two months?"

"Maybe."

"Maybe? Why the hesitation?"

"I'll only agree if we have a first-class compartment. All

to ourselves. No more soldiers. No more anyone. Just Marco and me in some place I can lock."

"Easily arranged."

~~~~

Major Fred Smithson, forty-five-years-old, short and wiry with floppy ears and a pointy nose, sought out the man he was replacing. When he found him, Colonel Tucker Cranston was alone, stretched out on a wooden picnic table in back of Bagram's officer's mess. His eyes were closed, a smile on his lips, his breathing slow and regular. A very warm sun beat down on him.

Not wanting to disturb the man, Smithson sat on the ground, back to the building, waiting for the officer to stir. When Tucker began to rouse, Smithson stood and came abreast of the bench. "Colonel Cranston, sir?" No immediate reaction. He repeated himself.

Tucker sat up and turned to the man. "Major Smithson?"

"Yes, sir. Smithson, sir."

They shook and Tucker waved to the bench, inviting his replacement to sit.

"You just get here?"

"Yes sir. Me and my 1st Cavalrymen landed two hours ago. I've been looking for you. Hoping you might . . . ."

Tucker ran his hands through his hair then massaged his face. "Hoping I might fill you in on what the fuck you'll be doing here in God-forsaken Afghanistan."

Smithson laughed once and nodded. "Yes sir. Exactly."

"Tell me about yourself, Major. Your background. Family. Can I call you Fred?"

"Please do, sir."

"I'm Tucker."

"Thanks. I'm married. Three kids. We live outside of Waco, close to Fort Hood. This is my sixth overseas posting. One near Tikrit, three in wonderful downtown Baghdad, then ten months at CentCom. Now I'm here." He looked skyward and spat out, "Christ."

Tucker chuckled. "I appreciate your attitude, Fred. Sums up the supreme shambles that is the country you've come to democratize. Or pacify. Or save. Pick one of 'em." Tucker paused. "Hope I haven't overstepped."

"Not at all, sir. I have few illusions."

Tucker took a deep breath. "Almost a trillion dollars spent, near twenty-four hundred KIAs on our side. No telling how many of the locals we've been shooting at since oh-one have been killed." He frowned and shook his head. "You were at CentCom. Ground Zero for the self-delusion and bullshit about 'progress' in Afghanistan. One step forward, two steps back is how we ought to mark that 'progress.' The brass there can't tell the difference between a mirage and an oasis. You still with me, Fred?"

"Every step, Tucker."

"Maybe you'll do okay here. I hope so. Here's the inside skinny. Things here never change. *Ever.* There's corruption at every level of the Afghani government. Just like in Baghdad. You were there, you know. Exact same thing here. Everyone's on the take. People's loyalties are to family, to tribe, and to religion. In that order. And maybe, just maybe there's a teensy bit of loyalty to their government. And don't forget, we have another record poppy harvest on the way. Your skepticism is well placed."

Smithson stretched his neck, hunched his shoulders. "Granted it's supremely fucked. No one at CentCom—at least in private conversation—will say otherwise. In public, however, as you've all too correctly noted, they have to spin a different story, one that reflects this administration's skewered priorities." Smithson closed his eyes. "So tell me, please, Tucker. What should I do for the next twelve months? How do I insure the safety of my guys?" He opened his eyes and stared at the man whose job he was taking.

"A good question. And for my mind, the *only* question. Here's how. Watch out for green on blue. That'll be our supposed allies shooting at us. Wear a sidearm at all times. Keep the *gung-ho* in your duffle bag, and . . ." Tucker hesitated, smiling inside, "and there's an Afghani cook who works here in the mess. Right here in this building behind us. He'll find you. When he does, listen to him very carefully, trust him, and do what he says. He won't steer you wrong. Name is Jabari Hajji Murad. He's related to the local war lord."

"An Afghani cook? Really?" Smithson chuckled. "And I'm supposed to listen to him and trust him?"

Tucker looked directly into the dark eyes of Major Fred Smithson. "That's exactly, precisely, what I'm advising you to do. Listen to him, you prosper. Don't listen, you don't prosper. It's just that simple. Please believe me, Fred. For your wife's sake. And for your kids. Please."

~~~

They were almost clones of each other. Both short, skinny, swarthy, frizzy-haired with pock-marked skin that their 1960s sideburns and sparse mustaches didn't do much to hide. They were both in their late twenties. Both had dropped out of school by the sixth grade, and both had numerous family members either behind bars, awaiting trial, or scarred, crippled, or dead from stab wounds, bullets to the body, beatings with blunt instruments, and, in the case of one uncle, tossed from a helicopter cruising at four thousand feet.

They were Sultan Abdulin and Chingiz Nabiyev, a pair of Kazakh small-time criminals born and raised in Chelyabinsk. What set them apart from most of their countrymen was that the two dared to dream dreams no small time Kazakh criminal ought to dream: they were plotting to rob—and kill if necessary—one of David Osinchuk's Vladivostok-bound mules.

They'd come up with idea when Sultan traveled to that Pacific Coast city with his *own* very small load of illegal substance—nine kilos of hashish. As he waited in the Red Flag Tea Room for the outbound TransSiberian, he spotted Osinchuk, known to him and to Chelyabinsk's criminal underground as a person of stature, and someone with whom one did not lightly fuck. But this was different: his mule was a woman. *Easy pickings,* thought Sultan.

The Kazakh noticed Osinchuk carrying a bag of some weight. He took a seat next to a woman and a young man. Sultan watched as Osinchuk placed his bag on the floor next to the woman's bag, one that looked identical to hers. The Kazakh, himself having been involved in several such schemes, realized at once what was afoot. And when Osinchuk stood up and reached for *her* bag, leaving *his,* Sultan patted himself on the back. *Knew it all the time. Saw it coming.*

Sultan understood full well the level of crime at which David Osinchuk operated and guessed that there was something in the bag perhaps even more precious than his own hashish. *Meth, maybe? Heroin? Opioids? Fentanyl?*

He phoned Chingiz, his partner in crime, and filled him in. "Since I'm going to Vladivostok anyway," Sultan said, "I'll keep an eye on her. Wherever she gets off, I'll follow her."

"Just what I would do," agreed Chingiz.

Although Sultan's compartment was two carriages down from Osinchuk's mule, he managed to be near her whenever the train stopped. During the next five days at stops in Tyumen, Omsk, Chita, and Khabarovsk, either the woman herself or the young man got off, but never together and never carrying the black-strapped bag. Sultan deduced that the one who remained on board guarded the valuable cargo.

They rode together all the way to Vladivostok. Sultan followed them off the train to the back of the rail terminal where they sat themselves on a bench. It was close to two in the morning, foggy and damp. He watched and waited twenty meters away, hiding in a clump of bushes.

Within minutes, a man carrying an identical bag came up to her, spoke briefly, sat for a moment, then picked up *her* bag, leaving his own.

Sultan gloated. *Amateurs.* He didn't bother following the man. *Guy's wearing a uniform, maybe he's armed. Let's just scope this out for the time being.* He taxi-trailed the woman and the young man to the Hyundai Hotel. There, the Kazakh was able to bribe the desk clerk and learn the woman's name. He phoned Chingiz.

"Chingo. It's all good. Her name is Tamara Stoikova. She's staying a night here in Vlad with her son. They handed off the bag already. Find out everything you can about her."

"Will do, Sulty. Good work."

~~~

Two days before he and his men were to leave Afghanistan, Tucker and Jabari drove the now familiar road to Shaikh Murad's compound. *For the last time,* Tucker hoped.

"My nephew, Hakeem, he sad see you go," the driver said. "Me also."

"Thanks, Jabari," Tucker said, unanswered questions bumping around in his brain. *I wonder how you'd treat me if I hadn't sold myself to the Shaikh. How did you treat Contreras? Did you know he was going to be shot? Do you know the shooter? Did you yourself, perhaps, pull the trigger?*

They stopped, as usual, in front of the steps that led up to the warlord's fortified home. And, as usual, Hakeem was there, this time with a pair of bulging woven bags by his side.

Hakeem took Tucker's hands in his own. "Congratulations, *Lieutenant Colonel* Cranston. Jabari told me. The Shaikh and I are pleased that the information we provided might have helped in securing your promotion."

"Without that intel, Hakeem, I'd still be a major. I'm grateful. Please thank your grandfather for me."

"I'll be sure and do that. Meanwhile, you are in your final few days with us. What plans have you and your family made?"

"When I return to Alaska, I'll still have a few months to serve. I'll have put in my twenty and don't plan to re-up. I'll call it a career. I have a degree in history. In the fall, I'll be enrolling at university and looking to get a high school teaching certificate. Something I've wanted for years."

Hakeem nodded his pleasure at the news. "You'll remind them about Bismarck's failings as Kaiser Wilhelm's chancellor?"

Tucker grinned. "I might mention it, but I'm not sure it's proper to cite my own dissertation."

"Don't be shy, Colonel. I told you how much we appreciated your insights."

"Thank you, Hakeem."

"I'm glad you've taken the time to bid us farewell. And

I am equally pleased to tell you that your replacement, Major Smithson, visited us yesterday."

Tucker guarded his silence. He knew that Smithson had come here the day before, but hadn't yet heard the results of his meeting with the Shaikh.

"A very bright gentleman. Very agreeable," Hakeem concluded with the barest of smiles.

Tucker thought his host's smile a bit too smug, as if signaling to him, 'Here's one more American we've been able to corrupt.' Tucker didn't respond.

Hakeem gestured to the two bags at his feet, filled with apples.

Tucker's heart softened. "You remembered. Thank you, Hakeem. My wife will be very pleased."

"I'm glad. How soon will you see her?"

"We leave in two days. A day to travel and we'll be home in Alaska."

"So, three days from now. Wonderful. I'm sincerely happy for you, Colonel. The Shaikh is, too. He would like to speak with you. Please." Hakeem guided his guest up the stairs.

In the greenhouse, the old man was sitting and talking with his great-grandson, Akbar. At the sight of the American, both Afghanis rose and advanced toward Tucker. Akbar arrived first. He carried a large envelope.

"For you, Colonel Cranston," the young man said in English, presenting the gift, a broad smile on his face.

"Can I open it now, Akbar?"

"Yes, please, Colonel. Now."

Tucker opened the unsealed envelope and removed a set of large color prints: three showing Akbar riding a stallion in the midst of a crowd of horses, playing *buz kashi*. The fourth and last photo showed only the young man's leg, ready to mount, with booted foot in a stirrup. And attached to the boot, a Mexican spur with a beaten silver rowel.

Hakeem and the Shaikh had come to stand next to Akbar. They were smiling proudly.

"You like my pictures, Colonel?" Akbar asked.

For all of Tucker's bitter feelings, for all his guilt and self-loathing for what he'd done, and for all the anger directed at this family for how cleverly they had tempted him, he felt himself tearing up. In English, and slowly so the boy would understand, "I love this photo, Akbar. I will show it to my family. I will put it on the wall of my home. Thank you." He opened his arms and gave the boy a long hug.

The Shaikh spoke a few words to Akbar, who bowed to Tucker and left the three men.

"We sit, Colonel," Murad offered.

They arrayed themselves around a table laden with fruits and nuts. Hakeem spooned a portion of pomegranate arils into a bowl and handed it to the Shaikh.

"Colonel?" Hakeem asked, indicating the ruby-red seeds.

"Absolutely. One of my favorite fruits."

Handing the bowl to Tucker, Hakeem said, "The Shaikh thanks you, Colonel, for sending us Major Smithson."

Tucker only nodded to the Shaikh. *It was send him or he might take a sniper round in the throat. Not much choice.*

"I've told my grandfather that you'll be home, back in Alaska, in three days. He wishes you a safe flight and a happy reunion with your wife and children."

"Tell the Shaikh that I thank him for his good wishes. I remember at our first meeting when we spoke about our families." He looked at the old man. "You are right, Shaikh Murad. Family is all."

Following Hakeem's translation, Murad placed a hand

over his heart, smiled, and in English, "Family all, sir." Then Murad stood, signaling the end of the conversation.

Tucker put down his bowl of fruit. "Well . . ." he also rose, ". . . time for me to get back to Bagram. Lots to do before we head out."

Murad extended a hand. Tucker took it and wondered, once again, how such an enfeebled looking man of eighty-five had such a vise-like grip. Tucker turned to Hakeem. "Please tell your grandfather that I have learned much during my time here." He paused. "Some pleasant, some not so pleasant. But I value all of our time together, nonetheless."

After Hakeem's translation, Murad said, again in English and nodding slightly toward his guest, "Colonel Cranston, sir. You very wise man."

Tucker suddenly and unexpectedly felt saddened that his time with this family was coming to an end, even as he recognized their corrupting influence on him. "Thank you, Shaikh Murad. You are . . ." he searched for the proper word, ". . . you are generous."

Murad's smile indicated he understood. "Good bye, Colonel," he said, then turned and left the greenhouse.

A minute later Tucker and Hakeem were walking down the steps toward Jabari's waiting Jeep.

"Grandfather respects you, Colonel Cranston. As do I," Hakeem said. "My son more than respects you. He truly reveres you. I'm glad he got the chance to meet you." Hakeem looked off into the shaded oasis. "All of us here know how we used your good offices, Colonel. We won't pretend that our relationship was based on anything more than my family's business interests. We are not hypocrites here. We recognize that we are lawbreakers. We know it. We admit it. We are not necessarily proud of the fact, but neither do we shun the truth of the situation. Please believe me when I tell you that both grandfather and I have sincere and great affection for you. And we will always and forever value our brief time together."

Tucker was at a loss for words. He felt himself—despite himself—again growing misty.

They walked down the rest of the stairs in silence as Tucker digested this interchange. He was grateful that there had been an acknowledgement of how the Murads had used him. *Bottom line, however—I allowed myself to be used. No question about it.*

They came to Jabari's Jeep. The two bags of apples were in the back seat. Tucker turned toward Hakeem, nodded once, then got in the Jeep. A minute later, he was driving out of the warlord's compound.

~~~

Anatoly Suvorov viewed his life from polar opposite vantages. At this present moment, on the Thai island of Phuket, relaxing in a chaise lounge under a warm, winter sun, he was tolerably contented. He and Sofia were in the sixth day of a seven-day tour package. Tomorrow, they'd return home in time for him to fly to Alaska. Why shouldn't he be happy? How many of his countrymen have ever vacationed in Thailand, worrying about nothing more than what delicious fish they'd order for lunch?

Added to that, Anatoly was now a proud father. His almost year-old son, Marat, was home in Vladivostok in the care of his doting in-laws. Sophia had deigned to become pregnant only after he agreed to hand over to her the entire proceeds of his smuggling ventures. He'd kept hidden from her the thousand he skimmed every two weeks.

With her part of the illegally earned money, Sophia

shopped. And shopped. It seemed to Anatoly that she was always buying things, needed or not. Mostly not, he thought. He warned her about being too obvious with her spending. "Someone's gonna start wondering where the hell the money's coming from," he told his wife. "They'll ask about me and discover that I'm a pilot, making only so much. How'll you explain all the shit you buy?"

She hardly acknowledged him. "I'm not worried, so why should you be?"

Because his wife's profligacy added to his fear of discovery, he began to seriously consider escape, ideally into the arms of Olga, his Anchorage sweetie. Hardly a day passed that he didn't allow his imagination to take flight: he and Olga setting up home in some warm, foreign country, maybe even here in Thailand.

He'd never spent any of his deposit box money in Russia. Since Sophia knew, to the ruble, how much he made as a pilot, any irregular expenditures on his part would immediately draw her laser-like focus. In America, however, a different story, with Olga the recipient of his generosity. His twice-monthly visits to Anchorage saw him lavishing his favorite prostitute with dinners at the area's best restaurants, over-nights at the Alyeska Prince Hotel with skiing the next day, the occasional visit to the town's furriers. And, of course, baubles. Many baubles.

But despite being able to vacation abroad with his wife, despite finally having a son to carry his name forward, and despite his Olga-interludes, Anatoly was *not* a contented man. His job as a drug trafficker had turned him into a ball of nerves, unable to sleep through the night, unable to shake a persistent sense of doom. After all, he was an international smuggler. Of heroin. And if caught—on either end of his bi-monthly flights—he'd be spending most of the rest of his life in prison. If he were taken in Russia, it'd probably be Vladimir Central. The thought of it made him concentrate on keeping his butt cheeks squeezed together. And if he were grabbed in America, well . . . he wasn't sure what prisons there were like, but he'd recently found himself Googling stories about Attica, about Sing Sing, about Alcatraz, about Riker's Island. Dreadful stories.

From his chaise lounge, a deeply troubled Anatoly Suvorov watched as his wife emerged from the hotel's heated pool. She took off her bathing cap, allowing her thick blond hair to spill across her still damp shoulders. She toweled off, put on a robe, then sat. She took up her latest reading, *'Fifty Shades of Gray.'* Before opening the book, she put on her sunglasses and announced, "Next vacation, Toly, Greece. I hear Rhodes is wonderful."

He didn't respond.

She turned to him, "Rhodes, next vacation. Hear me, Toly?"

He slumped deeper into the chaise lounge. *Olga. Olga.*

~~~

If her first foray into drug trafficking had been a heart-stopping fright, Tamara's second trip to Vladivostok was a delight. David met them in the Red Flag Tea Room well before their departure. She and Marco took possession of their first-class compartment, locked themselves in, spread out, and successfully remained in isolation the entire trip. The bag-switch in back of the Vladivostok train terminal went smoothly and their over-night at the Hyundai Hotel followed by their flight back home were happily unremarkable.

It was on their return to Chelyabinsk that provided unexpected excitement. When she phoned David, letting him know of their arrival, he asked that she grab a cab and join him at an unknown address, 47 Chapayev Street, near Smolino Lake. He met her on the sidewalk outside the five-story apartment building.

"Where's Marco?" he asked.

"He was going to see some young lady. He'll catch up later. Why are we meeting here? What is this place?"

"I have your money. Come, I'll pay you inside,"

"Inside? Who lives here?"

He looked at her and shrugged, "Why, you and Marco do. And maybe me, too." He walked up the stoop stairs, leaving her frozen on the sidewalk below. "C'mon," he urged. "You need to start arranging, unpacking. I've moved all of your stuff out of that chicken coop you were living in. It's all in cartons upstairs. And I've taken the liberty of ordering a couple things, although you'll still need to buy most of the furnishings. I've paid you an extra two thousand dollars. We'll need nice stuff."

Climbing the steps to take his hand, Tamara was overcome. "We? We'll need?" she asked. He didn't reply.

She was silent as they took the lift to the fifth floor and entered the apartment. As David had indicated, her and Marco's few possessions were in a pile of boxes in the center of a large and bare living room. Hanging from one wall was a Samsung 65-inch television, its flat screen still wrapped in plastic. In the kitchen stood a huge new refrigerator, humming quietly. She went and opened it and saw only a single bottle of champagne. She read the label. "Veuve Cliquot. We must be celebrating something."

"There's a lot to celebrate. We'll need a long couch right here in front of the TV. Big enough for the three of us."

"Three of us? 'We,' you said before." She moved closer to him.

"One more thing. I almost forgot," he said, reaching into

his pocket and smiling as he brought out a small velvet covered box.

"What the hell, David?" she whispered, reaching for the box.

He held it tightly in his palm and laughed as she greedily began prying his fingers away, while with his other hand, he gently moved a lock of hair off her face. He allowed her to open his fingers.

"David. This better be what I think it is."

"Of course it is, Tama. I've wanted for a long time to make an honest woman of you."

She punched him lovingly in the stomach, opened the box, saw a large emerald ring, gasped in astonishment, and without hesitation, slipped it onto the fourth finger of her right hand. "It's gorgeous," she managed through tears. She took his face in both of her hands. "It's you and me from now on, David."

"It's only and always been about you and me since I woke up in intensive care, Tama. You know that." He drew her to him.

She smiled then pushed him back, not allowing him a complete embrace. "And all this," she waved at the apartment, "the new flat, the TV, the fridge, this giant stone, this is all supposed to make an *honest* woman of me? If you were really serious, you wouldn't have tempted me into being your mule in the first place."

He laughed out loud. "Remind me how hard I had to try, Tama. And how hard did you actually resist? You were easily seduced. But you're right. Yes, you're a mule, but you're my *favorite* mule. You're my *favorite* person. And as I've told you before, you don't have to do this. You can quit right now, right this moment, if you want."

She kissed him full on the mouth, then nestled into his

arms. "I'm thinking about it. Really. I'll do a few more trips, then decide." She disengaged. "But right now, I'm writing you a shopping list. You go to the market, I call Marco, let him know where he lives, then we unpack, make dinner, and think about furnishing this place. I'm not sure the two thousand extra is going to cover what we need."

"What *we* need?"

"That's what I said."

Marco was delighted to be best man. At the reception, he suggested to his mother that he might like to help out David in his business.

Tamara, champagne glass in one hand, grabbed her son by the collar with the other. "Over my dead body. Put that notion out of your brain. You're at tech school, and that's where you're gonna stay." He laughed as she pulled him closer so they were face to face. "Got it, buddy?"

Marco embraced his mother. "Mom, I was kidding. Just wanted to see how'd you react. It's bad enough I'm a part-time drug courier. I don't need more." He held her at arm's length, smiling.

Tamara pointed with her head across the crowded hall. "Why don't you go introduce yourself to Tali, my boss's daughter. I think she likes you."

Marco followed his mother's gaze. "Likes me? Tali's crazy for me. Been telling me that for three months now."

Tamara gave Marco's cheek a gentle pinch. "My secretive son. What else are you doing behind my back?"

"Best you don't know."

During the next three trips east, Tamara and Marco experienced a few minor hiccups: a compartment door that wouldn't easily lock on the third trip; a derailment of another train ahead of them on the fourth causing a delayed meeting in Vladivostok; Marco becoming deathly ill the fifth time after eating fish sandwiches they bought from a vendor in Omsk.

Tamara saved enough to pay for her son's tuition at the Yuri Gagarin Voc-Tech Institute where he enrolled in a course of rough and finish carpentry. When the school's director grew concerned about Marco missing classes every other month, she soothed his worries by donating a variable speed drill press and a band saw.

Their new home on Chapayev Street was within walking distance of Smolino Lake, ideal for rowing and picnics in the summer, skating and cross-country skiing in the winter.

The neighbors wondered about her husband. They delicately probed about his occasional coming and going at all hours of the day and night. Tamara explained that he was a busy motorcycle mechanic, owned his own garage. They remained dubious but when she offered very excellent and free medical advice, their suspicions were put aside.

~~~

Colonel Tucker Cranston arrived back in Alaska one year and five days after leaving home for his final combat tour. Three Hercules aircraft carrying him and his battalion landed at Joint Base Elmendorf Richardson around noon. They were deluged by joyful family members, and following a short welcome home ceremony by the base commander, Tucker and his men were dismissed and encouraged to enjoy ten days of leave.

It was a glorious and sunny afternoon. Hardly a breeze, hardly a cloud. He and Luellen were alone on Tucker's second day home. They steered their mounts toward the Susitna River. From this vantage, the Glenn Highway, miles away, was invisible, the sound of traffic undetectable. They stopped on a low bluff, the shin-deep and meandering Susitna river thirty feet below. A pair of hawks wheeled slowly overhead. The couple dismounted and found seats on the ground. They leaned against smooth boulders. A comfortable silence surrounded them. Neither felt a pressing need to break it. Finally . . .

"We had a great time in India," Luellen said.

He laughed, looked at his wife and took her hand. "Did we ever."

"Despite the fact that you scared the shit outta me."

"You're not easily scared, Lulu. You're a tough cookie."

"And Switzerland was lovely. The woman at the bank, Giselle Bisset, invited me—and you, of course—to come back and visit. She showed me photos of her home. Humongous chalet on Lake Leman. Said we'd be welcome any time. Interested?"

"Sure, but it'd have to be sooner rather than later. Like I told you, soon as I finish my service, I want to start working toward my credential. So if we're going to go, it'll have to be in that small window, about five weeks long."

"We might visit our money. Something over a hundred and eighty grand, right?" She smiled at the thought.

"Hundred and eighty-four and change. I checked just before we left Bagram."

"So you come back safely to us with all that cash *and* two bags of apples."

"A parting gift from Hakeem, the war lord's grandson." Tucker paused in thought. "An intriguing guy. I'm actually glad I met him."

"Even though he corrupted you?"

Tucker shook his head back and forth. "Sweetheart. I had

no choice. I'll tell you why sometime, but not right now. It's a rough story."

"What about the letter that was waiting for you? It came two weeks ago. Hand written but no return address. Just a Utah postmark. What gives?"

"From Jed McHenry, the guy I replaced at Bagram. He was the one who told me about Murad, told me to trust him, told me I'd be better off if I did."

"And you are, aren't you? We are."

"Yes, we are. I guess we are. I'm not super proud of myself, but I'm happy for our secret Swiss account."

"Amen. So how come there wasn't a return address?"

Tucker hesitated, tossed a pebble off the bluff. "He doesn't want to be found. He's hiding out in a houseboat on Lake Powell, in Utah or Arizona. Big lake. Lots of places to hunker down. Doesn't want Murad to find him and extract further favors."

Luellen turned to him, a worried look on her face, her body rigid. "What about us, Tuck? I mean, what if Murad got in touch? Wanted you to do . . . whatever. You couldn't refuse, could you?"

Tucker picked up several more pebbles and began lobbing them into the river below. He answered his wife's question with a shrug.

"Tuck? Talk to me."

"We live about as far from Shaikh Murad as is possible and still be on the same planet. No way he'd be in touch."

~~~

"I thought we settled this already," a very annoyed Tamara said. "Before that first trip to Vlad, I told you I wouldn't take a gun."

David Osinchuk sat in their kitchen, finishing the last of

the pelmeni and sour cream Tamara had prepared. He'd waited until Marco had left for the evening, uneasy about broaching the sensitive subject, especially after his wife had so vocally objected to the idea months earlier.

"I know we talked about it, Tama, and I remember your decision. But things are getting a little weird."

"Weird? What's that supposed to mean, weird?"

"It means *both* the fucking Kazakhs *and* the fucking Azeris are wanting a bigger slice of the trade. They're putting pressure on my boss."

"Didn't you tell me that the Afghani guy, what's his name, had things under control?"

"Murad. That's what I thought, too, until last week." He hesitated. "There was some shooting out in Pershino, by the Red and White Grocery. A drive-by. No one got hurt. I think it was just a couple warning shots."

Tamara's face hardened. She got up and left the kitchen, went to their bedroom, and slammed the door behind her.

He didn't dare follow her. When she'd been in there for half an hour, he knocked softly.

"Tama, come talk. Please."

She opened the door and stormed out, went to the kitchen and put the kettle on. With her back to him, she said, "Two things, David. One. I won't carry a gun. And two. We've talked about me quitting. After this Friday's trip, we're going to sit down and make a decision. Understand?"

He'd followed her into the kitchen and now came up behind her. He gently placed his hands on her shoulders. "Got it."

She shrugged off his hands, made herself a mug of tea and took it back into the bedroom.

~~~

Book 3
February - March 2019

Sasha was in a lousy mood. Had she been in a better frame of mind, she might have admired the view from her Hotel Ukraina window: eight floors below, the Moscow River meandering around three sides of the building. A building—despite the current Radisson owners' insistent denial—that was commissioned in 1947 by Joseph Stalin himself.

She glowered at the two people standing in front of her. "Minister Konovalov promised me there would be at least four of you, maybe more," she growled. "Where the fuck are the rest?"

A woman and a man in their late twenties stood squirming on the suite's deep pile, living room carpet. She was round and geeky. He was thin and geeky. They both wore glasses, both wanted desperately to smoke, and both had hair that cried out for attention. His was straw blond, spiky, and unkempt, while hers was dark brown and crammed into a huge uneven ball bunched on her nape. They wore casual American attire—Jeans, pullovers, and Adidas. Neither rushed to answer the question thrown at them by this pissed off American cop. The young woman raised her eyebrows to the man, urging him on. He shrugged and turned self-consciously to Sasha, speaking in English, "I didn't know we would be more. Only two of us got assigned last week."

"Bullshit," Sasha spat out. "Konovalov promised that I would have someone physically close to me at all times. Someone who can come get me when things go south. Which one of you is that person? And answer me in Russian."

Shuffling her feet, the woman looked up, and in Russian, "I am Vera Yaroslavna Chekovskaya. Please call me Vera. I'm your tech support. I've brought those three large pieces of luggage in the entryway. They're filled with all the gear I thought we'd need."

"Great." Sasha glared at the man. "And you are?"

"Martyn Pavlovich Shevchenko. Martyn. I do all of the coordination—transport, food and lodging, even safe houses and an escape plan. Any tasks at all."

Sasha leaned back in her chair. "Shevchenko? A Ukrainian name? How'd a Ukrainian land a job in a Russian ministry?"

He sniffed. "Just talented, I guess."

"We'll see about that. Please tell me that one of you is a Special Forces commando and you come heavily armed. Please."

Stares back and forth again until Vera spoke. "Sorry. Neither of us is trained in weapons, so it looks like we don't qualify for your protection unit."

Sasha covered her eyes and let her head roll back. *On my own. Again. Unarmed in Russia. Unh-uh. That ain't gonna happen.* She opened her eyes, rose and walked deliberately toward Martyn. "Coordinator, huh?"

He took a step back. "Yes, ma'am."

She jabbed a finger his way. "OK, Martyn, coordinate this. Here's your first job. You are to go immediately to Konovalov and let him know that since he's short-changed me on my protection, I'll need to protect *myself.*" She looked at her watch. "It's now ten-fifteen. If in the next five hours I don't receive an efficient handgun with a ton of ammo, I'm on the first plane out of Russia. And Konovalov can keep his promised payment and shove it up his ass. Got it?"

Martyn retreated another step. "Y . . . yes, ma'am. Got it."

"Just so I'm sure, repeat the entire message back to me. Word for word."

He did.

"Excellent. Beat it now and convey my message just as I spoke it to you." She turned to Vera. "And you, while he's gone, you'll fill me in on what's in those suitcases." She looked at Martyn, still standing there. "Well? The fuck you waiting for? Go do the errand I just sent you on."

Wide-eyed, Martyn grabbed his briefcase and fled the room.

Vera hid a smile and walked to the room's entryway. She rolled one of the large suitcases into the living room. "Mind if I smoke?" she asked.

"Go ahead."

She lit up. "Want one?"

"Don't smoke any more, but thanks."

Vera dropped to her knees and started unpacking, the lit cigarette dangling from her lips. The room soon filled up with harsh smoke. Sasha cracked a window. "Maybe next time in the corridor?"

Vera nodded an OK, coughing.

"You think there might be a connection between your smoking and your hacking?" Sasha asked.

Vera shrugged. "Almost certainly."

Sasha laughed. "What's your background?"

"I'm a graduate of the Moscow Institute of Electronic Technology. I also teach there part-time. We consider the place superior to anything in your Silicon Valley."

"You think your institute has bragging rights, huh? We'll see. What did you study?"

Vera reached for an ashtray, laid her cigarette down, and

took five various sized sets of Zeiss monoculars and binoculars from the suitcase. She passed a pair to Sasha. "Three years in the Department of Microdevices and Technical Cybernetics." She gave Sasha a confident smile. "Most of the gear we'll be needing, I can order from the Ministry, make from scratch, borrow and adapt, or if I have to, steal. Some stuff, naturally, is off limits."

Sasha took the binoculars to the window and adjusted them. "These are great. I can see the Bolshoi. And next to it, if I know Moscow, ought to be the Lubianka, your country's most notorious prison. My grandfather used to tell me that from the Lubianka's basement, you can see all the way to Siberia."

"An old joke. Not really funny then. Not funny now. We're not even going to think about that place. We're going to keep it positive."

"I like your confidence. But if you're as talented as you say you are, what are you doing working for the Ministry of Justice?" Sasha laid the binoculars next to the other sets on the floor. "Why aren't you part of that hackers' group, the one that influenced our election a few years back?"

Vera removed two shotgun microphones from the suitcase and began mounting one on its stand. "You mean the GRU hackers? Those dicks?"

"I guess those are the dicks I mean."

"Actually, they wanted me. Asked me to come and help them out with encryption. I wasn't interested." She reached for her cigarette, saw it had gone out, and left it in the ashtray.

"How come?"

"Too many horny guys. Too much machismo. I would've been only the third woman in that group of over a hundred men. No fun."

Sasha nodded her head in sympathy.

Over the next hour, Vera brought out and demonstrated

a variety of Canon, Olympus, and Sony gear—camcorders, cameras, and voice-activated audio recorders.

Sasha waved at the gear arrayed in front of her. "Hold it a second, Vera. You told me that the place you studied was better than anything in Silicon Valley. Yet all this stuff, every bit of it so far, is foreign-made. Nothing Russian here, nothing to rival Silicon Valley."

"True enough, but now have a look at these, Russian made." Vera took out the last item in the suitcase—a small hinged box that she opened and turned for inspection.

~~~

First Officer Anatoly Suvorov arrived back in Russia feeling greatly relieved to be on his home turf. The wholly unexpected meeting with the two cops in the Anchorage hotel room had seriously unnerved him. He still had the yips.

His wife, Sophia, expecting the return of a jubilant husband following a successful bit of smuggling was dismayed to see him strangely un-buoyant. She ignored her son, who was pulling on her apron, crying to watch *The Flying Ship,* a Russian cartoon she had just turned off. She walked toward her husband, still standing in the doorway.

"Toly," she said, "you look so edgy. Why the long face? Did everything go okay?"

When he didn't immediately answer, Sophia's eyes narrowed. "And the money. Where's the two thousand? Have you picked it up yet?"

The pilot staggered into the apartment. He wore a weepy expression: mouth turned down, chin trembling. "Haven't picked it up yet. Problems, Sophia."

"Problems?" she repeated, an edge in her voice. She

grabbed at her son and pushed him toward the bedroom. He resisted, howling. "Shut it, Marat," she threatened, squeezing his shoulder.

In fear, the toddler slunk off.

Anatoly watched the mother-son interaction with indifference. His own situation was much more dire. He fell into an armchair and spoke in a monotone. "I handed off the shit at the airport as usual. Not a hitch. But the customs guy was killed later that night in a car crash. I saw it on the news. I don't know if he made the delivery or not. But he's dead and there's no one around anymore to hand off to." He purposely omitted telling his wife about being visited by the Anchorage police and their warning to him to avoid returning to Alaska. "I don't know if I get to do this again."

"What do you mean?" Sophia roared. "You can't do it again?"

"Just what I said. No more deliveries. No more payoffs." He brightened a bit, a smile slowly replacing his downcast expression.

"And you want to know something, Soph? I'm relieved. It's like a great weight taken off my shoulders. I'm gonna ask Dima for reassignment. No more flights to the U.S. I'll fly domestic, to Novosibirsk and Irkutsk."

Sophia moved threateningly toward her husband. "No more payoffs? Are you kidding me, Toly? I was counting on them. We were going to Rhodes. You can't do this. I mean, what the hell?"

He put up his hands, trying to placate her. "It's over, dear. Greece is out. And, like I just said, I'm okay with it."

"Well, I'm *not* okay, Toly. Not at all." She stamped her foot.

Marat snuck back into the living room and used the

remote to turn the TV back on. In a fury, his mother rushed to him, grabbed the device, turned the set back off, and wielded the remote like a cudgel to strike her son on the head. He fled screaming to the bathroom and locked himself in. Sophia grabbed her parka and stormed out of their apartment.

The next day, Anatoly went to the Slavianski Bazaar. He thought the chances of him collecting were slim, but why not try? He was hoping the paymaster didn't yet know that the drug he flew to Alaska almost certainly never made it to its final destination. If they asked him, he'd play dumb, tell them he did his part, tell them it's not his fault the dopey customs guy got himself killed. And he hoped like hell they didn't know about the visit from the police.

When he entered the hotel's cabbage-and-cheap-vodka-stinking lobby, the man behind the mesh cage looked his way and frowned. Anatoly understood right away that they knew about the death of the customs agent. Why wouldn't they?

Seated next to the front desk, sunken into an ancient and severely frayed armchair, was the same balding man he'd dealt with at the Café Pyatnitsa. When the man saw Anatoly, he smiled knowingly, came to his feet, and met the pilot halfway into the room.

"Toly," he said, still smiling. "How the hell are you? Just back from Alaska? How'd it go?"

Glued to the spot in mid-lobby, Anatoly couldn't answer.

The man clicked his tongue. "We know about the accident in Anchorage and that our package was lost. Police probably have it. But never mind. Wasn't your fault, was it? We also know that they visited you in your hotel room a couple nights ago. Threatened you, did they? Told you not to come back anymore? But, like I said, not to worry too much."

Anatoly felt better. "So, my work is over?"

"Over? Far from it. Let's just say that no matter what happened in Alaska, you *still* work for us."

The pilot blinked stupidly and inched back. The man moved with him in a two-step.

"So, Toly, here's what. Since the shipment you delivered in Anchorage disappeared, you can't expect us to pay you. Can you? No. Of course not."

When Anatoly was about to object, the man put a finger to his lips in a shushing gesture. "Shut your mouth and listen carefully. You'll continue with the pick-ups at the train station, same as you've done all this time. But instead of taking the product on board your plane to Alaska—which we understand you can't do anymore because the American cop wants to kill you—you'll fly it north to Provideniya."

"Provideniya? What . . ."

"Yeah, Provideniya. On Chukotka. Troika flies there. New route for you. New plan. Your flight schedule's already been arranged. You'll fly there, hand the stuff off to a fisherman. We'll let you know who. You won't have to do this very often. Maybe two, three, maybe four times a year. Maybe more often. We can count on you, I'm sure."

The man behind the mesh spoke, "You deliver it up north, come back here and I pay you. Way less, of course, since the risk is minimal. Shouldn't be a problem, should it?"

All Suvorov could do was shake his head. "No. No problem," he managed. "How . . . how much do I get?"

"We'll figure it out," the bald man said.

Two days later, Anatoly prepared to be first officer on a domestic flight to Irkutsk, in Siberia.

"Tell me your schedule," Sophia asked. She had just

emerged from the bathroom, smelling of lavender. She was drying her hair. She was wearing a bathrobe, loosely tied. He saw that she was naked underneath. Her milky thighs flashed white as she walked to the kitchen table, reached for a cigarette and lit up. She saw him checking her out and drew her bathrobe closed.

"My new schedule?" he asked. "We leave here about five-thirty this afternoon, get to Irkutsk about nine tonight. Be free all day tomorrow. I might go out to Baikal, take a tour of the lake. Come back the next morning. Easy."

"Great," she said. "Bring me something fun."

"Will do."

Around seven that evening, Sophia called flight status to confirm her husband was in the air. She then phoned Dima, Toly's boss at Troika and the man who had performed their marriage ceremony.

"Dimushka, the idiot's gone flying. Not back for two days. The brat's at the neighbor's. Come over here right away. Don't bother knocking, just come in. Surprise me. I'll be naked and playing with myself on the bed, waiting for you to come and do what you do so good."

~~~

Sasha saw eight tiny objects, each encased in foam. She reached into the box, took one, and examined it closely. "These are the tiniest bugs I've ever seen," she said.

"They're omni-directional microphones," Vera said. "They can pick up sound up to six meters and will transmit back to us, up to three hundred meters away. Cool, huh?"

"And how."

"Made in Novosibirsk, by the way, though you're not

supposed to know that."

"I suppose I don't get to take one of these home?"

Vera shook her head, smiled and re-lit her cigarette. She took a deep inhalation. "I grabbed eight for this job and I need to return all eight. If I don't . . ." She blew out a cloud of smoke.

"Not healthy for you. Just like your smoking."

Vera laughed. "Right. Just so you know, I can also do landline taps if I have time and opportunity."

"Super. What other goodies have you brought?"

The second suitcase was crammed with a variety of GPS gear, three laptop computers, a pair of printers, three sets of night-vision goggles, and assorted other gadgets. Vera took a GPS watch and handed it to Sasha.

"Wear this at all times. You'll be tracked by us twenty-four/seven. Any trouble, all you have to do is press on the tiny knob on the side. That'll activate an alarm."

"What happens then? Paratroopers fall from the sky? The KGB rushes in to save me?"

Vera smiled. "Not quite. Konovalov will know immediately that you're in trouble. So will we."

"Whew. That's a relief. I'm saved. And the third piece of luggage, that big trunk?"

"The best for last," Vera said. She rolled the trunk into the living room. Inside were a variety of drones. Vera took a tiny one out of its foam and held it on her palm.

"Pocket-sized. Very quiet. Good for close in work, seeing around corners." She returned it to its protective casing. "We make even smaller ones that weigh hardly thirty grams, but they wouldn't let me have any of those. Too hush-hush." Vera took a larger drone out of the suitcase.

"Hexacopter. We have two of these. We can be eight kilometers away and still operate them remotely. They have enough juice to go for almost three hours."

"But won't whoever we're tailing spot the drone? Or hear it?"

"These guys can fly really high up. Pretty much out of visual range. And as far as sound goes, all drones make *some* noise. This one here is the quietest one we've produced. We'll test it and you'll see." Vera held the hexacopter above her head. "These are by far the most sophisticated and fun toys we have. They can spy, record, follow, hack, photo, jam, bomb, even skyjack. Just about anything you might want to do, these babies can manage."

"And you know how to fly them?"

"I should. I designed a fair portion of their operating systems."

"Good for you, Vera. I'm impressed. But to keep someone under surveillance, we'll need to follow. Right?"

"Yes and no. I mean, we don't really have to. We can keep a suspect vehicle under surveillance remotely. Just like the US does with its Predators. They fly them over Afghanistan while the pilots are sitting in Las Vegas."

"Yeah, but we'll want to be able to scope out where the vehicle stops and what happens after that. So, we'll probably need a car. Is that something Martyn can arrange?"

"Ask him when he comes back."

~~~

Mirza ibn Murad never enjoyed driving through Turkmenistan. Even in good weather, there was hardly a tree or a rushing river to be seen. The place was all desert, the Karakum, covering three-quarters of the country. And right now, blanketed in snow, the terrain was even more depressing.

He was taking the shortest south-to-north route, headed toward Mary, Turkmenistan's fourth largest city at just over a hundred thousand souls. *Poor souls,* Mirza thought, *having to live in this piss-poor country.*

After five hours of uninterrupted and frigid tedium, Mirza came upon the immense natural gas complex at Yoloten. He'd driven past this site dozens of times and noted, once again, the glacial pace of development. *Here they are, with the second biggest natural gas reserves on the planet. So how come the dummies can't manage to finish a pipeline that'll make them some money. Idiots!*

His stop in Mary was brief: gas, lunch, and a quick restock of his cooler. He hoped to cross north into Uzbekistan before the border closed for the night, usually at nine. He still had several hours before it shuttered and was fairly sure he'd make it. A bottleneck changed his plans.

The driver of the lorry in front of him—parked on the highway with its engine off—walked up to Mirza's idling Atego. The driver noted Mirza's Afghani license plate and spoke to him in Pashto. "Looks like we might be here a while. I heard on my CB that a gas line exploded, couple kilometers up. Guys are dead, road closed 'til further notice."

Mirza sighed heavily and looked at the long line of parked lorries that were strung out ahead of him, motors silent. He shut his rig and carefully climbed down from the cab. He was having spasms in his lower back and his knees were stiff and puffed up. He and the other driver stood and watched feathery wisps of gray smoke in front of them rise into the desert air, to be whisked away by an chill afternoon breeze.

"This means I'll be sleeping at the border," Mirza said. "Hate that place. Right next to the canal. Nothing but a zillion bats and the smell of shit."

"No fun," said the other driver, who introduced himself as Daoud Ghulam, from Kunduz.

The two men bundled blankets around themselves and sat down on a roadside berm. The line of lorries in back of them lengthened, soon extending a kilometer south. Mirza brought out a pack of Marlboros and offered one to the other driver.

"Great. Thanks," Daoud said, lighting up. He leaned back and blew smoke into the air. "What're you hauling?"

"Nothing important. Lotta crap," Mirza answered.

Since Daoud had often transported 'crap', he was curious, but discreet. "Nothing important, huh?"

"Nah," said Mirza. "Small stuff. The usual. How 'bout you?"

"Would you believe dried fruit?" Daoud asked, smiling. "Two hundred and forty cases of raisins and figs and apricots."

Mirza returned the man's grin. "I'll believe anything you tell me. Figs? Sure. Why not?" He looked at his watch, got up, and flipped his cigarette out into the snow. He climbed the Atego's steps and reached into the cab, foraging under the driver's seat. He felt the revolver he kept hidden, then searched further until he found a small piece of carpet remnant. He pulled it out, climbed down, and swatted dust off the rug.

"You actually going to use that?" Daoud asked, eyebrows arched. "Here? In this weather?"

Mirza shrugged. "I promised my wife I'd honor *Salat* every day." Then, as an afterthought, "I always promise her . . ."

"So you prayed today, at *Fajr* and *Zuhr*?" Daoud asked, a note of skepticism in his tone.

"Not quite," Mirza admitted. "I *thought* about it, but, you know . . ."

"I know. No apologies needed."

Mirza grinned. He kicked the snow off of a level spot on the highway and tossed down his rug. He leaned over and adjusted the carpet so that it faced generally southwest, towards Mecca. He rubbed his back vigorously and as carefully as he could, lowered his bulky body down onto the rug, one throbbing knee at a time. Once settled, he fulfilled his afternoon's spiritual obligation.

~~~

A breathless Martyn returned to Sasha's apartment around two-thirty in the afternoon. He was sweating. There was a large bulge in his briefcase. He went to the kitchenette's table, moved aside some of Vera's gear, and began emptying the briefcase. He took out four boxes of ammunition and a cloth bag. He pointed to the bag with a shaking forefinger. "It's a silent pistol, they call it a Stechkin. Konovalov himself brought me to the ministry's armory. They didn't want to give him the weapon but he started screaming, threatening. The guy in the armory was scared to death and finally gave him this thing. Said it's used by the Alpha Group. Supposed to be super quiet."

Sasha took a small revolver from the bag. She checked to see that it was unloaded, passed it from palm to palm, and cold fired the weapon. She noted '7.62' written on the ammo boxes.

"This'll work, Martyn. You done good. Now, how 'bout I order up a late lunch and we'll go over, *in very minute detail*, how you two are gonna help me while protecting my ass."

The makings of lunch—beef and ham sandwiches, cheeses, olives, pickles, and potato salad—were spread before them. Sasha's two helpers were drinking beer. She looked longingly at the frosty bottles of Baltika, her preferred Russian brew. *Six hundred and thirty-six days dry. And still counting.* She worked on her Pepsi. "Be specific, Martyn," she said. "Remind me what you do?"

He put down his bottle of beer and wiped his lips. "Like I told you already, transport and tickets, clothing, places to stay, places to hide, places to store things, find us food, phony documents, maps, medical supplies. Drugs, even. Just about whatever you need that's *not* electronic. I'm your gofer and I'm good at it. The minister hand picked me for this job because I also speak fluent Pashto and a smidgen of Dari."

"Bravo. Where'd you learn those?"

"At the Foreign Ministry's language school. They run intensive, full-immersion programs."

"And you chose Pashto because?"

"Well, I actually wanted Arabic, but those classes were full. I wound up in a very small class, just five of us for four years of immersion." He took a bite of sandwich and wiped mayonnaise from his mouth. "The Minister told me you're super important."

Sasha scratched the back of her head. "But not important enough for him to provide all that he promised me." She sipped her Pepsi. "Do you both know *exactly* who I am and why I've been shanghaied to Russia?"

Vera said, "You're an Alaskan cop. With a history."

"Let's hear what you know about my history."

"Three years ago, you arrested someone in Vlad. Someone who killed three Alaskans in a hotel. The guy who did it got knifed in jail. And I heard that you killed a couple guys out on the Pacific Coast, in Anadyr. Don't know much about that one. And you shot some Russians in Alaska. Drug dealers, I think. Don't really know if any of this is true."

"The Alaska part I can confirm. Russian Mafia guys in a

big fishing port, place called Dutch Harbor. They were dealing heroin." She had a memory-flash of Kostya after she'd wounded him, lying there in the parking lot of the B and B, begging for his life. *Didn't do any good, did it, pal?*

"And that's why Konovalov brought you here. Heroin. Right?" Martyn asked.

"Is that what he told you?"

"Pretty much. He told us we'd work with you in Chelyabinsk. It's known as a heroin distribution center."

"And when we get there?" Sasha asked.

"We are to help you find out who, what, why, when, and where," Martyn said. "*Without* any help from the local police. Off the books, according to the minister."

After passing through the Bugristoye customs station at the Russia-Kazakhstan border, it's another 140 km to Chelyabinsk.

"Correct," Sasha said. "Shouldn't be a problem, right? We just show up, corral the bad guys, and go home."

Vera gave her new boss an indulgent smile. "No, Sasha. *If* we even show up in Chelyabinsk, I set up an electronic listening post. I install bugs and tap phone lines. I listen to private conversations. I hack what needs to be hacked. I jam what needs to be jammed. I provide instantaneous communications with our base at the ministry. I operate drone flights, and I make life totally miserable and confusing for our adversaries. And when they are sufficiently unhappy, we swoop in and only then do we corral them. How does that sound?"

Sasha laughed out loud. "Sounds great, Vera. But first thing is finding them. And right at the beginning of that long list of things to do, you said, '*If* we even show up in Chelyabinsk.' What am I to understand about that?"

"Because I think it's best if we don't start in Chelyabinsk." She took a forkful of potato salad and washed it down with more beer. "We start on the border, at the Bugristoye crossing, and work our way north."

"I'm glad someone has a plan. Let's hear more of it," Sasha said.

They gathered around an unfurled map of southern Russia. It showed the seven thousand, two hundred kilometer-long Russian frontier with Kazakhstan, the second longest international boundary on the planet. Vera used a fork to point out Chelyabinsk, just north of the Kazakh border.

"Place has a million-two population," she said. "Big, rough, complicated place. Lots of industry, lots of drinking, lots of unemployed. Although the guidebooks talk about how interesting and lovely the place is, it's really dangerous, especially for outsiders. I heard it's the sixth city for crime in Russia."

"There's another reason Chelyabinsk is dangerous for

you, in particular, Sasha," Martyn said.

"Why's that?"

"Here in this room, your spoken Russian is pretty perfect. Outside, however, I'm afraid it won't cut it."

"Explain."

"Well, your Russian is archaic. You speak correctly, don't get me wrong. No grammatical mistakes and your accent is almost native. But you speak like someone who stopped talking Russian in 1950. You have no sense of current usage, no sense of slang. And the double entendre I used earlier would have been understood by any modern Russian. It went right over your head. So, you need to limit your public exposure in Chelyabinsk, which, like Vera said, is a dangerous place for outsiders."

Sasha nodded. "You're right, of course. I learned from my grandfather. I speak his Russian. He left here in 1945 and only came back once for a short visit. I'll take your very good advice, Martyn, and try to keep my mouth shut when I'm in public. And thanks."

"You're welcome," he said. "Although there's room for improvement. I'd imagine after a month together with us, your Russian might sound a bit more up to date."

"We'll find out." Sasha finished her Pepsi. "A minute ago, Vera, you suggested we *don't* start in Chelyabinsk, but at the border station, at Bugristoye. I agree, but tell me what you're thinking."

"Well, we know for sure that heroin passes through the border. We also know that it comes from Afghanistan. And we're certain that some of the Russians who are supposed to be guarding the frontier are being bribed. This is all well documented. As soon as Konovalov told us what we were going to do, I hacked into the Afghan Department of Motor Vehicles in Kabul. Took all of four minutes. Their commercial license plates are long, with light blue letters and numbers on a black background. A little hard to read, but no mistaking them for Turkmen or Kazakh. Now, I'm going to assume that the smugglers are *not* using private cars, but rather, lorries or vans. Easier to hide stuff. And those vehicles have even more distinctive license plates."

"Go on," Sasha said.

"OK. There are cameras at all Russian border crossings, cameras that record all arriving vehicles. It was simple to get into the system that monitors those passing through Bugristoye. And what I noticed is helpful. But *only partially*. I was able to identify four Afghani commercial vehicles being inspected in the first hour. That was during mid-day."

"You said only 'partially' helpful," Martyn said.

"Because the cameras are set in a fixed position to record *only* license plates. There is no video record of any interactions between drivers and guards."

"Which is where bribes presumably are offered and taken," Sasha said. "So that means that the cameras won't do us a whole lot of good. Added to that, we're making some huge assumptions," which she ticked off on her fingers. "We're assuming that the goods are smuggled in on Afghani *commercial* vehicles. What if the heroin is being brought in by car? And a car with *Kazakh* plates? And if the bribe is sent to the guard's bank account rather than handed to him? We're counting on an Afghani commercial vehicle *and* seeing money change hands. We could be here forever."

Martyn leaned forward. "And what if we set up on one side of the highway and the guard and driver are passing money on the other? Or inside the back of the lorry? Jesus."

"Sure it's a long shot, but we have to start somewhere," Vera said.

"I know we do," Sasha said. "But let's flip your scenario into something that might work better."

"Like?"

"Well, you propose to find the vehicle, *then* find the border guard who takes the bribe. How 'bout we find the guard *first*, then have him lead us to the vehicle?"

"And how do we do that?" Martyn asked.

"We follow the money." Sasha looked at Vera. "Go ahead. Tell Martyn how we follow the money."

Vera smiled, the better idea dawning on her. "Sasha's right. I'll make us an Excel file of all the FSS staff at Bugristoye. We'll enter all of the variables—age, length of service, marital status . . ."

"Gender, kids," said Martyn, getting with the program. "Living arrangements, former postings, criminal records . . ."

"Those are all valid criteria," Sasha said. "But at the heart of the problem is finding which of the border guards has extra money, needs extra money, who owes, who spends. So we look at alimony payments, outstanding loans, business dealings, and all the indicators of sudden and unaccounted for wealth."

"Right," Vera said. "I can search bank accounts and credit cards. I'll do a sort, eliminate those who we feel wouldn't qualify . . ."

"We'll be left with the most likely candidates who are probably on the take," Sasha said. "If we can narrow the list to . . . let's say fewer than eight, find out from their duty roster when they're on the job, then our search becomes easier, more focused and more efficient."

"So, it looks like I'm busy for the next several days," Vera said.

"One more thing to note," Sasha said. "The border guards are most likely being bribed with dollars or Euros."

"Which they can't spend in this country without drawing attention," Martyn said. "And since they can't make the exchange from dollars to rubles in a bank, they'll need to deal with the black market money exchange. I've done it myself, lots of times here in Moscow."

"Who hasn't?" Vera added.

"Exactly," Martyn said, grinning. "We'll need to learn about the exchanges in both Troitsk and Chelyabinsk. Though I'd be surprised if a border guard would be so stupid as to try and exchange dollars in Troitsk, so close to the border."

"Never, ever underestimate the stupidity of your common, everyday border guard," Sasha said.

~~~

Just past six o'clock and the line of lorries began to inch forward. Mirza started the Atego and a few minutes later, drove past the smoldering wreckage of an unknown structure, a hundred meters off the highway to his left. The building was all crispy and charred and covered with white fire retardant. An ambulance was parked close by, its doors flung wide and its crew standing around, smoking. The acrid smell of burned natural gas blew into the Atego's cab, only dissipating as Mirza drove north, toward Turkmenabat. By ten that evening, he had skirted the city, crossed an iced-over Amu Darya River, and arrived at Farab Alat, the border crossing with Uzbekistan. As he expected, the place was shuttered until the next morning. He parked his truck at the rear of a long string of cars and lorries, grabbed a roll of toilet paper, and donned a heavy jacket and fur cap. He shuffled to the rude, cement out-house, did what he had to do, then returned to the relative warmth of his cab as quickly as his aching back and puffed up knees allowed. *Don't* *know how many more times I can make this trip. I'm a wreck. I hurt all over. Maybe I can retire. But if I do, I won't get to see Her again.*

He knew this hole-in-the-wall didn't have cell service so he didn't bother trying to phone his wife. *Just as well. She'd probably ask if I prayed all five times today. I'd have to lie.*

He ate the last of Medina's roasted chicken and washed it down with cold coffee. Then he lay across the seat, covered himself with three heavy wool blankets, and was asleep at once.

The sound of lorry engines starting up awakened him around six. He ate a piece of stale pastry, drank more cold coffee, and left his Atego parked and locked. He walked toward the border barrier and was gratified to see the old soldier, Emek Failani, standing customs duty on the Uzbek side.

Failani escorted Mirza through the complex barrier of drop-down gates, fences, and cement blocks. After finding a replacement for his border guarding duties, the Uzbek insisted on Mirza sharing breakfast.

Inside the crossing post's small kitchen, the two men shared a modest meal: bread and goat cheese, lamb jerky, tomatoes and cucumbers, dates, and tea. Emek found a pair of throw-pillows and pressed them upon the driver, "For sick back, dear friend," he said in English.

Mirza thanked his host, passed him five, fifty-dollar bills, returned to his Atego, and drove into Uzbekistan.

~~~

Late that first afternoon, Vera asked when they'd be done for the day, explaining that she had a date with a girl friend to go to the movies.

"You're kidding, aren't you?" Sasha asked.

"No. I'm serious. I need to go home and change. We have tickets for the eight o'clock."

"You can go home. Both of you. But only long enough to gather two weeks worth of clothes and personal stuff and then get your asses back here."

"I don't understand," Martyn said.

"What's not to understand?" Sasha asked. "You're in it for the duration. Both of you belong to me."

In unison, the Russians slumped. Neither argued, however. Vera sighed and grabbed her carryall. "I'll be back in a couple hours."

"Me, too," Martyn said.

"That's the spirit," Sasha said. "Do or die." She laughed. Her helpers didn't.

That night, Sasha and Vera slept in the suite's bedroom, each on her own queen-sized bed. Martyn spread himself out on a long sofa in the living room.

They awoke the next day to an apartment that had quickly become a smelly testament to close-quarter living—food, blankets, clothes, and electronic gear spilling over into every corner. Sasha took control. She reserved the maintenance of the bedroom and living room for herself. Martyn was appointed kitchen scullery maid, while Vera was in charge of her electronics and keeping the bathroom habitable. Sasha chased the two Russians into the hall whenever they needed to smoke.

It took the rest of the week for Vera to prepare the Excel spreadsheets that now lay before her. She'd first hacked into the FSS database and downloaded the names of the personnel who work at the Bugristoye frontier crossing: sixteen men and five women. She guided her partners through the spreadsheets.

"On the horizontal axis, running along the top, are the twenty-one names. And on the vertical axis, on the left, are the variables we established. We might see that we may need to add others. But we spent a lot of time considering what these criteria ought to be and I can't think of anything we left off."

Sitting on either side of her, Sasha and Martyn both nodded.

Vera continued. "I've prepared a folder for each of the twenty-one, supplementing the information you see checked on the spreadsheet. So, for instance. If I've checked someone's criminal past on the spreadsheet, all the details can be found in that person's folder. Follow?"

"Easy," Martyn said.

"What I'd like to do is review the variables just one more time," Vera said. "Read them out to you. And if anything seems amiss, something left out, or something needs to be added, speak up."

"Carry on," Sasha said. "You're doing great."

Vera began pointing and reminding her two partners what their thinking had been when they established the criteria.

"The first things are pretty standard—age, gender, length of service in the FSS, along with rank and salary. Previous work is next, other federal jobs or private work. Then education. Note that two of our candidates didn't graduate high school. And two have college degrees. A mixed bag. Next is marital status. Single or married, and number of times married. Then divorce, number of divorces. And this is important—any alimony payments, child support, or large settlements. Next is family. Age and gender of children, parents, and any history of criminality. Then housing. Where they live, in the barracks, or renting, or maybe they own their place."

Martyn said, "I'm betting the people we're looking for

have all used their new-found wealth to move out of those crappy FSS barracks. Moved to Troitsk."

"Makes sense," Sasha agreed.

"Total sense," Vera said, then continued. "The next thing is banking. Do they have a checking or a savings account? Or maybe both. And how much ready cash? Do they have a deposit box and how often do they visit? Have they paid off or still have outstanding loans? Then credit card use. Do they keep a zero balance or are they paying the minimum? Then legal problems. Were they ever sued or did they ever sue anyone? And with what outcome? Any liens or other civil penalties? Then the big one, any criminal records showing the crime, conviction and punishment—fine or jail time." Vera took a breath.

"This is a really good start," Sasha said. "We might be missing something important, but I can't think what it could be. So, let's find out who're the prime suspects and who's off the hook."

Five of Bugristoye's FSS staff were eliminated right away.

"These guys are all office-bound administrators," Vera said. "Folks who never actually make it down onto the pavement to inspect vehicles crossing into Russia. I can't imagine someone in admin orchestrating what's going on at the drop gate. This seems to me to be a crime committed by a single person, not a group."

"For the sake of argument, I'll go along," Sasha said, "even though I've arrested enough administrative and executive types who managed their crimes from on high. But for now, we can move on."

By lunchtime, they had agreed to eliminate three married people, each with three kids and each with a spouse making a good living.

"Unlikely they'd be into something so chancy. Too risky

for the kids," Vera said.

She got an argument from Sasha. "I know all about lousy and uncaring parents." *Myself included. At least up 'til now. Maybe I can make amends when I get back. The fifty grand'll help.*

Three new recruits were crossed off—two men and a young woman. They were all under twenty-three-years-old, and had been in the FSS for less than a year.

"They're too raw," Vera argued. "They certainly know *that* it's done, but they're probably not sure yet *how* it's done. So they haven't yet dared to give it a try. Plus, they don't have the seniority to fix their work schedules, make sure they're at the border crossing when they need to be. And besides, the three all come from good families. And all of them live in the FSS barracks."

"I agree," Sasha said. "And if barracks living is a serious criterion for kicking folks off our list, then there are three more who qualify."

"Let's have a look," Vera said. "See if they have red flags."

They spent ten minutes with each of the three and eliminated two. They kept a young man who had a bank account, which, at first glance, looked to be too large for someone in his economic bracket. He was struck off the list when both parents turned out to be higher ups in the FSS.

"Looks to me like the kid is being groomed for bigger and better things," Vera said. "He's had two quick promotions. He'd be nuts to try something so risky. I mean, his future is guaranteed. Why would he chance it?"

Sasha chuckled. "You don't think kids from good families can be tempted? Kids with money and bright futures? I've seen loads of 'em. *B.J. Lewis for one.* "But again, for the sake of argument, we can drop him. At least for now."

"Great," Martyn said. "Let's stop here. I need food. It's past two. I've looked at the menu at Il Forno, the place in the lobby. I'm ready for Italian. Osso buco."

"My treat," Sasha said. She waved Konovalov's credit card.

~~~

Eight months had passed since the Kazakhs first discovered David Osinchuk's mule. Now they sat in Sultan's mother's tiny, ninth floor apartment in Chelyabinsk's warehouse district. The two were busy eating *shuzhuk*—horsemeat sausage and rice.

Chingiz spat out a piece of tendon, then flushed down a mouthful of food with half a glass of *samogon*. They'd brewed the vodka in the apartment's bathtub, forcing Sultan's mother to bathe at the neighbor's. Chingiz made a face as he downed the nasty tasting swill, then belched loudly.

When they'd learned the nurse's address, they were immediately stymied: there was no way just the two of them could manage an adequate surveillance of the woman.

Sultan had solved the problem. "That group of Uzbek kids we sell hash to? Let's get *them* to watch the nurse for us. There's a dozen who'd do it. We pay 'em with ganje but don't tell 'em nothin' about *why* we're watchin' her."

Chingiz found eight likely urchins who divided up the task and spent their days observing Tamara, her son, and her husband.

The kids began their scrutiny in July 2018. At the end of that month, on a Friday, they watched as the nurse and her son took a cab to the terminal and boarded a train bound for Vladivostok. A few days later, the woman returned and the Uzbeks resumed their surveillance. Nothing for two months until the last Friday in September when, once again, the nurse and her son, following the same routine, trained to Vladivostok. And then again at the end of November. And when the same thing happened at the end of January of the new year, Naim, one of the Uzbek gangbangers, called on his Kazakh bosses.

Sultan handed Naim the hash pipe he was working on. The Uzbek teenager took a long draw, held in the smoke, blew it out and recapped his gang's findings. "She didn' go to work any of them Fridays. Every two months." He handed the pipe back to Sultan. "And it's always the last Friday in the month."

"Good work, kiddo." Sultan put another lump of hash into the bowl. "OK. So let's think." He took out his smartphone and called up the 2019 calendar.

"The last Friday this March is the 29th. If she doesn't go to work, she's goin' to Vlad. And you gotta let me know fast, I mean, right away."

"Don' worry," the Uzbek said. "I call you. And when she leave for the train, I follow on my motor scooter and call again when she at the train station."

"Sounds good," Sultan said. He lit the hash pipe and handed it back to the kid.

"Take your last hit, then scram," Sultan told Naim.

When the Uzbek gangbanger had gone, Sultan turned to his partner. "Chingo, you listenin'? End of March, we move. I'll get us tickets right away. But we can't tell nothin' to nobody about this. So not a word."

Chingiz zipped his lips together, only opening them long enough to take a gulp of *samogon*. "When we rob the nurse, should we take guns? Wouldn't that be cool?"

"Jesus, Chingo. I keep tellin' you. No guns. We get caught—a couple guys like us with no creds and no connections—it's life in the can. So knives only."

"Shit, and I was hopin'."

~~~

Returning from Il Forno, they spent the rest of the day reducing their list to the five most likely suspects: Valentina Andropova, Pyotr Bondarchuk, Gavrilo Mandelshtam, Tanya Morozova, and Dushan Rodchenko.

Sasha emailed the names to Konovalov, asking him to find out if they had bank accounts and deposit boxes. He answered that afternoon: all had accounts and safety deposit boxes in banks either in Troitsk, in Yuzhno-Uralsk, or in Plast. He said court orders were being prepared that would grant access to their banking information.

After a quick dinner—borscht, burgers and fries ordered up from the hotel's Lobby Bar—they began to examine the dossiers of their prime suspects.

"First on the list is Valentina Andropova," Vera said, opening the woman's folder. "She's thirty-four, not married now, but divorced in 2018."

Martyn looked at her photo. "Wow. Nice looking lady." He showed Sasha the picture: big green eyes under beautifully curved brows. Luscious lips, a dimpled chin. Curly blond hair. A knockout.

Sasha shrugged. "Yeah? So?"

He laughed.

"What's her story?" Sasha asked.

Vera read from her notes. "She moved from the barracks in 2016 and has a *very* nice place in Troitsk. One hundred and ninety square meters."

"Why is that nice?" Sasha asked.

Vera said, "The average Russian apartment is around sixty square meters. This'd be three times as big. And here's something really crazy. She's a lavish spender. I checked her credit cards. In the past six months, she's made three high-end purchases, an HD TV/stereo set up, a Danish sofa, and a set of Le Creuset pots and pans. The total comes to about half of her yearly salary."

"If Andropova's on the take," Sasha said, "she's not being very careful about spending. Reckless with her credit card. Does she have another source of income? Rich family, inheritance, other work?"

"None of that," Vera said. "And there's more. She vacations every year in Europe. In 2016, Barcelona. Sicily in 2017, and Malta last year. She likes the Mediterranean. She keeps a deposit box in a bank in Plast. That's about sixty kilometers from here. She drives a 2005 Ford Focus. Don't know where she got it or how much she paid. But she owns it outright. And one more point. She's got a boyfriend, a Kazakh guy. He's a car dealer. So maybe . . ."

"Maybe," Sasha said. "Maybe if you examined her divorce papers, the Kazakh's name just might show up as . . . ." Sasha had to fish for the word in Russian, ". . . a co-respondent."

When Martyn shrugged his non-understanding of the term, Sasha explained, "The co-respondent is the guy Valentina was fucking who was not her husband."

Martyn slapped his forehead. "Shoulda known. You've got a suspicious mind, Sasha."

"Normal cop mind. Everything is suspicious. So we start listening in on her phone conversations. She has a smart phone for outside stuff, but whatever comes in on her landline, we can monitor."

"We're not done with Comrade Andropova," Vera said. "Seems she owns several pieces of property around Samara—two were inherited, but she bought four since she began working at Bugristoye. I was able to track down the purchase agreements and title concerning those land buys. Way more expensive than she could afford."

"You said no money in her family?" Martyn asked.

"They're all lower middle class prols. Just poor ex-commies."

"Maybe her Kazakh boy friend helped her out," Martyn suggested.

"I like that possibility," Sasha said. "By the way, Vera, something I wanted to ask you. I know you Russians have the technology to monitor smart phones. How come *we* don't get to use it?"

"I asked Konovalov," Vera said. "He said he applied all kinds of pressure, but got push-back. Government wouldn't give us access to that technology. Shame."

"A real shame," Sasha said. "Makes our work so much harder."

"We'll manage," Vera said. "Meanwhile, if we're done with Andropova, next in line is Pyotr Bondarchuk." She looked at Sasha. "We done with her?"

Sasha nodded. "We can move on from Andropova."

"OK. Pyotr Bondarchuk's thirty-one, moved to Troitsk from the FSS barracks last year, about the same time he married Svetlana Kuzminskaya. Bondarchuk has been at Bugristoye for almost six years. He's a sergeant. Nothing special. According to Konovalov, he has both a checking and a savings account at the local Russian Agricultural Bank in Troitsk. And a deposit box that he opened there last year. His wife is the co-signer on the box and his accounts. They traveled to Moscow after they were married. They spent ten days at the Moscow Marriott. I have a copy of his credit card receipts for that month. It's weird. There's very little there. You'd think he'd put all their meals and entertainment on the card, but only the hotel bill."

Sasha said, "Which means they paid cash for the fun stuff."

"Looks that way. And here's something else interesting," Vera said. "Bondarchuk's father is a former FSS border guard. Worked for years at several places along the Amur, the border with China. And Bondarchuk's uncle, Nikita, was also a border guard in Mongolia. And guess what?"

Sasha said, "I'm gonna take a wild stab. He got popped for crimes at the border?"

"Your suspicious mind again," Vera said. "The FSS sent in an undercover agent. Uncle Nikita was caught with his hand in the till. Spent seven years in Lefortovo for taking bribes. Released in 2012 and died the next year."

"What about Bondarchuk's living arrangements in Troitsk?" Martyn asked.

"One bedroom apartment. With a landline."

"Our kinda crook," Sasha said. "Bondarchuk could be a possible winner. Who's next?"

"Tanya Morozova. She's thirty-eight-years-old, married to an unemployed sheet metal worker. He used to work at a place called Chelyabinsk Pipe Rolling. Got injured and laid off. That was eight years ago. He hasn't had a regular job since. She began work with the FSS after that. No kids. They live in a two-bedroom place in Yuzhno-Uralsk, which they bought outright a couple years ago."

"Makes you wonder where the money came from," Martyn said.

"Does it ever," Sasha said. "What else for Miz Morozova?"

Vera read, "She's from Moscow. High school graduate. From 2002-2006, she served as a clerk in the Navy's Coastal Military and Artillery. Stationed in various spots on the Black Sea. She received two reprimands and a light court martial.

Suspected of pilfering in each instance."

"Sticky fingers," said Martyn.

"She banks near her home," Vera said.

"Credit card info?" Sasha asked.

"She shops a lot on Avito, small stuff."

"What's that? Avito?" Sasha asked.

"We don't get Amazon in Russia, so Avito—a Russian company—is where we do our on-line shopping," Vera said.

"Parents, siblings?" Sasha asked.

"All Moscovites," Vera said. "No one exceptional. All employed but no red flags."

"OK. Put her on the list for landline listening." And as soon as Konovalov sends the court orders for deposit box and account searches, we'll go banking."

Vera said, "Which means, Sasha, that sometime soon, we'll need to relocate to the border, to Troitsk, closer to the action."

"Way ahead of you, Vera," Sasha said. "Konovalov's arranged for us to use an office in Troitsk. Seems the Ministry of Justice has a temporary holding facility there for people who get nabbed at the border. We get a big empty office on the building's second floor.

"Available right away?" Martyn asked.

"Right now," Sasha said.

"So what's keeping us here in Moscow?"

"Only your appetite for osso buco," Sasha laughed. "Let's pack up."

"I'll make plane reservations," Martyn said.

"No need," Sasha said. "Your boss has arranged a Ministry plane for us. It'll be available at Vnukovo this afternoon. It's a six-hour flight, due east, to Chelyabinsk. And he's supplied us with wheels when we get there, a rental car that we pick up at Avis.

Vera looked around, equipment everywhere. "All we have to do is pack. Christ."

~~~

Petya Bondarchuk was aghast. He could hardly catch his breath. "Say that again," he wheezed.

"I'm pregnant. Six weeks," Svetlana repeated. "Isn't it wonderful?" There was a tremor in her voice.

The FSS border guard wanted to answer in the most forceful way, telling her, 'No, Sveta, it's not wonderful at all. It's a disaster.' But he held his tongue. He plopped down on their new hide-a-bed, purchased just last month with the extra-legal proceeds from his work. Svetlana sat down beside him, took his hands in hers.

"I know it's a shock, Petya. I know it's not what we wanted." She hesitated and looked away. "Well, not what *you* wanted, anyway."

He stared at her. "You mean *you* wanted to get pregnant? After all we talked about? I thought we decided to wait."

She shrugged. "Things happen."

He removed his hands from hers and stood, not knowing what to say, which way to walk, how to react to this wholly unexpected and wholly disastrous announcement.

Svetlana leaned forward. "And if we ever decide to have a second child, Petya, the government'll give us more than a half million rubles. Think of it."

He turned to her, mouth agape. "A second one, Sveta? I don't even want a first one! I don't like children, remember. I have no interest in being a father. My own mother hated being a parent. And she let me know about it every day."

Svetlana began to tear up.

He gentled his voice. "Please Sveta. Not now. Not yet. Please do like every other woman in our country does. Get an abortion."

"But the church . . ."

He flapped his hands at her. "Spare me your Russian orthodoxy. Your Kalinin is as rotten as our Ukrainian Metropolitan, Onufriy. Both crooks. And as for the half a million the government claims it would send us for a second child, that's bullshit. I don't know anyone who's been able to cash in on that. Besides which, money-wise, we're doing just fine, thank you." He pulled out a roll of American bills from his back pocket and waved it in front of his wife. "Look at this."

She looked. She reached. He laid the money in her hands. She counted.

"Nine hundred and fifty dollars. How . . .?"

"Old business and some new business. My contact in admin put me onto three drivers coming into Russia this morning. Two tractor-trailers from Turkmenistan, and a lorry from Uzbekistan. The drivers apparently weren't interested in having their cargo looked at."

She held the money tightly and sniffled.

He sat down next to her and counted out four hundred dollars. "Take this, go to the money changer. You've done it before."

She dried her eyes and took out her smartphone. She spent a minute then said, "The official exchange rate today is seventy-two rubles, twenty-six kopecks to a dollar."

"Right. The guy'll offer you just a little above, maybe seventy-three. Hold out for seventy-five and not a kopeck less. Should amount to just under thirty thousand rubles."

She nodded.

He took her hands. "Dr. Oblonskaya is where all the

women here in town go. At the Tverskaya Clinic. Shouldn't cost more than ten thousand rubles. She's quite nice, I hear."

"So I hear," his wife said. "And the with rest of the money?"

"Buy yourself something nice."

"Thank you, Petya."

~~~

They arrived at Chelyabinsk around nine that night. A freezing rain was pummeling the airport. They piled into the ministry-arranged rental car, an older model Lada that was barely large enough for the three of them and their mountains of gear. They headed south, and an hour later, drove into Troitsk. Another half hour to unpack and get moderately settled in their new quarters, a ten-meter by seven-meter room the Ministry of Justice used as holding quarters for unsuccessful smugglers. There was a bench along one wall, a table, and two chairs. One long window looked out onto the Miass River flowing just a few meters away. The bathroom was down the hall.

"Hopefully, we won't have to be here long," Sasha said. "One or more of our suspects will give himself away."

"Or give herself away," Vera added.

"Maybe the nimble-fingered Morozova," Martyn said. "But not the gorgeous Andropova." He shook his head. "She can't be a criminal. She's too good looking."

Sasha shook her head and looked at Vera. They exchanged smiles. "Let's each take a corner for sleeping," Sasha said. "Martyn, Mr. Coordinator. Go find us mattresses, bedding, pillows etcetera. But first, go find us some food. I looked at Google Maps. There's a place that sells shwarma near by. Get us all full plates."

"But before that, find tables for our equipment," Vera added. "And knives and forks."

"And more chairs," Sasha said. "And a wall map of the area."

"And see about getting us a landline phone installed. And a TV," Vera added.

"Food first, then the rest of that shit," he said.

Martyn brought plates of shwarma, which they devoured. He didn't find beds, cots, or sleeping bags, but was able to score twenty heavy blankets, which doubled as mattresses and covers. By midnight, they'd set up Vera's gear on tables along one wall and converted their new office into a usable listening post.

"We're done for tonight," Sasha said. "First thing in the morning, we go tap some landline phones."

Vera looked at Martyn, already in bed. "As soon as our coordinator there finds me something resembling a Troitsk utility suit. Size small, please, Martyn."

His back was to the women, blanket over his head. "Ask me tomorrow," he mumbled.

Dressed in cobbled together utility-man's attire, Vera placed taps on the landline phones of Valentina Andropova, Pyotr Bondarchuk, and Tanya Morozova. The three lived in different apartment blocs in Troitsk. Using Konovalov's credit card, Vera was able to rent vacant apartments in each of the three blocs. She was then able to re-route the conversations of the trio of suspects to her voice-activated recording machines in the rented apartment. Since the listeners had downloaded the Bugristoye duty roster, they knew when the suspects would be at home. Vera hooked up a notification alarm that rang in their headquarters whenever the recording device was activated by a phone call. That necessitated a trip to the rented apartment to listen to the recorded conversation.

"Kinda tedious," Martyn said. "Why can't we stay here in our office and monitor their conversations?"

"That would require close cooperation with the local phone utility," Vera explained. "Something Konovalov doesn't want us to do. Might somehow alert the suspects. Yeah, it's tedious. But it's the best we can do."

Sasha decided to hold off on the two remaining serious suspects—Mandelshtam and Rodchenko. "Three is about all we can handle at one time," she said. "Besides, the other two don't have landline phones which means we'll need line-of-sight mics or some other means of surveillance. We'll see where these two live, consider how to snoop. But for now, we'll focus on the first three and see what we can see. Hear what we can hear."

Over the next week, they monitored the phone taps, visiting their rented apartments as soon as a call came through. They often stayed there through the evening.

Andropova's calls were long and involved. She spoke mostly to friends (about her next trip abroad) and family (about her dying aunt). Carmi, her Kazakh boyfriend, never phoned, leading Sasha to believe that they spoke only on her cell.

Bondarchuk used the phone rarely, his wife almost ninety percent of the time. In the week since the surveillance began, he made a single call to his father and none to his sister. Mostly, he spoke to his co-workers at the Bugristoye crossing, never for longer than a minute and only about their work schedule. He seemed to have no friends.

The phone conversations of Tanya Morozova were frequent, at least one an hour when she was home. Three people took most of her time: her younger sister who complained about her current lack of a boyfriend; her mother who inquired about

Tanya's husband and questioned why she continued to live with the SOB; and with an unidentified man about a meet-up some time in the near future.

The listeners reviewed what they overheard at the end of each day. So far, a big nothing. On the morning of their eighth day of eavesdropping, Sasha received an email from Konovalov with several enclosures.

~~~

Anatoly's speculation about his wife fooling around changed one evening from mere suspicion to near certainty. It was something Sophia said, an offhand remark. They were having dinner.

"Toly. Have you ever flown up to the Chukotka Peninsula?"

He raised his eyebrows, shook his head. "No, never," he answered, not wanting to let on that Provideniya, on the Chukotka, was the village to which he'd flown twice recently to drop off shipments of heroin.

She'd looked at him questioningly. "Funny. I thought you'd been there."

"No. Why would you think that?"

"No reason, really." She paused, took a bite of the shashlik she'd prepared. He hated the way she made the lamb kabobs, always overcooked.

"Chukotka. Horrible place," she said. "Only Eskimos live there, I heard."

"Why horrible?" he asked. "And why the sudden interest in Eskimos?"

She didn't answer, but rose, collected her dishes, and took them to the sink. He watched her, feeling somehow, that she knew about his trafficking flights up north. *But how could she know?*

Sophia put on her parka and made to leave.

"Where to?" he asked.

"Visiting," was her terse reply. "Back in a couple hours."

He was left alone with Marat, happily watching Sesame Street. Anatoly sat and brooded. *Why this sudden interest in Chukotka, in Eskimos?* He knew that his wife was someone who had only the barest knowledge of the geography of her own country. She invariably exhibited an uncertainty about where exactly the Volga was, where the Gulf of Finland was, where Irkutsk was. "Is that close to Moscow," she'd ask.

No. He was fairly certain his wife had no knowledge of Chukotka's location. And no knowledge of who might live there. Something was up. But what?

He shared hot chocolate with his son, then bathed him, put him to bed, and returned to his living room to continue obsessing. The more he thought about it, the more he was certain that she'd learned about Chukotka from Dmitri, his boss. It was he who set the flight schedules and arranged for Anatoly to fly to Chukotka. Why? *Because he knows exactly what my cargo will be each time. Because he's the one who told me, two years ago, to go to the Slavianski Bazaar to meet someone who might ease my financial problems. Because only Dmitri could have assigned me as first officer on those Alaska flights. He's involved. And he's been talking to my wife. Only talking? I need to find out.*

~~~

Armed with court orders from Konovalov's Justice Ministry, Sasha and Vera drove to Plast, a small town northwest of Troitsk. They visited the SovKomBank and inquired about the accounts and the deposit box of Valentina Andropova. The bank manager was absent, but the woman's assistant, a very nervous young man who was properly intimidated, offered no resistance and quickly produced what was requested. The checking account showed nothing interesting—a balance of a few thousand rubles. Inside the deposit box, however, a different story: a large pile of dollars, Euros, and English pound notes. Vera and Sasha gave each other long smiles. The deeds to the woman's several parcels of property, a few vintage photographs, and a handful of heirloom jewelry made up the rest of the contents. They listed and photographed everything they discovered, returning all the items as they found them. They made it clear to the assistant bank manager that their visit was not to be mentioned to Andropova.

The manager of the Russian Agricultural Bank in Troitsk was Mikhail Sergeyevich Kutusov, a short, round man with thick glasses and a thin mustache.

Sasha and Vera crowded into his small office.

"We're investigating one of your clients," Sasha began. "Pyotr Bondarchuk is the subject of an investigation the Ministry of Justice is conducting." She presented the manager with Konovalov's court order.

Kutusov scanned the document, seemingly unimpressed. "And what precisely is the nature of this investigation?" he asked, not bothering to disguise a yawn.

Sasha smiled at the man. "We're not keeping you from your work, are we, Mr. Kutusov?"

When he didn't answer, she rose and came around to his side of the desk.

"Sasha? What . . .?" Vera asked, her eyes widening.

Sasha looked at Vera and patted the air in front of her, reassuringly. "I got this one. Not to worry." She turned back to the bank manager and hovered over him. "*What* precisely? Is that what you asked?"

The man looked up at the woman hovering over him and could only nod.

"Precisely this, mister bank manager. We're going to wait here, this young lady and I, while you bring us the account information and deposit box of this man." She pointed to Bondarchuk's name on the court order. "That's *precisely* what the fuck you're going to do. We'll wait here. If we don't have what I've asked for in, let's say, twenty minutes, I'll call Minister Konovalov in Moscow and let him know you're impeding a federal investigation. Questions?"

She backed up, giving the man room to rise and scoot out of the room.

Vera exhaled. "That's how it's done, huh?"

"You can scare the shit out of ninety-nine percent of the population. Scare 'em enough, they'll do whatever you tell 'em. It helps that he was smaller than me."

"And if he'd been bigger."

"Depends on how much bigger."

Eleven minutes later, Kutusov was back with the FSS border guard's account information and deposit box.

"Make yourself scarce," Sasha said to the man.

Kutusov fled the room, closing the door behind him.

Vera laughed, "No mercy."

Sasha smiled and opened the deposit box. The contents made her smile even more broadly.

~~~

After a quick drive through Uzbekistan, Mirza arrived at Ghist Kuprik, the border crossing between Uzbekistan and Kazakhstan. Over the years, he'd learned that the guards here were all young men without skills, without brains, and without futures. Young men who were easily bribed with bottles of Stolichnaya pepper vodka, cartons of Marlboros, a handful of hydrocodone tablets, and an assortment of women's lace undergarments.

After the gift giving and the "thank yous," Mirza was invited into Kazakhstan, no inspection necessary. "See you on your return."

Now, the last and longest leg of the journey—a two and half day, two thousand kilometer slog north to the border with Russia.

The first time Mirza had driven through Kazakhstan, years earlier, he planned to take the highway that ran past the Russian Cosmodrome at Baikonur. He hoped to catch a rocket launch, maybe even a moon shot. But at the highway junction near Kyzylorda, he was stopped by security forces and told that particular road was off-limits to foreign license plates. No use arguing. He'd turned back and never again attempted his rocket ship watching.

In those early years, he could manage seven or eight hundred kilometers a day without a thought. But now, because he'd averaged barely five hours of sleep a night, and because his legs were aching and his back was still killing him, Mirza needed help. He took out a bottle of Percocet, popped one into his mouth, and washed it down with grape juice. He knew the drug made him sleepy, but with his radio blasting and with thoughts of *Her*, his teenage lust-child, Mirza was confident he'd manage. He'd tough it out for the next several hundred kilometers to Zhezqakghan. *However the hell the locals pronounce it.* He'd overnight there and then continue north another eight hundred kilometers to Kostanai in a single, very long day. From there, Russia was only a few hundred kilometers beyond.

But when a combination of smoke and clanking began rolling out from under the Atego's hood, Mirza's plans again took a hit, a blown piston the reason. He had the lorry towed to the Avtomasterskaya Garage in Zhezqakghan where he learned that they'd have to send out for parts.

"Maybe a week. Maybe a little longer," the mechanic promised.

"So be it," Mirza replied. When he tried to call Hafez on his smartphone, he discovered it, too, had succumbed. *"Fucking Apple. I shoulda bought a Samsung."*

Despite being warned about landline usage, he went to a local phone and called Jalalabad, where Hafez arranged to have money wired to the local bank. And he called ahead to Troitsk where his conversation with the border guard was purposely short and vague. They used simple Russian.

> Mirza: *It's me. Atego break. I late.*
> Bondarchuk: *When?*
> Mirza: *Eight days. Maybe more. No Mercedes place here. Need to send to Karaganda for parts.*
> Bondarchuk: *Call again when you're close.*
> Mirza: *OK.*

~~~

All three of them were away—Sasha and Vera checking the contents of deposit boxes, and Martyn buying food—when the tap on Petya Bondarchuk's landline finally produced.

Vera drove to Bondarchuk's apartment bloc. She went to their listeners' rented flat and tuned in. Initially she suspected the wife had made a call, but when she heard the conversation, her eyebrows popped up. She took the recording back to their headquarters. Sasha listened. And then again. She and Vera looked at each other with happy faces.

"This could be really good," Sasha said. "What's your feeling?"

"I like it," Vera said. "Not only for the very suspicious sounding content, but also because the Russian that the other man speaks is definitely *not* native. He's got a Caucusus inflection."

"Afghani?" Sasha asked.

"Maybe. Martyn's the one to ask."

"Definitely Afghani," Martyn confirmed when he returned from shopping. "They have a peculiar cadence that's not like any Uzbek or Turkmen speaker. And they have special trouble with the hard Russian consonants, zhe and che, shch."

"The driver says maybe eight days 'til he gets here," Sasha said. "We're going to be really careful and be totally ready to roll five days from now. Just in case whatever's wrong with his vehicle is fixed quickly. Not the usual way garages work, but we'll stay on the safe side."

"Should someone be monitoring Bondarchuk's line all the time now?" Martyn asked.

"Unfortunately," Sasha said. "This is what real police work is all about. Waiting. We'll do shifts in the apartment. Boring like crazy but no choice."

They waited a week for the second call. When it didn't come, they began to fret.

"The lorry driver has got to be in touch," Sasha told her partners. "I mean, he can't just show up, unannounced. He runs the risk of Bondarchuk not being on duty."

"Right," Vera agreed. "But here we are on the eighth day after the first call and no second call. He was due today."

"So what can we assume?" Martyn asked, then answered his own question. "That, one, the driver contacted Bondarchuk by other means. Maybe by cell. Or, two, that he simply hasn't shown up yet. Or, three, the driver was arrested."

"OK, let's examine those possibilities," Sasha said. "Maybe he contacted Bondarchuk by cell."

"Then why didn't he use his cell phone for the first call?" Vera asked.

"Dead battery, no signal," Martyn answered.

"Both possibilities," Sasha said. "In which case, we could be royally screwed. We have to hope that Martyn's number two—that the driver has not shown up yet—is the reason. Maybe the parts for his Atego didn't come and he's still stuck somewhere."

"That's what we have to hope for," Martyn said. "Otherwise, like you said, we're probably screwed."

"So we need to keep to the same schedule over at Bondarchuk's apartment bloc," Vera said, "listening, waiting and hoping for a second call."

"How long do we give it before we move to a different suspect? Morozova, maybe?" Martyn asked.

"Let's just play it by ear for now, not put a time limit on it just yet," Sasha said. "Meanwhile, whose turn is it to monitor Bondarchuk's landline?"

"I'm up," Vera said. "I'll leave soon. Bondarchuk should be back from work in an hour. Martyn, you're next. See you in eight hours."

"I'll bring you dinner," he said.

~~~

The promised week for repairs turned into sixteen long and boring days. The hotel where Mirza stayed was infested with bedbugs, cockroaches, and a variety of spiders. Small and medium-sized rodents had the run of the place. Hot water ran intermittently and was usually gone by eight in the morning. And the food at the hotel and at the local restaurants was mysterious. Not until after he ordered and took his first bite did Mirza ask the waiter exactly what *'qarta'* was. He was sorry he asked.

He checked out the local whorehouse. He waited across the street to assess the women and the clientele. After a couple hours of observation, he took a pass. For want of something to do, he went once a day to the local mosque. He'd be able to tell Medina that he'd observed *Salat*.

The single bright spot came when he scored a load of Oxycontin at a ridiculously low price. He stocked up.

Not until two and a half weeks after his rig had broken down was Mirza able to get back on the road. The Atego was running smoothly, thanks to the professional work done at the garage in Zhezqakghan. It had cost a small fortune, but Ghafoor had sent enough funds to the local bank to cover the lorry's rehabilitation.

He drove into Kostanai, just south of the border with Russia. While gassing up, Mirza landline-phoned his Bugristoye connection.

Mirza: *It's me. I come visit.*
Bondarchuk: *Great. When?*
Mirza: *Tomorrow okay?*
Bondarchuk: *Good. Between ten and eleven at night.*
Mirza: *OK.*

~~~

Vera was on duty in Bondarchuk's apartment bloc in the afternoon when the call came through. She phoned back to headquarters. "We're on," she said. "Guy is due tomorrow night between ten and eleven." She put her cell phone on speaker and played the tape for Sasha and Martyn.

"Come on home," Sasha said. "Let's get ready."

"I'll bring pastries and lattes," Vera said.

Twenty minutes later, drinking hot coffee and eating donuts, Sasha said, "So, just as we planned and rehearsed. We know the make and model of the lorry, a Mercedes Atego. We use the FSS cameras to spot an Afghani commercial license plate, then we cue the drone to confirm if it's our guy. We wait for it to go by us while we wait up the highway next to the Lukoil gas station.

"We'll test the drones one more time tomorrow morning," Vera said.

"Good idea," Sasha said. "Tomorrow, we pack up everything and get ready to set up in a new location. I'm thinking the lorry driver'll deliver whatever he's carrying to someone in Chelyabinsk. We might come back here to Troitsk, for one or both of our lady suspects, but no telling when. So everything in the car tomorrow. Martyn, make sure the Lada is gassed and ready to roll. You're in charge of the packing. And be sure and get us travel food and fill up a Thermos with coffee."

"Will do."

"OK," Sasha said. "I'll call Konovalov, let him know where we're at."

~~~

The time at the border was twenty minutes to eleven. The Bugristoye crossing was bathed in bright spotlights.

Mirza climbed down from his cab and greeted his long-time ally. They walked to the rear of the lorry through six inches of snow. The driver opened the doors, swung them wide, then lowered the automatic lift gate. The two men got on the heavy steel plate and Mirza raised them up. Bondarchuk spent three minutes pretending to examine the cargo. The lorry driver passed him six, fifty-dollar bills that the guard accepted without looking, then signed off on the manifest, indicating it had passed inspection. The two men returned to the auto-lift and Mirza lowered them to the ground. Bondarchuk nodded to the Afghani and walked toward the next vehicle in line. Mirza climbed back into the Atego's cab, let out a huge sigh of satisfaction, and drove into Russia.

And now the last leg—one hundred and forty kilometers to Chelyabinsk, delivery of the rugs, two, maybe three nights relaxing, score some Percocets, and return through the frontiers with small gifts to distribute to his friends guarding their international borders.

They waited five kilometers north of the border. Vera was sitting in the Lada's passenger seat, toggling her laptop between the FSS license plate scans and the drone's-eye-view of the border crossing from two hundred meters above. Martyn was behind the wheel. Sasha, crammed into the back seat, leaned forward to watch Vera's laptop.

From ten o'clock, only three Afghani lorries had passed through. Each time, Vera had dropped the drone down to take a closer look. But no luck: two Isuzus and a Toyota. No Mercedes yet. At twenty minutes to eleven, another Afghani license plate showed up. Vera again piloted the drone down. "Here it is," she said. "Here's the Atego." She steered the drone close to the vehicle. "There's an eagle on the side, easy to follow."

The drone transmitted images of the lorry driver getting down from his rig and greeting Bondarchuk. The two of them walked to the back of the vehicle and stood on the auto-lift as it raised them up. They entered the back of the lorry and were lost from sight for a few minutes. When they emerged, they parted.

"Bet you anything money changed hands when they were inside the lorry," Martyn said.

"No takers," Sasha said.

When the lorry began to move, Vera raised the drone and locked it on the Atego as it left the border checkpoint and entered Russia.

A few moments later, the Atego passed the Lukoil gas station. Martyn pulled out behind it, but stayed far back. Vera piloted the drone down to a hundred meters above and slightly behind the vehicle.

"No need to get any closer, Martyn," Vera said. "Our eye in the sky has him in clear view."

Martyn kept a safe four vehicles in back of the Afghani lorry. "What's the plan when he stops?" He looked into the rear-view mirror at Sasha, stuffed into the back seat with all of their personal gear as well as Vera's electronics.

"We watch, hopefully see what happens, and take it from there," she said. "I know it sounds a little vague, but we're not really after Bondarchuk or the driver of the lorry. We want to take it up the ladder, nab whoever is the final recipient of whatever the driver's carrying."

"Vague seems to be our working principle," Martyn said.

"Like a lot of police work," Sasha said. "You try to put the pieces together as you find them, try to guess which end is up, and then move to the next step. Sometimes they fit beautifully, sometimes it's a mess."

"Uh-oh," Vera said. "Martyn, you have to close the gap, quick. Get the lorry in sight."

"What's happened?" he asked, speeding up, passing two cars and closing to within sight of the lorry.

"I totally forgot the tunnel we need to go through. The lorry will be lost from the hexacopter's view for the time it takes to go through the tunnel."

"How much time?" Sasha asked.

"The tunnel is about a kilometer long, so at this speed, not quite a minute. Just stay in sight," Vera said.

"Got it," Martyn said.

They passed into and out of the tunnel. The lorry was still in view of the trailing car but the drone had lost contact.

"What gives," Sasha asked. "How come the drone hasn't picked up again?"

"Good question," Vera answered. "I wish I knew. Happens sometimes. You lose sight, lose focus, and the target needs to be re-acquired. Easy to do in the desert in daytime. Like Clooney in *Syriana*. Way harder at night and when we enter a city with lots of traffic." Vera fiddled, adjusted, fine-tuned, but the drone did not find the lorry. "OK Martyn. It's up to you. Stay on him. Keep him in sight."

"Will do."

They entered Chelyabinsk and got off the main highway on Igumenka Street, bordering Smolino Lake. With less traffic now, Martyn dropped back. After passing the Café Panda, the lorry turned right into an unnamed street crowded with grim, multi-storied apartment blocs. Martyn followed and watched as the Afghani vehicle entered a business district, all the shops closed, the streets deserted. The lorry slowed, drove past an unmarked store, and turned into a dark alley.

They drove past and saw the lorry parked, the driver getting down from the cab and moving toward an alleyway door.

"What do we do now?" Martyn asked.

Vera said, "I've got to collect the drone and gas it up, get it ready if we need it again."

"You do that," Sasha said while opening one of Vera's boxes of electronics. She grabbed a pair of night-vision goggles.

"You two find a safe place to park and collect the drone. I'm gonna go around the block, scout out the alley, see if there's another way in. You wait here. If you see the guy come out and get into the lorry, honk twice. I'll get back here as quickly as I can." She adjusted the goggles over her wool cap, then stepped outside the heated car.

The cold hit Sasha like a polar vortex. She huffed out a visible breath, then walked quickly along the empty street, the pavement slick with ice. She entered the alley from the opposite side. Sasha had never worn night vision goggles and was astounded at the clarity and range. She approached the front end of the lorry to within ten meters, but when the door the driver had entered opened and three men came out, she ducked behind a Dumpster.

Guided by the light from a single flashlight, the men spent the next half hour dragging out rolled-up carpets and hauling them into the building. When they finished, another vehicle, a step van arrived, backed into the alley and stopped a few feet from the lorry's rear end. A short man exited the van. He was wearing a Chelsea FC hoodie and thick work gloves. He opened the vehicle's side door then turned and entered the building. A few minutes later, he carried out two cardboard cartons. He put them into the van and drove off.

Sasha retraced her steps and arrived back at the car a minute later. She hopped in the back.

"What's with that van?" Vera asked her. "It was only there for a few minutes."

Sasha took off her gloves and vigorously rubbed her hands together, then blew warm breath into them. "Just long enough for the driver to collect two cartons. I'm guessing they were full of what was probably stored in the rugs."

"Rugs?" Martyn asked.

"Right. They spent half an hour unloading over forty rugs."

"So what's next?" Vera asked.

"You two take a snooze. We'll keep in touch via our wireless mics." Sasha re-packed her goggles.

"And you?" Martyn asked.

"There's a sign in the place's front window, says the store opens at 7 a.m." She checked her watch. "Still a few hours from now. I'll watch what happens, wait for the place to open."

"That's crazy," Martyn said. "It's too fucking cold to hang out. Wait here in the car. Keep warm."

"Nah. Let me have a blanket. I'll be OK. Go find yourselves a spot close by, behind one of these apartment blocs. I'll call."

~~~

On the western bank of Smolino Lake, there's a depressed waterside neighborhood of twelve-story apartment blocs, each containing hundreds of Khrushchev-era tiny flats, named in honor of the former First Secretary. Thousands of working-class families live in the apartments. The blocs are surrounded by dismal parks, sparse greenery, and an all-pervading feeling of disillusionment and abandon.

Standing chockablock with the buildings are a variety of small stores: repair shops, second-hand emporia, appliance outlets, a pair of shoe stores, several groceries, and, of course, the state-owned vodka outlet—for those who can afford it. For those who cannot, there is always 'samogon,' the creative Russian's solution to getting blasted.

Just around the corner from the liquor outlet, tucked between a corner newspaper kiosk and an open-air fruit and vegetable stall, there is not quite a store, more a storefront, its lone, dingy window nearly always curtained closed.

Inside, there is a single empty room measuring seven meters on a side. There are no furnishings, no shelves, nothing hanging on the peeling-painted walls, nothing that might provide a clue as to what once might have been sold here. Tucked into a corner, there is a loosely hinged wooden door that opens to a small, rear office. This room contains a table with an electric samovar perched on it, a file cabinet whose three drawers have disappeared, a pair of spindly wooden chairs, and two chipped mugs in a sink. A door leading into the back alley is secured by a pair of sliding bolts.

This empty shell of an enterprise has irregular operating hours. Usually it's open only one day every other month. Occasionally, it's open less frequently. Occasionally, more.

Two days before the store is ready for business, a sign shows up in the window, announcing the opening.

The night before the big event, a lorry sporting Afghani license plates—the sides of the truck adorned with golden eagles—pulls into the back alley. Three men unload over forty rolled-up rugs and carry them into the store's main room.

Mirza ibn Murad points out three or four rugs. Cords are sliced and the carpets unrolled to reveal several carefully wrapped bundles, each weighing between twelve and twenty kilograms. Destinations are written in code in black marker.

David Osinchuk uses his treasured Swiss Army knife to gently poke one of the packages. He withdraws the blade, its tip now covered with a small coating of white powder. He samples the powder, smiles, and nods to the Afghani.

David tapes over the small hole so that none of the precious cargo be lost. They carefully pack the drug into two cardboard boxes.

They are soon joined by a third man who carries the cartons out the rear door, loads them into his van, then drives away.

Once the cargo is safely off, Mirza and David roll out half the rugs and stand the others upright, leaning them against a wall. That done, they return to the store's back room where the samovar is bubbling. Cream-filled strawberry cakes have appeared, bought by David. He and the driver always enjoy each other's company, though they see one another for barely an hour, only a few times a year.

Mirza's Russian is rough. David's Pashto is limited to curse words and a few appropriate slang expressions. They both know a little English. But for the next hour, they happily manage. They talk about how the rugs and their hidden contents have made it across four international borders, about the next day's rug sale, and how all the carpets will be sold before noon. They laugh. They are relaxed, relieved. Being a solicitous man, David asks about the driver's health after the long drive. Mirza confesses to having a throbbing back and painfully puffed up knees. He complains about being out of Percocets. David assures him he'll find an adequate supply of painkillers before the Afghani starts home.

After the strong tea and sweet cakes, the Russian bids the Afghani farewell, slips a hundred dollar bill into the man's hand, and wishes him a safe journey home.

Because word of mouth about the availability of a bargain galvanizes the neighborhood, the next morning, there will be a line of people waiting for the chance to buy a decent piece of carpet at a surprisingly fair price.

Some, if not most of the customers know that there's probably something fishy going on. Afghani rugs? Brought all the way to Chelyabinsk? And sold for affordable prices? Definitely something fishy. But it's Russia, after all, a place where no good bargain ever goes unbought, and upon which no illegal endeavor is ever looked askance—*na levo* being the guiding principle of Russian economic life.

~~~

Very cold and still dark, the sun not due to rise for another hour. The noise of early morning traffic is muffled by the low mist that has settled on the streets.

Sasha waits in front of the store, stamping her boots and blowing into gloved hands. She's wrapped in a wool blanket. She's been here almost three hours, waiting for the 7 a.m. opening. She's walked around the building twice through the back alley. She's scouted out the lock on the store's rear exit.

A half dozen women join Sasha in line, their breath visible. They are all heavily bundled up with thick woolen scarves and mittens.

By first light, just before seven, there are twenty or more people in a line that stretches down the block and snakes around the corner.

Sasha turns to a group of three women behind her. They exchange "good mornings." She listens attentively to the women's conversation and hears that rugs will be sold. Afghani rugs. Good quality and at a reasonable price.

"It's my first time here," Sasha says to the woman second in line. "Rugs any good? I don't want to spend my money on poor quality merchandise."

The woman looks at her skeptically, but answers, "Yeah. Very good."

"Have you bought here before?" Sasha asks.

The woman continues her questioning stare, but responds, "Yeah. Twice." And now with a tinge of suspicion in her voice,

"You're not from Chelyabinsk, are you?"

Sasha remembers Martyn's warning about her archaic Russian. "No. Khabarovsk. Just visiting." She turns from the woman, hoping that the faraway place she named—sixty-five hundred kilometers to the east—will somehow account for her unusual speech.

"Khabarovsk?" the woman counters. "You talk like an Evenk. Or a Chukchi."

Nothing to do but respond. Sasha turns and smiles at the woman. "I'm not Evenk. I'm Russian." *Leave it there*, she thinks.

Happily, the curtains on the store's front window split wide and a moment later, the door opens. The crowd, Sasha in the lead, surges forward.

Inside, she sees at least forty rugs, either spread out on the floor or rolled up and leaning on the walls. Most are at least two meters long, some even longer. They appear to be as the woman described them—good quality. And the prices attached to each seem to Sasha to be more than fair. She looks at several, even as the crowd surrounds her, shoves her out of the way, and begins to grab up the carpets.

"Folks, take your time, please," a voice implores.

Sasha looks toward the rear of the small store where a skinny young man stands in the doorway. He is thin, pale, and bushy-haired. He wears sweat pants, a Chelsea FC hoodie, and sneakers. He moves to stand next to the front door.

Several buyers have hefted the carpets and carry or drag them toward the door. They pause at the exit to pay. The young man collects the money, gives change, thanks the buyers. Within twenty minutes, every one of the rugs is sold and has been carted away. Sasha is soon left alone with the man.

"I guess I missed out," she says. "I couldn't decide."

"Not to worry. Come back in a month or two. They'll be another sale."

"Really? I hope so. You'll be back in a month? What day? What's your name?"

The man is counting a fistful of rubles. He pauses and gives Sasha the same questioning look the woman gave her while she waited in line. Though not as threatening.

"I'm Motke. Next sale is April. Might even try to be here before Easter." He finishes counting, takes out a set of keys, holds them up and jingles them, letting her know he's ready to lock up.

"Sorry," she says. "April, you said?"

He nods an affirmative.

Sasha leaves the store as Motke shuts the door behind her. She hears the lock's tumblers fall into place and a dead bolt shot. A moment later, the sign announcing the sale is removed from the window and the curtains are drawn. The three women who stood in line behind her are gathered across the street at a bus stop. Their newly purchased rugs are leaning against a fence. One of the women looks Sasha's way and nudges the other two. All three stare at her. Sasha smiles at them and walks around the corner and into the alley. She ducks behind some large trash bins and watches as Motke comes out the back door. He padlocks the door and hurries off. Sasha dumps her blanket onto a trashcan, phones Vera, and tells her she's following the man who organized the rug sale. "Same guy with the van, the one I saw last night carrying the carpets into the store, the one who drove off with the goods. I'll let you know soon what's what. Stay close."

Sasha easily trailed the rug seller for several blocks into a more upscale neighborhood. They arrived at Chapayev Street where Motke stopped in front of a man sitting on the steps that led up to number 47. Sasha stopped and watched from across the street and down half a block.

Chapayev 47 was a five-story apartment house, considerably newer and nicer than the ones closer to the rug store. The man on the steps was wrapped in an oversized down parka. The dark blue watch cap drawn down over his head didn't keep his shoulder-length, red hair from spilling out in all directions. He had a prizefighter's nose. The rug salesman passed him the bundle of rubles he collected at the carpet sale. The sitting man peeled off a chunk and handed it back to Motke. The two talked a bit more until the rug salesman walked off. The red-haired man rose, climbed the stairs onto the building's stoop, and entered. Sasha considered her options: continue following the rug seller, or stay with the man who got most of the money from the sale. The choice was obvious. She followed the red-haired man into the building. The small, tiled lobby was empty and smelled of disinfectant. Three locked bicycles, each with fat tires, were chained together in a corner. An elevator with a moving arrow above it showed the floors. The arrow slowed and stopped on the 5th floor. Sasha went to the tenant mailboxes set into the wall and was pleased to see that all of the boxes were intact and had names attached. There were two apartments on the fifth floor: 5A—Maxim Gordiev. 5B—Tamara Stoikova/David Osinchuk.

Sasha wrote down the names and left the building. She phoned Vera, gave her the names and told the techie to dig.

"On it. Won't take long. We meeting soon? Martyn's getting coffee and pastries."

"Yeah, let's meet. I'm standing in front of Chapayev Street 58. It's a new apartment building across the street from where the guy went in. There's a sign advertising rentals. Might be a good place to set up."

~~~

Mirza found lodging at the three-star Meridian Hotel, just a few kilometers north of the rug store. Happily done with his business, he settled into his room and made two calls back to Jalalabad. He spoke with his wife on the first call (*Yes, dear, I prayed five times a day*) and to Hafez on the second (*Perfect delivery*). He took the last of his Zhezqakghan-acquired Oxycontins, luxuriated in an hour-long bath, and fell asleep at once.

He planned to start back to Jalalabad in three days. But for now, he needed to recupe, to let his body mend before he got back into the Atego. He needed *not* to sit for half a day, immobile behind a steering wheel.

He rose at eight the next morning, dressed in warm clothes, and took a long walk. A kilometer into it, his knees began to feel better and he was able to properly straighten his back. When he returned to the hotel, the desk clerk called to him, "A phone message for you, sir."

Mirza went to the house phone. The message was short. "Come by the garage this morning," David said. "I have something for you." Exactly what the driver was hoping to hear.

In a buoyant mood, he enjoyed a continental breakfast at the hotel's restaurant. Later, he'd drive to David's garage to collect the promised supply of painkillers. *Hopefully enough to get me back home.* Following that, he'd trash his Apple Smartphone and buy himself a Samsung Galaxy. *Fucking Apple.*

~~~

Before Martyn and Vera showed up, the red-haired man left the building and started walking away from Sasha. No problem following the man, his long red hair leading the way. Sasha was able to lie back, never losing sight of him. After a fifteen-minute walk, he arrived at a garage, SportMotoServ. Sasha waited across the street, next to a diner, and watched as he used a set of keys to unlock the front door. He entered, and a moment later, one of the two roll-up garage doors opened. Sasha called Vera again. "Guy I'm watching seems to operate a garage, place called SportMotoServ. I'm on Christopolskaya Street 26. How soon can you get here?"

"No time at all," Vera said. "Maybe three minutes. I'll go to Burger King, get us breakfast."

"Really? Burger King? That's what I'm eating for breakfast?"

"I'll keep it simple. Coffee and a piece of pastry. OK?"

"I guess."

Twenty minutes later, Sasha was grateful to be warming up in the back seat of their car with the heater on high. They were parked across the street and three doors down from the red-haired man's place of work. She was finishing her second chocolate croissant.

Martyn was behind the wheel, Vera in the front passenger seat, her computer open on her lap. "I think I've pretty much eliminated the other guy on the fifth floor, Gordiev," she said.

"Let's hear it," Sasha said.

"Nothing there. No previous arrests. No weirdness in his past life. He's a groundskeeper at the South Ural State University. I was able to access the university's personnel files."

"Could be a front," Martyn said. "The shy and unassuming groundskeeper is actually the heroin kingpin of south Russia. Kinda like the dude in *Breaking Bad*, the guy who owned the fried chicken restaurants."

"I don't think so," Vera said, holding up her computer. "Here's his picture."

Sasha leaned into the front seat and looked at a bearded and round-faced man with glasses and crew cut blond hair.

"No way," she said, laughing. "This is not the guy I just followed, not the guy who took the rug sale money."

"Totally agree," Vera said. "The guy over there in the garage is David Osinchuk. And he is definitely, one hundred percent our guy. Here's his photo. I downloaded it from the local police's criminal archives."

"That's the guy I followed," Sasha said.

"And the rug seller this morning?" Vera said. "Turns out he—Motke, you said his name was—he's Osinchuk's nephew."

"Tell me more about Osinchuk," Sasha said. She took a last mouthful of croissant and washed it down with coffee.

"You're going to love this," Vera said. "By trade, he's a motorcycle mechanic. This is his garage. But that's probably a cover. I found him in the local *and* the federal criminal registries. David Osinchuk is a drug dealer. Of some note, actually, with a long and distinguished police record."

"I *am* loving it," Sasha said.

"Oh yeah. Has a well documented history. Been in the business his whole life." Vera scrolled down and read, "Started in Odessa, where he was born. Busted when he was twelve for possession of hashish. He's been arrested five other times and charged with five different drug-related crimes. Convicted only once for possession of a small quantity of heroin. Did seven months in Kopeysk, a local prison. That was more than ten years ago. No arrests since. Not sure who he works for now but the Justice Ministry thinks he's active in buying and selling heroin, moving opioids, dabbling in minor stuff, hash and marijuana. That's our David," Vera said, pointing at the garage with an unlit cigarette.

"Great work. And by the way, Vera, you can't smoke in the

car without opening a window, and you can't open the window without us freezing our asses off," Sasha said.

Vera shook her head and reluctantly put the cigarette back into the pack.

"And the woman in Osinchuk's apartment?" Sasha asked. "How does she fit in?"

Vera returned to her computer screen, scrolled down again.

"Tamara Stoikova is the Senior Charge Nurse at Polyclinic Number 2." Vera opened to the hospital's web page. "Here's her photo."

Sasha looked over Vera's shoulder at the picture of nurse Stoikova: straight brown hair, cut short, large dark eyes over high cheekbones, full lips, a nose with a noticeable bump on it, and a welcoming smile. "Nice looking woman," Sasha said. "Are they married?"

"I checked Tamara's name on the ZAGs registry. She and David were married two years ago."

"Kids?"

"Marco. Twenty-two-years-old, her son by a previous marriage. He studies carpentry in a voc-ed school."

Sasha sat back, taking in all of Vera's information. "I need more coffee," she said. "Martyn, go do it, coordinate coffee and more pastries."

He was back in ten minutes with a bag full of cakes and cookies, and three tall cups of steaming coffee.

Just as they began to dig in, Martyn yelled and pointed through the front windshield. Sasha and Vera looked up. A lorry with a golden eagle painted on its side was pulling up in front of the garage.

"We've just connected all the dots," Sasha said. "At least those happening here in Chelyabinsk."

They watched as the driver got down from the lorry and walked toward the garage. The door opened and the red-haired man, now identified as David Osinchuk, came out and took the driver's hand. The two shook and went back into the building. The door closed behind them.

"And now?" Vera asked.

"Give me a little quiet, please," Sasha said. "I need to think." She sipped her coffee. After a minute, she spoke, "Martyn, go walk by the back of the lorry. You'll be hidden from the garage. Use your smartphone and get a photo of the license plate without being seen. Then walk around the block and come back."

Martyn left to do what he'd been told.

"What're you thinking?" Vera asked.

"The lorry driver is not worth following. He has an empty rig. He's already dropped off last night what he was carrying, probably wrapped in those rugs."

"Do you think the cargo might be in the garage?" Vera asked.

"That's a hard one. If I were Osinchuk, a known drug dealer, guy with a record, I'd be nuts to store drugs in my place of business. I could be wrong, however. I mean, criminals do all kinds of stupid shit. That's why most of 'em are in prison. But four of the five times he's been arrested, he's avoided jail. So I'm thinking he may be brighter than most. And he hasn't been arrested again in ten years, you said. So, no. The goods are probably *not* in the garage. Nor would they be in his apartment. He's probably already moved them."

Martyn returned and got in the car. "God, is it cold out there."

"Get the license?" Sasha asked.

"You ask, I deliver," he said. He showed them the photo on his smartphone.

"Afghani commercial license plate," Vera said. "Give me a minute and I'll tap into their department of motor vehicles and find us a name to go with the lorry."

"Driver'll be heading back home soon," Sasha said. "I think it's time to let the minister know where we're at."

She called Konovalov and filled him in on their work. She told the minister about the carpet sale, about her following the rug seller to Chapayev 47, trailing Osinchuk to his work, and the surprise arrival of the same lorry they'd followed the night before.

"David Osinchuk?" the minister asked. "We know about him. He's been on our radar for years. Excellent work, Sasha."

She listened, smiling. She put her hand over the phone and whispered to her partners, "Konovalov thinks we're all brilliant."

Vera and Martyn glowed.

Sasha spoke into the phone. "We'll concentrate on Osinchuk, put a bug on him. We'll leave the driver and the border guard, Bondarchuk, for you to deal with. Vera will send you the lorry's license and description." She nodded while listening. "Got it. We'll be in touch later tonight, when we're set up." She closed the call. "You two should be due for a hefty raise." They glowed some more and watched as the driver left the garage, got back into his lorry, and drove off.

"I think we're done here. Let's go back to Chapayev Street, see about renting a place in that apartment bloc across the street."

~~~

"Where are you off to this time," Sophia asked her husband.

"Novosibirsk. Leaving tonight at nine. Be there for a

- 349 -

couple days," Anatoly said. "You going to visit your sister tonight?"

"Yeah. Soon as I get cleaned up and take Marat to the babysitter."

Anatoly picked up his suitcase and went to the door. "I'll call when I get there," he said. "Have fun."

"You too," she answered.

Anatoly had told the truth about his destination, but lied about the takeoff time. He wasn't scheduled to leave until the next morning. He didn't go to the airport but, rather, waited across from his apartment bloc, hidden in the bushes. After an hour, Sophia had not left for her sister's, but Dima, his boss arrived by cab, and went into Anatoly's apartment complex. The cuckold drew in a deep breath. *Fuckin' Dima. Fuckin' Sophia.* After two uneventful hours of waiting, Anatoly took a taxi to the airport and sat in the crew lounge, drinking coffee and wondering how he should react to the not totally unsurprising news that his boss was screwing his wife. If he broached Sophia's infidelity to her, she'd deny it and find a way to use his accusations to divorce him, take Marat, and stick him for alimony. She could also threaten to expose his illegalities. No way out of his Sophia-situation. And his drug trafficking? An equally, if not thornier problem. There was no wiggle room with this band of serious criminals. He belonged to them, body and soul. Still, he did have a nice load of American cash in his safety deposit box, upwards of fourteen thousand dollars. He thought about how he could use it to help himself. Flee to another part of the country? Try to fashion himself a new identity? As big as Russia was, he knew it was a hard place in which to disappear.

~~~

David Osinchuk had long ago learned that women make the best drug couriers. He found them braver, cooler under fire, and less given to panic. The eleven women he employed carried product to all corners of Russia and by all means of transportation. By the afternoon of the rug sale, three of the four bundles of heroin brought to Chelyabinsk by Mirza ibn Murad were given to some of his most dependable workers: two retirees and a twenty-six-year-old university student.

One of the pensioner/mules was Anita, a sixty-eight-year-old former kindergarten teacher whose paltry pension failed to cover the costs of keeping her aged and infirm parents from starving.

The other older woman was Oksana, a seventy-one-year-old former clerk in the Paymaster Corps of the Russian Ministry of Defense. Her husband lost a leg to an Afghani IED near Mazan Sharif in 1983 and his veteran's pension doesn't come close to covering the cost of his acquired opioid habit.

These two women have never met each other, and if David has his way, never will.

The ladies are both bound for St. Petersburg, one by train, the other by bus.

The retired teacher's twelve-kilo package will be transported down the Neva River, past the Hermitage Museum—formerly the Czar's winter palace—to the city's harbor. A brief journey across the Gulf of Finland will bring the contraband to the North Sea port of Gdansk, in Poland. There, the product will be stepped on, further divided into smaller packages, and trans-shipped by boat to other Baltic ports: to Klaipeda, in Lithuania; to Liepaja in Latvia; and to Parnu in Estonia. Where the white powder goes from there is strictly the business of the local *capos*.

Oksana's slightly larger, fourteen-kilo bundle is headed for Leipzig, in the former East Germany. There, persistent unemployment has forced thousands to seek whatever solace they might find from heroin's intense downer.

The third parcel—weighing in at just over seventeen kilos—will be taken to Moscow by Liubov Ivanovna Karpova, an aspiring doctoral candidate at the prestigious Moscow State University. She'll hand it off to a handsome young man she dates occasionally, a chauffeur for a Moscow mid-level don. The heroin will undergo a stepping-on, possibly two such dilutions, and be sold locally, in Birbirevo, a crowded and depressed suburb in the capital's north end.

Liubov's doctoral thesis, *'The Long Term Social Consequences for Russia of the Soviet-Afghan War, 1979-89: Drug Use Among Veterans.'* is set to be defended next year.

The young courier knows better than cutting too close to the bone as she prepares her dissertation. What she has learned 'on the job' stays 'on the job.' David has made that unequivocally clear and intends to read his courier's PhD effort before her doctoral committee does.

The fourth and largest package of contraband—twenty kilos—is going on a long journey: by train to Vladivostok, by boat across the Bering Sea to Alaska, by barge to Seattle, and from there, by car, bus, and train to New York City.

It will be given to David's favorite mule, the nurse who saved his life, and the woman with whom that life has become inextricably intertwined.

~~~

They got lucky. The newly built twelve-story structure opposite Chapayev 47 was a multi-use structure with underground parking, ground floor stores, and flats above, most still available for rent. A sixth-floor apartment was vacant. Vera made the rental arrangements. She signed a year lease using Konovalov's credit card. When they were left alone in the bare apartment, she laughed. "I've done this before for him," she said. "Soon as we're done, he'll cancel the lease, leave the management holding the bag. They'll try and argue. Won't work." She turned to Sasha. "How long will we be here?"

"No telling," Sasha said. "We have to plan for the long haul. According to Konovalov, Osinchuk is an important local mob guy. We'll stick with him, so we'll need to make this place livable. Martyn, take Konovalov's credit card and fix us up. First thing we'll need are window curtains. And by the end of the day, bed and bedding, tables, chairs, a set of shelves, bathroom stuff, soap and shampoo and towels, toilet paper. Get us a small fridge and a hotplate. And a microwave. Plates and cutlery and mugs and a coffee maker."

"And sleeping stuff," Vera said. "I should probably go with you. There's an IKEA store on Bazhova Street, near First Lake."

"Guys, I'm beat," Martyn said. "We've been up since yesterday morning. How 'bout we nap for a couple hours, then re-group?"

Sasha looked around their empty apartment. "Let's unload the car and bring our stuff up. Then we can snooze a bit."

"Thanks. When we get up, why don't we *all* go to IKEA?" Martyn suggested. "I like their meatballs."

"The horsemeat ones or the beef ones?" Vera asked.

"You mean there's a difference?"

The first thing they did when they got back from shopping was to put up heavy window curtains which they kept drawn while they turned their apartment into a sophisticated spy site. By noon the next day they were ready to begin surveilling David Osinchuk. They added a second set of curtains—gauzy and see-through—that allowed them to carefully observe the comings and goings in apartment 5B, across the street.

When they checked in with Konovalov, he was furious. "I just got notification that my credit card was charged over two hundred thousand rubles at IKEA. Almost three thousand dollars. What the hell's going on, Sasha?"

"It's simple, mister minister. You want us to grab Osinchuk and put a dent into heroin trafficking in Chelyabinsk? OK. That's not going to happen tomorrow, probably not next week, and maybe, just maybe—if we get a lucky break—it may happen next month. Towards that end, we've rented a place opposite Osinchuk's apartment. We've set up a listening and watching post and we'll be here a while. We need to eat and sleep like normal human beings. We've bought the bare minimum to be able to do that. Any other questions?"

Konovalov was silent for a moment, then chuckled. "Right you are, Sasha. I won't complain. You've already done very well in the short time you've been here. Carry on." He closed the phone call.

Sasha looked at her two smiling partners. "We're cool."

~~~

Mirza's brightly decorated lorry was stopped as he attempted to leave Russia through the Bugristoye frontier crossing. He wasn't worried. Normal procedure. The back of his rig was totally empty.

An unknown border guard approached. He was armed with a pistol. Standing nearby, two other armed guards watched as the first man approached Mirza's lorry and climbed up on the driver-side steel steps.

"Name and papers," the man ordered with a snarl.

Mirza wasn't a stranger to such peremptory behavior. During the ten-year war the Soviets made on his countrymen, he had been subjected to numerous bouts of such brusque conduct. He knew how to deal with it. He used his limited language skills and asked in pigeon Russian, "What's going on?"

The guard sneered through his mustache and acne-pocked face. "What's going on?" he spat at Mirza. "What the fuck you think is going on, you shit-faced camel jockey?"

With as much *sang-froid* as he could manage, Mirza said, "My papers are in order. And my lorry is empty. Have a look." He took his entry and exit documents from an envelope on the passenger seat and offered them to the guard. "Read."

At that moment, he watched through his passenger-side mirror as one of the guards reached into the daypack draped over the other guard's shoulder. He took out two small red packages. Two small red packages that looked to Mirza similar to the ones he had just delivered recently to David Osinchuk at the rug store. The man held up the packages for Mirza to see, laughed, and walked to the back of the lorry. The driver heard his rig's rear doors clank open, then heard one of them yell, "Hey, what's this here? Looks like contraband."

This is it," Mirza thought. *I've been set up. I'm fucked.* The thought of spending the rest of his life in some Siberian forced labor camp made his stomach rumble. A burst of fatalism seized him. He shoved the guard off the steps. The man fell, sprawling on the ground next to the lorry. Mirza grabbed the pistol hidden below the passenger seat and shot the man three times in the back. A squad of guards came running toward the front of the lorry, their rifles at their shoulders. Other border personnel in front of him lowered the heavy metal crossbar that blocked the road and sealed him in. Mirza screamed out, "Medina," then put the pistol to his temple, thought about the schoolgirl, how beautiful her calves were, and blew his brains out.

~~~

They parted the curtains just enough to allow them to use their Zeiss spotting scope. From their throw-together headquarters, they could look down into the 5th floor kitchen, living room, and just barely into the bedroom of apartment 5B's three tenants.

Martyn brought a pair of beers for him and Vera and a Pepsi for Sasha.

"We figure out their schedules," Sasha said, "when they're all away. Then Vera can do her thing."

The spotters took turns watching and charting the schedules of the three residents of apartment 5B. The team was relieved to learn that the people upon whom they were spying kept their curtains open most evenings when they were at home, closing them only at bedtime.

Using a 500 mm telephoto camera lens, the spotters were able to put together an album of the Osinchuk/Stoikova family.

"Osinchuk's a funny looking guy," Vera said. "I mean, besides having a nose from hell, he's always making faces, acting the clown."

"And it works," Sasha said. "The nurse and her son are always laughing. It's a pretty merry household."

By the end of the first week, they learned that Osinchuk and Stoikova left together around seven in the morning. They returned home separately—she about six, he usually an hour later.

Sasha followed the nurse to her work one morning and

waited outside the hospital for half a day, not knowing exactly why. Nothing noteworthy except for a pair of pre-teen boys hanging around across the street from the main entrance. They'd arrived the same time as the nurse and were still there when Sasha left at noon.

Twice, Sasha and Martyn were at Osinchuk's garage before he arrived. They sat across the street in their rental car, drinking gallons of so-so coffee and eating too many croissants. The garage activity was limited to patrons delivering their ailing motorcycles or taking away their newly repaired ones.

Marco's ins and outs were student-regular. He left for school at seven-twenty every morning and arrived home a little after five. Sasha followed him to his school one morning. Again, nothing remarkable.

They also fixed the timetable of Maxim Gordiev—the other 5th floor tenant. They found his life to be unerringly normal. He left for work at the university at seven-fifty and returned at five-thirty in the evening.

With the schedules of all four of the 5th floor residents now firmed up, Vera decided it was time to visit. When the four had left one morning, the spotters went into action.

Vera donned the Chelyabinsk Department of Utilities uniform that Martyn had somehow procured, took her tool bag, and crossed over to Chapayev 47. Sasha watched Osinchuk's apartment through the spotting scope, while Martyn was down on the street, ready to alert Vera if he saw any 5th floor tenants return home early. He was bundled up against a light snow and a chill wind, looking unhappy about his sentry duties.

Sasha watched as Vera smiled at a pair of babushkas who squeezed through the front door of Chapayev 47. Vera entered the lobby and spoke into her lapel mic. "Inside, empty, getting into the lift."

"I hear you," Sasha told her.

"Loud and clear," said Martyn. "We're cool on the street."

Vera rode to the 5th floor. The door lock was trickier than she'd imagined. She usually was able to pick a lock and gain entry in less than two minutes. This one took her four.

Sasha watched Vera through the spotting scope as she went about her work, placing five bugs: one near the flat's short entryway, one in David and Tamara's bedroom, two in the living room, and one in the kitchen. Vera spoke into them from varying distances and waited for Sasha's validation.

Before leaving apartment 5B, Vera did a quick search for a diary, phone book, something in which David Osinchuk might have entered data that would be of interest. "Nothing obvious," she reported. She looked around one last time, making sure she'd left no trace of her being there. She locked up, took the stairs down, and passed through a deserted lobby. Out on the street, she winked at Martyn, then walked to a nearby produce vendor, bought apples and pears, and returned to their apartment. Martyn followed a minute later.

"That was really, really cool," Sasha said. "I've set bugs a couple times, but they were big hunkers, and were wired, not the cute little things you just planted. And not with the range and clarity of these Russian-made jobs."

"You've done it only twice? I've done it maybe twenty times."

Sasha arched an eyebrow. "Am I allowed to ask where and when and who ordered it?"

"State secrets," Vera said, laughing. "Really, I planted them in some of the least intriguing places you can imagine. I'm not sure why we're at all interested in some of these mundane conferences—a meeting of Polish hog farmers in Lodz, or acupuncturists in Marseilles. I'm not kidding."

From their 6th floor spy-site, the three traded off at the telescope and the headphones.

Martyn kept a loose watch from bedtime—usually eleven—until wake-up, at six. Vera took the next shift until four in the afternoon. Neither had much to report since the three people they were watching were either asleep or away. Both complained about how boring the work was.

"Most of police work is terrifically boring," Sasha told them. "You wait for your suspects to do something. Sometimes takes days. You can't hurry the process."

Sasha took over at four every evening and worked until the folks she was watching went to bed.

At half past seven one evening, Sasha listened and watched the nurse and her son eat pizza in the kitchen. Their conversation was coming through loud and clear via bug #4, hidden between wooden slats in a kitchen cabinet. They made small talk, Marco telling about his day at his carpentry trade school. His mother paid close attention, often asking questions, seeking clarification. He left after dinner and half an hour later, David Osinchuk arrived. Tamara greeted him in the entryway. Sasha could hear them but couldn't see them clearly until they came into the living room. Sasha was captivated by what she witnessed. They embraced, kissed, smiled, kidded each other. He said something inaudible that caused her to laugh and push him away. He grabbed her hand and pulled her to him. She resisted happily, then just as happily, gave in and allowed herself to be dragged to an armchair near a window. She wound up sitting in his lap. They remained that way for a good ten minutes, chatting amiably, stroking each other's face and arms and neck, her fingers running through his long, red hair. She playfully tried to grab at his twisted nose, but he fended her off, batting away her hands. She whispered something in his ear that made him giggle. After kissing him on the mouth, she raised herself up and went to the kitchen. She heated two slices of pizza in the microwave, poured a beer, and set the food on the counter. He washed his hands in the sink and sat down. Tamara sat opposite him. The audio was clear.

"Bad news, Tama."

"What?"

"One of our Afghani drivers got killed leaving the country. I don't know how, heard there was a shooting at Bugristoye."

"Someone you've worked with?"

"Often. For years, in fact. A good guy. I just collected from him."

"Wait a minute. If he was caught, could they have traced him to you?"

David didn't reply.

"Answer me."

"It's possible."

"And what about Vlad? Are Marco and I still going?"

"Yeah, as usual, on Friday. I just made arrangements for you at the Hyundai."

They broke off talking. David took a brown bag from his pants pocket and put it on the table. Tamara regarded it with a frown.

"I know what's in the bag, David."

"I know you do. I'm sure you'll never have to use it. But for my sake, for my peace of mind, I'm asking. Please, dear."

She put a slice of pizza on a plate and pulled it toward her. "For your sake? I'm supposed to do it for you? To make you happy? What I'm carrying to Vlad is enough to get me twenty years in IK-14. Toughest broads in the country in that prison."

She took a bite of pizza and a swallow of beer. "If I'm caught with this weapon, David, the charges multiply, get more serious. I'll never see the light of day. Nor will I ever see Marco again. Or you."

He brought a pistol out of the bag. He held it in his palm. She sat back, dropped her hands into her lap. David explained:

"It's a Yarygina. Standard army pistol."

"Marco and I have done six train trips to Vlad without the need of a weapon."

"I know, dearest. But some things have changed. We're getting more heat from the Azeris."

"Do they know about me? Should I be afraid?"

"They know about me, and by extension, they probably know about you, too. Sorry."

Tamara slumped in her seat and rubbed her eyes with the heels of her palms. With her fingers, she massaged her scalp.

"Alright. I'll carry it. But I'll use it only as a very last resort, if then."

"I can live with that. You know, Tama. You can walk right now. I can replace you without any trouble at all. Really, I can."

"I've been thinking about it for a long time. We've talked about it before. But I need the money for Marco's school."

Sasha watched them with more than her cop's interest. *Look at what they have. A real partnership. They seriously care for each other. And they get to live in the same apartment, not separated by the equator.* She realized she was jealous. She took off her earphones and spoke to her partners. "They're a nice couple."

"For heroin smugglers, you mean," Martyn said.

"Sure, they're criminals, but . . . they're sweet together. They enjoy each other's company. They worry about each other."

"Love among thieves," Martyn said.

Vera looked questioningly at Sasha. "What's up with you?"

Sasha didn't reply. *David reminds me of my husband, Robin, dead and buried too many years ago. We had the same kind of relationship as these two.* She put her earphones back on and resumed listening.

"You've shot pistols before, Tama?"

"In Khost, when I was in the army. A captain took me shooting. He had a Nagant and he let me fire it a couple times. Weighed a ton. He said the Bolsheviks used them when they stormed the Winter Palace."

David took back the handgun and popped the empty magazine. "You can load as many as fifteen rounds, but I'd recommend half that many. Less pressure on the spring. And how many bullets will you really need, after all?" he chuckled.

"Not funny, David. Not at all. I'm still not sure if I even want to take the damn thing."

"Sorry, Tama. I am, really. I didn't mean to be flip over something as important to you as this."

"Where can I test fire it?"

"Test fire? You don't trust me?"

"When I was in Afghanistan, I saw the results of poorly maintained weapons, backfiring, even exploding some time. I'll want to give this pistol a trial run. You've fired it, I suppose."

"Actually, no. I got it only last week. Gave a militiaman twenty Oxycontin in trade."

"We'll do a test run."

"For sure. We can go north of town, top of Second Lake. The warehouses out by Zarya are usually deserted. I've shot there before. We'll go late. Tomorrow night, if you like."

"I don't like. But we'll go."

"Second Lake," Vera pointed on the map. "Close by. Do we need to follow them out there?"

"I don't think so," Sasha said. "No point, really. They'll shoot, come back, prepare to go to Vlad in two days."

"This Friday," Vera said. "And, do we stay with Osinchuk, or follow the nurse?"

"Both," Sasha said. "I've been thinking about it. We need to see where the drugs go, in whose hands they end up. That'll be my job. I'll follow her to Vlad."

"I thought you told us you'd never go there again. Too scary," Martyn said. "After your last time there and your problem with the mayor, what's his name?"

"Kollantai. Roman Kollantai. Mayor and mobster, all in one. You're right. I don't relish the idea of traveling there, but no choice, really. The deal I made with your boss. I'm committed to trying to trace the drug as far as I can, and if it means traveling to Vlad, then I travel to Vlad. Like it or not."

"And us?" Vera asked. "You want us to stay on Osinchuk?"

"That and another task. The other two women border guards? Andropova and Morozova. I know it's hard to do with only the two of you, and especially difficult since Osinchuk is here in Chelyabinsk and the two women are on the border in Troitsk. Think you can manage?"

"Frankly, no," Martyn said. "If we had a couple more helpers, then, maybe yes. But just Vera and I? Won't work."

"I agree with Martyn," Vera said. "We need electronics both here and at the border. Martyn isn't schooled in operating the gear we need at both places. So, it's a 'no' for me, too. I suggest that we stay here, keep an eye on Osinchuk. He'll be in contact with Tamara. We'll listen in on their conversations. They may give a clue to where the heroin goes after she passes it off. Could help you."

Sasha nodded. "Good argument, guys. I'm convinced. I'll call Konovalov, update him. I follow her. You stay here."

~~~

Hafez Ghafoor was worried. He hadn't heard from his driver for three days. "Let's give Mirza another couple of days," he told Kamal.

"And if there's no word, then what?"

"Then we have to assume the worst. We'll make inquiries, call up there, ask if there's anything about him in the newspapers. Usually, when the Russians make a drug bust at the border, they like to play it up, boast how impervious their frontier is."

"And his family?"

Ghafoor sighed heavily. The noise from the factory percolated into his office. "Depends on what I discover. If he's been arrested or . . ."

Kamal filled in, " . . . or dead . . ."

"Right. There's always that possibility. In either case, the Shaikh will do right by the family."

Two days later, Kamal was back in Ghafoor's office.

"It's bad news, Hafez. Mirza's dead. Shot himself when guards stopped him at the border."

"You're certain? How did you find out?"

"Hakeem read about it on line, on Ural News, or Ural Express. I'm not sure of the name of the news service. But the article, according to Hakeem, specifically named Mirza ibn Murad. Said he was stopped on his way out of Russia, refused to allow his lorry to be searched, pulled a gun, shot and killed a border guard, then shot himself."

Ghafoor exhaled, sagged, and scratched his unshaven

face. "I don't get why he didn't allow the lorry to be searched. He'd already dropped off the load days before. He called me and verified that. Said he was coming back soon. His lorry would have been empty."

"Hard to know. If we ever will," Kamal said. "You want me to tell Medina and his girls?"

Ghafoor swiveled his chair so he could look out the window. A lorry was being loaded with rugs. He turned and faced Kamal. "I think the Shaikh will want to tell his family. Mirza was his oldest nephew and was a regular visitor out at the compound."

Kamal rose and walked to the window. "Who's going to take Mirza's place up to Chelyabinsk?" Kamal asked.

"Soon as I put the word out that we're looking for a new driver, I'll have fifty applicants. Never a problem finding drivers. You want something to eat?"

"I wouldn't say 'no' to coffee and cake, if you have any."

"I'll fire up the Nespresso and call down for something. I think the kitchen made elephant's ears for lunch. Will do?"

"My favorite. Order at least four pieces for me."

~~~

Tamara and David drove north out of town, to the upper end of Second Lake, where small clusters of abandoned buildings and hollowed-out fish processing factories hugged the rocky shoreline. A full moon reflected off of an ice-washed beach. Tin cans and rusted oil drums lay scattered among large timbers left over from a pier built in the 1960s.

They walked down to the water's edge, their breath billowing out in front of them. David took a dented can and stood it on a flat boulder.

"I can't see any situation where you'd have to shoot from

more than a few feet. So stand here, a couple paces from the can and have a go." He handed her the pistol and a magazine.

She took the magazine in a gloved hand and examined it. "Cleaned it lately?"

"Just today. Scrubbed it. Pistol, too."

"How many rounds?"

"Ten."

"I brought these," she said, putting foam plugs into her ears, and giving David a pair.

He put the plugs in then pointed the weapon away from them and demonstrated: first he verified that the pistol was on 'safety,' slid the magazine into the grip, pulled back on the slide, and eased a bullet into the firing chamber. He handed her the weapon. "Ready to go. How 'bout that can?"

She reluctantly took the pistol. "Why did I let you talk me into this?" She turned toward the target, released the safety, spread her legs, held the weapon with two hands, and aimed at the large can that years ago had held cooked tomatoes. She squeezed off a round. The can flew backwards five meters and rolled toward the shore, stopping at the water line.

"Dead eye," David said, stooping down, searching for the spent cartridge.

Tamara was smiling. "I have to admit, David, that was fun. Let's have another go."

He laughed. "Carry on, dear. You're doing great."

She advanced toward the can and took up her same stance. Standing about three meters from the target, she fired.

Nothing but a very audible 'click.'

She tried again with the same results. She lowered the weapon, put it back on safety, and handed it to her shooting partner without a word, her gaze steely.

"Son of bitch," he bit off, taking the weapon. "Guy

guaranteed it worked to perfection."

Tamara remained mute, staring at him, shaking her head in rebuke.

He used a tiny flashlight that he held in his mouth, then removed the magazine, pulled back on the slide. The spent casing that should have been ejected was stuck in the barrel.

"Problem with the ejection mechanism," he said. "Let's try it again." He pried the spent casing out of the barrel, unloaded and reloaded the magazine, and chambered a round. He aimed toward open water and fired. The weapon worked perfectly, but when he went to fire off a second round, the same results—an infuriating 'click.'

David turned sheepishly to Tamara. "This is my fault, totally. I cleaned it, but I didn't think to test it before we came here. I'm so sorry, Tama."

She shook her head and smiled, then began to laugh. "Some gang of toughs we are, huh, David? The 'one-shot-gang.'" She went to him, took the pistol, and put it into her jacket pocket. "This is really the perfect weapon for me. Hardly works."

"Take it with you. By the time you get back from Vlad, I'll have something more efficient. Promise."

"Don't try too hard, David. This actually is as good as it needs to be."

He took her in his arms. "I hope you'll never have to use it."

"Fingers crossed."

~~~

Sitting astride an ancient Vyatka, a Russian knock-off of the Italian-made Vespa motor scooter, the Uzbek teenager waited down the street from the entrance to Chapayev 47.

Naim had begun his watching at seven that morning. By eight, neither the nurse nor her son had left the building at their usual time. He watched the dangerous David Osinchuk depart at eight-thirty. He phoned the Kazakhs. "Osinchuk is gone but the other two are still in the apartment."

"Good work. Let me know if and when they go out, and if they *do* go out with luggage and get in a cab, you gotta call me right away then follow 'em. Got it?"

"OK. Maybe someone can come by here, bring me something hot to drink? I'm freezing my balls off."

"I'm on it. Bring you coffee soon."

Knowing he might be in for a long wait, Naim had dressed in warm clothes, extra socks, gloves, and balaclava. From his parka pocket, he pulled out breakfast: Chicken McNuggets, still warm.

He started up the Vyatka and let it idle for a couple minutes. He'd do that every hour so's not to get caught with a cold and hard-to-start engine if and when the nurse came out with her baggage.

~~~

Tamara did not go to work on Friday. She and Marco slept in, then spent the rest of the morning packing. They ate a big lunch, and in the early afternoon, met with David.

"This may be the last time I'm going to do this," she told him. "I've pretty much had it."

"Fine with me," David said. "I've already spoken to several women about taking your place. When you get back we'll celebrate. We'll go somewhere. Take a trip. Wherever you like."

"Somewhere warm," she said.

He embraced his wife, kissed her on the lips, and left for work.

The watchers heard and saw almost everything.

Vera said, "You packed and ready to follow her?"

"Ready as I'll ever be. I'm taking something from your kit."

"No problem. Better not be one of the bugs."

"No, you're safe. Just a monocular. I'm traveling light. Leaving most of my stuff here."

"We'll guard it for you," Martyn said. "You've got the pistol I got you."

Sasha patted her carryall. "And a box of ammo. Hoping I don't have to use it. Give Konovalov a call. Let him know I'll be tailing the nurse all the way to Vlad."

"Your favorite Russian city," Vera said.

Sasha exhaled. "Right. Fucking Kollantai."

"I'll call a cab for you," Martyn said, "soon as we see the nurse and her son ready to leave."

"Good." Sasha stretched. "I guess that's it for now. You two have been wonderful partners. We got a lot done. Hopefully, your boss'll reward you."

"We'll see," Vera said. "I went on line and bought up the rest of the seats in your compartment. You've got it to yourself all way to Vlad. Same carriage as the nurse."

"Spending Konovalov's money," Sasha laughed.

"He'll survive."

Early that evening, Vera watched as the nurse and her son shared a light dinner. Their baggage was stacked in the living room, ready to go.

"They're all set," Vera said. "The train to Vlad leaves in just over two hours. They'll be calling a cab any minute."

Sasha got her gear ready. "Martyn, order a taxi for me right now. I'll follow them to the terminal."

Three minutes later, Sasha's cab arrived. She grabbed her backpack.

"Good luck, Sasha," Vera said. "Please keep in touch."

"You bet. Thanks you guys, for everything. I'll call again from the station and from the train."

"You can't call from the train," Martyn said. "No Wi-Fi. Only when you get off at a station."

"Christ, I didn't know that. OK, I'll manage somehow to stay connected. Bye." She hugged them and left the apartment.

Martyn kept an audio ear on the two people across the street. When she heard Tamara call for a taxi, he let Sasha know, sitting in her own taxi, down the block from 47 Chapayev.

Sasha's driver caught her eye in his rear view mirror. "Where we goin' lady?"

"The train station, but don't leave until I tell you. And then I want you to stay behind that cab across the street and keep them in sight. Got it?"

"Oooooh," he said in mock fright. "Sounds mysterious. But you didn't say 'follow that cab.'"

Sasha laughed. "I purposely avoided using the phrase, but . . . here they are, those two getting in the taxi. Just don't lose 'em, alright?"

"I'll need something extra. I mean this is above and beyond . . ."

She fished out a twenty-dollar bill and dangled it over the seat. When he went to reach for it, she tore it in half. "The other half when we get to where we're going."

"This is sooo cool," he said, and started off after the suspicious taxi.

~~~

As soon as the cab containing the nurse and her son left Chapayev Street, Naim started up his motor scooter and followed. When the taxi stopped for a light, the Uzbek took out his cell phone and called Sultan. "They're on the move. We're stopped at a light on Rustaveli. No more'n ten minutes from the terminal. Where you at?"

"We're already at the station. Got our tickets, sitting in the Red Flag waiting for them to show up. Stay with 'em. And call me again when they get out of the cab."

"Will do. The light just changed. I'll call again soon."

~~~

Their seventh train trip to Vladivostok was minutes away. Marco looked out the compartment window and saw a large group of travelers, Americans by their clothes, pushing and jostling their way along the crowded platform. After everyone had boarded, only a handful of militiamen, food vendors, and rail workers remained.

Right on time, the train lurched into motion, inching out of the station and gathering speed. When they came to the city's outskirts, an insistent knocking on the compartment door brought Marco to the front window.

Tamara lay down her book and very reluctantly put her hand under the shawl that covered her lap, fingers gripping the pistol. *Christ. Please don't make me use this. And if I need to, will I actually pull the trigger and shoot someone? Then what do we do? Hop off the train and disappear? Run home and barricade ourselves in? Right!*

Marco moved aside the curtain and looked into the

passageway. "It's the conductor." He slid open the door to reveal a tall and angular uniformed man. He wore a regretful but determined expression on his lined and mustachioed face. Two people slouched behind him.

The conductor took half a step into the compartment and leaned on the doorjamb. "Excuse me, please, but there's been a serious screw up." His up and down shoulders showed his inability to remedy the situation. "I'm so sorry, but these two young people have tickets for this compartment."

"What?" Tamara shouted. "Impossible. How the hell can that be? We were to have this compartment to ourselves for the entire trip to Vladivostok." She took her hand off the pistol and fished out their tickets from her carryall. "Look. You're mistaken," waving the tickets in the air. "We've paid for this first class compartment. It's private."

"You're right, of course," the conductor said, not bothering to look at Tamara's tickets. "That's exactly what your tickets show. But these two *also* have valid tickets for this compartment. Look. Here. Read." Now it was his turn to wave tickets in front of her. "It's an Eurorail screw up and there's absolutely nothing I can do about it. Sorry."

Tamara grabbed the tickets from the man's hand and examined them closely. "For God's sake," she spat out, exasperated. "How 'bout putting them in another compartment?"

"Can't do it. Their tickets say 'first class' and all other first class compartments are full." The man shrugged again and turned to the young couple, waving them forward. "Please, go on in." He glanced back apologetically at Tamara. "It's that goddamn Eurorail. There's paperwork I can help you fill out so you can recover a portion of your fare."

"Paperwork? Really? Don't bother. We'll live with it. Jesus Christ!"

When the conductor departed, Tamara turned to her two new compartment mates, still standing in the corridor. She sighed. "Nu. Come on in, bring your luggage. Nothing to be done about it."

The two Americans entered, stowed their baggage, and sat themselves. Marco closed and locked the door. He glanced at his mom. "Where do you think they're from? My guess is Los Angeles. Look at 'em. Both blond, blue-eyed and tanned, skinny surfer types. They have that California beach-bum look."

"Really? That's what you take us for?" the young woman asked Marco in textbook Russian, causing his eyes to widen.

Tamara laughed at her son's discomfort. "Be careful, Marco. Lots of foreigners these days have a passing knowledge of our language." She turned to the young woman. "Good accent. What's your name?" Sasha used the familiar form of 'you.'

"Jessica Brenner. This is Arnie Koenig."

Tamara introduced herself and Marco. "I'm supposed to say I'm glad to meet you. But . . . "

"Excuse us please for awkward," Arnie said in so-so Russian. "We not to predict the mixing."

"Don't worry about it. We'll survive," Tamara said. "You're far from home. You on holiday?"

"No," Jessica answered. "We're part of a group of students. We study Russian in Moscow, at M.G.U. for six weeks. An immersion course. We ride to Vladivostok and then drive home to Portland. That's in Oregon. We both study at university. I, Russian studies. Arnie, European History."

"Why Russian studies?" Marco asked, smiling. "Are we that interesting?"

"Very," Jessica said. "Your history is full of fascinating characters. Ivan the Terrible, Catherine the Great, Stalin."

Marco shook his head, still smiling. "Ivan the Great? The

tsar who killed his own son and blinded the architects who built the onion domes in Red Square? And Stalin? Killed how many Russians? And tell me about Catherine. The woman who rigged up a horse on scaffolding and . . ."

"Leave it there, son," Tamara interrupted, smiling. She turned to the two Americans. "It's a stupid story about Catherine. Unproven." She looked at her son. "And completely out of place." She couldn't help chuckling.

For their part, the Americans seemed puzzled by the Catherine-exchange. Arnie began to ask, but Jessica shook her head at him. "Leave it, Arnie." She turned to Tamara. "Are you riding all the road to Vladivostok?"

"Yes. Just a short visit."

"What do you make there?" Arnie asked.

"Visiting my sister."

"And here in Chelyabinsk. What do you make?"

Tamara saw no need to dissemble. "I'm a nurse and my son, Marco, is a student."

Arnie turned to Marco. "You are a student? What studies?"

Marco exchanged glances with his mother. "I'm studying rough and finished carpentry."

Arnie's expression indicated he didn't understand.

Tamara jumped in. "Marco works with wood." She knocked on the wooden compartment door as explanation. "He's learning to make buildings, build furniture."

"Excellent work," Arnie said, taking out a laptop computer and plugging it in. He began searching for something to download. Marco came over and sat by him, helping him navigate.

"You can get Netflix," Marco told him.

"Great. Maybe later. It make six days to Vladivostok, right?" Arnie asked.

"More like five days," Marco answered him.

A long silence ensued. Arnie returned to his laptop, searching Netflix. Marco pulled out his video player. Jessica took up a comfortable position next to the window and watched the dark countryside roll by. Tamara took out her favorite novel, *Anna Karenina*. She was halfway through the thousand-page book that she'd read twice before. In this section, Anna and her lover, Vronsky, have fled to Italy. Love is in the air. When they return to Russia, however, things will fall apart. Knowing what was in store for the couple, Tamara reluctantly put down the novel. "I'm going for tea," she said, taking a Thermos from her carryall.

~~~

It was bound to happen, Sasha thought. *But not quite so soon.* She and the heroin courier she was following bumped into each other at the end of their carriage, next to the samovar. Sasha was filling a mug from the spigot, adjusting her stance each time the train lurched. Tamara came up behind her, holding a Thermos.

Sasha turned and saw her. "They're out of sugar already," she said. "How is that possible? We just left."

"We have some in our compartment, just three doors down. Stop by. I'm Tamara Stoikova. Tama." She extended her free hand.

"Katya Rodina," Sasha said, using the name on the passport, internal ID document, birth certificate, and driver's license provided by Konovalov's Ministry of Justice. "Nice to meet you."

"You, too." She finished her pouring, closed the tap, and sealed her Thermos. "You don't sound like you're from Chelyabinsk."

Sasha opted for her earlier, storefront, answer. "Right. I was born in Khabarovsk, but I've been living abroad for years. Spend a lot of time in the Netherlands. Work." *Calm down. Not too much unneeded info.* Hoping to deflect further questioning she asked, "Where are you traveling to?"

"End of the line, Vlad. Going to see my sister."

Sasha nodded. She knew Tamara didn't have a sister. Only one sibling, a younger brother in Novgorod. She played along. "Be there long?"

"Not too long. A family visit."

"Nice."

"I'm afraid it won't be a happy occasion. My sister has ALS." *Why the hell did I offer that?* Tamara thought. *Keep it simple.*

"Oh, I'm so sorry."

"Early stages, but still . . ."

Sasha had listened to hundreds of liars. Tamara, she was pleased to learn, was pretty good, taking her time, not getting flustered, speaking with the proper emotion when talking about a sick relative, albeit an invented one.

"You said 'we,'" Sasha said. "Someone else with you?"

"My son Marco. We're going to visit my sister, Elena."

Elena? OK. Sis has to have a name. "How long will you be in Vlad?"

"Just a few days. I need to get back to work soon."

"What's your work?"

"I'm a nurse. Have been all my life, it seems. And you?"

When Sasha and Konovalov began devising her cover, they agreed to have Sasha work in law, for the Ministry of Justice, something about which she knew a good deal.

"I work at the International Court of Justice, in the Hague. I'm a glorified secretary to the Russian delegation to the court.

We split our time between the Netherlands and England. A great job. Don't get to speak enough Russian so I have a slang-deficit." *Way too fucking complicated. She'll ask if I speak Dutch. Jesus, I gotta get out of this.* "Why aren't you flying?"

Without hesitation, as if she'd worked it out and practiced it, Tamara answered, "My son is afraid of flying."

Sasha appreciated that Tamara said it with just the right touch of motherly indulgence and a hint of reproach. *Good going, Tama. But how come Marco flew to Prague last year with his schoolmates?*

"And you, Katya," Tamara asked. "Where are you heading?"

"Same place. Vlad for a visit—an old school mate. Might do some skiing. Blue Hill. Maybe Mount Falaza." *Or maybe meet up with the mayor. Talk about old times.*

The train swerved just as another woman with a foam cup in hand approached the samovar.

Sasha decided enough for now. "Can I swing by in a little for some sugar?"

Tamara nodded. "Sure. Compartment four."

~~~

The next morning, the two Kazakhs were having breakfast in the train's dining car when the woman and the young man they were tailing came in. And there were two people with them, obviously Americans.

"What the hell's goin' on?" Chingiz whispered. "Who're those two?"

"No idea," Sultan said. "Maybe people she met on the way here. We'll hang out and see, tail her back to her compartment."

Half and hour later, they followed as Tamara, her son,

and the two young Americans entered the nurse's compartment. When the Kazakhs heard the door lock click shut, they quickly retreated to their own carriage to re-assess.

Chingiz blew out a breath. "I thought it was just s'posed to be the woman and her son."

Sultan's jaw began working up and down. He sucked on the nail of his right thumb. "Dunno. Maybe those two are just visiting her. Maybe they have their own compartment and are just stopping in. Maybe . . . " His voice faltered.

"And maybe," Chingiz offered, "maybe they're in there in a permanent way and maybe our plans are gone to shit. I mean, how we supposed to rob the two of them if there are four in the cabin?"

Sultan stopped gnawing on his fingernail. "You know, Chingo, this may not be such a bad thing. Maybe it's actually better this way."

"Huh? How?"

"I mean, Americans always have cash, always have laptops, smart phones, valuables. So the plan stays the same, except we make it bigger. We grab the woman's package *and* take anything and everything valuable from the Americans. It's a better score, right?"

Chingiz nodded, smiling. "I get it, Sulty. It's better."

~~~

The pursuer and the pursued had lunch together on the second full day of travel. They were a hundred kilometers from Omsk. Outside their dining car window, the flat, low grassland of monotonous and frozen gray-white steppe extended to the horizon.

Since their unplanned meeting at their carriage's samovar,

Sasha had wanted to get closer to Tamara. Having watched with envy Tamara and David's shared intimacy, Sasha was interested in finding out more about the woman's marriage.

They started the meal by splitting a plate of salted mushrooms, followed by red caviar and black bread. They drank raspberry-flavored kvass.

"I'd kill for some black caviar," Tamara said, "but can't find it anymore since it's forbidden. Damn sturgeon."

Sasha was unsure how to respond. *Probably because of over-harvesting. Same as on the Bering Sea. Greedy fishermen.* "This red is pretty good, though," she said.

"Not bad," Tamara said. She finished off the last of the fish roe. "What were you doing in Chelyabinsk?"

"Nothing, really. I was just passing through. Never been on the TransSiberian and had some time to kill, so here I am."

The waiter came to collect the dishes and take their orders.

Sasha smiled up at the tall man, his uniform neatly pressed. "I'll have the medallion of beef with onions."

"Baked chicken, for me," Tamara told the man. "And a plate of mixed vegetables."

The waiter left and Sasha jumped in, eager to move the topic back to Tamara. "I see a ring. Married long?"

Tamara sat back and smiled. "Two years last month."

"A newly wed. And Marco's dad?"

"I was married long ago to Marco's father. We hardly lasted a year. Everyone's entitled to screw up. Me, too." She closed her eyes and shrugged her brows and shoulders. "And how 'bout you? I don't see a ring. Not married?"

Sasha didn't run from her reality. "I was married for three years. My husband died, unexpectedly."

Tamara's grief was real. She reached across the table and

covered one of Sasha's hands. "I'm so, so sorry. When was this?"

"Long time ago. Almost seventeen years."

"Do you have any kids?"

Again, Sasha felt a desire to tell the truth, at least partially.

"Yes, a daughter. Maria. She's almost seventeen." *How do I square this with my work in Holland?* "She's in school in London." *Really? For God sakes, stop talking.* Sasha looked out the window. The grasslands were covered with pockets of snow. "My husband died in an accident the same day I learned I was pregnant." *Mostly true. An on-the-job-accident.* "Tell me about *your* husband, Tama. You wore a huge smile when you spoke about him."

Tamara laughed. "You're very observant."

The waiter reappeared, pushing a cart. He asked if everything was as it should be and assured them that their entrées were on the way.

Tamara said, "I was almost fifty when we met. I'd pretty much given up hope of ever finding anyone." She made a wry smile. "Chelyabinsk is not exactly teeming with available men. So, I worked at raising my son as a single mom and gave my life to medicine. The plan was working, too. Then David showed up one day at the hospital. He was a patient, came into the ER with serious injuries to his chest and ribs. I was the nurse on duty. Patched him up. He got better, we dated, married, and have hardly been out of each other's sight since. This is really the only time . . . when I visit my sister . . . that he and I are apart." She smiled. "Sounds like some kind of fairytale, but that's the way it happened."

The entrées arrived. The waiter distributed the food and rolled the cart away.

Sasha slowly sliced into her beef. "Fairytale or not, Tama. I'm jealous. Really. What's he like?"

"David? Mostly positive. Rarely down. But when he's down, it's temporary, and fixable. He's very sweet and generous with his time. Funny in a Harpo Marx kind of way, always making faces. Loving and caring. He's become an extraordinary influence on my son. Marco adores him."

"Marco's dad is still in the picture?"

"Not at all. Not even in Chelyabinsk anymore. Artur was the un-David. *Not* caring. *Not* funny. *Mostly* down. And unfaithful from day one."

Sasha sat back "I can't believe it. Seeing you now, Tama, I can imagine what you looked like twenty years ago. He must have been nuts to screw around."

"He preferred blonds. Teenage blonds."

"What's with these guys?" Sasha laughed.

"It's actually good that we split. I'm so much better off now."

They concentrated on their food for a few minutes before Sasha asked, "What's David's work?"

"He owns a garage. He repairs motorcycles."

Sasha watched as Tamara seemed to drift off into a reverie. *Dreaming of David. Who can blame you? After watching you for close to two weeks, it's clear you two are crazy for each other. His nose and all.*

"And you Katya, you haven't found anyone?" Tamara asked between mouthfuls of chicken.

Sasha felt compelled to be truthful. "I *have* found someone, actually, but . . . " *There's that 'but' again.*

"But?"

"I spend most of my time abroad, in Europe. And he lives in Chile."

"Wow! A South American? How'd you meet?"

"At a conference in Amsterdam." Sasha realized her fictional story was fast becoming too complex. *Like the Marines. Keep it simple, stupid.* She decided to put off further inventions. "Beef is terrific. How's the chicken?"

"Great. Let me cut you some. Will you feel like dessert?"

~~~

It was a bright and crisp Saturday afternoon. Pyotr and Svetlana Bondarchuk had driven up from Troitsk to Chelyabinsk and were strolling down the Alleya Slavy. They were toasty warm in their newly purchased North Face expedition parkas. They took their time walking toward the McDonald's. The fast food eatery was crowded and dozens of customers spilled out onto the sidewalk. The Bondarchuks joined the queue.

"I'm gonna check the menu," Svetlana said. "Back in a minute." She walked to the head of the line and elbowed her way into the restaurant.

A moment later, Petya felt someone tap him on the shoulder. He turned and saw a short, stocky man with beady eyes. He wore rimless glasses. He was dressed in a heavy overcoat and a wool watch cap pulled down over his ears. The man reeked of tobacco. Somehow, he chillingly reminded Petya of Lavrenti Beria, Stalin's secret police chief. The FSS border guard shuddered.

"Pyotr Alexandrovich Bondarchuk?" the man asked in a gravelly voice.

Petya knew right away who the man was and why he had come, but needed to ask, "Who are you?"

"Alexei Sustak," the man said. He flashed Bondarchuk a badge. "Ministry of Justice. Criminal Investigations." Two other men, dressed similarly, suddenly materialized on either side of Bondarchuk. Sustak smiled. "My colleagues."

Petya's bladder let go. He stood frozen near the entrance to the McDonalds while his pee trickled warmly down his leg. He was unable to even twitch. *Uncle Nikita.*

Svetlana exited the restaurant and stopped short. The tableau that greeted her—her husband rooted to the ground, a small puddle of yellowing snow at his feet, and three smirking men surrounding him, one holding a sheaf of papers—made the blood rush to her head. She suddenly felt dizzy and slipped back into the restaurant.

"Looks like your wife's abandoned you," Sustak said. "Women. Impossible to understand." He laughed. "Let's go have a chat."

A federal agent on each arm, Petya was led away from the eatery. His feet somehow found the strength to move his rigid body as if he were walking on stilts. He turned from one to the other, hoping to see a sympathetic face. The one holding his left arm said, "Pyotr Alexandrovich. Tell us everything you know, and perhaps your sentence can be reduced to . . . well, let's say eight years. I think that's probably the least you can expect. In Novocherkassk, if you're lucky. If not, Vladimir Central."

Those last words caused the muscles in Petya's neck to freeze so that he was unable to turn his head. He had to swivel his entire body when the second man—on his other arm—spoke. "Otherwise, if you refuse to cooperate, you might never again see what's her name? Svetlana? She's a cute little thing. So, what's it going to be?"

The border guard's eyes filled with tears, soon rolling down his cheeks. His lips and chin were bouncing up and down. The noise of his lower bridgework hitting his upper canines was a discernable 'clacking.' He placed his palms together in front of him, reverentially. "I'll tell you everything you want to know. I'll cooperate. Just please, please, only eight years."

~~~

They met for lunch again the next day. The dining car windows were frosted over. The weather was typical Siberia-in-February—very cold and dry. The mostly treeless steppe was gradually giving way to forests of birch and pine, shrouded in winter-white.

They had sampled each other's entrées the day before and decided to get what the other had eaten: Sasha now ordered the chicken, Tamara, the medallions of beef.

Sasha said, "You haven't described David physically, but from the way you talk about him, I've formed a mental picture of him."

"I'd be surprised if you got anywhere near what he looks like," Tamara said. "He's one of the most unusual looking men I've ever encountered. Handsome in a totally weird way."

Sasha smiled her encouragement. "Let's hear."

Tamara sat back from her food. "He's a young and wild fifty-three years old. Crazy long red hair. Lovely hazel eyes. And a nose that's indescribable. Broken several times, twisted every which way. A catastrophe of a nose. But somehow it fits his face."

Sasha smiled. "You're right. My mental picture wasn't even close. *You* are *right, Tamara. He* is *handsome in a strange way.*

"And he has a generous streak that extends out beyond us, beyond his family. You remember the meteor that exploded over Chelyabinsk in 2013, in the middle of winter?"

Sasha hadn't the faintest idea what Tamara was talking about, but scrambled for a response. "I was out of the country then. Remind me."

"It was incredible. This huge meteor broke up before hitting earth, but parts of it bombarded the area. A couple thousand people were hurt, mostly from flying glass. David went around town in his van, driving people to the hospital. Did it for a week. The Ural Press did an article about him, with a photo." Tamara smiled. "He didn't bother saving the article, but I found a copy and have it at home."

"Sounds like a good guy."

"A very good guy."

~~~

At the stop in Krasnoyarsk, Sasha got off the train and phoned Konovalov. The minister was up-beat.

"Good to hear, Sasha. The frontier guard, Bondarchuk, was taken yesterday. He's spilling his guts, hoping for a lighter sentence. And the lorry driver, the Afghani, is dead. Killed himself at the border after shooting a guard. So, your good work is producing dividends. I'm happy."

"Thank you, Igor Semyonich. I had lots of help from your two, very able assistants. I hope you'll give them their due when they're back at work."

"Without question, Sasha. They'll be amply rewarded. But what about Stoikova, the nurse? Where are we at with her?"

"I've actually met her. We had lunch together already. I'm looking for an opportunity to search her luggage. Soon, I hope."

"And Osinchuk?"

"Vera and Martyn are continuing the surveillance on him.

We should be able to implicate him as soon as we find the woman in possession of the contraband."

"Excellent. I'll look forward to that. As I mentioned to you earlier, we've wanted Osinchuk for years. An elusive criminal."

"We're working on it, Mister Minister. Hold on, the train whistle just blew. I need to get back on board. I'll be in touch again soon."

"Keep up the good work, Sasha. Goodbye."

~~~

Marco Stoikov was built like his father, short and thick set, with massive, tattooed arms, and a barrel chest. Facially, he resembled Tamara with her short cut, brown hair, high cheekbones, and deep-set, dark eyes. Marco had a mouth the opposite sex found alluring. For all his brutish body, he was soft spoken, well mannered, and hard working. Not especially book smart. Extremely street smart.

Very early in the morning of the third day, Sasha saw Marco in their narrow passageway. He was standing in front of his compartment, looking out the window. She came up to him, leaned, and looked out. He acknowledged her with a nod and threw a thumb over his shoulder, aimed at his compartment.

"Everyone's still sleeping. The heat in our compartment cut out around three this morning. Too cold to get out of bed."

Sasha looked in Compartment 4, saw everyone heavily swaddled in blankets. "Same in my compartment. I came out to the corridor to exercise, warm up. Let's you and me grab some hot chocolate."

"I'm game."

They made their way to the empty dining car, the busboys

still setting the tables. They sat and asked one of them to send a waiter.

Their train was heading southeasterly, toward Lake Baikal. A hazy early morning sun flowed through rime-etched windows, casting the dining car in a dim glow. A waiter came to their table.

"Two hot chocolates and four croissants, please," Sasha said. She looked across at Marco.

"Just what I would have ordered," he said.

When the waiter left, Marco asked, "You're from Khabarovsk, mom says. Born there?"

"Yeah, but we moved to St. Petersburg when I was two. Been there?"

"Last year, with my class."

"Your carpentry school classmates?"

His face lit up. He seemed pleased that she knew about his school.

"Exactly. Last year we spent ten days there, walking up and down Nevsky Prospekt, studying the architecture."

"The pre-Bolshevik stuff, of course." Sasha said.

"Of course. From Peter the First's time. But don't be so critical of Soviet architecture. I mean, in Moscow, the Seven Sisters and MGU are really cool."

She remembered the Hotel Ukraina and it's Soviet stylings. "I'll take your word for it," she said.

The waiter showed up with a pot of hot chocolate and a covered basket of croissants. Sasha poured. "Tell me about yourself. How'd you get into carpentry?"

He took a sip of chocolate. "A long story. I dropped out of high school after only a year and went to work in the building trade. I was a grunt. Whatever needed to be carried, I carried— bricks and hand tools, lumber and heavy machinery, re-bar and bags of concrete mix, spools of wire and boxes of tiles. A grunt. And paid accordingly. One day, I watched a carpenter working a lathe. He took a long, rough piece of lumber, started shaping it on the lathe, and five minutes later, it was a beautifully formed bannister post. It seemed like magic. That was it."

"Your mom says you're good at it."

"She's a big fan of mine," he said and finished off a croissant.

"I really like your mom. Classy lady."

"She really is, thanks." He tore a second croissant into bite-sized quarters. "It was hard for her for a long time."

"How so?"

"My dad left us when I was one and she raised me by herself. I wasn't the easiest kid to raise. A handful. But she managed."

"Do you have anything to do with your father?"

"I've met him exactly three times that I remember. The last time was twelve years ago." Marco paused. "I haven't really thought about this before, but David fills in."

"Fills in?"

"Yeah. I mean, he's been a dad. And a partner to my mom that she never expected."

"Tamara told me she didn't have much hope for the men of Chelyabinsk."

Marco laughed out loud. "She always complained about that. Always threatened to move us to some place where there was a better selection of guys. Then David shows up."

Sasha refilled Marco's cup with chocolate. "David's the one, huh?"

"He's definitely the one. She laughs all the time now. Never seen her this happy. Never even knew she could *be* this happy. It's really cool."

~~~

The Kazakhs were in the dining car where Sultan was nursing a cup of tea. He was reviewing, once again, the plan they'd devised. He knew he had to keep reminding his partner what they were going to do, keeping it uncomplicated. They were a few hours from their intended heist.

"So, Chingo. Like I tol' ya, we're on our way to Ulan Ude. That's where the TransSiberian meets the TransMongolian. That's where we do our business."

"Got it."

"A little before we get there, we go into her compartment, take the bag, take whatever shit the Americans have, and jump from the train in the rail yards, before the station. I got a car arranged and a safe house. Same place we scoped out six months ago, remember?"

"Sure. The place that smelled like a barn? Horse shit all over the place?"

"It smelled like a barn because that's what it is. My uncle's place. You with me?"

"With you."

"We stay there two, three days, then head back home."

"Got it. How 'bout food while we're in the barn?"

Sultan sighed. "Chingo. We'll have a ton of food. My aunt's gonna cook for us. Don't worry."

"I ain't worryin'. Just askin'."

"Right. Now we only got half a litre of home-brew left. But we be gotta be smart. Can't get shit-faced."

"Right. Can't get shit-faced. We gonna kill 'em?"

"We don't wanna *kill* 'em, Chingo. Just *scare* 'em enough so they give us what we want."

"Right. No problem. And if everything goes smoothly . . .

" Chingiz prompted.

"If everything goes smoothly, we're back home in Chelyabinsk a few days the proud owners of..." Sultan paused.

Chingiz's eyes were wild. "Of? Of?"

"Of an unknown amount of a precious substance."

"That we think probably is ..."

"Probably heroin, or meth, or opioids."

"Or maybe even fentanyl. How great is that?"

~~~

In his father's arms, Marat Suvorov looked in wonder at the pair of caged tigers. Anatoly had brought his son to Sadgorod, Vladivostok's premier zoo. It was the toddler's first visit to the zoo and he was enchanted. His father was much less so, having escaped the home under threat from his wife. Sophia continued to fume about the sudden and drastic change in their fortunes. On an almost daily basis, she harangued him about the lost revenue, challenged him to replace the extra and illegal four thousand dollar monthly income. His pleadings did him no good.

"The U.S. Customs agent is dead, for God's sake, Sophia. There's no one to hand the stuff to. Why can't you understand that? They've taken me off the job, given me a different flight schedule, Irkutsk, Novosibirsk, Khabarovsk. I don't fly to America any more. It's over."

Despite the logic of his explanation, Sophia was not persuaded. "How do you expect us to live," she shouted at him, "now that you've fucked us out of the money?"

Nothing to do but dress his son in warm clothes, put him in his baby buggy, grab a bus, and head for the zoo.

They stopped in front of the polar bear enclosure. The beast was lounging by a large and icy pool. Anatoly coached his son, "Bear, Marat. See the bear."

Marat looked at the bear, turned to his father, and smiled with his whole face. Anatoly felt a great release. *Someone appreciates me.* He gave his son a hug then moved his thoughts to someone else who appreciated him, at least some of the time: Olga, his Anchorage part-time-for-hire lover. As his wife's tirades had become more and more strident and filled with vitriol, Anatoly had retreated deep into Olga-fantasyland. He conjured wild scenarios in which he hijacks a Troika aircraft, and then he and Marat fly to Thailand where Olga meets them in Phuket. In another dream-scheme, he goes to the American Consulate in Vladivostok. He imagines himself being forgiven for his own sins and given asylum in America when he exposes the extensive drug cartel in his hometown. He knows about America's Witness Protection Program. He fantasizes that they'll find him a beachfront home on the Gulf Coast. He'll fish all day and return home to his tanned and well-adjusted son and his loving Olga.

The hooting of a trio of Japanese snow monkeys, splashing water at each other, brought Anatoly back to real time. Their screeching frightened Marat who began to fuss in his baby buggy. Anatoly wheeled him away and made for the exit.

On the long bus ride back to town he faced the ugly truths of his life: since he would almost certainly never again fly to America, the prospects of re-coupling with Olga were virtually non-existent. And then there was the more immediate cause for depression and fear: he had to go back to the rail station in two nights for another pick-up. The desk clerk at the Slavianski Bazaar had outlined exactly what Anatoly was to do: go to the terminal and collect the woman's parcel; come back to the hotel for several more packages collected over the past months from other sources; take them all to the airport and load them onto the

Yakovlev Yak-40, the commercial aircraft he'd fly up Russia's Pacific Coast to Provideniya; then deliver all of the goods to an Eskimo man.

Of course, he hadn't breathed a word of this to his wife. And the amount of the payment for this service had not yet been clearly stated, either by the clerk or the bald man, the one who seemed to be organizing the rest of Anatoly's life.

~~~

Seventy miles from Ulan Ude, the Kazakhs left their compartment and made their way toward the next carriage where David Osinchuk's mule was carrying something they hoped was a valuable drug. They had drunk the last of their *samogon* and were feeling confident. They were armed with hunting knives, five-inch blades in scabbards stuck in the side pockets of their camo pants. A few doors down from the mule's compartment, they paused in the passageway to collect themselves. They were sweating and breathing hard. They leaned on a handrail and looked out the window as the train passed through a dark and snowy night.

Four doors down from the nurse and her son, Sasha had just finished *Out of Sight,* an Elmore Leonard favorite of hers that she re-read in a Russian translation. In the novel, Karen and Jack fall in love. Doesn't work out—she's a cop and he's a bank robber. Both knew it would end badly but neither shied away from taking the plunge. She winds up shooting him in the leg and arresting him. It made Sasha think of her own love interest, Tomás, her Chilean. He was no bank robber but their situation appeared to her to be equally star-crossed, the two of them living at opposite ends of the planet and neither one having a mind to move.

While conjuring up Tomás's image, Sasha lay back and glanced through her inner window, out onto the carriage's passageway. She saw a pair of young men—non-Russian, Asian maybe, scruffy faced, both dressed in camo—standing in the corridor and gazing through the window. They weren't talking, but their body language, to her cop's trained eye, seemed furtive, suspicious. As they moved down the corridor, she rose to a sitting position.

"You ready?" Sultan asked. His voice quavered. His forehead was beaded.

"Whenever you want," Chingiz whispered.

They took their knives from their scabbards and hid the blades behind their backs as they inched forward along the empty passageway. Well before they reached the nurse's compartment, her door slid open. The American man came out. The Kazakhs hurriedly slipped their knives back into their pockets as the young man walked past them. The smell of their combined nervous sweat was strong enough for him to wrinkle his nose as he passed by. He went into the bathroom at the end of the wagon. They heard the door lock.

"When he comes out, we follow him back," Sultan said. Chingiz nodded and wiped his brow with his shirtsleeve.

A minute later, they heard the toilet whoosh-flush. The American appeared at the open door, drying his hands on a paper towel, then tossing it into the trash bin. He walked past the Kazakhs. The two men followed him closely, trying to appear nonchalant. The American arrived at his compartment and knocked. When it was opened and he made to enter, Sultan rushed forward, pushed the man inside, and followed him. Chingiz came after and slid closed the door behind him.

Marco heard the knock, and opened the door. As soon he did, Arnie was shoved from behind and crashed to the compartment's floor. Two Asian-looking men, brandishing long knives, followed him into the room. One of them hissed, "Quiet. Not a fucking word."

A five second scene ensued during which no one spoke. Jessica melted back into her seat. Arnie crawled to the side of the compartment, rose and sat next to the window, across from Jessica. Frozen, Marco stared at the two men. And Tamara, her pistol hidden in her lap, her shawl masking the weapon, sat thinking that she'd have to do what she swore to David she'd never do. *Do I threaten, try to scare them?*

One of the men stood in front of the door, his blade slicing back and forth through the air. He wiped the sweat from his forehead with the back of his other sleeved arm. "Nobody move," he said in heavily accented Russian. "You'll all be OK. Just keep still."

The second man, standing in the middle of the compartment, scanned the room. He climbed onto the seat next to where Marco was sitting, opposite Tamara. He reached into the overhead bin and tried to wrestle free the black-strapped bag.

Tamara felt for the hidden weapon, gripped it in a suddenly clammy palm, and flicked off the safety with her thumb, just as David had taught her. *God help me. I guess this is where I man up.* She took in a deep breath and at the end of her exhale, she swiveled toward the man standing in front of the door—not three feet from her—and pulled the pistol out.

"Drop the knife. Now," she commanded.

For a moment, the Kazakh was frozen into inaction. Then he shuddered and lunged at her.

Tamara threw out her left arm, fending off the knife thrust and buried the gun's muzzle into the man's stomach.

"Drop the knife," she ordered. He looked into her eyes, then gritted his teeth and tried once again to stab her. Tamara pulled the trigger. Because the muzzle of her weapon was pushed into the man's stomach, the noise wasn't as deafening as she would have thought. But the force of the bullet smashing into him was brutal. He groaned loudly and fell in a heap, as if every muscle in his body had suddenly gone slack. The knife fell from his hand.

The man standing on the seat could only stare, mouth agape, his eyes as big as melons.

Without hesitation, Tamara raised the pistol, aimed, and fired. The usual click. Another try, another click.

When the man jumped to the floor and raised his knife hand, ready to strike Tamara, Marco grabbed him from the rear. They grappled and fell, struggling over the body of the one who was shot. The man struck out at Marco, gained some freedom, scrambled to his hands and knees, and crawled for the door. Tamara took the pistol by the barrel and hit him on the lower spine. He screamed once and flexed backwards. Before she could strike again, he slid the door open, and lunged—half in, half out—knife-hand leading the way.

Sasha heard a single gun shot and immediately jumped from her seat. She opened her compartment's sliding door and stuck her head out into an empty passageway. She was surprised no one had been alerted by the obvious sound of a gunshot. She thought to bring her own pistol but realized she couldn't afford to be caught with it. She went quickly down the aisle toward Tamara's compartment. As she arrived, the door flew open and one of the Asian-looking men hurtled part way into the corridor. He whimpered while clawing at the corridor's carpet, looking for a handhold to escape whoever was dragging him back into the room. His face was a terror mask and he thrust behind him with an ugly hunting knife.

Sasha stepped into a kick, hitting him in the forearm of his knife-hand. He yelled, dropped the weapon, then turned full frontal, allowing her a second kick—a toe to his jaw. The man let out a heavy 'oooooph,' his resistance slackened and when he grabbed his face, he was hauled back into the room. Just before the door closed, Sasha saw Tamara. She held a pistol by the barrel and swung it down on the man, landing a fierce blow on his shoulder. He shuddered and gave a low grunt. As Tamara was about to deliver a second blow, she looked up, saw Sasha, then quickly closed the door.

The corridor remained empty. Sasha heard the muted sounds of a struggle coming from within the compartment. She picked up the hunting knife and returned to her own compartment. She threw the blade out the window. Farm house lights winked through the snow.

Tamara saw Katya kick the man twice. She closed the compartment's door then swung down at the man again. He fell on his partner's inert body. Marco climbed onto the man's back and wrapped a forearm around the Kazakh's neck. The man thrashed weakly, but Marco maintained his chokehold, stood up, and lifted the much lighter man off the floor. The Kazakh kicked wildly, one boot striking Jessica in the mouth, knocking her against the window.

"Grab his legs," Tamara commanded Arnie.

Up until then, Arnie had been a spectator, but now he lunged for the man's flailing legs and hugged his calves. Under the pressure of Marco's chokehold, the Kazakh's strength ebbed. He soon went limp. Marco continued to strangle him for another minute, until Tamara said, "Enough, son. He's done for."

Marco let the body flop onto the floor, next to the man his mother had shot. Tamara bent over the two men, now lying side by side. She felt for each man's carotid artery. No pulse from either.

The four survivors collapsed into their seats, breathing deeply. Jessica, sitting next to the window, held her bleeding nose and sobbed. She'd raised herself into a fetal position, arms around her knees. Arnie tried to comfort her.

Marco looked at Tamara, nodded. "Good job, mom."

She let out a long breath. "You too, son." She looked toward their outside window. "Arnie, open the window."

He looked at her uncomprehendingly. "Huh," was the best he could do. With more authority, she said, "Open the window as wide as it gets. We need to get rid of these two."

He followed her orders. The large, main window was sealed shut. Below it, however, and extending almost the length of the compartment, was a narrow, slat window that was hinged on the bottom and opened in. When Arnie opened it the sounds of the train clattering through the night flooded the compartment.

"Marco, grab his shoulders," Tamara said, pointing to the man he'd strangled. "Arnie, take his middle. I'll take his legs. Out the window with him."

Marco complied, but Arnie needed more prompting.

"Do it," Tamara ordered the American.

He obeyed. One after another, and with much squeezing, the two would-be thieves were pushed through the window and dumped out onto the nighttime taiga.

Ten minutes later, the train pulled into Ulan Ude. The four travelers, sitting now in a darkened compartment, were barely holding it together in the wake of their life-and-death struggle.

Tamara broke the silence. "We're still two days from Vlad.

We need food. We'll be here for less than twenty minutes." She handed Marco a wad of bills. "Son, go out and get us coffee, sandwiches, cakes. And a bottle of vodka."

She looked at the two Americans. The terminal's lights illuminated the interior of their shadowy compartment. Jessica appeared to be in a daze, still curled up, arms embracing her knees. Arnie was immobile, staring out the window.

"Go on, son," Tamara urged.

Marco buttoned up, put on his heavy jacket, fur hat, and left the compartment.

Arnie reached up and turned on his overhead light. He stared across at Tamara. His face was tear-stained and ashen. She crossed over to his side of the compartment and sat by him. She took his hands. He leaned into her and wept.

"We're safe, Arnie. Not to worry." Then she glanced down at the floor. A dark and damp stain covered the carpet.

"Oh shit." She began rummaging through their carryall, finally producing a pair of Marco's t-shirts. She poured some bottled water onto the bloodstain, then vigorously swabbed the incriminating evidence. Most of the stain, however, remained. She thought for a moment, returned to her carryall, and after a minute's search, came out with a toothbrush from her toilet kit and a small bottle of hydrogen peroxide from the medical supplies she always carried. She went down on her knees again, soaking the area with the peroxide, brushing the dried blood, then using Marco's t-shirts to sop up the mess. After ten minutes, most of the blood had been removed. *It'll have to do.*

Arnie had watched Tamara at work. He'd been mostly immobile, his movements sluggish.

Tamara put a hand on his knee. "You should lay yourself down. Try and sleep." When he slowly stretched out the length of the seat, Tamara covered him with a blanket and turned off the overhead light. "Marco'll be back with food soon. Rest until he comes."

Over the next two days, their moods bounced back and forth between dark depression and hysterical laughter. Between relief and tears.

Arnie couldn't forgive himself for being complicit in the strangling of the Kazakh.

Marco tried to reason with him, "It was him or us. You had no choice." Arnie remained unconvinced.

Jessica openly wondered about continuing in her college major—Russian studies. "What's the point?" she asked. "Everything I study, everything I learn about Russia will always be colored by what happened on this train." She looked quickly at Tamara and Marco. "Not that meeting you two hasn't been wonderful. But the rest . . ."

Marco and his mother were less vocal about what had happened. Whenever they were alone, they looked long and questioningly at each other.

"Is it worth it, son?"

"Not sure, mom."

At the stop in Chita, the Americans got off and paced up and down the platform until the whistle blew, urging them to re-board. When they returned to their compartment, Jessica spoke: "Arnie and I talked about what happened and we came to a surprising conclusion."

"You've decided you want to move to Russia?" Marco offered, laughing.

Jessie smiled. "Not likely. No. Arnie and I agreed that because of meeting you two, if we had to do it again . . . we most likely would. Crazy, isn't it?"

Tamara sighed. "You're so sweet. But if it were up to me, and for your sakes, I'd wish the opposite: that you two would have been spared such trauma. I mean, thanks for your feelings about us. We totally reciprocate. But, if you had missed the train, or found another compartment, it would have been so much better for you. As it is, I'm afraid it'll take a long time to put this trip behind you."

"But worse for you and Marco," Jessica said. "At least we get to leave here and put physical distance between us and Ulan Ude. You two will always be close to the events. Harder for you to put it behind you."

Tamara took her son's hand. "We'll manage. Actually, I think we've even begun managing." Marco gave his mother's hand a squeeze. The train slowed as it reached the Vladivostok rail yards.

~~~

Anatoly was at home taking care of his son. He and Marat had just eaten the dinner that Anatoly had prepared for them—potato soup with sausage and vegetables. Sophia was out, promised to be back in time for him to get to the airport and fly up the coast. He hadn't told her that he needed to collect a load of heroin from the woman at the railroad terminal. If Sophia returned home late, he'd miss the connection.

For the past several days, he had Olga on the brain. He knew his fantasies for what they were: escapist dreams. But he couldn't help himself. He tried several times to phone her, but she never answered.

And now, the clock showed eight. He and his son watched a videotape of Sesame Street. Afterwards, Anatoly gave him a bath, tucked him in bed, and read to him a brilliantly illustrated *Father Frost,* his son's favorite Russian fairytale. Marat kissed his father goodnight, turned over, and fell asleep.

Nine o'clock and no Sophia. Then ten, then eleven. At quarter past the hour, she showed up and breezed in without a word. She went straight to the bathroom and closed the door. He heard the shower running. He knocked on the door, shouting, letting her know he was leaving for work, back in two days. No response from within. He went to Marat's small room, peeked in, and was gratified that his son was quietly in dreamland. Anatoly gathered his coat, slung his small backpack over his shoulder, and left his home.

~~~

The four travelers sat silently in their compartment as their train slowed and entered the Vladivostok rail yards. They looked at one another and smiled, but no words passed between them. They gathered their baggage and shuffled their way toward the carriage doors.

Once on the platform, still silent, they walked slowly toward the terminal. At the end of the platform, they stopped and faced each other. Jessica looked at Tamara and Marco, "I'm super happy that we met you two. Although I wish the circumstances had been more . . . less . . . I don't know."

"Less chaotic?" Tamara offered.

"More peaceful?" Arnie suggested, chuckling, then caught himself. "I'm surprised I can even laugh. I mean . . ." He began to choke up.

"I know exactly what you mean," Tamara said. "Come here." She opened her arms wide and both of the Americans closed into them. Marco joined them in a group hug. They clung together for a good minute, until Tamara gently pushed them apart. "I don't want to be an alarmist, but it's probably for the best if you two don't come to Russia again, at least for a lot of years. You never know."

"This is my first and last visit," Arnie said.

"And mine," Jessica agreed. "Though I'd come if I had the chance to hang with you two again," she said.

"And we'd love to host the both of you, but for your own safety, please. You have our address and our phones. We have yours. We'll stay in close touch."

Marco offered his hand to the Americans. "Go to the airport directly, stay there until your plane leaves. In eight hours?"

Arnie checked his watch. "Nine and half. If we really feel the need to hurry, there are shuttles every half hour. We'll manage."

"Well then," Tamara said. "Let's say our goodbyes. We'll remember you two always and the Eurorail screw-up that brought you into our lives."

Final hugs, final goodbyes.

When the Americans left for the shuttle, Tamara and Marco gathered up their baggage and began walking to their rendezvous.

"I'm feeling old, son. And tired out. And frightened. I don't like feeling this way."

Marco hooked his mother's arm through his own. "I'm also feeling scared. We got away with one, mom. It was close. Way too close. Let's go meet the guy and get rid of this shit."

From her vantage behind a thick platform stanchion, Sasha had witnessed the entire scene between the Russians and the Americans. Although she wasn't able to hear what was spoken, the body language of the four compartment-mates was telling. And when the two Russians made for the exit, she easily kept them in view. Sasha's single piece of luggage, a small backpack, was draped over her shoulder.

Mother and son left the terminal. The weather had warmed, the snow turning to a light rain. They walked to the usual meeting spot at the rear of the station, found the low-lit wooden bench, dried it off, and sat. Tamara placed her strapped bag on the ground next to her. Marco scrunched down into his coat, buried his hands deep in his pockets, and let his head droop.

Sasha found a spot in the shadows of a thick stand of bushes thirty meters from the sitting couple. She used Vera's monocular and watched.

After ten minutes, a man approached the bench. His back was to Sasha. He appeared shaky, nervous and kept looking side to side, as if expecting some unforeseen tragedy. He was dressed in a knee-length overcoat and a wool cap and was carrying a piece of luggage identical to Tamara's. He said something to her. She responded and smiled. The man sat, placing his bag next to hers.

Sasha used the monocular and could now see him front-on. *Well lookie here. We've met, haven't we? In Anchorage, and not that long ago. You ought to be nervous, Anatoly.*

Tamara roused her son, then the two of them collected themselves, switched bags, stood and made off, moving away from Sasha. The man rose, picked up Tamara's bag, and began walking in Sasha's direction.

As soon as he passed her, she stepped out from the shadows and forcefully shoved him in the back, sending him into a deeply shaded corner of the building. He caromed off the station's brick wall, and spun around, the bag falling from his grasp. "What . . ." he began, but Sasha was on him at once, the barrel of her Russian Special Services pistol shoved into his mouth. His teeth cracked audibly against the metal. The pilot's eyes went wide.

"Anatoly Suvorov," she whispered. "I thought I warned you—when we met in your hotel room in Anchorage—what

I would do if I ever saw you again. And here you are, still trafficking in heroin. You should've listened to me."

Suvorov's legs gave way and he would have collapsed had not Sasha grabbed him around the collar with her other hand and, with her body, pinned him to the wall. She pushed the pistol further into the pilot's mouth. He gagged and sputtered.

Sasha did a quick mental review of her options: she could deliver him to the first militiaman or local cop she'd find. But then she'd have to identify herself and explain what she was doing here in Russia—an American policeman with a pistol. *No. That definitely will not work. Konovalov would deny any connection to me.*

She could take the bag, leave him—unconscious or not—destroy the contents, and flee Vladivostok. *Again, no. Suvorov skates. I can't have that.*

She could leave the bag, leave him unconscious, call it in and hope the cops find him and the goods. *Once again, no. He might name Tamara, might identify me.*

Or she could continue her tracking, switching to Suvorov. *A non-starter since he's seen me. And even if he hadn't, no way I could manage a one-person surveillance. No choice left, really.*

"I'm glad you're wearing a wool cap," she whispered.

"Wha . . . ?"

"It'll collect the spray."

Suvorov grasped her intent and his bowels and bladder simultaneously gave way. The noise preceded the smell by a few seconds.

"I gave you fair warning." She took the pistol out of his mouth and placed it under his jaw, facing up. Tears flooded his eyes. "I have a son," he begged.

"And I have a daughter who doesn't have a father because of drug dealers like you." Sasha looked quickly in every direction.

Seeing no one, she fired a single shot up through the man's jaw and into his brain. His wool cap jumped as the slug tore through the top of Anatoly Suvorov's head. There was very little blood-spray. Sasha dragged the dead pilot deeper into the shadows, behind a hedgerow. She recovered her backpack, looped it over her shoulder, took up the bag of heroin, and walked into the train station's parking lot. There was an older man fiddling with the keys to his car. He didn't pay her the slightest attention. She continued through the lot, past Lenin's monument, and out onto Posyetskaya Street.

It began to rain harder, fat drops splashing into puddles. Water quickly collected in the gutters and streamed into nearby sewers.

Sasha hitched up the collar of her coat and ducked into an alleyway in back of the Café Pizza. She saw half a dozen trashcans. She disassembled the pistol, wiping her fingerprints off of each piece. She dropped the barrel into one trashcan, the body of the weapon into a second, the bullets into a third. Rainwater was flooding into a nearby manhole. She dropped the black-strapped bag onto the ground, opened it, and spilled out the contents. For the next five minutes, she tore open each of the more than twenty packets and dumped the drug into the running water, flushing the heroin into the manhole. When she finished, she stuffed the packing paper into the strapped bag and retraced her steps toward the rail station. After carefully wiping away any fingerprints, she tossed the bag into a trashcan.

A few steps later she was again inside the station. She squeezed out her soaking watch cap then shook the moisture from her hands. She bought a ticket on the *Rossiya,* the first train out of Vladivostok, heading west, leaving in four hours. She opened her phone and texted Vera.

"in vlad. heading back soon."

"why soon? job done?"

"job done. searched T and M bags. found NOTHING OF INTEREST."

"nothing? how can that be?"

"don't know. nothing more to do."

"coming back here?"

"alaska."

"will you tell kono?"

"no. you tell him. I contact him later."

"we miss you. Martyn says good luck. me too."

"you two were great. will miss you a lot. million XOXOXOXOs. bye."

Then she made a local call and began composing a letter.

~~~

Victoria Romanova fumbled on the nightstand for her buzzing cell phone. Groggy, she sat up in bed, trying not to jar her husband awake. She glanced at the clock—quarter past three in the morning. She found her phone and hit the green and listened.

"Good morning Vika. Guess who?"

"Sasha?" she whispered. "What the hell? Three in the morning. You sound close. Where are you?" Vika stood, grabbed her robe and moved to the next room. Her husband, a deep sleeper, hardly moved.

"I'm close, but only for a couple more hours. I need to see you. It's very important. Can you come right away to the central train station?"

Vika couldn't help but smile. "I hope it's not as serious as the last time you were in Vlad."

"Different situation, but just as serious. Can you come? I'll be waiting in Lenin Square, next to the monument."

By a quarter to four, the earlier, serious rain had morphed into a fine mist. A wash of ground fog covered Lenin Square. Wet snow blotched the ground.

Vika approached the monument and at once saw the only person crazy enough—besides herself—to be out on such a rotten and bone-chilling early morning. The two women embraced, exchanged multiple cheek-kisses, never leaving off holding onto each other, laughing at their preposterous situation.

Five minutes later, inside the terminal and over steaming cups of Ceylonese tea, Sasha told her friend the abbreviated version of what she'd been doing the past several weeks. She ended by giving her a letter to be hand-delivered later that morning.

"It goes to a couple staying at the Hyundai Hotel. You should deliver it and wait for their answer. Have a read."

Vika read the letter from start to finish. Twice. "Fucking hell, Sasha. What have you gotten yourself into *this* time? And why this letter?"

Sasha sat back, let her shoulders relax. "It's too long and complicated a story. But please, trust me. It's the right thing to do. Will you deliver it?"

"Of course I will. No question. And how should I let you know their answer?"

"You can email or text me. Just write 'yes' or 'no.'"

Vika stored the letter in her jacket. Over tea and cream-cheese filled vatrushki, they brought each other up to date. Sasha avoided talking about her daughter's drug bust and was vague about Tomás; Vika told about her teacher training, about her family, and especially about Yuri Gregorich, her father.

"Dad's still working at the fish plant, still whining

about being stuck in dry dock instead of on the ocean, still complaining about Putin and Kollantai. And still rhapsodizing about the visit we made to Alaska two years ago. He longs to go again. He was grateful to have met your grandfather. We were sad to hear about his death."

"Thanks. About Alaska, come anytime at all. As soon as you're able."

"Can I tell my father that we've met?"

"Yes, but not for a few days. Not 'til I'm out of the country. Tell him I'll write or call him soon."

"He lives for the adventure you put him through last time you were here. Especially when the cops came looking for you at his home."

The terminal's loudspeaker crackled to life with the announcement that the *Rossiya* was ready for boarding.

"That's me," Sasha said.

The women rose.

"Where's your baggage?" Vika asked.

Sasha pointed to her daypack. "This is it. I left a bag of stuff I didn't need on the train. Didn't want to be encumbered."

"What was the rush?"

They began walking toward the passenger platforms. Vika studied the face of her American friend. "Since you're not answering, I'm going to assume I shouldn't press you. Though I'm dying to know what you've been up to these past few hours."

Sasha hunched her shoulders. "Nothing dangerous. Promise."

"I know you too well to believe that."

They arrived at the *Rossiya*. Passengers, porters, and railway personnel were hustling about.

The friends stopped on the platform in front of Sasha's carriage. They embraced.

Holding her Russian friend close, Sasha whispered, "Better you don't know what I've been up to in Vlad. It wasn't very . . . pretty."

Vika pushed her to arm's length and gazed steadily into Sasha's eyes. "Sounds way too similar to the last time you were here."

Sasha shrugged. "I gotta go. Bye Vika. Thanks so much for this favor. It's very important to me. And love and kisses to your father, an all-time favorite of mine."

"I'll tell him. Bye, Sasha. Love you. Stay in touch."

"For sure."

~~~

Marco and his mother rose at ten to a room service wake-up call. They showered at length, dressed, and went down to the Hyundai Hotel's breakfast buffet. Just as they settled in, a woman came up to their table. She carried a cup and saucer and said, "You are Tamara Stoikova, from Chelyabinsk."

Tamara was taken aback. "Yes. But I don't know who you are."

"I'm someone with an important message for you and for Marco, here. And for David. May I sit?"

When Tamara didn't answer, couldn't answer, Vika sat and placed her cup and saucer in front of her. "We don't know each other, but someone who wants the best for you *does* know you."

"Who . . . ?"

"You've never met her, at least officially. But she knows you. She's followed you closely, on the train, and before, in Chelyabinsk, across the street from your apartment on Chapayev Street."

Marco stared at their uninvited tablemate. "Who the hell

are you and whattaya want?"

Vika looked at Marco. "Who I am is unimportant. What I want is to read you a letter that my friend wrote last night. It's addressed to both of you. May I?"

Again, Tamara was without words.

Vika began reading.

"Dearest Tamara and Marco: The man to whom you passed the bag of heroin last night in back of the railroad station is dead. The contents of the bag have been flushed away."

Vika paused long enough to watch an expression of frightened disbelief take possession of Tamara's face. Marco looked vacantly at his mother.

"I'll continue," Vika said.

"I know what happened on the train. I was a witness, and for a moment, a participant."

"Katya," Tamara whispered.

"Mom, quiet," cautioned Marco.

Tamara looked at Vika. "What do you want?" she gasped.

Vika sat back. "Me? I want nothing. I'm doing this as a favor to my friend. And as a favor to you and your son."

"How do you know us?" Marco demanded.

"*I* don't know you two from Adam. But my friend does and she warns you . . . advises you, perhaps a better term . . . But here, let me finish reading."

"I know what you and David have been doing. I know about the Afghan rug sale. The driver of the lorry that delivered the

rugs is dead and the FSS guard who took the driver's bribes was arrested just a few days ago. You and David are still free. At least, for now. If you want to stay that way, you must immediately and forever stop trafficking in drugs. If I learn that you or Marco or David are again dealing drugs, I will tell the police everything I know. And you can see from what I've already written, I know a great deal, enough to condemn you to a life in prison. The person reading this letter to you is my messenger. Tell her what I want to hear—that you are done with the business. If you do not tell her immediately, you will not make it home. You will be arrested in Vladivostok and probably never get home. For years, at least.

Vika paused. "My friend didn't sign the letter. But as you can see, she wishes nothing but the best for you, for Marco, and for David. Will you promise me what she has proposed to you?"

Tamara had her hands to her face and was quietly weeping. Marco seemed frozen in his seat.

Vika asked them again.

Tamara looked at her son and took his hand. "I swear to quit the business." She looked at Marco.

"Me, too. I swear," he whispered.

"Excellent," Vika said, folding the letter and putting it into her purse. "I'll let my friend know of your promise. She will be deeply gratified. You will, of course, convince David. If you cannot, well . . . ." Vika took a final sip of her tea, then rose and walked away.

When she was gone, Tamara managed a faint smile, tears still dotting her cheeks, "It's good, Marco. It's a good thing."

"I know, mom."

~~~

Sasha had a lone compartment-mate: a blind man traveling to Khabarovsk with his service dog, a beautiful golden lab. She introduced herself to the man as Katya Ivanovna Rodina, her assumed name.

"I am Pavel Michailovich Shirokin," he answered. "And my dog, Queenie."

Somehow, the presence of the blind man and a mostly sleeping dog put her mind at ease. When he reached into his hamper and came out with a Thermos and sandwiches and offered to share, she accepted gratefully.

"I'm heading home from a conference of teachers of blind children," he said. "And you, Katya Ivanovna? What brings you to my compartment?"

"Came to see a friend and to ski. Been here less than a week. Heading home back to work now."

"And where is that?"

Here we go again. "In Holland. I work for the Russian delegation to the International Criminal Court in the Hague."

"You're a lawyer?"

"No. More of a para-legal secretary."

"Been at it long?"

"Close to ten years. *Let's change the subject.* "And you, Pavel Michailovich, tell me about your work." *Take your time.*

He took his time. For the next two hours, he held the floor, telling about blind children and their triumphs. He told about his family, his wife of forty years and his six children, all grown and all teachers. By the time they were half way to Khabarovsk, he trailed off, got comfortable, and dozed. Queenie remained vigilant, raising her head to look at Sasha each time she went in and out of the compartment.

When he awoke, they were riding into the outskirts of his hometown. Pavel Michailovich stretched and cleared his throat. "It's always interesting to me, Katya Ivanovna, to listen to the way strangers talk. Being blind from birth, I've developed an acute sense of hearing, and being a teacher of the Russian language, I get to hear my native tongue spoken by all kinds of people. Your Russian, my dear, is *almost* native. Ninety-nine percent native. But . . . a tad old fashioned. Strange for someone as young as you. You've used some expressions and words that I haven't heard in years. And, one more thing. I hear the *barest* hint of a foreign inflexion. It's the way you pronounce the hard and soft consonants. Not quite what I'm used to hearing. So, I'm guessing that your time abroad has been an influence on your spoken Russian. I sense that you are speaking mainly another language—English perhaps?"

The train slowed to a crawl as it entered Khabarovsk's rail yards. Pavel began to gather his things. Queenie rose and looked to her master. Pavel reached down and stroked the dog's neck. At first, Sasha thought to lie to the man. But given his obviously keen powers of observation, she thought it best to tell the truth.

"You have a great sense of hearing, Pavel Michailovich. You have found me out. In fact, when I was much younger, I attended university in the United States, in Seattle."

"Hmmm. And what was your major course of study?"

"Criminology," she answered truthfully.

The blind man then smiled a smile that made her stomach flip-flop, made her imagine that he saw through her imaginary story. She wouldn't have been surprised if he now told her that he saw her for exactly who she was—an American police officer come to Russia in disguise and having just a few hours earlier shot a drug dealer in the head.

"Criminology?" he said, grinning. "Huh. Yes, that fits."

He reached out his hand toward Sasha. "That makes complete sense now, Katya Ivanovna." He took her hand in his and shook it once, gently. He laughed to himself. "Please stay safe . . . Katya Ivanovna. A lovely name." He laughed lightly again then bent toward his dog. "Come Queenie. Time to go home. Say goodbye to . . . ," he paused, ". . . to Katya Ivanovna."

The way he had made a point of her name sent shivers down her spine. She helped escort the man down the carriage steps to the platform. They said their final goodbyes. Before reboarding, she checked her smartphone. Vika had texted a 'yes.' Sasha closed her eyes and smiled. *You're in the clear for now, Tama. Better not screw up.*

Sasha reboarded, found her compartment, and slumped onto her seat, wondering about her brief but creepy interaction with the blind man. *How did he know? It's as if he'd read my mind.* Her thoughts were interrupted when four teenagers—two boys and two girls—stormed into the compartment, laughing, shoving, and falling all over each other. Sasha was glad for the company. She and her new friends stayed together, sharing food and stories until the station at Chita. There, she transferred to a branch of the TransSiberian that took her south, first to Harbin, then, a day later, to Bei Jing. She flew from there to Seattle, then home to Anchorage. She took three days of R and R, visiting with her daughter every day at the youth center. When she finally arrived back at the precinct, there was a FedEx letter waiting for her. She tore it open and found two envelopes, both with Russian Ministry of Justice embossed logos. She opened the larger envelope and took out a single piece of handwritten paper. She read.

Dear Sasha: You have done exceedingly well. The work at Bugristoye was outstanding. We are very pleased.

However, since you have seen fit to fabricate the innocence of Tamara Stoikova, her son Marco, and the notorious David Osinchuk, I feel our 'deal' somewhat compromised.

Sincerely,

Igor Semyonovich Konovalov

Sasha now turned to the second, smaller envelope. She greedily tore it open and found a cashier's check for five hundred dollars.

"Motherfucking Russians," Sasha screamed, crumpling up the check.

#

~ Epilog ~

A hundred and forty cartons of Afghani raisins, apricots, and figs are neatly stacked on two dozen pallets in a Chelyabinsk warehouse owned by Agro-Partnyori, LLC, one of the largest dried fruit importers in western Russia.

Inside of every carton are five plastic bags of fruit, each weighing three and a half kilos. A closer inspection of a select number of cartons reveals smaller bags—one kilo each—of another Afghani product, hidden deep among the raisins.

Well before dawn, two men stand in the dimly lit warehouse, inspecting the cartons.

"So how do I know which of these has what I'm looking for?" the man asks. "I mean, they all look the same to me."

"Come. I'll show you," says Daoud, the lorry driver who has brought the fruit to Chelyabinsk. "Agro Partnyori is not the final landing place," he explains. "The address of the final consignee is stenciled on each package. Look for 'Borzoi Fruits' in Ufa. That'll be seventeen cartons of raisins. Your stuff'll be in those."

A quick search by the two men reveals the correct cartons, stacked on two pallets. The men unseal those cartons, empty them of their hidden treasure, then re-seal. They pack the illegal product into three smaller, sturdy cardboard boxes that the man loads onto a hand truck. They pause to light up.

"You get through the border OK?" the man asks Daoud.

"No sweat. I didn't recognize the frontier guard. Good looking woman. Valentina Andro . . . something. Couldn't read her whole name tag. A great big blond woman. Tall with the most gorgeous green eyes. She apparently got word I was coming and was waiting for me. We went into the back of my lorry and I stuffed four, fifty dollar bills in her palm. She signed off and waved me through. Didn't even bother looking at my manifest."

"Easy. So, we'll see you again soon?"

"Next month probably," says Daoud. He takes a long drag on his cigarette. "Just wondering. What happened to the guy I used to deliver to?"

The man shrugs. "David? He kinda dropped out of the business. Spends all his time now in his garage. Works as a motorcycle mechanic."

"So he's not in the trade anymore?"

"Appears that way."

"The gang in Jalalabad? Do they know about this? Did he tell them he's no longer dealing?"

"No idea. Why?"

"It's just . . . I hear they don't like guys who've been a long time *inside*, suddenly on the *outside*. Too dangerous for them having someone who knows so much not working for them anymore."

"Think they'll react?"

"Count on it," says Daoud. "They always do in these kinds of situations."

~~~

Busby Moranis had his heart broken on a Saturday night. He and Luisa had just come from eating out—Café Paris for steaks. During the meal, Busby felt the wall solidify, the one that had been growing between them for the past month. He asked her about it but she wouldn't engage. On the way back to her place—a place he'd come to know as his second home—she suggested they take a drive down the highway. Fifteen minutes later they pulled off at Beluga Point. A stiff breeze roiled the waters of Turnagain Arm.

She took a deep breath and let it out slowly. "I told you about my ex," she began.

Busby felt his stomach knit tight. *Jesus. Please don't go there.* "You did. Augusto. Doing three to five for robbery, out of state."

"Yes. Augusto. Well . . . he's getting paroled in a month."

Busby didn't want to hear another word. He wanted this conversation to end here and now. He wanted to go back to their early days, when they had just met, wrestling in bed, naked and laughing hysterically. It staggered him to realize that was not going to happen again.

She gently stroked his sleeve. "He wants to rejoin his family."

He couldn't look at her and stayed silent.

"The girls miss him, Busby. They adore him. He's their dad."

His tongue felt thick. He stared out the windshield. "I get that, Luisa. Let him be their dad. Let him be a real father to them. I can live with that. But . . . from the tone of your voice, it's clear that . . ." He turned to her. "That you miss him, too."

She nodded, looked away from him, out onto the water. "I do," she whispered.

"Your girls adore him. And so do you."

She nodded.

"More than you adore me."

When she didn't reply, he started up the car. "I'll take you home." He didn't want to argue. From bittersweet experience he knew that you can't talk someone into loving you. They either do or they don't. The chemistry is there or it's not.

"Box up my stuff," he said. "Call me when I can come and pick it up." He felt his heart break into pieces, then felt the pieces somehow begin to reassemble and harden into something he didn't much like. He kept silent during their drive back to town.

She wept quietly all the way home and got out of the car without a word.

He drove off, thought to get a beer, and drove to Chilkoot Charlie's. As soon as he wedged himself onto a seat at the crowded bar, a woman squeezed in next to him. She smiled up at the handsome man. "What's your name?" she asked.

He noted her lithe figure and slight Russian accent. *Russian. Jesus.* "I'm Busby. You?"

"I am Olga. You look unhappy, Busby. Maybe I can help."

~~~

The weather in Anchorage continued drizzly and gray right through the end of October. The parking lot at Colony High School was peppered with deep puddles. The school buses had long since departed and late-working teachers, umbrellas opened, filed out of the building. At a quarter past four, a hooded Tucker Cranston left his work and headed for his car, carefully picking his way between the wet spots. He carried a briefcase full of essays that needed grading. The topic: the failure of the United States poppy eradication program in Afghanistan.

He heard a voice call out from behind him, "Colonel Cranston."

Tucker turned to see a slight female figure, shrouded in yellow rain gear. He paused and sheltered his briefcase inside his rain coat. "Yes. Can I help you?"

The woman came up to him, stopping a few feet away. "You can, Colonel Cranston. You absolutely *can* help me."

She pushed her hood back, exposing to Tucker a beautiful face surrounded by long, dark hair.

He gave her a broad smile. "Do I know you?"

"No. But we have mutual friends."

"Really? And who might they be?"

"The Murad family. The Shaikh, his son Hakeem, and *his* son Akbar. You remember them, of course. I spoke to Hakeem just last night. He asked me to tell you that Akbar is still using the spurs you gave him when you were at Bagram."

Tucker sagged. He couldn't respond.

"Perhaps, Colonel, it's best if we don't stand in the drizzle and talk. Is there a place nearby where we can sit?"

Tucker remained mute, rooted to the pavement. Heavy rain drops splatted on his hood. More than anything right now, he wanted to do a re-boot on his past idiocy. *Stupid. Stupid. Thinking we would be free. McHenry's free, hiding away, floating on Lake Powell. Me, in plain sight. Stupid.*

"Somewhere nearby, Colonel Cranston?"

He came to. "Yeah. The Vagabond Blues in Palmer."

"I don't have a car. I'll drive with you."

Sitting across from the woman at a table near the café's front window, Tucker noted her husky voice and her subtle Russian accent. The woman sipped at her hot chocolate and regarded him with a warm smile.

"Your daughters have returned for their next year at Columbia University. Congratulations. And since leaving the military, you've become a teacher. Something you always wanted to do, according to Hakeem. He raved to me about the breadth of your knowledge of Afghanistan. He and the Shaikh were very impressed." She blew across the top of her mug. "And I spoke to Madame Bisset this morning. Your account at *Dubois Freres* is doing very well. Something approaching one hundred and ninety thousand dollars." She saw Tucker's surprise and hastened to explain. "The Swiss these days understand the need to be more forthcoming about their banking practices."

Tucker felt beaten, felt as if the great burden he shed after his tour in Afghanistan had once again been dumped onto his shoulders. *Lulu will freak tonight when I tell her.*

He sighed heavily. "What do you want from me? Just tell me straight out. Get it over with."

The woman sat up in her seat and took a paper napkin to her lips. "Thank you, Colonel, for choosing the direct and honest approach. So, a week from this Thursday, you will fly to St. Lawrence Island. There, you will collect a single passenger, a young woman and her several pieces of baggage. You will bring them here to Anchorage. The woman will leave with her two private suitcases. Someone will be waiting at the airport to take the remaining several parcels. You will fly there every few months. And there will be other occasions when your piloting skills will be needed."

"Every few months?" He heard the whiny tone of his voice. He felt disgusted with himself. "How the hell am I supposed to do that? I have a job, I work every day."

She gave him a frozen smile. "Hakeem said you were resourceful. You'll figure it out."

He realized there was no point in telling the woman that his Cessna 150 didn't have the range to fly from Anchorage to the middle of the Bering Sea. *No, don't even bother arguing. There are several villages where I can to stop to gas up. And these packages? Pretty clear what they contain. And pretty clear they've got me by the balls. Stupid me. Stupid. Stupid.*

The woman seemed to read his thoughts. "We'll cover the costs—gas and maintenance of your plane. And, of course, you can expect a deposit into your Swiss account. That goes without saying." She took a small piece of paper out of her jacket pocket. On it was a phone number. "Before you take off, call this number.

And when you've landed back in Anchorage, call it again." She slid the paper across the table.

Tucker took the slip of paper, looked at it briefly, folded it, and placed it in his wallet. He stood and walked out.

Larissa Bunina sipped her hot chocolate, took out her cell phone, and called her husband.

"Done," she said.

~~~

She'd just returned home from visiting her daughter at the youth center. Robin was adjusting to the tedium of incarceration. Seven months and she'd be out and would hopefully decide to come and live with her.

Sasha sprawled on her sofa and opened her laptop. She went to her email account and saw that Tomás had written. She hastily opened the email.

Sasha: This is the hardest thing I've ever had to do.

Her vision blurred. She read the next two sentences, then slammed shut her laptop. She sat for a moment, re-opened the computer, read the rest of Tomás's letter, then trashed it. She went to the 'search mail' option, entered his name and deleted all previous exchanges between them. She went to 'sent mail' and deleted all of her messages to him. She went to 'trash,' found all of their correspondence and hit 'delete forever.' She went to her contact list and deleted his name.

She rose, put on her parka and left her double-wide. She got in her pick-up and drove to the Brown Jug. She put two six-packs of Corona and a fifth of Cuervo into her cart and pushed it to the cashier. She stared straight ahead, not moving, not reaching into her pocket for her credit card.

"You ready, ma'am? Anything else?" the old guy behind the register asked.

When she didn't answer, he asked again. "Anything else ma'am? Should I ring it up?"

She stood there. *Seven hundred and seventy-two days.*

~~~

"Roald Amundsen?" Boris asked his wife. "Of course I know the name. He was the first man to the South Pole. There was a race between his team and some Englishman."

"Scott," said Larissa. "Who died there. But Amundsen was also famous for something else. Know what?"

"I give up. Tell me." Boris was stretched out in their bed, the comforter pulled up to his chin. He looked cozy.

Larissa was next to him, her glasses on, reading something she had just downloaded and printed. "Amundsen was the first person to navigate the Northwest Passage, across the Canadian Arctic."

"Wonderful. But why are we talking about this?"

She dropped the papers, turned to her husband, and scrunched down under the comforter. She pushed her legs into his half of the bed and found his toes with her toes. "We are talking about this because there is a Norwegian ocean liner named after him."

Boris tried to grab her legs in his. "Why should I care?"

"You should care because that particular ocean liner will sail across the Northwest Passage next summer. From Nome in Alaska, to the East Coast. Now do you care?"

Boris Bunin was giggling. He ducked his head under the blanket and began exploring.

BIOGRAPHICAL NOTES OF MAIN
CHARACTERS

Full name: **Gordon (Busby) Moranis**

Place and date of birth: Yakima, Washington. Dec. 16, 1978

Height: 6'2" / *Weight:* 204 pounds

Color hair: blond / *Color eyes:* blue

Distinguishing features: Scar, left knee (football injury, 1995). Scar left wrist (football injury, 1997). Scar right collarbone (football injury, 1997). Tattoo of football championship trophy on right upper arm.

Skills: Small arms gun collector.

Family: Parents: Helen (father unknown). Marriage: none. Children: none.

Education: BA Kinesiology, Pacific Lutheran University, Parkland, Washington, 2000. Graduate, Washington State Patrol Academy, 2001. (21 of 59)

Work history: Washington State Patrol, 2001-2004. Bethel, Alaska Police Department, 2004-2008. Alaska State Troopers, 2008-2010. Anchorage Police Department, 2010-present.

Full name: **Gary Rafael Hernandez**

Place and date of birth: El Monte, California. January 12, 1973.

Height: 6' 1" / *Weight:* 225 pounds

Color hair: brown / *Color eyes:* brown

Distinguishing features: Limp, left leg (gun shot wound, 1996). Corrective lenses (reading). Pacemaker.

Skills: Fluent Spanish speaker.

Family: Parents: Jorge and Georgia. Married: Florencia, 1994. Divorced, 2001. Children: Octavia, Romano. (Both children live with mother in Los Feliz, California.

Education: AA in Business Administration, California State University, Los Angeles, 1993. Graduate, Los Angeles Police Academy, 1994 (33 of 165)

Work history: Los Angeles Police Department, 1994-2008.

Anchorage Police Department, 2008-present.

Full name: **Aleksandra (Sasha) Kulaeva**

Place and date of birth: Fairbanks, Alaska. August 18, 1978

Height: 5' 9" / *Weight:* 141 pounds

Color hair: blond / *Color eyes:* light green

Distinguishing features: One-inch scar on left knee (cause unknown).

Skills: Private pilot certification, 1995-present. American Translator Association Certification, (Russian) 2017-present. EMT I, 2007-2009.

Family: Parents: Roberta and Peter Kulaev, both deceased. Married: Robin Hutchinson, 1999-2002. Children: Robin.

Education: BA in Criminology, University of Washington, 1998. Graduate, Alaska Public Safety Training Academy, Sitka, Alaska. 1999. (5 of 32)

Work history: Sitka Police Dept. 1999-2002. Anchorage Police Dept. 2006-present.

Full name: **Robin June Kulaeva**

Place and date of birth: Big Lake, Alaska. June 21, 2003.

Height: 5' 6" / *Weight:* 120 pounds

Color hair: light brown / *Color eyes:* light brown

Distinguishing features: mole on right calf.

Skills: student pilot

Family: Parents: Sasha and Robin (deceased)

Education: eleventh grade

Work history: no known work history

Full name: **Artun Utkan Ozil**

Place and date of birth: Istanbul, Turkey. October 30, 1961.

Height: 5' 7" / *Weight:* 185 pounds

Color hair: brown / *Color eyes:* brown

Distinguishing features: Three knife wounds on left forearm. Missing left ear lobe. Slight stutter.

Skills: apprentice mechanic. Fluent Greek. Conversant Arabic, English.

Family: Unknown

Education: Unknown

Work history: Unknown

Full name: **Mehmet Sevket Ozil**

Place and date of birth: Kavakli, Turkey. Nov. 24, 1960.

Height: 5' 5" / *Weight:* 220 pounds

Color hair: brown / *Color eyes:* hazel

Distinguishing features: Scar on right thigh. Wears bifocals. GERD (Barrett's low grade dysplasia). Kidney stones.

Skills: Fluent Greek, Russian, French. Conversant Arabic, Spanish, English.

Family: Parents: unknown. Marriage: Nicole. Children: Laura, Monique.

Education: unknown

Work history: unknown

Full name: **Stanislav (Stan) Mikolai Babiarsz**

Place and date of birth: Feb. 22, 1957. Lodz, Poland. Emigrated from Poland to the United States, 1961.

Height: 5' 10" / *Weight:* 204 pounds

Color hair: gray / *Color eyes:* gray

Distinguishing features: Corrective lens. Hearing aids. Scar in left armpit (knife wound). Appendix scar. Hirsute.

Skills: Fluent Polish, Russian, Ukrainian. Plays accordion, bandura, and dombra.

Family: Parents: Mikolaj and Teresa both deceased. Marriage: Louisa Symanski. Children: Stepan, Jakob, Loretta.

Education: BA History, Loyola University of Chicago, 1980. AA Criminal Justice, Harry S. Truman College, Chicago. 1982. Graduate, Chicago Police Department Education and Training Division. 1982 (4 of 83)

Work history: Chicago Police Department, 1982-2007. Dutch Harbor/ Unalaska Police Department, 2007-2018. Anchorage Police Department, 2018-present.

Full name: **Larissa (Lara) Kirillovna Bunina**

Place and date of birth: Kirovsk, Soviet Union. July 1, 1974. Immigrated to Israel, 1997. Immigrated to United States, 1998.

Height: 5' 2" / *Weight:* 109 pounds

Color hair: black / *Color eyes:* black

Distinguishing features: Deformed left big toe (ballet injury, 1989. Tattoo of a rose above right buttock

Family: Parents: Kirill and Maria. Married: Boris Bunin, 2000. Children: Peter, Michael

Education: Vaganova Academy of Russian Ballet, St. Petersburg, Soviet Union (two years) 1989-91. BA History, Yaroslav-the-Wise University, Nizhny Novgorod, Russia, 1993. MA Political Science, St. Petersburg State University, St. Petersburg, Russia, 1995. PhD. Economics, St. Petersburg State University, St. Petersburg, Russia, 1997.

Work history: Sales clerk, Russian Book Store #21, 1998-1999.

Full name: **Boris (Borya) Davidovich Bunin**

Place and date of birth: West Babylon, New York.
March 11, 1962.

Height: 5' 8" / *Weight:* 170 pounds

Color hair: brown / *Color eyes:* brown

Distinguishing features: Corrective lenses. Broken right ankle, soccer game. Nocturia.

Skills: Fluent Russian.

Family: Parents: David and Maria. Marriage: Larissa, 2000.Children: Peter, Michael

Education: BA Business, Hunter College, Manhattan, 1981.

Work history: Owner, Sunny Day Cleaners, twenty-two dry cleaning stores in Brooklyn and Staten Island.

Full name: **Leonid Maksimovich Bulgarin**

Place and date of birth: Moscow, Soviet Union.
July 30, 1962.

Height: 6' 1" / *Weight:* 185 pounds

Color hair: blond / *Color eyes:* hazel

Distinguishing features: Pockmarked left cheek (acne). Corrective lenses. Chain smoker. Diabetic.

Skills: Pilot. Fluent English and Ukrainian.

Family: Parents: Maksim and Liudmila. Marriage: Dorotea. Children: none.

Education: Graduate, Higher Civil Aviation Academy, Ulyanovsk. Soviet Union 1990 (12 of 32)

Work history: Pilot, New England Flight Service. 1995-2003. Pilot and owner, Grizzly Air, Anchorage, Alaska. 2004-present

Full name: **Dorotea Konstantinovna Bulgarina**

Place and date of birth: Kiev, Ukraine. December 2, 1968.

Height: 5' 3" / *Weight:* 146 pounds

Color hair: blond / *Color eyes:* blue

Distinguishing features: Tattoo of trident (Ukrainian national symbol) on left thigh. Chain smoker. Bifocal glasses. Sleep apnea

Skills: Accountant

Family: Parents: Konstantin and Antonina. Marriage: Leonid.

Education: Graduate, Praktykum Accounting School, Kiev, Ukraine, 1991.

Work history: KDD Group, Kiev, 1993-1997. Oschadbank, Kiev, 1997-2004. Assistant Manager, accountant, Grizzly Air, Anchorage, Alaska. 2005-present.

Full name: **Anatoly Maximovich Suvorov**

Place and date of birth: Saratov, Soviet Union.
August 19, 1979

Height: 5' 10" / *Weight:* 168 pounds

Color hair: blond / *Color eyes:* blue

Distinguishing features: Slight stutter. Ulcerative colitis. Smoker.

Skills: Pilot.

Family: Parents: Maksim and Yekaterina. Married: Sophia. Children: Marat

Education: Graduate, 2005, Aeroflot Aviation School, Moscow, Russia. (56 of 82)

Work history: Smartavia, Archangelsk, Russia. 2005-2009. Troika Aviation, Vladivostok, Russia 2009-present.

Full name: **Pyotr Aleksandrovich Bondarchuk**

Place and date of birth: Perm, Russia. February 22, 1980.

Height: 5' 11" / *Weight:* 195 pounds

Color hair: blond / *Color eyes:* brown

Distinguishing features: appendix scar, ingrown right big toe nail, flat feet, diabetic.

Skills: Fork-lift loader driver

Family: Parents: Ivan and Maroushka. Married, Svetlana Kuzminskaya, 2018. No children.

Education: Graduate, Secondary School No. 136, Perm, Russia, 1998

Work history: Day laborer, Novomet-Perm, Perm, Russia, 1998-2003. Expeditor, KennaMetal, Perm, Russia, 2003-2013. Federal Security Services, Troitsk, Russia, 2013-present.

Full name: **Kamal Saifi ibn Murad**

Place and date of birth: Jalalabad, Afghanistan. September 19, 1964

Height: 5' 6" / *Weight:* 195 pounds

Color hair: brown / *Color eyes:* brown

Distinguishing features: multiple scars on left rib cage, scar on right knee, polio survivor, hepatitis A.

Skills: Fluent in both Pashto and Dari, conversant in Uzbek and Turkmen. Instructor in land mine detection and demolition, Afghan Army, 2001-present.

Family: Parents: Aleem and unknown. Married: Farhana, 1984. Children: Unknown

Education: Unknown.

Work history: Afghan Army, 1981-present.

Full name: **Tucker Harrison Cranston**

Place and date of birth: Willow, Alaska. June 16, 1973.

Height: 5' 11" / *Weight:* 180 pounds

Color hair: light brown / Color eyes: brown

Distinguishing features: chipped front upper tooth, corrective lenses, appendix scar.

Skills: small aircraft pilot.

Family: Parents: Jack and Heather. Marriage: Luellen. *Children:* Raylette, Tessa, Elizabeth, Rory, Trent.

Education: Graduate. BA History. Texas A & M. 1995.

Work history: US Army, 1996-2018.

Full name: **Luellen Pearl Cranston**

Place and date of birth: Laredo, Texas, March 30, 1976.

Height: 5' 2" / Weight: 115 pounds

Color hair: brown / *Color eyes:* light brown

Distinguishing features: tattoo of Rosie the Riveter on left thigh. Missing top joint of right pinky. Seasonal allergies, allergic to bee sting.

Skills: Conversational Spanish speaker, accountant, taught stained glass at El Paso Community College, El Paso, Texas. 1997-1999.

Family: Parents: Bernard and Evangeline. Married: Tucker Cranston, 1999. Children: Raylette, Tessa, Elizabeth, Rory, Trent.

Education: BBA Business Administration and Accounting, University of Texas at El Paso. 1998.

Work history: Bookkeeper, Cranston Flight Service, Willow, Alaska, (intermittently) 1999-present.

Full name: **Tamara Ivanovna Stoikova**

Place and date of birth: Chelyabinsk, Soviet Union. July 5, 1968

Height: 5' 8" / Weight: 132 pounds

Color hair: dark brown / *Color eyes:* black

Distinguishing features: Appendix scar. C-Section scar. Mole on left shoulder.

Skills: Combat nurse, Conversant French, German, and English speaker.

Family: Parents: Ivan and Lydia. Marriage: Artur Vinogradov (divorced). Children: Marco

Education: Graduate. Kirov Military Medical Academy, St. Petersburg, 1987.

Work history: Combat nurse, Afghanistan, 1987-1989. Nurse, Municipal Polyclinic #2, Chelyabinsk, Soviet Union. 1989-present

Full name: **David Jakovlevich Osinchuk**

Place and date of birth: Odessa, Soviet Union. January 2, 1966.

Height: 5' 11" / Weight: 175 pounds

Color hair: red / *Color eyes:* hazel

Distinguishing features: Deformed nose. Scar on left malleolus. Scar on right upper arm. Multi-freckled.

Skills: auto mechanic, chef, baker.

Family: Parents: Jakov and Leah. Marriage: Tamara Stoikova. Children: none.

Education: Odessa Professional School of Rail Transport and Construction, 1987, (completed one year). Kiev International Culinary Academy 1988, (completed three semesters).

Work history: CTO Garage 2424, Soviet Union, 1982-87, Odessa, Soviet Union. Bike Garage and Lab 632. Chelyabinsk, Russia. 1989-2001. La Petite Bakery. Chelyabinsk, Russia, 2002-2005. Owner, SportMotoServ, Chelyabinsk, Russia, 2009-present.

Full name: **Salar Murad ibn Sayed ibn Habibullah**

Place and date of birth: Ghazni, Afghanistan. September (?) 1935 (?)

Height: 5' 4" / Weight: 146 pounds

Color hair: gray / *Color eyes:* brown

Distinguishing features: Disfigured left thumb. Scar over right eye. Scar along right rib cage. Scar down right thigh.

Skills: no known skills.

Family: Parents: unknown. Marriage: Larmina, Shiren. Ramineh. Children: (Murad is suspected of having sired at least twenty children. Their identities cannot be verified.

Education: no known education

Work history: no known work history. (Murad is reputed to be 'war lord' of the province of Nangarhar)

Full name: **Hakeem ibn Salman ibn Murad**

Place and date of birth: Herat, Afghanistan. March 1, 1975

Height: 6' 0" / *Weight:* 180 pounds

Color hair: brown / *Color eyes:* brown

Distinguishing features: Corrective lenses. Dyspeptic. Scar on right knee. Slight hearing loss.

Skills: Fluent English, French speaker. Conversant in Russian.

Family: Amir Salman (mother unknown). Marriage: Reha, Naheed. Children: Akbar, Daamin, Baahir.

Education: MA in Middle Eastern Studies (double first), Cambridge University, Great Britain, 1996.

Work history: no known work history

Full name: **Mirza ibn Murad**

Place and date of birth: Jalalabad, Afghanistan. January 20, 1965.

Height: 5' 8" / *Weight:* 195 pounds

Color hair: brown / *Color eyes:* brown

Distinguishing features: Scar on left cheek, scar across lower back

Skills: truck driver, auto mechanic

Family: Parents: Abdul Hannan and Damsa. Marriage: Medina. Children: Berezira, Hamdiya, Esin, Moska, Yasmin.

Education: finished fifth grade

Work history: no known work

End Notes

#1   Two of the Russians were shot and killed by Detective Kulaeva in the second floor hallway of the Bering Bridge Bed and Breakfast, in Dutch Harbor. The third Russian fled, was wounded by Sasha, and tracked down to the B and B parking lot where she shot and killed him. That man was Konstantin (Kostya) Zhuganov, twin brother of Taras, Boris Bunin's consigliere. It was the death of Kostya, at the hands of Kulaeva, that drove Taras to seek revenge.

#2   Barbiarsz told Raymond that two witnesses reported hearing a different sequence of shots than that reported by Detective Kulaeva. They deduced that after she had wounded the man, pursued him, and interrogated him, she executed him. A full account of the conversation of the two chiefs of police can be found in Traffic North, by Richie Goldstein, pages 282-288.

#3   In 2016, Detective Kulaeva and FBI Special Agent Charlie Dana traveled to Dutch Harbor to investigate the disappearance of Jimmy Lasorda, an American High Seas Fisheries Monitor, missing off of a Russian trawler. The two policemen discovered a quantity of heroin in a restaurant freezer, heroin stored there by the missing fisherman.

#4   Viktor Kulaev was a Soviet Air Force pilot who ferried American-made fighter planes from the Territory of Alaska to Russia during WWII's Lend Lease Program. When the war ended, Kulaev remained in America, married, and raised a family. His oldest grandchild is Sasha Kulaeva. When her parents were killed in a plane crash, Viktor raised her and taught her how to fly.

#5   Artun Ozil's victims and the reasons for their demise. Antonia – Portuguese, cheated the cousins out of sixteen ounces of gold bullion. Danny – Israeli, tried to steal hashish the Ozils were smuggling into Eilat from Egypt on a glass bottom boat. Eduardo – Brazilian, tried to muscle in on the Ozils' theft of a large cache of rare coins. Gerhardt – Austrian, insulted Mehmet's wife. Georges – French, tried to blackmail Mehmet with information about an arms theft in Sofia, Bulgaria. Gabriel – Dutch, attempted to steal data off of Artun's personal computer. Igor – Slovakian, reneged on debt incurred when Mehmet loaned him 80,000 Euros. Katerina – Russian, stole Artun's 1955 Citroen DS. Laurentina – Dutch, called Mehmet a "rag head." Lonzo – American, tried to horn in on the Ozils' stake in a cannabis farm in Humboldt County. Mickey – Honduran, spat at Artun, then threw a bottle of Pauli Girl at him. Muhammad – Bahrainian, forged Mehmet's name on a check. Mutto – Moroccan, chased Artun through the Marrakesh Casbah. (This was really self-defense). Olivier – Basque, wanted money back from an arms deal that crashed when the shipment sank in the Bay of Biscay. Orestes – Greek, ratted on Artun and Mehmet to the Greek National Intelligence Service. Pascal – Belgian, cheated Mehmet of his proper portion of the proceeds from the theft of a 2014 Kenworth T800. Rudy – American, stole the cousins' heroin for his own use. Shakira – Lebanese, laughed at Artun in a bordello in Rhodes. Turko – Greek, the first. Called the cousins "scum." Artun cut his throat. Wesley – English, gay man who came on to Artun. Xerxes – Macedonian, tried to blackmail the cousins over their theft of four Greek amphorae. Yolo – Egyptian, stole a HDTV from Mehmet's mother.

#6   After the problems in Vladivostok in 2016, Sasha needed to flee Russia, but was captured in Anadyr by the Kerensky brothers, two small-time Magadan criminals. They took her to the woods with the intent of shooting her, but she was rescued by Vika Romanova, who shot and killed the brothers then flew with Sasha to Provideniya. There, she took a boat captained by Buster Kopanuk to his St. Lawrence Island home. From there, Sasha flew back to Anchorage with Grizzly Air, on a plane flown by Leo Bulgarin.

#7   Sasha and Chilean Detective Tomás Morales captured Taras Zhuganov in Vladivostok's Hyundai Hotel, in the room of Alla Kollantai, the daughter of Vladivostok mayor, Roman Kollantai. Zhuganov and the young woman were both naked. Detective Kulaeva forced them into staged in flagrante postures, then photographed them. She used the photos to threaten both the woman's father and Zhuganov's brother-in-law and employer, Boris Bunin. Zhuganov had come to Vladivostok to kill Sasha in order to avenge her killing his twin brother, Kostya. After his arrest, Zhuganov was taken to the Partizanskaya Prison and murdered that night by order of the mayor, Roman Kollantai, with the approval of Boris Bunin. Sasha has retained the photographs as an insurance hedge against Bunin and Kollantai.

#8   In 2016, four Alaskans were caught skimming Bunin heroin. They were disposed of. The four were Jimmy Lasorda, a high-seas fisheries monitor who was tethered to a crab pot and thrown into the sea; Isabel Castro, Jimmy's girl friend, who was given a lethal drug cocktail; Rudy Castro, Isabel's brother, who was shot in a motel room; and Rose Nakamura, Rudy's girlfriend, who was pushed in front of a train. For a more detailed description, see Traffic North, by Richie Goldstein.

#